The Maiden Voyage of New York City

Gary Girod

Milton, Ontario
http://www.brain-lag.com/

Brain Lag Publishing
Milton, Ontario
http://www.brain-lag.com/

Cover design by Catherine Fitzsimmons

ISBN 978-1-928011-31-6

Library and Archives Canada Cataloguing in Publication

Title: The maiden voyage of New York City / Gary Girod.
Names: Girod, Gary, 1990- author.
Identifiers: Canadiana (print) 20190204540 | Canadiana (ebook) 20190204559 | ISBN 9781928011316
   (softcover) | ISBN 9781928011323 (ebook)
Classification: LCC PS3607.I76 M34 2020 | DDC 813/.6—dc23

To my loving parents, and Peter, Emily and Daniel.

Prologue

Marko Sverichek sat at the prow of the motorboat as it sped down Wall Street Canal. At nearly seven feet, his gaunt figure towered over the boat's captain and the two armed bodyguards who rode with him. A gentle breeze blew against his black suit and neatly trimmed dark hair. His nostrils filled with the scent of salt and seaweed. Just beneath that, the ever-present stink of sewage made him clench his teeth.

To his right and left were the skyscrapers of Manhattan. Most had been built over a hundred years ago. In that time, the sea had risen up to cover their first two floors. The gentle ebb and flow of the tides rested three feet below the high water line, halfway up the second floor windows. Circling each skyscraper were makeshift plastic walkways where a ship could dock and one could enter the new 'first' floors.

Plastic bags, tin cans, and a thousand other knickknacks floated in the water. There was a bump against the boat as it hit something large. Marko had learned to ignore those, but a metallic *clank* made him peer down into the water, where he spotted a tin lunchbox. The cover's faded paint depicted a man firing lasers from his eyes at a robot as the box bobbed and sank into the water amidst so much other debris.

As the sun began to set, lights rose up inside the skyscrapers all the way to their tops. It was only the first few levels that remained unlit, leaving the canals in darkness. Marko looked down. The water was murky and filled with trash, but he thought he saw a street sign labeled 'Avenue of the Americas' in the water. He grimaced. There was always the chance that a boat's underside might accidentally scratch a lamppost, street sign, or statue and start to sink. Marko hoped that their captain was expert enough to dodge the old signposts that threatened to scrape the bottom of the boat; he didn't want to swim in the cold Atlantic Ocean all the way to his destination.

"Beautiful night," the captain remarked. He had been a local hire, Marko's own, not a company man like the bodyguards. He hadn't learned to be solemn and silent. For the past few years, Marko had been in and out of meetings with the richest New York City had to offer and normally would have leapt at the opportunity to banter with someone who didn't look down their nose at him. But he didn't feel like talking, not now, not tonight. Marko just wanted it to happen.

Marko turned, smiling at the man. He had a thick beard, callused hands and leathery skin, but his eyes looked younger than Marko's. "Couldn't have asked for a better night. There aren't any storms, barely even a wind. The weather report says there aren't any clouds," Marko concurred while looking up. Nearly every window above him was shining with light and the sky between the buildings was a thin black abyss.

"You think it'll work?" the captain asked innocently.

Marko gave him an irritated look, which the captain appeared to have missed. "I wouldn't be here if I didn't."

"I sure hope so," the captain continued, entirely missing his tone. "If it has to happen, I hope it works. Of course, I might be out of business if it does."

"No, you won't," Marko stated, unsure but sounding as if he wasn't. "Things will be better than ever before."

The man scoffed and looked past Marko. Marko turned, trying not to show his angry grimace. He preferred his workers to speak their minds to him in theory, but the people of New York City had an incurable strain of pessimism. *Must be because they have to live in claustrophobic conditions within the skyscrapers. It drives them insane. There have been tests from decades ago where rats were put in the same cramped conditions as New Yorkers. They eat each other. And I'm pretty sure the rats weren't surrounded by water.*

Marko only had a few seconds to fume at the tactless captain of the most pathetic boat in the lagoon that was New York City when they finally arrived at their destination: the Empire State Building. While the other skyscrapers looked like lifeless blocks being swallowed by the sea, Marko thought that this tower barked defiance. Even as the first two floors had fallen beneath the waves, the monolith reached toward the sky, its segmented form growing thinner until its point seemed to reach up into the cosmos itself. Even the waves crashing against its eastern side looked majestic. It looked like the only skyscraper that could weather the storm, as if this spire was more eternal than the roaring seas themselves.

The captain drew them up beside the makeshift dock. The guards were the first to leap out. With the exception of the few wealthy people who hadn't abandoned New York to the waves, every New Yorker had to have some knowledge of ship-bearing. It was as if when the sea levels rose and the lights ran out, Gotham had turned into medieval Venice or Amsterdam. Or at least, that was one of the ways Marko described New York City as his mind tried to make sense of the improbability.

"Sir." A deep voice pulled Marko from his thoughts. Marko took the offered hand and stepped out of the boat. The crew paced around the building until they reached a window that had been expanded and fitted with a glass door. The single door was hardly as glamorous as the massive gilded rotating doors below, but those were filled with dogfish and eels.

There were two guards with assault rifles standing on either side of the door. Marko paused and turned on his internal computer. The neural interface came up in front of his eyes and a notification appeared, asking if another user could wirelessly link into him. Marko turned his right hand palm up and, with his left index finger, pressed on his right palm like a touchpad and pressed 'Grant Access.' The guard jumped into the digital part of his brain and scanned his ID.

When it had finished, the guard said, "Can you please step to the side?" The two bodyguards who had been accompanying Marko waited and did the same. Marko caught a flicker in their eyes as if they all knew each other, but protocol was protocol. When the men were scanned, the other security guard opened the door for them.

Marko turned and gave one last look at the doubting captain, who had returned to his boat. "Sail out past the edge of Manhattan. It will be safest there."

"You sounded so confident earlier." After a pause, the captain added, "I'll be sure to do that."

Marko glared daggers at the captain. He had only meant... but the man had pulled back the line tying him to the dock and had his motor revving in the water. Marko wasn't going to try to educate the man by shouting over the engine. He turned, nodded at the security guard while muttering the little-heard courtesy of 'thanks' and stepped inside.

He was immediately hit with such an overpowering concentration of pine and lemon air freshener that his eyes watered. Humanity couldn't stop itself from receding below the waves, but it could get rid of the smell.

I guess we deserve some credit for that.

Where once had been segmented office spaces, there was now a grand, open reception area. Couches rested in a line between the reception desk and the door, each with its own side table and antique lamp. Along the walls were Romantic paintings of peaceful European landscapes, filled with windmills and granaries and simple-dressed townsfolk. Despite their attempt to shut out the world, this place in its brightly-lit excess still carried an air of the impending doom in its over-perfection.

Waiting in front of the reception desk was a large man, half a head shorter than Marko, but with an enormous gut. The man had three chins; the first two and the rest of his round face were covered in white stubble that matched the thick hair on the top of his head. He wore a fine, dark blue suit and sported an antique golden watch with inlaid diamonds on his left wrist. His clear blue eyes, which were friendly but distant, had locked onto Marko. Marko walked towards him, hearing the echo of his black dress shoes as he spanned the gap between them.

"Sverichek," the man called as they approached. "Ready for tonight?"

Marko wondered if he was asking if he was personally ready for the ceremony or if all the plans were ready and functioning. "Yes, Mr. Stanhope." A response that answered both questions.

"Good." Stanhope nodded. "I managed to sneak away from the socialites for a second. I don't think they mind; they've mostly been congregating around me, but I suspect it's just because you haven't shown up yet. When you're ready, we can head to the observation deck."

Marko nodded nervously. He didn't like large social events, especially ones where he had to mingle with people above his social class as he endured their judgment. It wasn't a good quality for a scientist to have: the inability to socialize with financiers. The two stepped around the reception desk, completely ignoring the middle-aged woman sitting behind it, who was trying to look busy in front of her boss' boss' boss by typing madly onto a projected keyboard in between smiling at them. Stanhope pressed the button for the elevator. They stepped inside and were immediately hit with the cold putrescence of algae and salt water. Marko could imagine the pool of water that was just underneath their feet, filling the bottom of the elevator shaft. He looked at the buttons and saw that the first two had been removed. *Good,* he thought, and before he could stop himself, he imagined some careless pencil pusher stressed from an upcoming deadline accidentally hitting the wrong button and drowning inside a luxurious decorated elevator in the middle of what was once 'the Capitol of the World.'

The doors opened to a long, golden hallway cut with red carpet. Marko had to temper his long strides as Stanhope waddled beside him. Stanhope opened the door at the end of the hallway and they stepped onto the roof of New York City. There was a slight burst of wind that tousled Marko's hair. To his right, a shining cube of light filled with elegantly dressed people whose eyes had been locked down at the rest of the skyscrapers turned to him. Without pausing for a view over the side, Marko followed Stanhope underneath the observation deck and up the stairs, emerging in the center of the party.

Tables covered in white cloth with glasses of champagne and bouquets were spread across the room. All around them were men, the youngest in their thirties but most in their fifties, in finely-tailored suits, slick-gelled hair and satin handkerchiefs. The women were noticeably younger than their male counterparts, each dressed in a myriad of shiny gray, deep blue, and even a handful of red, green and black dresses. Marko guessed that the older women with austere clothing were the ones who had their own money. Marko noticed an exception to the age rule at the end of the bar, where a woman in her late fifties, or early sixties minus the plastic surgeries, stood beside a well-muscled, bronze-tanned, college-age boy who looked as if he were wearing his first suit. Marko smiled and saved that image. *You have to smile now, look friendly. This is a business world; it's all marketing, not the product. They'll trust you if you smile.*

The conversations began to die off as all eyes turned to the two giants, the one skeletal, and the other walrus-fat. They looked as if they didn't know how to respond. A few people broke out in cheers, more from a sense that that was what they were supposed to do than at any actual enthusiasm for Marko. The hollow cheer spread throughout the room and Marko was received to the least enthusiastic uproar he had ever heard.

Stanhope marched forward, walking directly into the throng. Marko kept pace, fearing the inevitable introductions that were to follow. "Esteemed guests, Marko Sverichek, the head of Project Sea Titan, inventor of the Sea Titan motors and the man who will save the city tonight."

A few glasses were raised.

"When does the show start?" asked one of the younger men, who stood beside a stunning Chinese woman in black.

Stanhope turned to Marko. Marko looked at his watch. "High tide is in thirty minutes, so an hour."

Stanhope turned his head, nodding at the semi-circular crowd. "I think we can drink all the booze before then."

That drew some laughter. An older man said, "You can!" which drew a second round of laughs. After that, the majority of the crowd returned to their previous conversations, to Marko's relief. He stood quietly by Stanhope as he talked to an older French couple. Marko caught a few key words, but wasn't listening to them as he let his mind and ears wander. The talk of the people in the observation deck was slow, expectant and almost dreading, but in a nonchalant manner, as if the specter of disaster was humorous. Every few seconds, Marko caught someone looking at him, then turning away. *I am a sight to behold. Seven feet tall in a three-year-old suit. I would have gotten a new one, but nice suits are expensive for a man like me to buy.* Marko looked down and was reminded that his tie was comically short. *They must all be thinking 'what a poorly dressed freak he is, who let him out of the lab? Or did he synthesize a muscle growth serum and break out? Maybe that's why he's so tall...'*

"Mr. Sverichek," a soft female voice called. Marko turned and looked down. A short Latina with soft up-turned cheeks, dark almond eyes and jet black hair looked up at him. She was wearing a green dress suit that looked somewhere in between stylish and business-like. Her smile seemed more genuine than most of the others at the party. She reached out to shake his huge hand. "It's good to see you again."

"Yes, Miss Mayor," he stuttered.

"So formal. Please, call me Sophia."

"Yes, Sophia."

"So, are you enjoying the party, Mr. Sverichek?"

"Yes."

"Are you lying?"

He paused long enough to give her a chance to answer her own question.

"It's all right. I get bored of formal events, too."

"Yes, you're right." He smiled awkwardly. "I would prefer that things got started."

Sophia's smile straightened and she nodded slightly. "Good, so you're confident?"

Marko nodded. "Yes, I checked everything again today. Everything should go by without a hitch. Every variable has been calculated, nothing is left to chance."

Sophia's smile widened. "I wish there were more people like you in politics; people who could only tell the truth. It seems we get too much of the opposite. Try to enjoy the party," she sang as she turned. Marko gave an awkward nod just after she walked away and watched her join another group of socialites.

Marko looked aside, trying to ignore his own thoughts. There was a waiter walking toward his small group with a tray of champagne. Marko grabbed a glass, wishing he could have grabbed two. Stanhope and the French couple each took a glass and Marko realized he shouldn't act the drunkard in front of the only man who believed in him while he was trying to impress foreign business magnates. The couple kept talking to Stanhope, although they would occasionally look at Marko as if to be polite and acknowledge that he existed.

Oh, to hell with this. Marko walked away, not even bothering to give an excuse. He didn't care whether or not they started forming opinions about him; he had already formed enough about them. He walked to the window. Everything faded as he gazed out at the still-drowning city; the gentle white waves upon the buildings looked like an almost peaceful struggle against the dark, cold water that was reaching up to claim them all. As high tide arrived, the water level began to rise until the first two floors of every skyscraper were fully underwater. The city workers were careful to scrape off the barnacles during the day, but there was a clear line on every skyscraper in Manhattan where the sea water had left its salty kiss. Marko glanced at his watch every few minutes until finally, the moon hung above Manhattan. *Not quite yet. It's not centered.*

Lights from every skyscraper were shining down on the dark brown waters. In the distance, smaller lights rose in a semi-circle around Manhattan. A third of the taller buildings in the Boroughs had their lights on. More light came from the houseboats that filled the bay.

Marko gazed down as far as the windows would let him. He had wanted to be as close to the ground floor as possible, but the financiers wanted to watch the spectacle from above. Marko looked down at the other skyscrapers and saw the bottom halves of each filled with people, staring at the water below. Caught between the sea and space, millions watched and waited as the water rose to its highest level.

Marko looked down at the engineering teams, who were riding the waves in their boats. They were barely specks from this height. It didn't matter; he knew exactly where each of his machines were and could imagine every single bolt underneath the towers. Even at the top of the city, he imagined he felt the gentle thrum of the machine placed a thousand feet below him.

"If this doesn't work, you will go down in history as a madman."

Marko didn't even glance at the portly, fine-suited old man who happened to be his only supporter. "You didn't have to be here. None of you had to be here."

Stanhope knew who he was referring to, as the two had broken away from the larger gathering of the richest industrialists and real-estate owners who had the misfortune of being unable to move their business out of the sinking city.

"Most of the time, innovation leads to disaster. Other times, it dominates the market, but either way, it is the future, and in this case, risks are unavoidable. If I don't die here now, I'll just die somewhere else in a less exciting fashion."

"Well, if this doesn't work," Marko choked out the nicety and imagined himself flinging the fat old man from the ledge, "we'll be the only ones killed."

"Us and whoever is in the buildings that we fall on."

Marko tuned him out. He looked at his watch, then back up at the moon.

"It's time!" someone from behind Marko announced.

Even with the handrails, no one dared to stand on the edge with Marko. Stanhope stretched awkwardly as he tried to put a hand on the tall man's shoulder, before letting it rest on his back. "Best of luck," he intoned and abandoned him for his young wife.

The last of the engineers emerged from the water, climbed into the boats and sped off. The rest could be done via remote.

Marko saw the bubbles before the tremor worked its way up the building. A few people gasped. The champagne glasses tinkled. Dirty foam rose furiously at the base of the skyscraper as the machine began to work. Marko held his breath, hoping that the tiny holes beneath the concrete wouldn't create too strong a stream of pressurized water that might unbalance the delicate procedure. The skyscraper continued to shake. Glasses fell from tables and cries rose from behind him. Marko looked out to the other buildings and saw the people watching open-mouthed as the tower shook.

The Empire State Building began to rise. The massive engines at the building's base sputtered out water and calmed as the long-lost concrete sidewalk emerged as its newly reclaimed base. Then the Empire State Building grew still, fully detached from the sunken land.

Cries of wonder became cheers and as the people below cried out, Marko heard them echoed from behind him. Marko looked up at the moon. They had only risen thirty feet, but he felt as if he could reach out and grasp it. Marko looked over his shoulder. Everyone lifted their glasses to him. Then the socialites and billionaires turned to the company heads who funded the construction of the machines, hired the engineers, the Congressmen and women who hadn't done anything except calling it a 'bold initiative' and gave tenuous support. Marko watched as they drank to their own futures.

Marko put his left index finger on his right wrist. He tapped it twice and the digital interface appeared before his eyes. He placed his left index finger on his open right palm and brought up a groupchat application. Video of the engineering teams scattered throughout the city appeared before his vision. "Is everything working according to plan? No malfunctions, even minor ones? No? Then activate the motors on the other buildings, too."

Marko tried to follow the engineering teams as they weaved through the canals, once streets, of New York City as he attempted to guess which building would be the next to rise. It was the one directly opposite him, and Marko almost laughed with joy as he saw the face of an astonished girl in a blue snowflake sweater clutching her mother, mouth agape as she looked down at the waves, then back up toward the stars, as if gauging the new difference.

A future scientist.

The buildings rose around him sporadically, sometimes a few in sequence; once, he saw five rise together in a line. By sunrise, every skyscraper was over two stories taller. Marko clutched the railing, exhausted, feeling as if he had just run a marathon.

Stanhope appeared at his side. "If only you had been at Atlantis!"

Marko laughed with joy and almost hugged him. Gulls cawed below him. *In a night, I have reclaimed a city from the waves. I am the captain of New York City.*

Chapter One

Night descended on Miles Buhari's deluxe apartment an hour before it fell on the city streets as the sun dropped behind the skyscraper opposite his window. Miles lay in the middle of his king-size bed, blue sheets strewn haphazardly as he tossed and turned, pillows on the floor. He opened his crusty, bloodshot eyes slowly. He couldn't decide which side to take, but after a minute, he rolled to the left and felt his long legs clumsily hit the ground. He rose to his full height, fingers reaching for the ceiling. He bent down and grabbed the soles of his feet as he flexed his aching muscles. When he had finished, he walked across the expansive room to the extended closet he had turned into a walk-in wardrobe. On his right were five suits, black, gray, blue, dark blue and brown, hanging next to a series of imitation leather coats of even more colors. Opposite them hung a dozen pair of faded navy jeans. Miles fingered through them absentmindedly. He needed something that felt energetic and dangerous. Club-goers were craving the dangerous and mysterious again, now that it was an option and not a facet of daily life. Everyone was annoyingly exuberant about the city rising up except him.

Very few people could afford an apartment like he had. He had heard that before the Miracle, luxury apartments like his were stuffed sometimes ten people to a room as the owners rented off their apartments to those people who had nowhere else to go. Miles was from London, a place that was booming with new commerce as its competitors were liquidated. He bought the most expensive class of apartments at the Halifax Tower for near the same price that a low-income worker in London paid for an apartment just above the heavily-dammed Thames.

That was a year ago. He had gotten the apartment so that he could blog about the daily lives of New Yorkers as their city sank beneath the waves. *Make big cash, maybe win a Pulitzer, then leave.* Crisis, crime, racism, drugs; any one of those was front page material. Mixed together and sprinkled with personal interest and Miles solidified his reputation as the most famous gonzo journalist in the world.

Miles had been watching the Empire State Building with everyone else that night. He had already prepared an article about the tragedy that occurred when the symbol of industrial America toppled and crashed, killing unknown thousands. What should have been disaster turned into a miracle. Atlantis rose up from the sea and Miles was stuck in the city, wearing faded jeans, a short-sleeve t-shirt with the wavy silver dragon around an orb logo of the band Eleventh Planet and a 'better-than-real' leather jacket. He looked at himself in the full length mirror against the far wall.

His muscles stretched the shirt, making it look like it could rip if he so much as turned. He put a hand on his head and felt his short, curly, dark hair which was barely darker than his skin. He hadn't shaved in two days and he had the lightest five o' clock shadow, broken only by a tiny scar on the right side of his square jaw. He caught his light brown eyes in the reflection. Ever since he was a boy, he had been told that they had a hypnotic effect on people. He had put it to great use before and found that his suggestions carried an almost overpowering quality to them. Tonight there were bags under his eyes, his head drooped and his eyes were placid, like the eyes of a long-worn painting. They still drew the eye, but lack of sleep cost them their sorcerous element.

Miles looked out the window, down thirty-two floors. Street lights were being installed on the newly raised bases, but his block still didn't have them. Every few minutes, a boat would pass by the canal, illuminating the newly-raised street.

Miles gave himself one last look over and walked out of his apartment. As he walked through the hallway, he scrolled through the photos he had taken the previous night. The shots were mostly of dark rooms cut by shafts of light; green, blue, purple and red with the silhouettes of revelers caught mid-motion on the dance floor, each of their bodies showing a different level of detail the closer they were to the illumination of a light beam. Miles had a few make-out shots, mostly men and their girlfriends, a few lesbians. He pulled up a photo he had taken of a bottle of rum being hit by a ray of light. He laughed; he had been bored and thought he might try an artistic approach. *Worthless. These photos could have been taken anywhere in the world.* He hit delete, wincing as he did. He didn't want to be left with nothing, but he had too much pride to pump out a half-decent article. His readers wanted to know what no one else was telling them about the floating Sodom and Gomorrah.

Miles stepped out of his apartment and hit the elevator button. He stepped inside, pressed 'L' and immediately got a headache from the soothing elevator music.

Miles had catalogued so much change in culture in the city in the years he had been there, during the worst of its decline. Scavengers had been scrounging up old souvenirs of New York recently; snow globes and paper weights. Showing the city in its former glory had become all the rage. Food had become much spicier as Indians and Pakistanis set up food carts to the point that masala and chicken curry were more common than burgers and sandwiches. Two years ago, the supergroup 'Rising Demons' played on an aircraft carrier, trying to raise funds for the city. While some had seen that as a sign that New York still had some prestige and cultural power, Miles had written that it was just like when the Beatles played at the Red Square in Moscow before the Soviet Union collapsed. It was a kiss of death set to music. It irked him that reality didn't conform to great fiction.

Miles stepped out into the lobby. As he walked through the glass doors, he noticed that half of the windows facing directly outward were glass and only the windows to his left and right were still sealed off behind a sheet of metal and plastic covering. Miles stepped out and walked down the street, breathing deep the cold salt air. He tapped his wrist and called Andy, his local liaison, the man who served as the gatekeeper to the underworld. No response.

Miles walked north until he hit a series of blocks that held multiple smaller buildings. These were lucky enough to have risen with the rest of Manhattan. They weren't as luxurious, but they were the shopping centers and entertainment venues for the people who lived and worked in the skyscrapers, who couldn't bear to leave them behind. Night settled on the rest of New York as he arrived at the Asphyxia night club. There was a line of thirty people to get in. Miles walked alongside it, seeing if there was anyone he knew.

"Miles!"

He turned. A dark-skinned woman with braided hair, wearing a blue coat and black skirt, hugged herself for warmth.

Miles walked over to her and gave her a hug. "Mylie, what have you been up to? I haven't seen you in five months."

"I've been gone for five months." She shivered. "When I lost my job at the tourism board, I wasn't going to stick around in an apartment with those two mean bitches and that old creepy guy. I left for

Philadelphia, but I got a call a week ago saying they were re-hiring me."

"So now you're back in with the creepy guy?"

She bit her lip, widened her eyes and looked to the side, and nodded jerkily. "It took a whole city rising up from the grave to bring me right back to where I always was. Still, the job is a bit more rewarding. Before, it was like trying to sell coffins. That's what I was doing in Philadelphia; working for a funeral company. Copywriting for coffins, cremation, green-funerals."

"Wow. Welcome back to the land of the living."

At the front of the line, the bouncer in an over-tight black-colored shirt let the first couple in, then closed off the entryway with the rope.

"I noticed you are still doing that blog."

"Yeah, but it hasn't been very good recently."

"I noticed," she said.

It stung because it was true. Miles rolled it off with a laugh. He turned his hands over, palms upward, as if asking for forgiveness. "Not too much of interest has happened. Everything is right joyful."

Mylie smiled at the quaint phrasing. "You were never good at writing about that."

Another couple entered and they stepped forward.

"It's worse; now this place is teeming with reporters from everywhere. When I was the only one here scoping out the dark undersides of the city, people had to read my articles or fuck off. Now there are journalists everywhere in the city and people are following them now because they are 'respectable'; because they are pawns to the media."

They moved ahead in line until they were just behind the red velvet rope.

"If you are still looking for dark and unwholesome, you could always go to the Boroughs."

"I don't want to get shot."

Mylie laughed.

"You laugh, mate, but that's the trick. Everyone in the business sells just enough of the truth to shock people into watching, but not enough to make them vomit. Here, Africa, parts of Asia where there is still war and starvation. They see three-year-old kids with distended bellies and visible ribs and they think that's the worst, but that's just the censored version for middle-class Americans and Europeans."

"Have you ever been to Africa?"

"I haven't even been to Italy, but I know how it works."

They were laughing as they walked into the club.

Inside, red, green and blue lights flashed on and off while a brighter white light blazed on and then went out, seemingly at random. A DJ with blond dreadlocks and glasses played on a raised platform, mixing the electronic sound. The dance floor was crowded as Miles and Mylie began to dance at the edge until they could make their way closer to the center. A curly red-haired girl that looked barely legal danced next to Miles. Miles looked at Mylie, who was moving away from him, having found a man who had taken an interest. After moving on to two other women, Miles worked his way to the bar. Alcohol of every type covered the shelves. There was a vertical line of golden rums and scotches, followed by white vodkas and whiskies, then green absinthe. There was a line of red and blue, though Miles was sure that most of those were just the color of the bottles and not the drinks themselves.

A woman in a dark t-shirt with a picture of a gas factory with different colored lights rising out of the pipes between the letters of 'Asphyxia' walked up behind the bar and looked at him. "What'll you have?"

"White Russian," he shouted over the noise. She brought it out and he turned around, rested his back against the bar and surveyed the crowd.

Nothing.

He looked to the side and saw a dark-haired man in a fedora turn his head sideways and hold that position, obviously taking video of the scene.

Nothing and it's already being covered.

Miles looked down the length of the bar. Three twenty-something girls were drinking and talking. Behind them, a lone man tried and failed to slyly stare at them. *He doesn't stand a chance.* At the end of the bar, a pale man with ice-blue eyes and near-white blond hair was looking at Miles. He nodded at Miles, who mimicked the gesture. Miles stood up and walked to the men's bathroom. From inside one stall, he heard gasps and moans. He tried to ignore it and turned to see the pale man behind him.

"Miles." The man smiled.

"David, how's it going?" He shook his hand, sliding him three ten thousand dollar bills as he did. David looked around, making sure no one was watching. Still cautious, he slipped Miles a small plastic bag with a single dark purple pill in it. He nodded one last time and left. Miles stepped into a stall and tried to ignore the sound of the moaning couple. He opened the baggie and took out the pill. He threw his head back and swallowed.

He waited a minute, until he began to feel fuzzy and warm. He unzipped his pants. The yellow stream hit the bowl and the sound exploded into an array of colors. He looked to his left. The moaning grew louder as the couple had given up on any privacy. Splashes of color flew over and below the divider with every moan while the divider wall was glowing. Miles zipped up and walked back to the dance floor. The speakers turned into fountains of color. Dark purple rolled out as the deep bass played, blue flew out as the high-tempo electronic hum took over, and the mash-up of guitar and drums with a synthesizer sprayed out orange, red and green hues over the dance floor. The sounds he could now see mixed with the flashing multi-colored lights and Miles could barely tell what was real. He chose not to care, picked a girl to dance with and used her as a fixed point to keep him from completely losing all sense of reality. Pretty soon, he forgot he was supposed to be writing anything. He was back at the bar with one of the three girls he had lured away from the others, a margarita in hand.

A phone icon danced in front of his vision with the word 'Andy' floating beside it. Miles let it go. Andy called again. Miles tapped his palm. "I can't talk," was all he said, while letting the blaring sound in the background explain the rest.

Andy said something from the other end.

"What?" Miles asked, kicking himself for even bothering.

"You have to come here, this is amazing."

"Hang on!" This time he did shout and realized his voice was a royal purple. Miles put his drink down on the bar. The glass 'clinked' on the tabletop and sent out a soft, near-white vibration. "Hang on, I'm going to the bathroom, excuse me, love, only a minute."

He walked to the bathroom, where the music was a muffled violet blaring against the walls. "What is it?" Miles growled.

"Wherever you are, get out and meet me at the intersection of 33rd Street and Avenue of the Americas. Trust me."

"What the hell for?"

"We're jumping off the buildings."

Miles furrowed his brow. "What?"

"We're jumping off the buildings. Get here now, otherwise you'll just have to watch us from below."

Andy hung up. Miles looked off into space as the thrumming purple sound mixed with the gauche wallpaper.

He opened the door and stumbled out. He glanced at the bar and saw that the girl was gone. *Damn you, Andy.* With no excuse to stay, he weaved his way through the crowd to the exit. He ran out of the club and down the street. The cold silence brought him back to reality, as the gentle passing of the current was the only sound he could see. There were hardly any people out, just the odd couple going to a club or bar. All along the street were boats tied up to the newly installed cleats in the old concrete sidewalk. There were a few nice ones on the main streets, but then there were dirty ones in a long line, clearly from the Boroughs, poor folks working as a taxi service to the rich drunks who wandered out at night, needing a ride home. As Miles ran, he saw a man with a thick black beard standing up in his boat, staring at people who passed. Miles averted his eyes and kept running.

He was a block away from the intersection when he nearly ran into three women walking side by side, talking excitedly. Across the canal, more people walked parallel to them. Nearly a hundred people were standing on the corner. Miles squinted as he looked for Andy. By now, the synesthesia had worn off and his eyes and ears were functioning normally, but he still felt fuzzy and light-headed.

A short, curly brown-haired man in a blue blazer and worn jeans saw Miles and jumped up, waving. "Miles!"

Miles ran over to him, joining the crowd. They locked hands and hugged.

"Glad you could make it. We're about to go up."

Miles looked up the skyscraper. The lights were on at the base and the building's top faded into the blackness, merging with the sky. In between the two, near what must have been the twentieth floor, was a sky bridge.

"From there?" Miles pointed at the bridge.

"Yeah." Andy nodded. "Faisal, come here." He waved over a well-muscled man with jet black hair and goatee. "This is Faisal." He clapped a hand on his shoulder. "Faisal, Miles." The two shook hands.

"Miles Buhari?" he asked.

Miles nodded.

"I've read your blog for a year now, all the crazy things you've covered. That's why I organized this. I thought it might be worth an article."

"So what is this?" Miles asked.

Faisal turned to the crowd. "Everyone shut up!" he yelled, an angry scarlet.

The crowd turned to him, though most continued to talk.

"All right, everyone, follow me. We're going inside the Walton Building. There are a lot of us, so we're going to take turns with the elevator. Make sure it stops at the 23rd floor. From there, I'm going to open the door to the sky bridge. There are no railings, so stay near the center until you jump. If any of you are drunk or high, or tripping, you can't come. That's the breaks. Oh, and to get in, it's ten thousand dollars per person, has to be cash or non-government issue e-currency, nothing traceable. Okay? Good, let's go."

The whole crowd turned with Faisal. The lights in the Walton building were on, but there was no one in but a lone security guard. Upon seeing them approach, the guard stood up and walked to the door, tapped out a combination on his hand and opened it. The guard looked at Faisal. "Make sure they only stop on the 23rd floor. The video cameras are only disabled here and there."

"I'll ride with them."

The guard nodded, let them through and started collecting bills from the people behind him. The crowd slowly filtered inside the lobby. When fifteen people had gone through, Faisal waved them over to the elevator. They crowded inside. Faisal pressed the button for the 23rd floor.

"How did you get this many people?" Miles pressed. "Are they some sort of group?"

Faisal looked over his shoulder at him. "I know maybe three of them. But I started a thread, they re-sent it to their friends. It always works like this, every time I come up with something new. Always hundreds show up."

He forwarded the message to Miles. *Come to 33rd Street and Avenue of the Americas and jump with us* appeared in front of Miles' eyes.

After an uncomfortable few seconds wherein Miles was pressed against thirteen strangers and one of his drug dealers, the doors opened to a long hallway with modern art pieces on the walls, interspersed with chairs and coffee tables. Faisal stepped forward and walked halfway down the hall, pulled a key card from his jeans pocket and opened a door on the left. The others followed him through into a maintenance room. He waved them over, towards a large double door with warning labels all over it. Faisal pressed a few buttons on a side panel, waited for a metallic 'click' and opened it. A gust of cold air tore through the room. Faisal turned, smiling.

"Come on!"

He ran out onto the top of the sky bridge. The crowd stepped up to the edge of the door. Miles looked down and saw, twenty-three stories below, the cold water as black as night between the two sidewalks. The wind tousled Faisal's hair, but his pace was steady. He walked until he reached the center. Hanging off the south side, there was a giant metal spool wrapped with a long black elastic rope. The machine was tied to numerous sandbags that were stacked around it. Any relief that Miles may have had from seeing the bungee equipment dissipated when he realized that it had not been installed into the bridge and was instead being held down by makeshift weights.

"Line up!" Faisal called. "You each get one jump, then I'll reel you up. Watch your head as you come back up. After that, go to the back of the line if you want to go again. Who's first?"

Miles looked at Andy. Andy grabbed his arm and pulled him into the forming line.

"Stop it, are you mental?"

"What?"

"I'm not jumping off of that."

"Why not? Tons of people have done this before. It's perfectly safe."

Miles stopped. He wanted to tell Andy the meaning of 'perfectly' and 'safe' but his curiosity was piqued when he said that this had been going on before. How many other people had counted on this wobbly machine to keep them from certain speeding death? Then Miles realized that if Andy wasn't full of shit, a real possibility, then this strange part of New York culture had gone on without his notice. He felt a stab of professional guilt for not having done something this uniquely stupid in a while.

The first person in line was a skinny blonde who was chatting with her two girlfriends. Faisal smiled at her and attached the two straps around her ankle. He said something to her that Miles didn't hear and then she jumped. Everyone else was looking down, but Miles was looking at the spool as the rope spun wildly from it. Then it suddenly ran out with a *twang*. The girl screamed and Miles looked over just as a few people behind him gasped. She was bouncing a dozen feet above the cold water. Her friends cheered and pretty soon everyone else took up the call. Faisal reeled her up, then slowed as she neared the bridge, being careful not to bang her against it. He helped her up, making Miles wince as he kneeled so near the edge without any protective gear. He pulled her up, gave her a hug and detached the rope. The girl ran back to one of her friends, who looked so similar she might have been her twin. The girl's friend hugged her and cheered, "Yeah, Kate!"

The next girl jumped off the side, flipping and turning as she did. The rope *twang*ed and she hung above the water. Three more people went, and Miles was seriously considering jumping, if only to make up for his previous failure as a journalist. He was fifth in line behind Andy. He turned, looking over his shoulder, and saw a heavy-set man behind him, whose gut hung out of his shirt.

"Want to go ahead of us?" Miles asked.

Andy gave him a confused look. "No, he can go ahead of you; he's not going ahead of me."

"Come on, I need to gather my courage."

Andy shrugged. "All right."

The man huffed, obviously insulted, but didn't turn down Miles's offer to let him go ahead. He muttered "pussy" as he passed him.

Miles ignored that. He felt the blood rushing through him and heard his heart pound in his ears as they neared the front of the line. As the fat man approached, Faisal gave a worried look. He attached the straps to the man's ankles, despite his reservations. Faisal began to say something when the man jumped. Miles looked down at the fat man as he flew headfirst at the water. There was a *twang* and then a slight screech of moving metal. Everyone fell silent. Faisal put his hand on the machine, as if that would have done something. Then the screech ended.

Faisal looked visibly worried and quickly reeled the man up. With some struggling, he climbed back onto the bridge.

"See?" Andy backhanded Miles on the chest and walked forward. Faisal strapped Andy's ankles while still breathing heavily from trying to lift the fat man. Andy jumped and Faisal reeled him back up. Miles looked over his shoulder. The entire crowd from below, minus a couple that must not have paid, were crowded in the maintenance room. There wasn't even enough room to walk back through the crowd behind him. Miles's panic at being trapped on the bridge, combined with the after-effects of the pill, made his heart pound in his ears.

"Come on, Miles!" Faisal called.

Andy walked back, put a hand on his shoulder and said, "All right, your turn," and pushed him forward. As he took his first step onto the bridge, Miles felt like the whole world was tilting, then as he steadied himself, he felt as if the world was too straight, as if the bridge he stood on was too hard and too real. The world continued to reassemble and change its mass with every step.

"Go or get back in line!" someone from behind yelled angrily.

Sweat beaded his forehead. Faisal walked over to him. "Come on, you can do this." It was then that Miles realized this must be the first time he had come face to face with a genuine admirer of his. He had been praised by a few fellow thrill-seeking journalists and on the internet, all outside New York. Everyone in the city hated him for tracking their decline. But Faisal seemed to be the first person he had met who genuinely admired him. *Because I seek the truth? Because I occasionally glorify or publicize the nuts like him?* Miles nodded and let Faisal attach the strap to his legs. *If I survive this, I will have to ask him why he likes me and pretend I'm not surprised.*

Miles walked to the edge and looked down. It was the same sight, a black river between two raised blocks of concrete, but somehow it looked ten times closer than it had before. He closed his eyes and jumped headfirst. The sensation was better than anything he had ever felt. It seemed more like flying than falling. Then the rope stretched to its end, his eyes flew open and he saw that he was less than ten feet from the water. *If there had been a boat there, I could have been impaled on the mast!* His heart exploded in his chest again as he bounced back up into the air before falling down again. He thought he heard faint applause, but it was less than a whisper from twenty stories up.

There was a whirring and a light shone above him, blazing on the sky bridge. From above, a voice on a loudspeaker called, "This is an illegal gathering on private property. You are all under arrest. Calmly step off the bridge and re-enter the building."

Blood was rushing to Miles' head as he hung limply below, straining awkwardly to see the helicopter whirring above him. He lurched forward, swinging himself back and forth, trying to see what was happening. As he swung forward, he saw Faisal trying to force the opposite door, to no use. A policeman jumped on him, but Faisal elbowed him hard and swung around and punched him. Miles swung forward again. When he swung back, he saw Faisal flying through the air. He hit the water, the splash accompanied by a sickening *crack*. His body floated up, face down.

Miles tried to look away and he suddenly felt like he was going to pass out. His right leg was numb and his other hung awkwardly, pressing against his stomach. His eyes began to close when a sudden pang of nausea made them shoot open. Animal instinct rushed into him. He strained the muscles in his stomach and lifted himself up, feeling instant relief like the breaking of a fever as the blood began to flow out of his head. He reached for the straps and tried to undo one. He was fumbling, and couldn't undo it. He fell back down, his stomach muscles exhausted, the blood continued to flow down into his brain and his lower body felt as if it were disappearing. He roared and lifted himself up again. This time, he managed to undo one of the straps. He fell back down, jerking as he did. He finally succumbed to exhaustion and let himself fall for a second. His head pounded in pain and he forced his eyes open. Faisal's body had drifted until it was nearly underneath him. Miles lifted himself up again, his roar little more than a cringing moan as he fumbled with the last strap. He hardly felt it when he fell.

Then the freezing water engulfed him, forcing the air from his lungs. He tried kicking, but his legs wouldn't respond. He clawed pathetically at the surface, his strokes stiff and awkward as the cold made him jerk and spasm. He watched as the lights drifted away and the darkness consumed him. He felt light-headed again, and then a feeling of warmth overcame him. He saw the dark outline of Faisal's body above him. Miles thought he was smiling at him.

Pain shot through Miles' legs. He kicked madly and felt himself rise up. He was writhing more than actually swimming, but he was nearing the surface. He reached out his hand, cresting the water. His head broke the surface and he gasped for air. The helicopter's blades continued to break the night silence. More lights had come on all around him. To his left, at the skyscraper's entrance, cops were carrying people off. Two were yelling at Miles, telling him to swim towards them.

Trespassing, illegal and dangerous activities. This would be great if I weren't a part of it.

Miles dog-paddled the other way. The cops kept yelling at him. Miles grabbed onto a decrepit, small motor boat and with the last of his strength, he flopped in. He was panting and shivering, with his face pressed against the cold metal of the boat. He heard the cops continue their shouting, only this time they were moving farther away. He looked up and saw them running back toward the bridge. They were going to cross and catch him. Miles tried to stand up, but the boat wobbled and he fell down again. He hit his head painfully and shivered. The cops had crossed the bridge and were rushing him.

Frantically, Miles raised himself to his knees, leaned over the side of the boat and untied it from its cleat. He grabbed the side and pushed it with his hands. He fell backward as one of the cops nearly stepped on his hands. They were cursing him. Miles covered himself as if expecting blows. But they weren't stupid enough to jump in after him. Miles leaned backward and revved up the motor. It started on the second pull and he was off. As he sped down, he caught a glimpse of the group of people being arrested cheering him as he fled.

Miles sped down the canal, stopping after three blocks and pulling into an open spot. He jumped from the boat. He was about to run off when he decided to tie it to the dock. He didn't know why, but he figured he shouldn't add to his growing list of crimes. His numb fingers could barely make the knots, but miraculously, they managed. He ran off, as fast as he could, trying to force some warmth into him. After a while, he had to lean over, panting but still freezing, the biting cold water and the frigid night air cutting into him. His heart pounded furiously and he felt as if he might have a stroke. Resting against a wall hardly helped. He kept running, passing the odd couple who would gasp and step out of the way, knowing that a drenched man running in the dead of night can't be up to any good.

He finally arrived back at the Halifax Tower. He let the building connect to his internal comp. The system identified him and the doors opened. Shivering, he stepped inside and pressed the elevator button and when it came, he pressed '33.' Miles ran down the hall to his apartment. He burst inside, slammed the door behind him and without even locking it, started stripping down. He threw off his clothes, ran to the thermostat, turned it on full blast heat and rushed into the bathroom, turning on the shower. Once it started heating up, he stepped in. Scalding water poured down his body, but the pain felt good as feeling coursed back into him. Eventually, it was too much to bear and he turned it down. He sat down in the shower, covering his face. Not a single thought passed through his head, which had gone from feeling as if it weighed nothing to weighing a ton. He let it fall into his hands.

After what must have been ten minutes, steam filled the bathroom. It was getting harder to breathe. Miles reached up and turned off the water. He pressed his palm against the shower door and pushed it open. He crawled slowly to his feet, wrapped a towel around himself and collapsed on his bed. It never felt so good. He closed his eyes. Everything was dull. A long time passed, but he couldn't sleep. He tried opening his eyes, but his eyelids were too heavy and he quickly gave up.

Go to sleep! Go to sleep.

It was a futile effort. After lying down for what felt like hours, he raised himself to his elbow and forced himself to look at his antique clock. *3:23 A.M.*

Miles sat up, feeling pain course through him as he did. He didn't realize how stiff his back was, then he remembered the fall into the cold water. He walked over to his desk and sat down. On the desk was a clear white cube. He pressed a button on it and it hummed to life, projecting a desktop screen. He opened up a document and began to write, detailing everything, minus his own involvement. A few minutes later, he leaned back and re-read the article through tired eyes. It wasn't his best. There wasn't even a photo. But it was the best thing he had written in a long time. His finger reached for the screen and hovered over the 'post' button. He wondered if the cops would follow him. *Surely they wouldn't? They have enough on their hands, trying to turn Manhattan into a gated community to keep out the people from the Boroughs. They wouldn't chase after me, not without any hard proof, not with just this.*

He clicked 'post.'

When he had finished, he felt a wave of relaxation wash over him. He turned, walked over to his bed, slid inside, lay his head back, looked at the ceiling and closed his eyes. He was too exhausted to have nightmares.

Chapter Two

Alex Waverly walked across the circular road that formed the center of the spider web that was once Brooklyn. More accurately, the borough underneath the thousand piers was Brooklyn. The single-story buildings sank beneath the waves, the grocery stores, pharmacies and offices taken over by schools of fish, which were barely visible in the dirty green water. Above that was a floating city balanced on a layer of plastic and steel. Alex stood in the center of it, the 'Eye,' as the circular shopping center was called. He leaned back against the railing and watched as hundreds of people rotated around it like a dour carousel, filtering out on one road or another. A salt-scented cool breeze broke against his navy-blue jacket and worn jeans. All around him were buildings that rose two to four stories high. Boutiques and fashion stores built of black steel arches that supported a multitude of clear glass windows to mimic the Parisian galleries, restaurants made of faux brick that spilled their scents of lab-grown fish meat and imitation beef onto the street, and all the haute culture the Boroughs could muster was concentrated here. Alex picked out certain people as they walked by and tried to gather as much information on them as he could with just a cursory glance.

An olive-skinned woman made eye contact with him. *Nose piercing, neat black eye-liner, pale pink lipstick. Brand new black t-shirt with shiny golden design of music notes turning into a gothic castle; faded jeans, definitely imitation. White canvas shoes with black roses on them. She is middle-class, has a good job, probably fashion, entertainment or modeling-related. Has a wild side. She thinks she's classy but she has bad taste...*

Two hands reached around and closed over Alex's eyes. "Tell me my life story by what you see."

"You're not sweating, which means that you didn't run here, meaning that you didn't have a problem with being late and keeping me waiting. From the way your fingernails are digging into my nose slightly unevenly, I can tell you haven't trimmed or clipped them in a while, which means you've gone back to your habit of biting them because you're nervous about something. Considering I don't feel a ring anywhere on my left eyeball, men must still find you unattractive."

The blinders came off. He looked down to his left. His partner Cassidy Kikia looked up at him. She was in her mid-twenties, lanky, with dark brown hair, a sharp nose, and cheekbones that cut clear lines across her face. Alex knew Cassidy didn't have much money, though neither did he, being a cop in the Boroughs. Early on in their career, he had worried she wasn't getting enough to eat or perhaps she was addicted to drugs, as so many cops he knew were. But every time they ate together, she was stuffing her face with cheap Asian food. She didn't show any signs of having an eating disorder, and Alex assumed she was just naturally unnaturally skinny.

Alex was Cassidy's age, with bright blond hair and sea blue-eyes; proper sea-blue, not like the dirty water around the city. Like him, she wore plainclothes, though hers were normally more colorful than his. He had sculpted biceps, thick legs and at six feet was a bit taller than most, and a head taller than his partner. Even with his tan, he was still a shade lighter than her, which bothered him because when they weren't on patrol, she stayed inside all day and watched anime or played video games.

"You're not one to be giving dating advice, now are you?" She smirked.

"Your hair..."

Cassidy scrunched her nose. "What about it?"

"You changed it. It used to curl at the ends, but it's straight, and it smells different than normal, meaning you must have styled it. You didn't care at all about being late, did you?"

Cassidy tried to maintain a harsh look, but failed.

"Oh..." he said, realization dawning on him. "Or maybe you didn't plan on changing it. I'm guessing your newest boyfriend uses mango-scented conditioner, which is why your hair is different. Are you sure he's not gay?"

"I'm sure." Cassidy grinned.

"Point taken."

"And it was just a one-time thing," Cassidy clarified.

"Well, thanks for that info. Now that you've finally showed up, where shall we eat before our shift starts?"

Cassidy shrugged.

"Not sushi again."

"All-American?" she said with a hint of annoyance.

Alex was about to say, 'what's wrong with that?' but knew that once they started bickering, it would never end. "I'm not really hungry."

Cassidy shrugged. "Coffee then?"

He nodded.

Alex and Cassidy merged with the crowd and exited the Eye westward. Each shop along their route had a different shape and color. Some leaned forward precariously, some were falling back, and there was one butcher's shop with real wooden boards laid over a crack between the pier and the shop's entrance. The red imitation meat dangling from steel hooks in the window hung noticeably backward. A designer shop on their right was five stories tall, almost unheard of. A gable stretched from the roof with a long hook. Alex had heard that because of the narrow staircases in Amsterdam, the Dutch moved all their furniture into the higher floors through the window, until Amsterdam was swallowed up by the waves, that was. He looked up at the hook, wondering if the people inside had ever used it to lift any heavy items through the window.

The walkway narrowed, forcing Alex and Cassidy to meander single-file as passers-by did their last bit of shopping before the stores closed. They turned down a side street, continuing to look for an uncrowded coffee shop. The problem with the Boroughs was that there was no pattern to the stretch of shops, no sense to their placement. Antique stores were next to electronic stores, general stores were next to restaurants, where any shop was located was anyone's guess. It wasn't a problem for his partner, who seemed to know every corner of the city by heart, but Alex was always focused on other things and routinely got lost.

"Our jobs should be getting a lot easier soon," Cassidy said to Alex as they passed a sex shop with flashing red neon lights.

Alex raised an eyebrow. "Why would you say that?"

"I would think someone as observant as you should know." She grinned. She looked at him and laughed. "Are you trying to judge whether or not that was sarcasm? Maybe you're less observant than I thought."

"Well, now I definitely don't care about your opinion."

"Oh, don't be like that. It's all over the news; Manhattan is booming now. Businesses are relocating back there and tourism is flooding in—

no pun intended."

"Maybe by you, I am sure the news sources you are quoting—"

"Yeah, yeah. The point is, that money is going to spread out to the Boroughs soon."

"'Soon' as in two days, or when I'm collecting a social security check?"

"I'm not an economist. But things will be better, you'll see."

With most other people, he would have argued, but Alex had resolved not to kill Cassidy's optimism. When she wasn't being annoyingly cheerful, she had a hell of a bitter side. Her optimism was the other side of her see-saw personality, her good angel, the side of her he knew how to deal with.

Alex took a step forward and nearly tripped on a chunk of a broken plastic barrier. He awkwardly jumped over it and cursed, making Cassidy laugh.

Alex scowled at her. "Someday you're going to fall over the edge, right into the water, and I won't pull you out."

"I won't fall in." She smiled. "I know every single inch of the Boroughs. I still find it hilarious that you manage to get lost with an internal GPS and all your maps and charts. Your sense of direction is so bad I'm amazed you can find your own apartment."

Alex turned away. "Let's stop in here," he dodged, walking into a café called the Purple Frog. The inside was imitation wood, quaintly decorated, with green wallpaper and red rose designs.

Antique, dark wooden chairs and couches with a near-similar rose over green design decorated the room. The floorboards were old, though, and Alex could hear a whistling from what must have been a hole somewhere near the center of the room. The sound of the waves lapping against the beams that held them up echoed through the invisible hole. *I wonder if that was intentional or just poor craftsmanship.* There were only five other people in the room, each scattered around the small shop. There weren't any servers to be seen.

The two sat down at a table with a chess board drawn into it, though there didn't seem to be any pieces or sets anywhere in the establishment. An aging woman in a teal and blue skirt with wrinkles around her eyes walked up to the table.

"You two had a chance to look at the menu?"

"Just coffee," Alex replied.

"Same."

The woman nodded and walked back behind the counter.

Alex was examining the odd setting when Cassidy asked, "How's your romantic life going?" though she didn't sound genuinely concerned.

"I'm not looking."

Cassidy raised an eyebrow. "Not looking? Why not?"

"I've been out of it ever since... well, you know. Now that I'm back, I need to stay focused, especially since there's been a spike in crime."

"What are you—"

The server returned, placing their coffees on the table.

"Thanks. What are you talking about? You can't make an excuse that you aren't looking to date because there's crime. There's always crime. You just don't have any prospects, do you?"

Cassidy was right, but Alex never let her win.

"I'm worried. There's a bad feeling in the air. You can sense it on people. Their excitement at seeing Manhattan rise up is hollow. And there's been a big spike in violence."

Cassidy took a sip and waved her hand at him. "Just the birthing pains," she said.

"What?"

"Every great change is met with some blowback. If things are getting worse, it means they are getting better."

Alex shook his head. He couldn't argue with that level of optimism any more than he could argue with someone who thought they were an orange. Still, Cassidy was the good kind of crazy today.

Cassidy downed the rest of her coffee. "We have bad weeks sometimes, but we're supposed to get through these, that's our job. And besides, look at that."

"What, what is it?"

Alex looked out the window, but didn't know what he was supposed to be looking at.

"Made you look!"

Alex gave Cassidy a sour look. Before he could ask her how old she was, Cassidy explained, "The American flag."

Alex looked again. He saw the stars and stripes mounted on the next building over, gently waving in the slight breeze. It did look out of place the longer he looked at it, like it belonged in a textbook, or in the halls of a government building, not out in public.

"When was the last time you saw one of those waving from a house or shop somewhere?" Cassidy prodded.

"I can't remember," Alex remarked, sipping at his coffee.

"And you think you're so observant! I've seen three today. Ever since we've been cops, we've had to take on different racial gangs: Puerto Ricans, Russians, Haitians; because government was a far-off entity, no one cared about America. When things went to hell, everyone divided up by neighborhood or family ties or race or religion. But now people have something to believe in. What's happening in Manhattan is giving people hope, and people are proud to be Americans. You'll see. Soon, people will care less about their different gangs, clans and whatever other group and more about their city and their community and life will get a lot better for us and for them."

Alex thought that over as he downed the rest of his coffee and waved the waitress over for the bill. They stood up and walked out.

When the door shut behind him and the cold evening air began to nip at their faces, Alex turned to his partner and remarked, "We could be driving cars now."

Cassidy looked sidelong at her partner. "On these walkways? Be sure to run that to the chief."

"I meant if we weren't cops here," Alex explained as if it were obvious. Cassidy knew what he meant, but she had an annoying habit of forcing Alex to spell everything out. "Police in New York used to have horses, and not just until cars were invented. Long past that, right up to the point that the city started sinking, there were cops riding around on horses."

"Where would they keep them? Not in the station. They didn't have stables in the station, did they?"

Alex couldn't tell if she was being purposefully stupid. "No, I'm sure they kept them somewhere else."

"Bad planning. If they did take them somewhere else, that means that they would have had to take a car to get to the horses."

For a second, Alex thought she had a good point. "No, you idiot! They used the subway." It was a guess, but it felt right, even if it didn't sound right.

Cassidy shrugged. "Makes sense. What do you suppose they are going to do with that?"

The subway was currently abandoned. A thousand miles of concrete tunnels lay underneath a city that rose skyward, leaving it behind. As far as anyone knew, the subway was a destination for the occasional photographer taking pictures that would appear on a news website or scientific journal demonstrating just how much the world had been damaged due to the changing climate. Aside from the photos, the subway, once the lifeblood of the city, was forgotten.

"No idea. Say, Cassidy, have you ever driven a car?"

They continued walking across what was once the southeastern side of Brooklyn, heading south as they discussed what it must be like behind a wheel. There had been people cramming the walkways in the center, to the point that one person was pushed into the water in front of them. Whether it was an accident or not, Alex couldn't be sure and he wasn't going to try to arrest the man who might have pushed him over if it meant risking throwing more people into the chilly water. The soaked man managed to pull himself back up, looking both ways angrily, but the man who had bumped him had disappeared, leaving him to curse as he wrung out his jacket.

The farther away from the center they moved, the fewer people there were. There were two old men on Alex's right playing an old board game with a cup and multiple dice. To his left, a father and his young daughter were kicking a soccer ball back and forth carefully in front of their house. Two Arab teenagers in blue and red jerseys relaxed on a boat, smoking.

"Officers Kikia, Waverly, there has been a report of suspicious activity at 603 Warner Road. Neighbors reported signs of struggle. Investigate," Alex heard inside his head. Alex pressed down on his palm and pulled up his GPS app. A green arrow appeared in front of his vision, down the road and curving to the right.

"I know a faster way to get there than the main streets." Cassidy turned around, leading the way back toward the center of the city. The streets on one side didn't perfectly line up with the others and they had a habit of winding, turning, and changing into other streets as the floating city had developed haphazardly, so Alex could only guess where she was taking them.

They turned onto Garibaldi Way, one of the main streets that cut from the ocean to the circular Logan's Square that served as the center of Queens. Cassidy turned down a side street with a signpost marked Warner Road. Once the two had gotten through the main thoroughfare and past the last edges of the crowds, they broke into a run. To his right, Alex read '357' on the nearest house. The run became a sprint as the two tore down the sparsely populated street.

603 was a blue houseboat whose paint had been so dried by the sun that it was almost white. There was one window, which had its thick purple shutters closed. Alex tried looking through the pinhole on the front door and saw that a light was on inside.

Alex opened up his internal comp and searched for a wifi signal. If there was anyone inside with a similar neural interface, he could see what their position was before engaging. There was only a standard router signal, not a surprise, considering how few people could afford bio-mechanics in the Boroughs.

"Go around back, I'll take the front," Alex ordered. Cassidy nodded and stalked to the right. Alex knocked on the front door hard. "Hello?

Anyone there?"

No response.

Alex pounded on the door. "Open up, police!"

He kept pounding. Only silence met him. He looked over his shoulder. Two Cuban men were watching from their own house across the street. A Thai woman pushed at the backs of her two sons, driving them forward, away from the scene. Alex turned around. The pinhole was black.

Alex kicked the door. The old door's lock gave and it swung inward. A second, louder *bang!* exploded as a bullet flew through the thin door. A scream burst out behind him; one of the onlookers had been hit. The door knocked against the man inside. Using the door as cover, Alex stepped into a dilapidated living room and saw a tall man with blood across his face lying on the floor. Alex saw his partner kick open the back door across from him. He looked to his right, into the bedroom and saw that another man had a gun aimed at his head. Alex jumped left into a decrepit kitchen just as a bullet exploded into the TV in the corner of the room, sending sparks flying. Alex hugged the wall for cover. He grabbed a lamp from a nearby side-table and flung it at the prone man just as he was lifting his gun. It shattered against the man's head and he collapsed. Another blast of gunfire sounded, this time from Cassidy. There was another blast from the man in the bedroom, then another. In between the gunfire, Alex heard the man's footsteps getting farther away. *He's trying to escape.*

Alex peered outward. His partner was taking cover behind a worn couch in the living room while the man in the bedroom opened a window. Alex leapt forward and sprinted after him. The man spun at the noise, but he was too slow. Alex barreled into the man's stomach, knocking him against the window frame. Alex suddenly stood up and grabbed the assailant's wrist as the man struggled to bring the gun down on Alex's head. With his left arm, Alex held the gun upward and away from him; with his right, he held the struggling man down. The man punched Alex with his free hand in the corner of his eye. Alex let go of the man's chest, leaned backward and landed a solid kick against his chest that sent him falling backward until he fell out the window and onto the walkway circling the house. Blood streaming down his head, dripping off his chin, the man staggered to his feet. He looked at Alex and his eyes went wide as if he remembered just then what he had done. By the time Alex opened his mouth, the man had bolted.

Alex ran to the back door, Cassidy in tow. They looked out and didn't see him.

"BACK!"

Alex fell backward, throwing out a hand to keep Cassidy in with him, as a blast sounded from their right as the runner fired his pistol. Alex stopped, leaning against the wall. He didn't hear any movement, then a loud *thud* from farther away. The man had jumped from the back of the house to the street.

"Watch him!" Alex motioned at the unconscious man in the living room, bolted out the back door and leapt onto the street. The gunman was ahead a good twenty feet and he was running fast. Alex sprinted after him as a handful of people watched, wide-eyed. A teenage girl saw the chase, gasped, and leapt to the side, falling back onto the street's handrail. The man ran past her, then Alex. An elderly couple wasn't so swift, and the man nearly stumbled into them. Alex wondered when he would tire and decide to take a hostage.

The fleeing man looked over his shoulder. Alex raised his gun. From the look in his wide eyes, Alex saw that the gunman knew he could never draw in time. The man's eyes returned to the street and he turned right at the intersection. Alex anticipated the man's turn, stepped onto the railing and leapt to his right across the water, clearing to the next street. The fleeing man turned at the thundering noise behind him just in time for Alex to tackle him. The two tumbled down the street. Alex rolled, grappling with the man until he had him pinned. Alex reached down with his left hand, grabbing the man's right wrist. He punched the man hard enough to stun him and the gun clattered to the ground. Alex rolled the man over to his other side and handcuffed him.

Alex tapped his right palm and brought up the police com-line.

"I've apprehended an armed man who fired upon my partner and I. I am currently at... Olive, in front of house 345. Requesting backup."

"Sending backup, over."

Alex tapped on his right palm, smearing more blood across it. "Cassidy?"

He waited. Every second that passed worried him.

"Yeah, Alex? Get 'em?"

"Yeah, I got 'em. What's the situation on your end?"

"Took you long enough. I was worried. I got backup here already, was about to call you. He's being rushed to the hospital in cuffs. You wouldn't believe this, though. I found about twenty kilos' worth of black tar heroin here. HQ is sending down Detective Harrah at some point to sweep the area."

"As soon as my backup arrives and carts off this man, I am coming to join you, look over the scene." Alex stated, pushing the man down as he put up a pathetic struggle.

*   *   *

Alex walked into his and Cassidy's office with bandages covering the knuckles on his shaking right hand. He closed his eyes and told himself the adrenaline rush would pass. After a moment of calmness, he sat down. On his desk was a small projection cube for official work and a notebook for himself. He found it easier to connect the dots in a case when he could actually draw lines between the things he had written. Next to the cube was a miniature sailing ship with masts and little cannons that he had constructed from a kit when he had a lot more free time on his hands. Cassidy's desk was pressed up against his. She had replaced the company issue cube with one that wasn't so ancient. They had a single window in their office, which afforded a view from the back of the building. The concrete walkway only serviced the front and sides of the old police headquarters, so Alex could stick his head outside the window and look straight down at the sunken building's base, which was teeming with algae and mussels. Alex knew that the electric system from the first floor had been disconnected and now the power came from a generator at the top of the building, but every time he plugged something in, he imagined himself being electrocuted.

Cassidy's side of the room was completely bereft of things, with white marks on the wallpaper from where photos had been hung by the previous occupant. Meanwhile, all along Alex's half of the room were maps of the Boroughs framed by charts and pictures of criminals.

Cassidy looked up as he entered and said, "Your half of the wall looks like what you'd find in a serial killer's lair."

Alex wrinkled his nose. "This is important work."

Cassidy gave him a disbelieving look.

"I honestly have no idea what you mean by that face."

"You keep picking up every clue from every crime scene, every print you can store, looking for a connection. But just because there's a connection doesn't mean that'll lead to a cartel, or the bosses behind it all. This city is terribly poor; everyone deals a little bit with drugs or with bootleg items and the contraband has a way of changing hands between a lot of people. Connecting one criminal to another supposedly unrelated person won't unravel a thread that brings down the crime lords; it'll just put one more petty thief in jail while we are all still tangled."

Alex recoiled a bit. He contemplated insulting her back. *No, best not to get on her nasty side, especially now that we have to file a report and will be stuck in the same office together for the next few hours.* "Bringing down criminals with evidence of connection to others makes the sentences harsher because it's evidence of organization."

"A drug trafficker giving a discount to a man who everyone knows sells bootleg t-shirts isn't organized crime."

That stung, but Alex restrained himself. "Do you not think my work is important?"

"I think the work is important." Her eyes widened for a second and her eyebrows flew up in a way that could be cute if she weren't in the middle of insulting him.

"Okay, then how do you explain how no one has been able to find a supply line for all the weapons and drugs in the city?" Alex asked. "One day we find thirty assault rifles with long range wifi-radar scopes that can hook up to other people's internal comps and allow the shooter to snipe an unsuspecting person from a mile away with no vision other than the internet connection in them. The next day in the southwestern corner of Brooklyn, forty kilos of black tar heroin, the next in the center of Queens, along with a ton of unlicensed bio-mech hardware. Where is it all coming from? How does it get transported?"

"The same way all illegal material gets transported. In people's shoes, in innocuous containers and a few unsavory ones. The drugs get here because we have a severe shortage of people power and criminals aren't so stupid that they can't sneak past a cop who isn't there. That's a lot more believable than there being a big conspiracy theory about the drugs."

"I'm not a conspiracy theorist. Maybe the connections are tenuous, but the big players must be the ones with the most connections, and charting that could lead to a source which is all we need to roll back crime. Cut off one source, a gang loses power, then we just do the same to the other one. I think it can work."

Cassidy fell silent and looked back to her home page, projected in mid-air, and started clicking.

"What? Nothing to say?" Alex asked.

"You're finally an optimist. I win."

Damn it.

"But it's okay, I know you're not a serial killer."

"How's that?"

"Serial killers have a very high level of intelligence."

Alex rolled his eyes and turned his back on her to keep her from seeing his face turn red.

"You need a girlfriend. Whatever happened to that cute redhead you were dating?"

"Haley," he replied.

"Yeah, her. Why aren't you two dating anymore, aside from the fact that you're crazy? I remember that month off you spent recovering, you were with her all the time. Even after you came back, it was like you were always somewhere else, always talking about her, telling me what you'd been doing with her, what you were planning that night. There was actually a time when you were carefree and happy."

"Oh." He shrugged. "I don't know... I just, I guess we both got caught up in our jobs or something. I haven't seen her in a while."

Cassidy gave him a cold glare. "You chopped her up into pieces, didn't you?"

Alex turned his back on her.

"Oh hey, I forgot to tell you, I picked this up at an antique shop."

Alex turned again. Cassidy was holding up a snow globe filled almost to the top with water, with miniature skyscrapers inside and a base that read 'New York City.' Cassidy turned it upside-down and when all the white flakes were at the top, rotated it back right-side up and put it on his desk. "When was the last time you ever saw a New York souvenir? I guess they'll have to start making them again."

"That's a little morbid, don't you think?"

Cassidy studied the snow globe, then looked back at Alex. "What's morbid about snow?"

"Not the snow. The city is underwater completely, up to the tops of the skyscrapers."

Cassidy looked at it, then back at him. "It's just a toy."

"It's creepy," Alex retorted. "Seeing you play with it, it's like a little girl playing with a voodoo doll as if there's nothing wrong with it."

"'There is no good or evil. Only thinking makes it so.'" When Alex didn't respond, she quietly muttered, "Shakespeare," and returned to her computer.

On cue, Alex turned back to the map and studied it, falling immediately back into his investigative mindset. The profiles had come back and the two men from the bust weren't connected to anyone he knew. That backed up his theory that the drug dealers had some sophisticated way of trafficking. He had never heard of low-level people, with seemingly no connections to bigger gangs, winding up with such a high volume of drugs. The house had belonged to thirty-five-year-old electrical engineer, Garret Lorrie, who had been beaten unconscious and tied up in the closet when Alex and Cassidy had arrived. Both of the intruders had been identified and both had a history of violence, though never gun violence before. Half the men in the city were attached to some gang, though Alex didn't know which to suspect just yet. Both men were receiving medical treatment, along with Mr. Lorrie. With everyone involved in the hospital, Alex and Cassidy had to wait to continue their investigation. Normally, waiting was Alex's kryptonite, but he had been shot at more that evening than he had been in years. He could use the downtime.

After staring at the maps for another pointless five minutes, Alex pulled out his office chair, rolled it around the desks and sat next to Cassidy. On the screen, a highly stylized anime girl in pink priestess robes was yelling in Japanese at a stuffed bear with green wings. Alex read the subtitles, but they only made him more confused.

"Hey." Alex risked annoying Cassidy. "Did Harrah report anything new?"

Cassidy tapped the side of her palm, the show paused and she looked at him. "Since you got your hand wrapped up? No." She hit 'play' and the bear turned into a prince with white tights and a golden mask over one side of his face. "Next time, don't incapacitate every criminal who shoots at you. For god's sake, you have to leave one person to tell you what happened," Cassidy finished saying just as a large-breasted green dragon-unicorn fired a laser beam from her horn.

"You said things would get better for the Boroughs."

"Yeah." Cassidy didn't bother looking away from the screen.

"You said that with Manhattan rising up out of the waves, constructing permanent bridges, business and tourists pouring in, that things would get better here. So far, I can't see it. All the tourists, the businessmen, the money, they're all over there. Manhattan is less than a mile away from us, but we may as well be living on the other side of the planet. All the planes fly over our heads and all the people and money stay over there."

Cassidy fell quiet and watched the screen as the priestess broke into a song about friendship. "Things will get better," she stated with conviction in her voice. "It's been less than a month. Give it more time."

Alex looked deep into Cassidy's eyes. He couldn't tell if Cassidy was avoiding meeting his or was that engrossed in the friendship song. When she started mouthing along, he had his answer. After a few seconds, Alex turned his chair and watched with her, wondering if any amount of context would have helped.

Chapter Three

Lei Xu stepped out of her apartment and into the hallway while reaching into her designer Parisian handbag for her mirror, to give herself one last look over. Content for the moment, she walked to the elevator and instinctively pressed the '2' button, then corrected herself and pressed 'L.' The lobby had been sealed off before the water had risen, so unlike the first floors of most buildings in Manhattan, the building's base hadn't been flooded. Now there were two glass front doors instead of a plastic wall. Lei nodded at the manager, who stood beside the reception desk watching the repairs, and walked out.

Outside, the sun was rising over the city. Seagulls were nearly as common as people. They rested on the sidewalk for a brief moment, only to be spurred into the air again by a curious child or oblivious adult. All about her were swarms of day laborers picking up garbage and professionals heading to work, but most stared in wonder at a city that was sinking just two weeks before.

Lei side-stepped to the edge of the thronging masses. Growing up in New York City, she never had to deal with crowds before. Now every block was filled with them. Every other person was taking pictures of the city as Manhattan's natives weaved through them and passed over the retractable bridges that reached out from every skyscraper to their nearest floating counterpart. Along with the tourists, some workers from the Boroughs were walking on the raised skyscraper blocks, pouring chemicals on the sides that washed away the sea, or using small, high-powered laser pens that fried off sea urchins, barnacles and rot. Lei could tell the difference between the outsider tourists and those from the Boroughs, because the latter were dressed in old jerseys and worn caps, taking pictures and video with external cameras. The richer foreigners would look at a monument and tap their palm.

I should take a walk and discover more of the city myself. She started walking, her excitement tempered by her high heels, which hindered her purposed stride. *What should I visit first? The old U.N. building? Are they going to use it again? I thought I heard them say they were turning it into a museum. The Freedom Tower? Everyone sees that.*

Before she even decided where she would go, her feet were taking her there. When she stood on the bridge crossing 49th street and saw the blocks packed with people shoulder to shoulder, she knew she had reached the right place. In the distance was Saint Patrick's Cathedral. Of all the new wonders that the 'Manhattan Miracle' had brought, this was the one that drew the biggest crowds. A floating cathedral. Lei kept trying to understand why so many people were jumping over themselves, holding small cameras above their heads and snapping shots at random. Standing there in front of the actual building that had been featured in every report on every news station of the 'New New York' was the cathedral, suddenly holier than St. Peter's or Notre Dame de Paris. The Vatican had called it a sign of God's providence, that Christianity would endure in a post-flood world.

As Lei peered above the crowd at the cathedral, it seemed so... small. Her eyes trailed upward, all the way up, until she looked straight up at the massive buildings towering over Saint Patrick's. *How difficult was it to raise them? How many nights did Sverichek spend calculating every variable so the engines could lift up the Empire State Building or the Chrysler Building?* Saint Patrick's Cathedral must have been a few quick clicks into a calculator, its measure over in minutes.

But it's not about the numbers, she thought as she gazed at the cathedral, catching its roof and spire over the growing crowd. She turned away. As she did, she remembered hearing a statistic saying that the 2nd most popular destination was the newly risen Yankee Stadium. That she could understand, even though she wasn't a baseball fan. The thought of 50,000 people drinking beer, eating hot dogs and watching professionals play baseball in a floating stadium seemed a lot more impressive than a floating cathedral, even if no teams had agreed to play there yet.

After roughly twenty minutes, in which she learned for the first time how to weave through a crowd, she arrived at the massive square hole that divided the city; or as it was once known as, Central Park. The edge of the sidewalk was lined with tourists. Lei spotted a Vietnamese family of six and waited behind them. The father kept snapping photos, but the four children were getting anxious, clearly not understanding the significance of the vast expanse of saltwater. The son pushed his older sister and spat something in Vietnamese. Their father turned around, grabbed his youngest child's chin and said something fierce and commanding in return. He then pushed at the child's back and the family was off.

Lei walked up to the edge of the sidewalk hesitantly; there was no handrail between it and the open water. To her right, Belvedere Castle sat perfectly on its hill, its dark brick structure mostly untouched by the debris and murky water. Two workers in the castle's lone tower raised a new American flag, its bright colors crowning the flooded park. Beyond that was Cleopatra's Obelisk, its tip high above the water, its base covered in dark algae. A seagull circled it and landed on its point. A group of American tourists to Lei's left was pointing and taking pictures. She followed where they were pointing and saw a large café submerged underwater. Her eyes followed the pathway from the café and saw bridges and fountains scattered throughout the lake.

Lei stepped back and her place was immediately taken by someone else. She walked behind the rows of people until she arrived at a makeshift pier with an extremely crude shed marked 'Changing Room' that looked as if it would tip over the minute anyone stepped in it. She walked up to it and noticed a sign marked "Scuba equipment for rent, $200,000 1 hour."

"Sir, where have you come from?" A woman in a low-cut tank top and jeans asked from behind the wooden counter.

A man with a trim beard in a white suit said, "Iran."

"Iran? That's the other side of the world! I bet you're familiar with ancient Egypt, pharaohs and pyramids and such. Well, you wouldn't think it, but we have our own ancient Egyptian pillar right here. You don't read hieroglyphics, do you?"

The man shook his head.

"Well, that obelisk right there," the woman behind the makeshift desk pointed at Cleopatra's, "is a genuine ancient Egyptian obelisk, and if you want to read the whole thing, you have to go under the water for it. If you've got an internal comp, I can upload the translation for you and you can read it yourself."

Lei tapped her wrist and brought up her own interface. *10:44 A.M. Not enough time for today, I will definitely come back for this though.* When the woman working the stand had gotten the Iranian man suited and seen him jump off the end of the dock into the water, Lei approached the desk.

"You looking to rent some gear today?"

"Maybe another day. That is, if it's still here. I hear there are plans to fix Central Park; I mean, to raise it out of the water."

"Then you heard different than me," the woman replied. "I heard that they are going to build over it and have two layers of Central Park. But there's going to be changes, so if you want to see Central Park before a bunch of contractors turn it into a strip mall, I can offer you a deal on gear. $180,000 for an hour, just for you. Come on, that's a steal, I'm practically paying you!"

"Thanks, I am busy now, but I will be back."

Lei turned, though she managed to just catch the unpleasant look the scuba woman gave her.

She was hungry, but decided to skip the over-priced hot dogs that the street vendors were selling. New York hadn't been selling hot dogs on the street since before she was born and she wasn't going to trust any vendor charging four times the normal price for half-cooked meat. She grabbed a chicken and stuffing sandwich from a nearby shop that she loved, which had recently relocated to the new street level. When she had finished, she continued her trek across the city.

Lei stopped halfway across one of the retractable bridges and looked across the canal, down the long line of floating skyscrapers. The wind tousled the strands of her short black hair and patted gently on her tan overcoat. She caught her reflection in the semi-clear waters. The muddy water had turned her tan skin darker, and her almond eyes were nearly black in the dirty water. Her face rippled as an Italian man with long, dark curls and olive skin rode his motorboat across the canal and then ducked as he went underneath the bridge she was standing on.

Most New Yorkers had taken to walking the newly installed bridges, having abandoned their usual habit of boat travel. From every other skyscraper, workers were turning the plaster and steel docks that were attached to the third floors, what were once the sidewalks, into makeshift awnings. Below them, workers scrubbed, scraped and chipped away the barnacles, mollusks and green algae covering the buildings' lower walls.

Lei figured she might as well head to her destination early rather than continue wandering. Even amidst a rolling sea of towers, the Empire State Building stood tall and proud above them. A semi-circle of tourists formed on the outside; those rich enough to have internal comps must have been recording and snapping photos through eye-cams while the poorer or those religiously opposed to bio-mechanics were using cellphones, which they bent and stretched as they tried to take in the whole building. Lei forced her way between a teenage boy and an old woman as she worked her way to the building's entrance. She slowly paced up the steps, which were still slippery, and smiled at the four security guards who stood at the building's entrance. After letting them check her ID, she walked in.

As she stepped inside, she was immediately hit with an overpowering stench of algae and sea water. The words 'Do Not Pass' appeared in yellow laser-light over sections of the floor that hadn't been cleared. Dozens of workers were on all fours, pouring chemicals and scrubbing furiously at the green grime beside buckets that were overflowing with starfish, mussels and clams. Lei eyed the nearest bucket and noticed a tiny crab crawling around the top. Giant fans stood at the back wall near the elevator, blowing the salty-grime smell of the sea outside. A handful of people were patrolling the lobby and spraying air fresheners, which did nothing to alleviate the smell and only made Lei light-headed.

She walked across the room to the elevator. A security guard stood in front of it. "I have an appointment," she said. "I'm—"

"Reception is on the first floor," the man said while pressing the elevator button.

He stepped inside and she followed, muttering 'thank you.'

The smell nearly disappeared as the elevator doors closed. When they arrived on the first floor, Lei stepped out, into the open reception area, and walked to the massive front desk made of imitation marble. Lei locked eyes with the bald, smiling man in a black sweater vest who sat behind it. She swung her briefcase in front of him, arched her back and kept her chin level. *Now is as good a time as any to act professional. Impressive for floor 1 should be passable for 101.*

"Lei Xu," she nearly sang. "I am here to see Mr. Stanhope for a one o' clock appointment."

"Wait one moment, please," he said. His sunny composure showed no hint that he was impressed as he casually clicked on a floating screen and called the office of New York City's owner. "Yes, I have a Lei Xu here for Mr. Stanhope. Yes, okay, sure." The receptionist clicked 'end call.' "Please proceed to floor 101."

Lei smiled, said, "Thank you," and turned back to the elevator. She pressed the '101' button. The elevator raced upward and in less than a minute, it was at the top. She stepped out into a giant marble hallway. There was a golden statue on the right side of the room that towered over her. She stared at it for a moment, realizing it was the famous statue of Prometheus that once adorned Rockefeller Center. Across the hallway leading up to another reception desk were marble statues, abstract art sculptures and even a lamppost with a street sign reading 'Broadway.'

A door at the end of the hall opened up and an electronic voice said, "Enter, Miss Xu."

The room on the other side was much smaller. It had wooden floors, walls and ceiling, and a chandelier that looked almost medieval and probably was. There were bookshelves filled with old tomes and artifacts, including an ivory Mughal dagger and a blue porcelain violin. A rotund man in a white suit with tufts of white at the sides of his head looked up from a desk at the other side of the room.

He waved her over. "Come closer," he greeted as he stood up. "Come, come." He took long, wobbling strides over to her. She sped up to meet him, her heels echoing in the high-ceilinged room. She switched her briefcase over to her left and shook his hand.

"Thank you for having me, Mr. Stanhope."

"Of course, Miss..."

"Xu. Lei Xu."

"Miss Xu." He turned around and returned to the chair behind his desk. "I was told by our R&D department that you have a brilliant idea for us."

"Oh, really?" She sat down.

Stanhope smiled. "You don't believe Arthur has any faith, in you?"

Lei began to blush.

As her face turned red, Stanhope's smile grew wider. "You should see yourself now, red as a cherry."

He was chuckling. Lei tried to compose herself when a bead of sweat appeared on her forehead and she knew it wasn't working. "Sir, my idea is—"

"Bet you wanted to impress me," he went on. "You couldn't convince your boss, and now you want to convince the big boss. You are a big picture person, aren't you?"

She could hardly breathe.

"Good," he replied. His lips fell back into a straight line, but his eyes began to sparkle. "I like big thinkers and audacious people, and to step out of protocol must mean that despite your personal timidity, you have great confidence in your product. So what's your idea?"

Lei was so put off that she could hardly begin. She reached into her bag and pulled out her projection cube and placed it on the desk. She pressed a button and the cube lit up and linked with her internal comp. She tapped a few times on her right palm and a hologram of New York City emerged. She centered the floating image on the Empire State Building. She pressed again and the image descended beneath the waves to the square block that the building rested on. The Sea Titan motor hung beneath them, and at the center was a fan which pushed the water downward, keeping the building level.

"You haven't changed anything, have you?" Stanhope asked. "Marko showed me this before, a year ago."

"Not yet." She pressed a side bar. Another, smaller motor on the building's northern side appeared, along with a series of smaller, interconnected motors scattered around the building's base. Lei touched the screen and the view returned to the full-scale Empire State Building, only now it was moving in the water.

"Sir, I have been working on developing a motor that could move even the heaviest skyscrapers in any direction without destabilizing them and it is compact enough that it can be installed on every moving skyscraper block in the city." She clicked a button and the screen zoomed out to Manhattan. Each skyscraper had a motor attached and they all began to move, circling together like one giant living organism. "It runs on cheap, renewable energy. If Stanhope Limited invested a few trillion dollars into additional hovering solar platforms out at sea, that would generate enough power for the entire city even with the new motors."

Stanhope nodded his head. He stared at the skyscrapers as they began a slow dance across the screen. His eyes were wide as the magnificent scene played out before him.

Stanhope watched in silence for a long time. Lei waited patiently, watching the skyscrapers rotate in his eyes. She thought they had done a full rotation before Stanhope finally tore himself from the projection, met her glance and with a puzzled look asked, "I don't understand, where would we move them to?"

Lei pressed a button and the process sped up. The buildings moved in a circle, then stopped. A clock appeared and showed that a day passed. At 7 A.M., the skyscrapers rotated and stopped again.

"Sir, I've developed an algorithm that calculates how we can move every building in New York City. The whole city could be re-arranged in fifteen minutes as each skyscraper moves over to take the place of another. Moreover, the retractable bridges that have been installed could easily reconnect the city regardless of which building it connects to. We could create a new New York every day."

"But why would we do this?"

Because it'll create something new, something never done before. "Think of all the money that the city is generating from tourism right now. Imagine all the tourists from the world over, who would flock to see New York City..." *dancing on the waves,* "...in motion. There would never be a permanent New York skyline. Every day, the city would change. They would have to stay here longer, come back again, to see it take a new form. It would change in such a dramatic way that the city is new every day, but at the same time, native New Yorkers wouldn't be disturbed by it as they move with the city."

Stanhope's eyebrows furrowed into a puzzled look. He looked at the scene again. This time his eyes dug deeper, as if seeing beyond the image itself. When he was finished, he looked up at her and asked, "How much will this cost?"

"The costs should be relatively cheap, sir." She pulled up projections for the project. "The motors don't use up much energy. The creation of the motors will cost a little over one hundred trillion, as you can see." She began to sweat as she said the figure. "But I am confident that the money we get back will far outweigh whatever we put in."

"You have left out the majority of the costs. And there is no 'we.' You aren't putting in any money. There is only 'me'."

She blushed again.

"I have to pay for people to install it. I have to get the permission of everyone else who owns a skyscraper to join along, otherwise it won't work. Then there's the cost of manufacturing, unexpected problems, and as New York's economy booms, everything here from labor to benefits will be more expensive than any projections my ambitious underlings give me; believe me, I know from experience."

Lei had turned bright red now. She wanted to say something, but could hardly form words. It didn't matter, Stanhope wasn't finished.

"Now, there's an even more important question: how do you know this will generate money? Who's to say that this will bring in any more business or tourists? New York City has risen from the waves; will any tourist look at that, unimpressed, and then when they hear that it now rotates, they will take the first flight from New Delhi to get here? You're asking me to build a custom factory to make the engines, get permission from all the other skyscraper owners in New York to have them installed and follow the program. That'll be a fortune and enough red tape to cover every leak in this city."

Stanhope put his meaty hand on his first chin. He paused again and turned to the screen. "I'm sorry, but your proposal isn't worth the money and risk I would be putting into it. Unless you can give me another reason to commence with this project, it's a no."

Lei knew it was her last chance. She forced herself to meet his eyes and delivered her speech:

"Last month, Marko Sverichek showed the world that there are no limits to the capability of the unrestrained mind. But we can't stop there. If we don't continue to challenge ourselves and push for new advancements, if we rest on our one great achievement, then we will have had the effect of inspiring the rest of the world to aspire to greatness, to build and discover new things and they will leave us behind. We should construct this because it will shock the world. A month ago, you saved the city and re-made New York. Why simply re-build the old when you could create something entirely new?"

Lei held her breath. A long moment of silence passed between them. She felt her insides disappear. *I thought this was the most brilliant idea I've ever had.* She had already imagined herself on news magazines and scientific journals being hailed as 'The next Sverichek.' She saw those headlines disappear in the unblinking eyes of George Stanhope.

"No," was all he said. The finality of the word hit her like a punch to the gut.

"The motors can be used to move the city in case of a hurricane or a foreign attack."

Stanhope burst out laughing. "I think the rest of the world is too busy treading water to attack us. And there hasn't been so much as a thunderstorm here in a decade, let alone a hurricane. As long as the federal government has an air fleet that can spray ice into gathering clouds until they dissolve, there hasn't been a natural disaster in New York since, well, I guess the flood. My answer remains 'no.'"

"I'm sorry for wasting your time," she said, hoping it sounded defiant, but feeling pathetic all the same. She grabbed her projection cube and put it in her bag. She shook his hand numbly and walked out.

She passed through the long hallway, biting her lip as moisture appeared in her eyes, trying to hold back the tears. She stopped as she noticed the statue of Prometheus.

You are not alone.

She walked to the elevator and pressed 'L.' When she arrived at the first floor, the workers scrubbing away the vestiges of the sea were in almost the exact same places as before. Most of the grime had been wiped off, but they were scrubbing the marble down to the surface, picking out the remaining specks of salt and sand. As she walked out, she noticed that the buckets with sea creatures had been removed.

She walked outside and pushed her way through the line of tourists. She kept her eyes to the street, not daring to look up at the buildings. She stopped two blocks away and finally looked up, imagining the skyscrapers moving and turning every afternoon.

Dancing on the waves.

As she walked back past the throngs to her apartment, she thought of her hermitical idol Sverichek, seeing him in the long hallway as one of those grand statues was saved from the sea. *How much did you change this city? After you lifted us up, did you expect us to stand? Will you continue to carry us?*

After a while, she tried not to think of anything.

Chapter Four

Rodney Maxwell's legs dangled over the sidewalk outside of the luxury boutique Il Maestoso Fiorentina. Holograms displaying opulent products from the world over were projected all along the open windows of the five-story gallery. Designer suits and light-colored skirts carrying opulent handbags passed by, wearing jewelry that glittered in the noontime sun.

Rodney was not one of them and neither was the girl whose hand he held. Rodney's deeply-tanned hand nearly matched Samantha's naturally darker skin. With his other hand, he held a half-finished strawberry ice cream cone. Rodney and Sam had their pants rolled up and were letting their feet dip into the water, which in the past few days was finally beginning to turn blue. The motors underneath the skyscrapers not only held them afloat, but acted as a filtration system, tearing through the garbage, leaving the water almost clear for the first time in Rodney's life.

"Remember when I told you that the other cleaners on the BlueSea and I found that safe?" Rodney smiled. "You'll never guess what was in it."

"Oh my god, you finally got that open!" Sam beamed. "Are we rich?"

"We?" He pulled back. "What makes you think I'd share the gold with you?"

Sam's eyes went wide. "No way. No way you found—"

Rodney started to grin and she pushed him. "I found something even better," he replied.

"What?"

"There were a bunch of family heirlooms; no gold or silver or anything, they must have cleaned it out before their house went under. But there was a book, seventy years old and perfectly preserved, called *Memories of Peponi*. It's amazing."

"Oh."

"It's about…" He looked over at Sam and sighed. "I'm sorry I didn't find a trillion dollars and an airplane for you, but what did you think the boys and I would dig up? Even if we found a safe stacked with money from a century ago, it still wouldn't be worth anything."

"Probably enough to buy a couple of books."

"Not a real one with paper pages. Hell, I don't think I've even seen a real book in my whole life. I think there might be laws against that, cutting down trees and all."

"So you think the book might be worth something?" Her curiosity suddenly piqued.

"Yes! It's invaluable. When I first picked it up, it felt strange reading ink instead of a screen. For a second, I was worried I wouldn't even know how to read it. Have you ever read anything that was actually written down? It's like something from another world."

Sam gave him a tiny smile. "Wow, you really love this thing, don't you? Is it any good?

"I've just gotten started. It's about this teenager living in rural Idaho with his girlfriend. He has the power to turn back time for objects and things."

"So he's a superhero?"

"No, this is really realistic. His girlfriend gets scared and runs away. He wants to chase after her. So one night he turns back time on the front doors of a bank, turns back time on the vault so it opens up and takes the money, but he misses the security cam. The government finds him, arrests him and tries to control his power when even he doesn't know how."

"So what happens to the girl?" Sam questioned, genuinely curious. "No, wait, don't tell me. You've got me interested, I want to read it myself."

"What makes you think I'll let you borrow it? It's too valuable for me to just be handing it out to any girl that smiles at me."

She glared at him, which only made him smirk. "Isn't it about time you went back to work?"

Rodney put his hand on his chest and feigned hurt. "The BlueSea should be pulling into the south harbor in about fifteen minutes, I have time."

Sam's eyes widened. "It's a fifteen minute walk!"

"It's ten."

"I live five blocks from there. It's fifteen."

"You're slow."

"Get going!" She pushed him.

He got up and started putting on his shoes, not caring that his socks were getting wet.

"Go!"

"Love you too, see you tomorrow!"

He started running south. Foot traffic was heavy enough that he got stuck behind a few crowds, and boat traffic was thick enough that three bridges were raised on his way south. He cursed and pulled out his cell phone. He might have been the only person in that block who couldn't afford his own Universal Neural Interface, and had to keep all his hardware on the outside. He checked the time and realized it had taken him twenty-two minutes to get to the southern end. He arrived, panting and peering at the horizon. He scanned all around him, but there were no boats marked 'BlueSea Waste Removal'; none that had the same crashing blue wave on teal background that he wore on his staff shirt.

He held a hand up to his forehead and gazed out to the open waters. Five minutes passed and he picked up his cell phone and called his boss. "Yiril? Hello?"

No response. He paced for another twenty minutes before he called again, then a third time. Worry overtook him. Without knowing what else to do, he headed east toward the ferry. It was a short trip from Manhattan back to the Boroughs, but it felt too long for Rodney. When the ferry docked, he broke into a run towards the northwestern edge of the Boroughs.

After a few minutes, he arrived at the company house. It was an extended pier, custom made of cheap plastics, like most of the piers in the area. There was no way it couldn't have been a violation of at least a few safety regulations, as the walkway would sway and sink a little as one walked on it, and more than once Rodney thought something would snap and he was either going to be swallowed up by the cold water or get wedged between cracked plastic on a trembling dock, but miraculously it held. The dock had a tiny office on its right side, barely larger than an outhouse, with one window. Rodney didn't know if this was his boss Yiril Zogheib's only home, but he never bothered to ask him.

There was a large boat with a line of brown around its bobbing hull with the words 'BlueSea Waste Removal' painted in dark blue on its sides. The boat was tied to the only cleat in the custom pier. The iron cleat clacked with every rise and fall of the sea.

Yiril was sitting on the boat in a folding lawn chair, looking off at

Manhattan.

"Where is everyone?" Rodney called as he climbed up the side of the boat to join his boss and captain. "I waited for you, I was ten minutes early even..." Before he could finish his sentence, he noticed that there weren't any extendable trash spears or garbage bags. The deck was completely empty.

"Go home, Rodney," Yiril called angrily, not bothering to look at him.

"What happened?" Rodney asked, stepping forward to stand beside him.

Yiril spat and phlegm hit the edge of the handrail and slid down the side. "We've been fired."

"What? Why?"

"Why?" Yiril asked. "The motors from the skyscrapers have cleaned out a ton of garbage as it is and now Manhattan is buying up their own licensed boats and hiring back all the people they laid off and then some. They don't want to pay any small-time clean-up crews, especially those that come from the Boroughs. Hard-working, sweating laborers picking up trash doesn't mesh well with the new décor of the city and now we're being replaced by 'professionals' and machines."

A pit in Rodney's stomach opened up. "What am I going to do?" he asked himself, but directed it at Yiril. "I need money."

Yiril gave him an angry look. "I have a stomach, too. I think my kids do as well. Go away." He waved him off.

"Maybe... maybe we can use this as a fishing vessel—" He spat out the words in panic.

"I said leave!" Yiril rose from his chair. Rodney backed up, stumbling as he did. Yiril walked towards him. Rodney didn't think he would hurt him, but for the first time since Rodney had known Yiril, there was a coldness in his eyes, as if he were looking at the one source for all his accumulated misery and was about to strangle it. Rodney leapt from the boat and jogged off the pier. He didn't think it was necessary, but he wasn't going to chance it. He looked behind him and saw Yiril glaring. He grimaced and spat, then returned to where he was sitting.

Well, shit, Rodney thought as he slowly trudged away. *I know what happens next. Now I spend the next few months begging and pleading for a terrible job. I can always get food at the mission and I've got the houseboat, so it's not the end of the world.* He imagined Sam's smiling face as they ate ice cream and watched the people walk by across the canals. The ferry wasn't free, Sam didn't make much as a waitress either, and he would sooner swim to Manhattan than ask her for money. He grimaced as he imagined what the next few months might hold as he realized he would probably see her a lot less often.

His feet started heading towards the only place that he could go now. Turning back west, he kept marching. Just before lunchtime, he was at the Saving Grace soup kitchen. The building was only a story tall, as nearly all of the oldest floating wooden buildings were, but it was four times wider than any of the plastic stilt-houses or houseboats. It had been painted eggshell white, and while the paint had chipped, the outside looked cleaner and more vibrant than the shops around it, which had dull blue, red and green paint. Rodney peered through the window and saw that the soup kitchen was almost completely full, mostly with older people and their young children. Those old enough to hold a low-paying job wouldn't be arriving until after work.

Rodney stepped inside, hearing a bell tinkle above him as he entered. Behind the counter, a mousy girl with bright green eyes, freckles and auburn hair strung up in a fishnet handed out trays with a bowl of soup, a cut of bread and a cup of water. Rodney got in line behind an Arab man and his wife, who wore a purple hijab. When someone ahead of them took a seat at a nearby table, they trudged forward. The wife said something soft to her husband in Arabic and he responded. Rodney guessed he was trying to reassure her, but he was of the opinion that Arabic always sounded harsh when men spoke it, so that he couldn't tell if he was being nice or berating. The girl behind the counter served him and he trudged to an open spot. Rodney tried to force down the tomato soup and biscuit, but after ice cream, the gruel made him want to vomit. *Probably two more months of this,* he thought and wanted to vomit again.

"Hey, Rodney." A dark-haired youth a few years older than him with thick eyebrows and the beginnings of a scraggly goatee smiled at him. He was wearing a blue hoodie of one of New Jersey's baseball teams and the cap of another, though Rodney doubted he was a fan of either. Beside him stood a lanky kid in a brown hoodie whose cheekbones, bony forehead, pale skin and dark eyes made him look like a walking ghoul.

"Hey, Antoni. Hey, Grease," Rodney greeted them half-heartedly.

Antoni sat down next to him on the bench. "Haven't seen you here in a while."

"Yeah, it's like you've been avoiding us or something," Grease remarked.

"I haven't. Times have just been good, didn't need to drop by here."

"Oh yeah?" Antoni sneered. "Off with the girl in Manhattan, livin' it up, right?"

"Pretty much," Rodney muttered and swallowed the rest of his biscuit.

"Why are you here now then?" Grease interjected.

"Just got fired a few hours ago."

"Welcome back to the poor house, then. We missed you down here. Oh well, cheer up. It's not so bad down at the bottom. You got food here. You still have that piece of floating shit to sleep in?"

Rodney waved his hands toward his bowl of soup as if to say, this food is bad enough already, don't make it worse. He swallowed. "Yeah, I do."

"The panel on top hasn't shorted or anything? So you have electricity at least?"

"I guess. I mean, there's not much there to power, just the lights, a fridge... actually, that's it."

"Damn, you'd think your parents would have left you a little something nicer." Grease laughed, but Rodney wasn't amused.

"So, now what?" Antoni asked.

"I dunno." Rodney sighed. "Look for a job, hope to get something as soon as possible?"

"You could always join us," Antoni suggested.

Rodney lowered his head. He whispered, "I'm not going to start dealing. Once you get marked as a convict, you'll never be hired again."

"There is the other thing," Grease mumbled.

"Pass," Rodney uttered.

"Since when could you just pass on something?" Antoni waved in front of him. "This is good. Grease and I have been thinking, all these billionaires and trillionaires coming into Manhattan. If we robbed even one of them, just caught one of them on the street, we could probably get enough jewelry or tech to last a month, maybe more."

Rodney gave him a long look. Antoni met it.

"Come on, don't tell me that doesn't appeal to you. You've been diving in for their trash like a trained monkey nearly a year now and what has it got you? A month's worth, maybe more, do you know how much stuff they carry on them? I have connections, I can get it pawned, do all the hard underground stuff. I figure the mugging would be the easy part."

Rodney looked over his shoulder. "I'm sure you've put a lot of thought into this." Rodney rolled his eyes. "Have you ever even done anything like this before?"

"No," he replied. "But look at us. We're young, we're intimidating. We catch some rich guy or some li'l ol' lady walking alone at night, they'll throw their stuff at us. Those rich bastards can afford to replace it."

"And how would you get away with it?"

"Run," Grease interrupted.

There was a long pause in which the both of them stared at him.

"Okay... after you run, then what?"

Antoni ran his thumb across his mouth. "We double back a few times, take a few odd turns, then we take the night ferry."

Rodney's mouth nearly fell open. "You two want to rob someone, run around in circles and then take public transportation as your getaway vehicle? You two are criminal masterminds, I can't believe you aren't running this place."

"Hey, asshole, we work with what we got."

"There's no way you could pull it off without a boat," Rodney concluded.

Antoni held his gaze.

Rodney looked aside. "Well, I guess there's no way you two would have come up to me acting like it's old times if I didn't have something you needed."

"So you can get us on the BlueSea and get it running?" Antoni suddenly latched on to the idea.

Rodney took a breath. "There's an access code... to his shed, that's where he keeps the key—"

"Do you know the code?" Antoni insisted.

"Yeah, me and the other boys would put up the equipment there, we had to know."

Antoni grinned wildly. He brought his hand up between them, shook it and exclaimed in hushed tones, "See, this is fate. I have been trying to come up with this for months, but I never brought it up to you because you were always busy with your girl. I knew you would never do it, not as long as she was distracting you. But now you're back with us and you deliver."

"I didn't say I would do it," Rodney replied.

"You might as well have. What do you have to lose? Yiril fired you. You have no loyalty to him and there's nothing he can do for you."

"I don't know," Rodney breathed.

Antoni stared him down. "And when will you? After two weeks of not seeing your girl and eating here three meals a day? How about a month? How about two? Three? Because by then, Grease and I will done it and moved on, with or without your help, because we aren't going to wait."

Rodney tapped a finger on the table and looked down. *They won't succeed without me. They'll get caught. Then I'll be broke and they'll be in prison.*

He nodded his head. "Okay, when?"

"Tomorrow night, we'll contact you with more info later."

Rodney bit his lip.

"Don't think about it." Antoni put a hand on his shoulder. "It's just like fighting in school, 'cept whoever we pick won't fight back. Easy."

Antoni and Grease stood up. "Knew I could count on you. Don't be such a stranger." Antoni patted him on the shoulder before walking out.

Rodney listened to their footsteps as they walked out. There was still some soup left, but he pushed it away. He watched the other people in the dining room with him. Their heads were down, they mostly ate in silence, and any conversation they had seemed grim. He couldn't believe that in one afternoon, he went from eating ice cream and lounging on a floating skyscraper outside Il Maestoso Fiorentina, to eating slop in a dirty soup kitchen with two dozen other misérablés. He moaned softly and closed his eyes.

He stood up and made the slow trek back to his houseboat. Once inside, he locked the door behind him, opened one of the kitchen cupboards, pulled back the panel and retrieved *Memories of Peponi*.

Chapter Five

Newly-crowned 'America's Mayor' Sophia Ramos sat in her plush reclining chair behind her oaken desk in her expansive and elaborate office. To her right, a marble framed window overlooked the canals of Manhattan from three stories up. Behind her to the left and right were bookshelves filled with old books on leadership, economics, one on great speeches of the last century, and a glass case with an old dueling pistol that belonged to Alexander Hamilton. Sitting directly across from her was Mr. Gao, the ambassador from China, next to New York Governor Andrew Dempsey. Gao was a pleasant enough man, the governor not so much. Sophia caught herself looking past them both to the door, as if hoping for an interruption that would never come.

"I hope you and your wife have been enjoying Manhattan," Sophia continued.

"Oh, yes," Mr. Gao replied, though he might as well have been a terracotta statue for how much emotion he showed. "She is taking my son diving in Central Park today."

Sophia winced. The people who ran the scuba businesses were unlicensed, many of them scavengers who were using their old gear for profit. So far there hadn't been any incident, but she had been told that some of the shadier vendors' gear was worn and the old oxygen tanks might burst if they dove down too deep. *Best not to worry the ambassador, though.*

"Well, that should be exciting," the governor interjected. "I might have to go do that myself."

Sophia decided to dodge by saying, "Since the Miracle, Manhattan has been rising and expanding faster than I could have imagined. It's hard to guess what wonder we'll take up next."

"Yes, this is why I am here. My government would like to give the city of New York and your country a gift; a Chinese garden over Central Park. It would float over the old park, giving it a harmony with the rest of Manhattan. My architects have already sent you some plans."

"I've seen them, they are quite remarkable." Sophia wasn't lying. The concept art that she had seen had shown a thousand tiny islands seemingly scattered around the park at random. Some were massive islands with gardens or a shrine connected by imitation wooden bridges. Others were tiny, inaccessible circular islands, no more than six feet across, with flowers of all different colors forming Chinese symbols, blue lilac waves under a yellow sun, a violet and blue symbol of yin and yang. And in the middle was what looked like a giant temple, though Sophia wasn't sure if it was a public building or an actual working monastery, perhaps the Buddhist response to Saint Patrick's Cathedral. "It is incredibly gracious of you, I am sure our Chinese community would love having a new Chinese garden, and I can't think of any better place to put it than somewhere over Central Park."

"Too bad Chinatown's on the other side of Manhattan," Dempsey remarked, "but I doubt anyone here would be opposed to a little walk to see anything like a floating Forbidden Palace."

"I think people will come much farther than just a few blocks to see it." The ambassador remained unfazed by the governor's attempts at a compliment. "There is so much that your new situation offers. We could set up a temporary worker program. We could send workers here and use the whole of Central Park, building platforms and floating statues."

"Yes," Sophia replied, "this could be a huge project. I imagine that the Italians, the Puerto Ricans, the Japanese and every ethnic group in the city will want some part of it. Your people could lay the ground work and we could make a park that reflected all the great cultures that make up our old and new city."

Mr. Gao's nose crinkled at the idea. Sophia held her wide smile even as the situation grew more awkward. As much as she liked the idea of skilled laborers giving a gift that would make the still-sinking Statue of Liberty look like a stocking stuffer, she didn't think many voters would like China 'taking over' Manhattan.

As a child, Sophia had been told by her mother that when she gave one of her ear-to-ear schoolgirl grins, her eyes beamed with a light of their own. As a teenager, she had even tried smiling at people to see how infectious her personality was. She regretted whoever came up with that saying, because now whenever she smiled at a crowd, she imagined she was spreading a smiling plague. Mr. Gao was apparently immune.

"The Chinese government would like to bestow this gift to America to commemorate this great occasion. We did not expect you would be so hostile to our offering."

Sophia let up on her smile, giving up on her attempts to infect the foreign dignitary. She sat back in her black reclining chair and drummed the fingers of her right hand on the desk.

Dempsey waved a finger and smiled. Before Sophia could stop him, he looked at Gao and mused, "I believe it says somewhere in the Bible not to turn down a gift, I wouldn't know for sure. But in any case, it would be discourteous of us to say 'no,' especially to a foreign dignitary that's come as far as you have."

Sophia looked back and forth between the two. Gao was unmoved and Dempsey remained oblivious. The governor was supposed to be on her side, but in that moment, she figured it was just as well that they were both on the other side of the desk.

"Yes, you're quite right. Ambassador Gao, I expect it to be quite the sight when it's finished."

Mr. Gao's thin lips hardly stretched and Sophia thought the look he was trying to give her was a fake smile. It needed work. "I have utmost faith in my people. And I think that visitors from all around the world will crowd the skyscrapers around it to get a view of the new marvel."

Sophia smiled, this time genuinely. She rose and said, "Thank you for meeting with me today. It's always a pleasure doing business, I hope you have a lovely rest of the day in the city."

Mr. Gao and Dempsey stood up. Gao donned a light grey hat that matched his suit and nodded, turning without so much as another word.

"Pleasure as always, Sophia," Dempsey noted. Without waiting for a reply, he followed Gao out the door. "'Manhattan Marvel,' that's a good idea, since we've already had the 'Miracle.'"

Sophia felt hot underneath her collar. She felt as if she had just been hard-balled by someone who was supposed to be on her team. Still...

Marvel...

As the door closed behind the pair, Sophia poured herself a scotch. She stirred the glass, watching the golden waves rise up and crash against the ice cubes. She walked over to the window and stared out at the lake that had once been City Hall Park and looked out to the canals beyond it. She raised the glass to her lips and drank. First came the cold, then the burn. She checked the time on her internal comp. She had five minutes before her meeting with Lei Xu. She looked past the canals to the outer rim of the city.

Sophia remembered growing up in Manhattan's outer limits. Freezing in the winters as the government heating oil was barely enough to warm up the tower they lived in. Panting in the humid summers before she and her friends jumped into the dirty bay. That had been before she had excelled in her business classes. Before she had under the table negotiations with the previous mayor and began a business selling old historical items that had been found on the sea floor. Before she took the job that no one wanted. Now, after surviving off of Manhattan's misery for nearly a decade, she was profiting from its revival. A twinge of patriotism prickled her skin. She remembered hearing about the American dream in old history books, how people could start off as nothing and then own the world. She hadn't risen that high, but she was determined to make the world remember her as the woman who had been born the daughter of a garbage man in a sinking apartment building and had lifted up the greatest city in the world.

Sophia looked farther, past the rim of the city, towards the Boroughs. Technically, she was still the mayor of that hell-hole. She paused, tasting the last drips of alcohol on her lips. She couldn't think of one person who had started there and made something great out of their life in a long time.

She set the glass down beside the cabinet and walked over to her desk, taking a seat. She found the contact number for her secretary Carol and sent the auto-message 'I'm ready for my next appointment.' After she spent a few minutes acting busy for no one, the large oaken door opened and a tall Chinese woman with dark hair and glasses and wearing a black dress entered. Sophia stood up, smile wide, hand outstretched.

"Miss Xu, it's a pleasure to meet you."

"Likewise, Miss Mayor."

Sophia had to steel her smile. "Please, call me Sophia." She always thought that the address of 'Mayor' made her sound like a cartoon character. "Please, have a seat." She waved to the chair Mr. Gao had just occupied as she took her own. Sophia put her arms out to the side and said, "I hear you were part of the team that lifted our city from the sea floor."

"Yes, though that was really Sverichek's work. He came up with the idea, made the plans, the engines. Our team just developed what he came up with."

Sophia's nose twitched. Humility was the last thing she was looking for in someone promising great new things. Manhattan might not have had much of a competitive political scene, but she had learned many lessons from her decades-long following of the news and pure common sense. One of the lessons she had learned was that when it came to technical work, leave it to the technicians. Every bridge that collapsed, every space shuttle that exploded was always, always the fault of some bureaucrat who rushed a schedule and pretended to know what she didn't. *Now's the time to prove your competence. Humility is a vice.*

"But I had read you were part of the team that made the engines, correct? Not the batteries, or any of the, um, accessories, you were part of the team that made the whole thing work, correct?"

Lei nodded her head. "Yes, I was on that team."

Better. Sophia had hoped that she would have said something else, but when Lei didn't, she continued, "So, show me the plans Stanhope turned down."

Lei grimaced.

Get some fire, girl! You don't like that? Prove me wrong.

Lei reached into her briefcase and pulled out her projection cube. She put it on the desk, pressed a button and a hologram of the engines appeared. She pressed another button and another hologram next to it of a segment of Manhattan moving appeared.

Sophia whistled. "That is pretty impressive. Are you sure these will work?"

Lei blushed. "Yes. I am sure of it. I have the models myself, my engines should be able to move any of these skyscrapers. Moreover, each has been adapted, so there are actually three different sizes, depending on the weight of the skyscraper. To be safe, each machine is capable of moving much more weight than the skyscraper they hold up."

"And these can be installed in tandem with the machines holding the skyscrapers up now?"

"Yes."

"Could you guarantee that there wouldn't be any disruption or... god forbid, a collapse while these are being installed?"

"Yes," she said without pause.

Good.

"One more thing. Could your skyscrapers... sail, if need be?"

Lei paused. "I'm sorry?"

"Not every skyscraper in Manhattan is grand and glorious. To be honest, many small ones, particularly those in northern Manhattan, are rather run down. They were inhabited by low-income people, then gangs. Some of them are downright putrid, no better than sewage dumps... some of them could very well be called sewage dumps. I've had some preliminary searches done of the abandoned ones, and a few bodies have turned up, too. Some only a few years old; one was a bleached skeleton, from maybe half a century ago."

Lei was visibly disturbed, but remained silent.

"I don't have to tell you that things were a lot different even just a month ago. Manhattan has no use for these. These will only stunt our growth. We need to get rid of them, to build anew... I dream, you see. I wasn't a dreamer, not really, until last month. My whole childhood, my world was sinking beneath the sea. Then one man lifted it all up. I intend to continue that work."

Lei crinkled her nose. "By moving the skyscrapers? Where to?"

"I intend to sell them," Sophia said. "To rich cities; those that benefited when the shoreline reached them and wiped out their rivals; cities on our new coasts which are rapidly expanding and need skyscrapers, but don't want to spend money on building material, which has skyrocketed in price. Do you think it is possible that if you adapted your machine to make it much larger, you could sail a skyscraper up to Paterson? Or down to Norristown? Somewhere along the coast, obviously... I don't mean to sail our skyscrapers across the ocean."

Sophia laughed, but Lei was still taken aback by the proposal. After a minute of thought, Lei said, "Yes, I think I can. But I still don't understand."

"Which part?"

"You really think selling off parts of Manhattan would benefit the city?"

Sophia raised an eyebrow. She wasn't sure if Lei thought she was mad or her idea was, or if that made any difference. *Yes, it does. She seems to worship Sverichek. He is a sane man, but he had a mad idea. Maybe I can convince her that I am just like him.*

"It's simple," Sophia explained. "Some of the mid-range skyscrapers we have are worth hundreds of billions of dollars in material. The engines to keep our skyscrapers afloat only cost the city ten billion dollars or thereabouts. If your machines cost about the same, then we could turn an enormous profit from selling off our garbage."

"I see." Lei still seemed unconvinced.

Sophia put her hands on the armrests of her chair. "Now we come to the agreement. If you can tell me you can do this, without any doubt in your mind, I will pay you one and a half times your normal salary and you will be running the R&D department you are currently working for."

"How is that possible?"

Sophia smiled. "I have hands and ears everywhere. I had heard about your idea and I've been pulling strings to make it a reality ever since. I called southern cities for potential offers, got quite a few back, and I talked to Stanhope. He still doesn't agree with the idea, but I am sending a great deal of money his way in order to hire off his staff who don't have anything to do since the Sea Titans were made, and I will be handling all the red tape myself."

Lei still looked apprehensive.

"It's yours if you want it. You can lead the team, lead the city. And if your machines work, we may just go ahead with your idea to have a rotating city. I can't guarantee it; it is a pretty flowery idea, if a bit impractical... but just maybe, you might get your way. Can you do this?"

Lei remained silent, but with the way she met Sophia's eyes, the mayor knew what she was going to say. "Yes, I can."

Sophia reached forward and shook Lei's hand. "Congratulations. We'll send a contract over later, but when it comes, you will officially be the new head of R&D at Stanhope Limited."

Lei smiled so widely Sophia was sure she was about to get a hug. Lei resisted, though when Sophia escorted her out, she nearly forgot her cube.

After she left, Sophia walked over to the window. She smiled wanly and looked outward. *I had convinced myself I would be the new Sverichek, causing civilizations to be reborn anew by my own will. I think that when Lei left, she thought she was the one who would be doing that.*

Silly girl.

Sophia traded her suit for a turquoise dress and sparkling deep green teardrop earrings. She applied a dark shade of red to her lips and a deep black eye-liner. She wore her highest pair of heels, which made her feel like she was walking on stilts. She put on white gloves for the finishing touch and stepped out of her apartment.

When she walked outside, a burly man with flaming red hair and beard and wearing a black tuxedo looked at her with shining green eyes and smiled.

"Hello, Charlie," she cooed.

She thought back to the first time she had met him. She was a sophomore at Bloomberg High School near the southern tip of Manhattan. They both knew they liked each other, but she had been too cautious.

"What do you think of me?" She had looked down into the video phone, trying to suppress a smile.

"What do you mean?"

"I mean, what do you think of me?"

"What do you mean?"

Boys are dumb.

"I mean, would you think anyone would want to date me?" She paused, thinking she had gone too far.

"Has anyone asked you?"

"Would you want to date me?"

She remembered Charlie had paused, his young face trying to work out the puzzle that was a teenage girl. In that pause, she thought a thousand horrible thoughts about how unattractive and undesirable she was.

"Sure, let's do it." He had smiled at her nervously. "I mean, I like you and you like me. Yeah, let's do it. Let's be boyfriend and girlfriend."

Sophia paused on the other end. "Oh... no, no. I was asking you if you wanted to be boyfriend and girlfriend, I wasn't asking you to be my boyfriend."

It took ten seconds for Charlie to furrow his brow and say, "What?" He turned off the chat-box. They didn't speak for a year afterward. But Sophia kept following him, eventually showing up at his marketing firm InspiringAds as a business liaison. Then, when she ran for city council, she hired the company for her campaign. Sometimes, she wondered if she only got into politics because she thought it might bring them together. When she thought about that question, she grinned, knowing the answer.

That night, Charlie smiled up at her from the bottom of the steps, standing in front of a polished silver cruiser. He reached out a hand that wrapped itself around her glove. He kissed it and beamed. "You look beautiful, Sophia, as always."

She smiled from ear to ear. "And you have never looked more handsome, Charlie."

Still holding her hand, he led her down into the boat. The engine gently thrummed behind them as the suited valet guided the boat through Manhattan. Sophia leaned back against Charlie's strong chest and looked upward. Two stars twinkled from between the monolithic towers that looked like hands reaching for the sky.

Charlie gently touched one of her emerald teardrop earrings. "Are you sure you don't want to celebrate your birthday with anyone else? You look so gorgeous, I expect you to be at a gala with hundreds of people."

"I can look gorgeous just for you," she said coyly. She thought she caught a hint of nervousness in his voice, and she had to steady herself.

"All right," he said, letting the word trail off. The usually talkative Charlie was silent the entire way over. Sophia tried to appear unconcerned, tried to keep Charlie from feeling her heart pounding in her chest. She looked over to the people walking on the sidewalks, then down at the white wake illuminated in the light. *This must be what lovers felt when they rode the gondolas in Venice.*

When they finally arrived, Charlie jumped out of the boat in his excitement, offering his hand to her again in a chivalrous gesture that made her laugh. They walked in to the Girabaldi, where Charles gave his name and they were escorted to a window-side table. Sophia was sure he had asked for it because it was romantic, but for her, the view from above could never compare to the view from below.

"How was work?" Charlie asked.

Sophia decided not to mention the earlier Chinese pressuring and was about to talk about her prospects with Lei Xu when she realized that those had to be kept under wraps, too. "Uneventful," she lied. "Aside from cake, the machine chugged on as usual."

Charlie nodded, his usual small talk failing him.

"Yourself?" Sophia asked, the first time she had to prompt him to speak in a long time.

"Fine," he replied. "Good, good. Been looking forward to this."

"Oh?" she asked.

"Well, I haven't gotten to see you much. You've been busy."

A waitress with wavy blonde hair stopped by their table. "Mayor Ramos?" she asked.

"Yes."

"My name is Cynthia, and I'll be your server tonight. Happy birthday!"

"Oh, thank you." Sophia smiled.

"Would you like the staff to sing happy birthday to you?"

"No, thank you, I'm trying to avoid the limelight."

"Okay, what will you have?"

"The pork tenderloin with carrot soup."

"And I'll have the lamb ragu," Charlie said.

"And to drink?"

"Um." She looked at Charlie. She felt she had already drunk enough and was feeling a bit light-headed. "Water."

"And a bottle of champagne," Charlie piped in.

"You'll be drinking it alone."

"You can have one glass... or I'll make them sing happy birthday to you."

Sophia laughed, defeated.

"Okay, I will bring the drinks right out." Cynthia smiled, took the menus and walked off.

Charlie seemed to find himself in the champagne glass as he joked and smiled his boyish grin. Sophia finished one glass, then another, feeling her professionally demure persona roll away with every giggle. The food was still succulent, even though she had it half a dozen times.

"They must be adding a pinch of extra spice every time I visit," she guessed, "so that the taste is never bland."

"Or maybe you are just happier than usual," Charlie proposed.

Maybe he was right. Sophia had been hoping to use her job as mayor to move to the mainland for some other political office. Now hers was the most enviable job in America. She could be anything; maybe even run for president.

"Dessert," Cynthia announced as she lowered a silver tray in front of Sophia.

"That can't be right, I didn't order—"

The waitress placed a small plate with a diamond ring in front of her. Sophia gasped loudly and the whole restaurant fell silent. She looked back up into Charlie's sparkling green eyes, the mischievous grin he had been poorly hiding reappearing on his face.

"Oh my god... Yes!"

Applause broke out among the restaurant. Since it was already a spectacle, Charlie stood up, picked up the ring, removed Sophia's white glove with the grace of a true gentleman and put the ring on her finger to hoots and hollers from the crowd.

"Happy birthday."

Chapter Six

A ring of darkness surrounded the divers as they swam down toward the sea floor. A school of fish swam out of their way as they descended. A crab scuttled along the seabed, kicking up dirt as it moved away from the giant kicking flippers above it. The sheer weight of the black box between the two men kept pulling them down until they were hovering just above the concrete base. In front of them, barely visible in the meager light, was a sign that read 'Fulton Street Subway Station (A) (C).' They swam down the stairwell into the subway.

The two men turned on the flashlights built into their suits and swam downward until the tunnel leveled out. They reached the base of the station and flashed their lights on the platform. Something huge lumbered past them, a black pupil-less eye catching the light. A tiger shark, fifteen feet long, lazily drifted past. Its skin was taut and it was too lean, as if it had been lost in the underwater tunnels for days, starving. Henry dropped the box and went rigid. He had seen sharks before, but never this big, never this close, never down in the subway. He watched the shark swirl around one of the algae-covered rusted metal beams, straighten and head straight towards him. Effortlessly, its speed quickened.

Henry felt as if he were watching it all happen from somewhere very far away, like a dream. The shark was a barely visible black shadow in the murky water, racing towards him at alarming speed, while Henry was paralyzed, helpless to watch as it launched itself at him. The blur flashed towards him. Henry fumbled for the harpoon gun, knowing that he would never reach it in time. He felt the gun's hilt just as the shark's teeth shone brilliantly in the light.

A harpoon appeared on the shark's side, lodged in its gills and the shark began to slow. Its mouth drooped wider and Henry watched the rows of teeth and pissed himself. The shark's nose crashed into Henry's stomach, and with a silent scream, he was pushed backward by the lean monster's momentum. The shark fell before him to the platform floor as dark blood rose in the water. Henry was shaking and gasping for air.

Suddenly, something was tugging his arm. Henry turned to Conner, who grabbed his hand and placed it on the handle of the black box, which he grasped, numbly. Conner pulled forward and Henry swam through a blinding stream of blood down a dark tunnel.

The iron and stone underbelly of a city that had been reclaimed by the sea surrounded them. Rusted metal tracks covered in barnacles and green algae led to an impenetrable circle of black just beyond their view. Conner turned and Henry lurched, missing what it was he had seen. Panic rose up in him as his mind toyed with dark fantasies until he saw the metal door with a sign marked 'Maintenance Room Employees Only' and then heard the thrum behind it. Conner swam up next to it and pulled open the door. They entered single-file, shifting the box lengthwise. They swam up, their flippers swiping against the worn concrete steps beneath them. A roar like the sound of a thousand screeching animals engulfed their ears, coming from above, below and all around them, vibrating in the water, stirring up the dirt and algae until their goggles were clogged and they were swimming blind. With every inch closer, the roar grew impossibly loud.

Then they crested the surface and the noise was clearer. Henry pulled off his mask and breathed in the dank, humid air. It tasted horrible; the air made him double over and gag as he suppressed a stream of vomit, swallowing painfully.

"Lift, goddamn you!"

Henry did as he was told, lifting up the now-heavy box. The pair struggled until they got it up three steps from the water and kicked off their flippers. As they did, two men appeared and pointed black handguns at them.

"Password!" one of them barked, aiming at Conner.

"Jesus Christ—"

"Wrong. Put down the—"

"Four Corners," Conner shouted as the air filtering machine nearly deafened them all.

The men lowered their guns.

"What are you carrying?" the imposing black-bearded guard in front shouted.

"Thirty pounds of heroin, usual shipment," Conner called back.

"Does that box have a lock on it? A strong one?"

"Yes, why?"

"Come along," the leading man ordered, pointing down one of the two ways in the intersection just behind him.

Conner nodded and lifted his end of the box. Henry hoisted his end behind him and they walked down the narrow hallway, lit by painfully bright lights strung up to the ceiling. At the end, there was another door covered in makeshift iron bars and locks. The guard undid them with three metal keys and opened the door. Inside, the room opened into a graveyard of electrical machinery. All the outdated computers, monitors, wires and other devices whose purpose was a complete mystery to Henry, were stowed there. Even if they weren't horribly outdated, they had all been destroyed when the subways were flooded. It seemed that in the decades since his gang had made air pockets in selected subway stations, they still hadn't fully cleaned them out.

But Henry wasn't thinking about that. The lead guard's flashlight fell on three sets of dark eyes in the middle of the room. They peered out, hungry, desperate, frightened. Three people, two older men in suits that were once worth more than most New Yorkers' houses, and a woman in a dress that was once bright and colorful, now dirtied and torn. The smell among them was horrible, and this time Henry threw up.

"Back! Back! Oh, god, you idiot, that's fucking disgusting!"

Henry waited for a hit, but it never came.

"Just put the box down and make sure it's locked!" the guard called.

Conner dropped it. Henry ran out, covering his mouth, while Conner made sure the chest was locked. Henry ran down the concrete hallway, feeling overwhelmed by nausea as the bright lights burned into his eyes and the roar of the giant air filter pounded into his brain, making him reach out blindly, clutching the wall for support. An image of the starved and terrified shark flew back at him. The shark was replaced by the wretched people in the room and he saw their anorexic corpses floating in the water, barely visible in the dark light. Henry dropped to the ground, lying in the center of the walkway. As he did, he heard the door close behind him and the bars being slammed back into place. He thought he heard a gentle pounding behind that.

A hand pulled at him and Conner shouted in his ear. "On your feet!"

Henry slowly rose as Conner pulled him to his feet and pushed him down the hallway. When they reached the flooded stairwell, Conner handed him his mask. As Henry put it on, Conner barked, "You'll be fine once we get out of here."

Henry nodded and felt a wave of dizziness roll over him as he did. Conner noticed and reached out a hand to steady him.

"Look, we can't go back the way we came. Other sharks will have smelled the blood. We have to go down the other way, to the next station. This time, if you see anything, don't hesitate, okay?"

Conner decided not to wait for his acknowledgement. Henry turned around, facing the dark water of the stairwell. He took a step downward and felt it cover his feet. As he did, he imagined an impossibly large shape drifting leisurely in front of him.

He dove.

Chapter Seven

Streaks of faint lamppost light were the only illumination in Rodney's houseboat. He sat in darkness, wearing a black sweater and blue jeans. Rodney's heart pounded softly, his breathing still in anticipation. *I'm not ready for this. I can't mug someone. I haven't been in a fight since I was a kid. No, it'll be fine. If you come across a lone man or woman in the dark, they won't put up a fight. They'll throw their stuff at you and run without remembering your face.* He clutched the kitchen knife in his hand, knowing he wouldn't actually use it. *All you have to do is show up and look intimidating. Antoni will handle the rough stuff and he'll sell whatever we get to the underground. You don't have to do anything and you'll be set. You'll be back to eating ice cream with Sam come tomorrow.*

There was a heavy banging on the door and Rodney jumped. He stalked to the door cautiously while slipping the knife into his pocket.

"Open up, it's us," came Antoni's harsh voice.

Rodney opened the door. They looked just as he had left them. Antoni was dressed in the same blue jersey, Grease still sported the brown hoodie.

"What are you dressed in?" Antoni laughed. "We need to blend in. You look like you're going to rob a liquor store."

Rodney blushed. He scanned behind them before waving them in.

"Go change," Antoni ordered, reclining on the couch. "Then we can go."

Rodney slumped into his room, flushing with embarrassment. He rummaged through the cabinet, searching for something that was unthreatening but still dark enough that it couldn't be seen easily at night. He finally settled on a navy blue jacket and jeans. He stepped out and the two rose off the couch. Antoni led the way out the door.

Rodney locked it behind them as they left.

The three walked along the road, circling towards the edge of town and the docks. The hairs on Rodney's body stood up in anticipation; the slightest breeze gave him a chill. He scanned the docks. A man sat outside on a lawn chair, wearing a hoodie that covered his eyes, but Rodney still felt the man's gaze on him. Rodney felt the knife in his pocket as he looked at the man. Aside from the odd man on his porch, no one else was out that night.

They turned left and stood in the shadow of Yiril's boat. Antoni had devised their meandering path, claiming that he had seen a lot of ship captains resting in their boats with guns ready to kill anyone who tried to steal their livelihood in the middle of the night. For some of them, it was their home anyway. The group slowed as they approached the boat. Rodney peered into the small hut to his right. No sign of Yiril.

They could have easily broken into the hut, but that would have triggered an alarm. Rodney walked over to a panel, entered '8836536' and stepped inside. He walked over to the small desk, opened it and pulled out the key to the ship, pocketed it and then opened the bottom drawer. There were four t-shirts with the 'BlueSea Waste Removal' logo. He grabbed three.

"Put these on, that way we can avoid suspicion if anyone asks us if the boat belongs to us," Rodney said while handing Antoni and Grease the shirts.

Grease kept pulling his down in frustration, as it was just short enough that it didn't meet his pants. Ignoring that for the moment, Grease pointed up to the ship's upper level. "You first," he said.

"Okay," Rodney said.

Antoni put a hand in front of him. "Whoa, whoa, you know why you are going up first, right?"

Rodney shook his head.

"Yiril knows you better than he knows us. If he's up there, he might hesitate before throwing you off the ship. Or shooting you."

Rodney nodded jerkily.

"Good. You go to the upper level, Grease and I will take the lower."

Rodney nodded and climbed up. Yiril wasn't at the top. He stepped inside the boat, then checked the stern to be safe, but Yiril was gone. Rodney sighed in relief, the first time that night.

Antoni climbed up to meet Rodney. "All clear?"

Rodney nodded.

"Good. You can pilot this thing, right?"

"Yeah, sure," he replied and stepped inside when he remembered the boat was still tied to the dock. He jumped out, undid the lines and ran back on. He turned on the engine and heard it rev in the water. As quietly as he could, he steered it towards Manhattan.

In between the spider web of houses and lampposts that were the Boroughs and the rising city of light known as Manhattan, there was a beautiful darkness, a calm, cold, relaxing place of solitude. Even with Antoni and Grease beside him, Rodney felt alone with his thoughts as he steered the vessel. In that darkness, Rodney looked up through the glass and saw a night sky filled with more stars than he had ever seen before. At the northern tip, there was almost a blanket of shining silver, which gave way to the golden lights of Manhattan, which consumed the night's stars and darkness like the rising sun.

Rodney slowed the boat down as they entered the canals. Panic came on him again as he saw boats tied up all along the sides of the buildings, without one opening between them. "Where do I tie us in?" he asked.

Antoni licked his lips and looked forward, as if hoping to spot an answer. "Anywhere you can."

"You don't think the police will ask us for proof of ownership of the boat?" Grease asked.

"Yeah, how can they prove it? Half the people in the Boroughs don't have deeds to their houses, which is why there is so much squatting. It's even worse when it comes to boating claims."

Grease paused. "You sure?"

"Yeah. No one knows who owns anything anymore. There was this one asshole who knew about these deed problems, broke into my uncle's house one day and called the police when my uncle returned. He jumped on my poor old uncle, beat the shit out of him, and when the police arrived, they arrested my uncle for breaking into his own house!"

There was a silence in the boat. "What happened?" Rodney asked.

"My father had to kill the guy. When my uncle got out of jail, he just went back to his house and tried not to cause a ruckus. Fact is, there isn't a lot of decent records in the Boroughs, so to keep order, the cops just arrest everyone."

Grease gave him an angry look. "Well, who's to say any cop won't see us sailing by at night, board, and arrest us for stealing?"

Antoni was silent for a moment. "I hear the cops are a lot more trusting this side of the bay. Just don't look suspicious."

Rodney pulled over into an empty spot. "You guys will need to tie up the boat," he told them while bringing it to a stand-still. Rodney watched them jump out and tie up the boat to the nearest cleat. He turned off the engine and breathed deeply.

Rodney stepped out and jumped to the swaying block. Pain shot up his knees. The hard concrete felt so solid underneath his feet. He walked around, feeling imbalanced, as if it were too stiff and unyielding. Most of the lights were still on all the way up to the skyscrapers' tops, and every now and then, he glanced a person in a fine business suit walking through a series of lit windows.

Antoni walked over to him, laughing. "Welcome to Manhattan. Come on, let's keep moving. We need to do the deed far away from the boat."

The three walked along the block, their heads straining upward. They passed one of the retractable bridges. It wasn't as hard as the concrete, but just as stable. After living their entire lives with the rise and fall of boats, the gentle sway of the houseboats and the gentle give of the streets, the solidity of Manhattan was like walking on the surface of another planet.

There was only a handful of people walking the streets; occasionally the odd group of men passed them by. As they walked forward and were forced to turn, they came upon a nightclub. There was a long line of men with designer jeans, sports jackets with the logos of teams that still existed, gelled hair and jewelry that must have cost more than everything in Rodney's house, *Memories of Peponi* included. Beside them stood a handful of girls, some who looked barely eighteen, in tight dresses that cut off mid-thigh and ended halfway down their chest. They wore diamonds on every exposed part of their body, earrings, rings, necklaces, belly button piercings, toe rings, a few designer watches.

As they approached, one of the two bouncers gave them a smirk. His eyes signaled over his shoulder to a sign that said 'Cover charge $100,000. Ladies enter free.'

"Come on," Antoni said. "We need to backtrack."

They turned around, walked down the block and headed to the left, following another bridge. They kept walking until the crowds of people started to thin and stopped when they reached an area with no one in sight.

Rodney asked, "All right, what's the plan?"

"We hide behind the corner of a building farthest from where we make the hit, jump out, put a knife in their face, tell them to keep quiet and hand over everything they have. Tell the unlucky bastard not to move, then sprint out around the first corner, then the second to throw off any cops. Then you jog back to the boat without bringing up any suspicion. When it all happens, just follow my lead. I can't signal us, you just have to pay attention, okay?"

"Easy as that?"

"You ever bashed someone's face in?" Grease asked.

Rodney shook his head.

Antoni threw his right fist into his open hand. "Punch them till they go down, then kick 'em. When I say so, turn and run, and when I say 'walk'... you get it."

The three kept going north until the skyscrapers got smaller and their lights were mostly turned off. They staked out a corner. There were streetlights all along the block and the light reflected off the canals, bathing the street in a golden glow that might have been soothing, but the lack of shadow and darkness set Rodney on edge. There was the odd man far off in the distance, though more often, there were a couple of people walking together. As he looked at the people, Rodney realized that there were so few out in this part of town and they were so far away that until they came to the next skyscraper block, he couldn't even make out their appearance. Rodney looked down the block. Someone walked by, glanced at them and continued across the bridge. Whether that was his path the whole time or whether he had altered it to avoid them, Rodney didn't know, but he was grateful all the same.

They leaned against the corner of the skyscraper, waiting for someone to walk by. Grease was saying something; no doubt he wanted to make them seem less suspicious by talking, but Rodney wasn't listening. He was looking up, watching the building fade into the sky. There weren't any stars up there, just endless blackness, the silver light having been washed away by the gold below it.

A tall, stocky man in a dark suit, well past his prime with hair so blond it was almost white, passed by them. He had a silver watch on his wrist, and held onto a briefcase. In that instant, Rodney knew what would happen next. As one, Antoni and Grease ran forward, knives drawn.

"Stop where you are," Antoni hissed.

The man swung his briefcase wide, knocking Antoni's blade away. He ran. Antoni and Grease chased him. Rodney followed. *Why am I doing this?* he thought, but pushed the thought out of his mind and sprinted after them. The man's giant strides threatened to outpace them, but soon, he began to slow. Antoni jumped at him and grabbed his shoulder. The man awkwardly fell to one knee. Antoni put his blade to the man's throat.

"Now stay down," Antoni panted. The man shuffled to his feet and the knife cut a thin, dark gash across his throat. Judging by the scream that pierced through the night, Rodney could tell it wasn't fatal, but painful. Grease tumbled into him, putting a hand over his mouth. The man swung wildly and knocked Grease hard in the stomach. He fell backward. Then the man continued to rise. He was pushing the stunned Grease backward, toward the freezing water. Rodney bolted forward, doubt and guilt driven from him as he knew he had to get to Grease before the pain-blinded man drowned them both. Grease hobbled backward awkwardly, trying to force the man back. Grease started to gain his footing and was pushing back against the man. They were on the lip of the block when Rodney put a strong hand on the man's shoulder and pulled back. The man didn't resist. He fell backward lazily, completely relaxed, but with eyes that met Rodney's with sheer horror as he fell backward. His chest was covered in blood from multiple wounds.

Grease had blood splatters all over his clothes. He was panting and looking at the other two blankly, as if they were supposed to tell him what he was supposed to do now.

Antoni stood up and looked around. His eyes darted across the canal. There was a group of two older men and their wives, staring at them. Rodney expected a scream. Instead, they turned, the men urging the women forward, trying to prod on the aging gals in high heels.

"I didn't mean to," Grease said breathlessly, "I swear."

Antoni gave him an evil glare as he looked up. There were lights on from numerous offices, though Rodney hadn't seen anyone walking around. His gaze shot to the surrounding buildings. In the commercial areas of the Boroughs, there were working security cameras. Rodney saw there were cameras on the street lights above them too, and prayed they could only see the canal to keep the boat traffic moving.

Antoni walked over to the body. He patted the man down and found a watch, wallet, and a set of keys. He pocketed the wallet and then threw the keys under Grease's legs, making him jump. Their splash was barely audible, but Rodney still winced and looked around. He jumped when Antoni put a hand on him. "Help me," he said. They both looked down. Rodney grabbed the man's arms, Antoni his legs. They side-stepped toward the lip of the block.

"Gently," he said. As gently as he could, they laid the man's body into the water. It bobbed, sitting on the top. Then, mercifully, it began to sink.

Antoni walked over to Grease, who was shaking. He grabbed his knife, walked over to the water and let the blood drip into the canal. When he was finished, he handed Grease his knife back. "Put it away," he spat through gritted teeth. When Grease did, he grabbed the man's coat and pulled them together. "Keep it zipped and keep your hand over your belly," he said, looking down at where a large splotch of blood was. "We can't clean it here. We have to get back to the ship, now."

The three walked back at a quickened pace, retracing their steps. Rodney felt a numb disconnection with the world, moving stiffly as they walked towards the more populated side of Manhattan. As they started to pace down one block, he looked to the end and swore he saw it stretch, connecting with the others, lasting for an eternity, but as they neared the end, it was shortening all on its own until, when he took his next step, he nearly slipped on the gentle incline of the metal bridge. He felt sick to his stomach again.

They passed the nightclub. The line was even longer as dozens of people were talking to their friends in excited voices as they shivered against the cold. He looked at one man walking away with a smiling Korean woman. An image of the dead man's final lurch backward flashed before Rodney's eyes and lingered with him. He saw those eyes when he blinked, not the scene, not the corpse, not even the fear, but the pleading, shocked brown eyes.

The three walked towards the last bridge between them and the boat. A siren roared and from behind, Rodney saw a police cruiser tearing through the canal. It spun wildly, stopping in the intersection. Rodney was shaking. Antoni put a hand on his shoulder, squeezing painfully. The bridge raised and the boat tore down the canal past them. The sound echoed and Rodney could imagine it tracing their path back to the murder scene. The bridge began to lower and it was only Antoni's hard grasp on his shoulder that kept him from running.

Rodney nearly bumped into the boat. They scrambled to get in, and it was only after they all jumped in that Antoni slammed his hand on the railing. They all jumped.

"You forgot to untie it," he spat at Grease. Grease began to babble an excuse, but then realization dawned on his face. He jumped out and untied the boat. They climbed up to the deck. Rodney put the key into the ignition and started it. Slowly, they pulled out of the harbor. Rodney did an awkward turn; the canal wasn't large enough for graceful maneuvering. After a bit of moving forward, then reversing, then forward again, he finally managed to get them going back toward the Boroughs.

"Slow down," was all Antoni said on the way back. Rodney realized he had been letting the engine roar, gunning at full speed. It wasn't even that fast, Rodney wanted to say, but Antoni glared menacingly at him.

When they finally reached the pier, Rodney brought the boat back into its place slowly. He stalled it. Grease didn't wait for a command. He rushed out, jumped out of the boat and tied it to the dock. Rodney turned off the engine. He looked at Antoni. Antoni didn't look back, but Rodney caught his eyes and saw that the anger hadn't dissipated; if anything, it had flared up. Antoni stood up, threw down his jacket and replaced his 'BlueSea' shirt with his brown one and walked out. Rodney grabbed the shirt, stuffed it into his pocket along with his and Grease's shirts, and followed in tow. They jumped from the boat. Antoni walked over to Grease. Seeing him, Grease put his hands above his head. Antoni started smacking him. As he pushed Grease backward, Rodney saw the same fear rise up in his eyes from before, when he was being forced towards the canal by the old man. Grease swung out, hitting Antoni in the chest with a loud thud. Antoni nearly leapt forward when Rodney stepped between them, pushing them apart. He felt cold, sticky blood as he touched Grease's shirt.

"What the hell was that?" Antoni shouted, not caring who heard.

"I didn't mean to."

"You weren't supposed to kill him!"

Rodney glanced around. The docks were usually dead at this hour, and with Manhattan becoming self-sufficient, it was becoming an unoccupied shell, but Rodney couldn't help but fill in the shadows with forms and horrors.

"Shut up," Grease spat.

"What did you say?" Antoni clenched his fist.

"Anyone could have heard that," Rodney hissed. "Look, we aren't out yet, we need to get as far away from here as possible, alright? Besides, you don't want to stand next to him, with all the blood on his shirt."

For the first time, cold reason came back into Antoni's mind. "I'm keeping the money," Antoni declared as he walked away. He had directed it at Grease, who looked defeated. Rodney felt a flush of anger rise in him. He threw out his arm and caught Antoni as he tried to walk past him.

"That's my money, too."

Antoni's hand curled up into a fist. He stared murder at Rodney, but couldn't think of anything to say against him. He had provided the boat. He hadn't screwed up.

"We're not sharing with him," Rodney said, nodding at Grease. "Payment for this time."

"Fine," Antoni growled. For a moment, Rodney felt a pang of guilt for betraying Grease. Then the shocked, dead eyes came back to his mind.

Antoni opened up the man's wallet. Inside, there were four one hundred thousand dollar bills and one five hundred thousand dollar bill, and even a few European bills.

"I'll take the five hundred thousand because it was my idea. You can have the four hundred."

Antoni made to hand it to Rodney. "What about the watch?" Rodney asked. "Anyone with a neural interface wouldn't need it to tell time, or even do anything. It's got to be an antique, maybe a hundred years old." Antoni tried to give him a surprised look, as if he had forgotten about it. Rodney had grown up with him and knew when he was bullshitting.

"Oh, right," he muttered unconvincingly. "Okay. You can have the five hundred k, I'll take the watch and the four hundred." Rodney nodded. He was sure he was being ripped off, but he wasn't going to argue, not now. Besides, he didn't know how to sell stolen things like Antoni did. Rodney took the five hundred thousand dollar bill. Antoni threw the business cards and everything he couldn't use in the water by the boat. He pocketed the watch and the wallet. Rodney nearly slapped himself, realizing that the wallet must have been worth a good deal too.

"We done?" Antoni asked, as if daring Rodney to accuse him of cheating. Rodney nodded stiffly. Antoni walked past him without another word. Rodney turned and saw Grease look away, ashamed. Rodney wanted to say something to him, try to tell him that it wasn't so bad.

"You need to wash that shirt." Rodney pointed at the bloodstains.

Grease looked down. He pulled off his jacket, then the 'BlueSea' shirt. He dipped it into the water by the boat and wrung it with his hands. Rodney stepped over him and handed him his red shirt. "That should be good." Without looking at him, Grease nodded, handing Rodney the 'BlueSea' shirt. He put on his own, then his jacket and walked away. Rodney changed and washed out the shirts with a cleaning solution until the blood disappeared. He replaced the shirts and key, hoping that Yiril wouldn't stop by anytime soon before the shirt dried. Rodney closed the door behind them. He saw the lights of Manhattan in the corner of his eye and turned away.

Rodney walked home under the glaring streetlights. He turned the key and entered, pressed the light switch and watched illumination flood the empty room. He closed the door behind him and trudged into his bedroom, sat down on the edge of the bed and stared at the floor. The hard plastic, imitation wood slowly turned into water and he watched a man's horrified face sink into its depths. He closed his eyes. He pulled out his phone; there were four missed calls, all from Sam. He stared at it. It began to flash 'Incoming video call: Samantha Harding,' and displayed a gif of her face. Rodney watched her tilt her head and smile. It repeated three times and disappeared, replaced by a notification that read, 'Missed Call.' Rodney tossed the phone aside and put his head in his hand.

Chapter Eight

Sophia had turned off her computer, put everything back in her purse and was about to walk out of her office when Police Commissioner Robert Kerry stepped inside. He had a chiseled face with steely gray eyes and silver hair in a crew cut. Sophia always wondered if he was using some sort of hair re-growth because it was so thick, but knowing him, he was probably too proud to do anything of the sort. He towered over her even from across the room, casting a lengthy shadow between them. The look on his face was somehow grimmer than usual and Sophia's eyes were drawn to a thick brown folder in his meaty hands. He crossed the threshold in five steps and stopped at the other end of the desk. He looked at the pitcher of water balanced on the dresser.

"You wouldn't mind if I poured myself a drink, would you?"

Sophia waved at Robert to do so, eyeing the clock as he turned. "I thought this was going to be a short meeting, since you scheduled it at the end of the day."

"No, Sophia. I scheduled it late because I didn't want to be interrupted by anyone else and this might take a while," he said while taking a seat in the chair opposite her. "You're so busy nowadays I can't ever find an opening. But what I have is worth your attention," he finished as he placed the folder on the desk.

Sophia eyed it before returning her gaze to Robert. "Still doing things the old-fashioned way, I see."

He ignored that, opened the folder and turned it towards her. The first page was a profile of a man named Gordon Mason. There was a picture of him standing at a podium, looking as if he was giving a lecture.

"I've met this man before," Sophia noted. Her eyes trailed down the page and under 'job description' it said, 'CFO of Sierras Financial.' Under that was a blue ink scribbling which read *Estimated wealth: $14 billion*. She looked through the file again and saw, "Whereabouts unknown, reported missing May 12, 2163."

Sophia turned the page and there was a rosy-cheeked woman named Sue Warner, COO of Browning PR, *Estimated wealth $7 billion*. Whereabouts unknown, reported missing May 14, 2163.

Sophia flipped through the pages of the three profiles, all billionaires. "What is this?"

"These three are billionaires located in Manhattan that have been reported missing by relatives and their businesses. I've tried to keep things quiet, I informed them that causing a media storm could only make things worse. But this is three high-profile people who have disappeared this month. I am afraid there might be a pattern."

"It's not just them. Last night, Brice Noble, CEO of Crazy Hornet Gaming, was found dead, his body caught against a Poseidon motor's filtration system."

Sophia opened the last profile to the grandfatherly smile of the elderly Brice Noble. She looked back up and met Robert's gaze, giving him a look that said *So what does this mean?* though he didn't seem to get it. As brilliant as he was behind a desk, he was inept at inter-office politics. If Sophia hadn't promoted him, he would have kept getting passed over by numerous other mayors who thought he was a moron because they failed to see his true talents.

Sophia chose to be blunt. "So what does this mean?"

"I don't know. I suspect that these people have been kidnapped; it's the only explanation for a bunch of rich people disappearing, with the killing of Brice Noble being a botched kidnapping effort."

"Are you sure it's kidnapping?"

"Yes, though there's been no ransom for any of the others so far."

"No ransom? Why?"

"I don't know yet, but there is no other reason to explain their disappearances."

"Well, what are you doing about this?" An edge of worry crept into her voice.

"I have detectives working overtime on each case and I am keeping them separate; all police in the loop know not to mention any of the other missing persons cases. If the city found out that rich entrepreneurs were being killed or kidnapped, then mass panic would break out. For the time being, I am trying to contain this, but you know that could end at any minute."

Sophia stiffened. She could see it happening before her eyes.

Everything she had worked so hard to build. The investments, the tourists, everything vanishing. In her mind's eye, she saw a row of skyscrapers still on the water, snow on the small blocks and bridges. The lights were out, the streets were empty and not a single footprint broke up the snow.

"I am doing everything I can," Robert continued. "But it's not enough. So far, there hasn't been much money that has made it to the Boroughs and the police there have no control over the streets. Security cameras are only installed on a few blocks in the heart of Manhattan so far, so their crime spills over. The streets and buildings are choked with tourists, many foreign, whose identities are almost impossible to track quickly. And Manhattan is a city of a thousand canals with boats everywhere, a police force that isn't nearly large enough and doesn't have enough boats to patrol or chase down any suspected criminals."

"Okay," Sophia said, trying to shake even worse images of chaos and violence from her mind. "Done. The city will hire as many cops as you like and equip them with high-speed cruisers."

"Can you guarantee that? The budget is in the hands of the city council."

"I will tell them it's due to expanding need or something generic. It won't be hard to get you what we need."

"Either way, that will take time." Robert leaned forward. "We face a crisis on our hands. If this goes public and every petty criminal finds out that we are impotent to stop these acts of violence—"

"I know."

"—it'll be panic and chaos."

Sophia looked at him gravely. She wished he wasn't so calm whenever he delivered bad news. It felt as if she had to do all the worrying for the both of them. "I will try to get some Coast Guard boats down to patrol the bay. Subtly, of course."

Robert nodded slowly, but Sophia could tell he wasn't reassured. "This still doesn't change the fundamental problem of Manhattan. Patrolling and watching a city on the water, with thousands of boats to make an easy getaway in, is near impossible without creating some sort of heavy surveillance that the public will call a 'police state.' Trying to put in the safety measures we need will be an uphill battle against civil rights groups and a scared public and in the meantime, things could all go to hell."

Thanks for phrasing it so gently.

Sophia paused and put her hands in her lap, almost as if she were praying. She hadn't in a long time, but she hadn't faced a crisis with anything this large at stake since the death of her father. The thought that Manhattan, after being pulled from the ocean, might endure another crisis...

She took a deep breath. "I met with one of the engineers of the Sea Titan motor a few days ago. She said she had developed and proposed a plan for a motor that would be added to a skyscraper, one that would give it the ability to move forward in the water. I am having her attach them to some of the older, crumbling skyscrapers in the Bronx area, the ones that have turned into drughouses and slums. We're clearing them out, and sailing the skyscrapers out to new coastal cities."

"So that's why you were asking for raids on those northern skyscrapers. That's a good start, fewer areas to patrol."

Sophia almost laughed. Nothing shocked Robert. Somehow, the thought of skyscrapers sailing up and down the Eastern Seaboard was an easily accepted fact.

"The development of the engines was all part of this idea she had, to make Manhattan constantly shift and change, the skyscrapers always moving one space to the right twice a day, once at noon, once at night. If we attached the motors to all the skyscrapers in Manhattan and went along with her plan, it would be impossible for untrained criminals and thugs from the Boroughs to commit any sophisticated plans, correct?"

Robert took a gulp of water. "Yes, it would. But it would also be impossible to patrol."

"Hire a computer specialist who can develop an algorithm that can predict where the skyscrapers are moving. I'll have a council meeting and voice your concerns and get the funding for everything you need."

Robert nodded. Sophia closed the folder and handed it back to him. Robert stood up.

"I expect you to solve those cases soon," she hoped. "I can get you everything you need to keep the city safe, but you have to work overtime to make sure things don't blow up before I can get everything approved."

"I have my best people on it."

That's not a guarantee, she thought. *No wonder Robert kept getting passed over for nearly a decade. He doesn't know how to promise what he can't deliver.*

Chapter Nine

Hope was a beautiful thing. Hope was like the high of caffeine without coffee, the rushed feeling of going down a roller coaster without actually taking the dive. That morning, Lei Xu woke with surety that felt like drowsy relaxation. She went through all the same motions as she walked out the now fully renovated apartment lobby: her head was held high, her back was arched, posture perfect. Today she was inspecting the operating teams at the Carlyle Building, who were putting her designs into effect. She had been told she wasn't needed in the early stages, but she couldn't wait.

She walked along the block, scanning the canal. She waved at a motor boat painted yellow with a stripe of white and black checkers on the side and a gray-bearded black man in a worn green hat pulled over. When the boat steadied, he reached out an arm and helped her step in.

"Where to, ma'am?"

"The Carlyle Building, 944 Westchester Avenue."

"That's quite a ways," he mused. "For that far, I would have to charge..." It was apparent from his hesitation that no one asked him to go anywhere near the city's dangerous northern edge. "In the area of a hundred thousand dollars."

"I can pay."

The man nodded, wiped some sweat off his brow and urged the dinghy forward. They had to turn around, and rather than deal with the hassle of going back and forth, doing a U-turn while trying to dodge other boats, he circled the skyscraper opposite Lei's apartment complex.

It was a cloudy day and it looked like it might rain later, making New York miserable again. On the two times that the rain fell since

Manhattan's rising, she had watched the water line. She knew it wouldn't rise, that the machines underneath would keep the buildings floating at the same level as it did during high and low tide. All the same, she and many other New Yorkers would watch the rain, worrying that even though their fair city had survived the melting of the ice caps and the rising of the seas, a few drops of rain would mean its doom.

As they skimmed between the floating obelisks, Lei had a familiar sensation, as if she was coming home after a long time. She watched the people as they passed on the streets in the late morning. It was strange observing the tourists who now swarmed New York, turning it into a lively place. Restaurants all along the waterfront were bustling, filling the air with the fragrances of a hundred delicacies from all around the world. There were French restaurants, Mexican restaurants with steaming plates, but the most present smell was Indian and Middle Eastern food. As they passed by a row of them, she could almost taste the curry. Now the restaurants were finally worth going to, despite their inflated price. Tourist money allowed them to buy finer products and the air filled with spices and oils, which were previously missing in the dark days when Manhattan food was cheap and bland. She saw waiters in black slacks and white buttoned shirts rushing to tables in the heat. She glanced to her left just in time to see a waiter drop a pitcher of water, proving that a change in the people came slower than a change of clothes. The supervisor came out and yelled at the idiot boy. The yelling faded behind her as the boat glided in the water and she tasted a hundred dishes of haute cuisine whose scents spilled out into the canals.

In between the restaurants, new specialty shops emerged, unlike before, when the only shops were food stores, alcohol stores and drug stores, or a mix of the three. An antique store was filled with people grabbing whatever stored or recovered treasures they could find. An electronics store was filling up with locals who could finally afford the newest gadgets and bio-mech upgrades that would grant them better vision, better hearing and memory storage. The tech was expensive, but on the off-chance they had any money left, there was a London designer store next door. At the end of the block, there was a leather fetish shop which had in bold red letters 'Manhattan Specialty Items.' Lei had no idea what that might mean and she was slightly curious, but decided she probably didn't want to know.

Soon, the shops and tourists became sparse, the buildings weren't as colossal, and the wait times for the bridges to rise were shorter. Near the edge of Manhattan, the first floors of the buildings were still covered in relics of the sea. The captain took them out to the rim of the city, where Yankee Stadium rested gently on the waves, surrounded on all sides by a mass of boats and people climbing inside, like ants retreating into an anthill during a storm.

Lei looked behind her, seeing the skyline, and beyond that, the Boroughs with their millions of makeshift houses and houseboats stretched all around Manhattan, looking like it might consume the newly risen city. Lei glanced forward and could even see land, true land, in the far distance. The land beyond looked like Central Park, its cedars and oaks now being choked and dying as their trunks lay beneath a layer of saltwater. There were houses in the far distance, but unless they were taken up by vagrants, they were unoccupied, the people having fled the encroachment of the sea years ago.

The faded red-brick Carlyle Building loomed over them. Even at only ten stories tall, it appeared massive, though its imposing stature was mostly just the aura of its newly remembered prestige. It was one of the first 'skyscrapers' the world had ever seen, competing for the title with a similar building in Chicago. Seeing it floating on the water, it was a reminder that Sverichek hadn't just lifted up a living city; he had rescued its history as well.

There were a dozen workboats beside the Carlyle Building as engineers in scuba gear rested on floating metal tanks, watching as a low-riding boat with a crane lowered her massive engine into the water. It gently fell, kissing the water and barely making a splash, despite its size. When it finally sank beneath the water, the engineers all rose in the ensuing ebb. They swam over and began to attach the tanks they had been holding to the motor. When they had finished, the motor had neutral buoyancy and with a bit of straining, the engineers made it sink and re-emerge before finally pushing it underwater.

"Are you sure this is the right place?" the driver asked. "It's sectioned off, the bridges are lifted."

"It is," she confirmed. "Just pull up somewhere where we won't be disturbing anyone."

"All right." The man nodded and steered the boat around the old brick building. Behind the building was a large trash boat where cleaning teams were dumping black bags. Hanging all along the side of the building were cleaners who scraped at the decrepit windows. Workers on the bottom floor were doing what had been done weeks ago in Manhattan, chipping off barnacles, removing anemones, starfish, and any odd crab that had decided to make the building its home.

Lei fumbled through her purse, pulled out two hundred thousand dollars and handed them to the driver, saying, "Thank you." He nodded and offered to help her out of the boat. There was a gentle hum and splash behind her as the boat began its long circuit back to Manhattan. Walking towards her from just inside the building was a short, pudgy man with one giant chin that blended into his thick neck, making him look like a frog. He had a bristly yellow mustache and wispy blond hair and wore a brown suit with white sneakers that had been caked in dust.

"Good afternoon, ma'am, I need to scan your ID."

"I'm Lei Xu, Stanhope Limited's head of R&D for this project."

"I'm sure you are, ma'am, I just have to see some ID."

She let him access her intercomp. After a second, he said, "Pleasure to have you, Miss Xu. My name's Harvey Tibbit."

"Pleasure to meet you," she replied. "Sorry I didn't call ahead. The city took my plans for the Poseidon motor and has run with them. So far, I haven't had any other assignments and I don't like being paid for nothing."

"That is my dream," Tibbit said wistfully. "I don't suppose you'd like to take over as supervisor? Everyone already knows what they are supposed to do, I just walk around and whenever someone from City Hall calls, I tell them everything's fine."

Lei smiled. "I won't deprive you of such stimulating work."

Tibbit shrugged. "I suppose not. By the way, when you have your next meeting with the mayor or Mr. Stanhope, don't let on that a chimp could do my job. Well, what do you care to see? I don't suppose you'd want to dive down there? We might be able to find another suit."

"No, that's alright. I was a designer on the team that produced the Miracle, I have seen motors installed on the underside of buildings dozens of times before. I was hoping to see what your team is doing inside."

Harvey nodded. "All right, let's step in."

That was easy enough, as the front doors had been removed. Leaning against the wall next to the entrance was a large, hand-carved oak door, and beside it there were painters who were trying to add a natural-looking gray color to the water-damaged first floor. Inside the sprawling brownstone lobby were cleaners everywhere, working under glaring portable lights. Garbage men were filling entire bags full of plastic bottles, batteries, a broken lamp and a host of other junk she couldn't begin to identify. There was a constant spray of pine air freshener, but the smell of warm filth was enough to make Lei gag.

"Whew! Sorry, should have warned you. At the edge of town, there was a lot of squatting, poor folks taking up home in the abandoned buildings. They were hardly the most hygienic people."

Lei nodded. She had seen poverty in her travels across the globe and was not surprised at the lack of propriety. Just the smell. "What did the city do with the people here? Where did they go?" She nearly had to shout to be heard over the hammering, binning and sloshing.

"Evicted them," Harvey bellowed back as they crossed the middle of the room, where the worst of the smell was. She noticed the other employees were wearing masks over their mouths and she looked around for a dispenser. "The police have been here for the last few days, kicking out loads of people, hundreds I think."

That made Lei pause. "What happened to them?"

"The city," he said, though she heard *Mayor Ramos*, "bought a bunch of cheap houseboats in the Boroughs and shipped them off there."

"So she just forcibly moved people? Without offering them aid or jobs when they got to the Boroughs? That's inhumane."

"Couldn't have been worse than here," he supposed. "There was rampant disease, starvation, people killing each other. I heard there have even been cases of cannibalism, though not here, to my knowledge. At least there is some help over there. There's nothing here for 'em."

Cannibalism? Here? In Manhattan? That gave her shivers. When she had visited central Africa, she had met an entire village of people with bloated bellies, ribs that you could count and thin, leathery skin stretched across their faces. Despite their starvation, none of them resorted to cannibalism, and it was rare even in cases of extreme hunger for people to do that. But that had been happening here? In what was once the greatest city in the world?

"The elevator's broken. Sorry, but we'll have to use the stairs."

Tibbit opened a door and they proceeded upward. They stepped out onto the second floor. Like the first, they were in an open area, though this was only half as large, as the room gave way to a hallway with a series of doors that were once offices. To her left, two burly-armed men were lifting a chipped desk towards the window. The crane from outside leaned near the window and stopped. The men tied a chain over the desk, then the taller of the two leaned out, stretched for the crane and tied the other end to it. The crane pulled back slightly. When it did, the two men gently lifted the desk outside. It swung back, so near that Lei thought it would fly through the open window, but it slowed and eased back. When it did, the crane turned and dropped it into the garbage heap.

Lei stepped forward, slipping past a group of workers in white coveralls who were pulling out the power lines in the now-skeletal wall of the building. She walked down the hallway, opening the first door on her right. The room was covered in white chips where the walls had been knocked down. A filthy, reeking carpet was rolled up against the side. Half a dozen workers were chipping and tearing at the walls and electrical sockets, paying her no attention at all. She closed the door behind her, turned around and nearly knocked into a man carrying a jingling garbage bag.

"Sorry," he called back as he jogged past her.

Lei turned to Tibbit. "Let's quickly go through the floors; I think if I passed through every room, I would just be getting in people's way."

Tibbit nodded good-naturedly. He was a jovial person, even if he didn't seem overly competent. The two marched up to the third floor, where much of the same was going on, then the fourth, fifth, until they reached the ninth and Lei let the now-panting Tibbit catch his breath. She walked over to the brick windowsill and looked out. The building was just a dwarf among giants, but in the 1880s, this had been a world wonder. *A building ten stories tall! If only the people in lace petticoats and horse-drawn buggies could have lived to see what New York had become.*

"What was this building used for?"

"What?" he panted behind her.

"What was this place used for originally?"

"It was founded as an insurance company in 1884. The cost of the building was too much for the company owners and drove them into bankruptcy. But this building always found new tenants and by the time that people were moving into the steel skyscrapers, this had been marked as a historic landmark."

Lei nodded. *Too precious to destroy, but not valuable enough to sell. Until now.* When she thought he had caught his breath, she stepped back to climb to the tenth floor when two policemen stepped out of the stairway, one of them tall, blue-eyed with gray hair, while the other looked so similar he might have been his brother, except that he didn't have as many wrinkles and still had some black hair amidst the gray. They were holding an empty body bag between them.

"What's this?" she asked.

They looked at her. "Who are you, ma'am?"

"I am the head of this project, Lei Xu, and you are?"

"James Malley, this is my brother Tahl," the older one said. The two policemen looked at Tibbit for confirmation and he nodded. "Ma'am there's no need to concern yourself, we are just removing some refuse."

"Refuse?" she repeated. "Did the crews run out of garbage bags?"

They looked at each other. The elder brother started, "Ma'am, there's no need to concern yourself—"

"Where is it?" she asked, not bothering to argue with them over her authority.

"Third door on the left," the younger man offered.

Lei led them down the hall and opened the door. A horrible stench hit her and she gagged, putting her forearm to her mouth. Near the far wall was a naked, skeletal figure. The face had multiple stab wounds where the blood had coagulated and took on the appearance of crimson sap. The skin and muscles of its lower legs had been removed, with tears visible at its stomach. Inside the stomach, visible through the pelvic bone, maggots were writhing and wriggling. Lei leaned against the opposite wall and vomited.

James closed the door, put his hand around her and said, "It's alright, ma'am, you need to sit down." He steered her away from the vomit, back into the main hall, and had her sit. Tibbit called a team to fetch her some water and in a moment, she didn't feel like she was about to pass out.

"How did that happen? How is that possible?"

The older cop looked at her. "I have seen some pretty horrible things in the evictions. With the poverty, hysteria and end of the world panic, there are a lot of crazies. The worst of it, like what you just saw, is thankfully few and far between. I'm sorry you had to see that."

Lei looked up, meeting his concerned glance. "What are you going to do with him?"

James looked as if he didn't want to say it, but refused to lie. "We are going to dump him on the garbage tanker."

"What?" Lei gasped. "But... that was a murder. He was a person."

James shrugged. "There's nothing we can do. We have no idea who that man was; even if he hadn't had his face torn apart, very few of the people living in extreme poverty have photo identification. Moreover, the tenants who lived here have been relocated to the Boroughs and it would be nigh impossible to find anyone who might know anything about this man. There is really nothing we can do, I am truly sorry to say."

"Then why are you here?" Lei asked, feeling a stab of guilt, as it sounded too much like an accusation.

"Only the police have the authority to move a body. Bureaucratic complications would have arisen if any of the other city workers did it, and the mayor has tasked the police force with giving all speedy cooperation to this project."

Lei was too stunned to say anything else. James looked at Tahl, then back to Tibbit. "You should escort her out, in case she gets sick again. We'll take care of it."

Tibbit nodded and helped Lei to her feet. They walked down the stairs. By the fourth floor, Lei was steady enough to walk by herself. When they arrived on the first floor, she remembered to hold her breath and walked outside to the block, breathing in the fresh sea air. She turned to Tibbit, who stood cautiously behind her, watching nervously as if she might collapse at any moment.

She smiled thinly at him. "I'm fine. Thank you for giving me the tour. It's good to finally feel useful."

"Of course, I am glad for the company," he added awkwardly. "It's always good to have a higher authority to walk around when I'm doing nothing; makes me seem important by association."

Lei chuckled awkwardly, trying to fight off the nausea. "All right... I am just going to call a cab, thank you."

Tibbit nodded and was about to offer to shake her hand, but then quickly pulled back, muttering, "Bye."

Lei called a cab service which charged one hundred and fifty thousand this time, though she hardly cared. After the call ended, she looked down the length of the canals back to Manhattan, watching eagerly for the cab. As she gazed outward, a horrible stench of warm, moldy flesh and disease came over her. She turned to her left and saw the brother cops carrying a body bag which sagged in the middle, only half full. They walked to the garbage tanker, heaved and threw.

Chapter Ten

A lex side-stepped a crowd of people and meandered onto a small walkway between two shops. The masses walked painfully slow for his taste. He tapped on his right wrist and in addition to his normal vision, an ultra-violet scan ran down his eye-sight every few seconds. The computer picked out the fingerprints identified by the scan and ran them across a criminal database.

Alex heard an unfamiliar flapping sound and looked up, seeing a new flag, bright red, white and blue breaking through the gray sky. There was something majestic in its defiance, and Alex felt a strange feeling that he had never felt before.

Patriotism? It can't be community or belonging.

"Alex!" a cheery, deep voice broke through his reverie.

He turned to see a man with cheeks freckled a deep red that matched his spiky hair. Slender fingers pulled back the locks that had been tousled by the wind, setting them back in place.

"What are you doing here?" he asked.

"Counting flags, Jason."

Jason looked up. "...How many have you counted so far?"

"One."

Jason smiled awkwardly. He hadn't gotten used to Alex's strange manner and had long ago given up on understanding it.

"What are you doing here?" Alex asked.

"Going to log it in a file? I swear I'm clean."

"That's just what a criminal would say.'"

"Nothing gets past supercop Alex." Jason smiled a bit wider. "Is this what you do on your day off? I just got done with lunch and was walking around. Care to join me?"

"Where to?"

"Nowhere. I am meeting a friend at two; until then I was just wandering."

Alex nodded and walked beside Jason. "So what have you been up to?"

Two flags.

"Still fixing plumbing systems and the like," he explained, "although recently I've pulled a side-job making antique souvenirs of Manhattan, real old stuff, the type you see in the movies. Snowglobes, miniature figures. They are all crap, but so far there aren't any machines pumping these out, so handmade plastic baubles are as good as you can get."

"How's the pay?"

"I make more doing that part-time work than my full-time job."

"Really?

"Yeah. Jackie, the girl who sells them for me, is an amazing saleswoman. Or the foreigners visiting Manhattan have no taste. How have you been? Do you have a girl yet?"

"I have a few prospectives."

"Prospectives?" Jason asked, confused. "As in, a few girls you are juggling, a few you haven't asked yet, or do they actually exist this time?"

Alex didn't have any good answer. "I have to be careful. I don't want to end up with a potential serial killer."

"So you're not a shut-in, you're just protecting yourself on the off chance that you'll end up in bed with a knife-wielding psychopath?"

"Yup."

Alex looked over at the massive, dark green tower that was One Court Square as it appeared between two rising shops. Alex squinted against the glare of light from the top. There were window cleaners on scaffolds all around the building's spire, wiping away at the filth and grime. For the longest time, the building had been a dark, dirty green, but now its spire gleamed like an emerald that was being unearthed. At its top, a giant American flag waved.

Three.

"Well, aren't you going to ask me how Sheryl and I are?"

"Oh, yeah... how is she?"

"Good..."

There was a moment of silence in which Alex got an intense feeling that he had forgotten something. "You still haven't picked a wedding date, have you?"

"Nope. The time is just never right. Some new work comes up and now this whole city's changing. I wish we could just elope and get it over with, but she insists on having a big ceremony." Jason tried to hold a placid look, but Alex saw concern in his eyes. After a slight pause, he added, "Cassidy's worried about you. She says you need to get out, have some fun. You haven't become a recluse since I've become too busy to hang, have you?"

"I saw Zack just three days ago. And I've been busy, too. I'm not a hermit. Just because I haven't asked a girl to make me her slave doesn't mean I don't have a social life."

Jason nodded. With each bob of the head, he seemed less worried. After turning down the next street, a grin began to spread across his face. "Prospectives," he over-enunciated the word as if that was enough of an insult in itself.

Alex ignored him and looked back up at the green tower, realizing for the first time how tall it was. Its color was so dulled by dirt and dust that it had appeared unimposing, like a far-off mountain nearly fading into the distance when storm clouds gather on the horizon. The spire hadn't received one of the motors and it continued to slowly sink.

"It makes you sad, doesn't it?" Alex breathed.

"What?"

"How much smaller we all are since the Miracle. Cassidy keeps saying that everything is going to change here; that the money from Manhattan is going to make everything better. Here I had hoped if anyone would make it better, it would be us, the cops, each of us putting our lives on the line. It's a hard pill to swallow, but the few successful pencil pushers and economists who could care less about the people across the harbor are the ones who are to thank for saving us from all our misery."

Jason looked at Alex, trying to understand, then gave up and asked, "What?"

"I just had this thought recently. I imagined Hercules, or some Greek hero, I get them confused, standing up against a hydra. Hercules is supposed to be strong and rip it apart with his bare hands. But then someone a thousand miles away with a nuke presses a button and blasts the monster and all Hercules can do is watch. I like my job, I always have. The mystery, solving difficult puzzles, facing off against people... occasionally getting shot." He smiled and laughed, even though Jason looked less amused. "If Cassidy is right, and this 'Miracle' cuts crime and pacifies criminals, then I'll know I was just a kid playing with toys before the adults showed up. Civilization has made good and evil the stuff of fairytales and stories."

Jason gave Alex a look as if he knew he should sympathize with him, but was having a hard time with it. "So you're saying that you don't want things to get better? You're a cop. That's your job."

"I want to make things better. It's just... I don't like how easy it's coming, I suppose."

That stopped Jason. He seemed to pull away, eyeing Alex with suspicion, like most people in the Boroughs eyed cops. "That's not healthy."

Alex looked back to the emerald tower as another layer of grime was peeled off.

"Sorry," he said. "I just realize how bad that sounded."

Jason sighed with relief. "I understand, the change has been messing with everyone."

"It's just weird," Alex reflected, looking up at the emerald tower. "Look at it. I know we see it every day and Manhattan in the distance, but it's almost as if these towers just sprang up out of nowhere, don't you think?"

"Yeah." Jason pulled back a few strands of red hair that had been blown into his face by the wind. "Yeah, it does." He squinted. "Jesus, are they actually going to use that building? I always remember cops patrolling it to keep some upstart gang from taking it over. You boys were always afraid some cartel or something would put up machine guns at the windows and act like they own the Boroughs just because they got their hands on the biggest building. I never thought anyone would actually use it."

"Yeah," Alex replied. "It's almost like this is too easy; that the recovery is too simple. We have all the space we need, the buildings are right here. Now we just have to go back to doing what we always had, and march back into the 21st century with wet boots."

"22nd," Jason corrected him, missing Alex's attempt at irony.

"My mistake. Sometimes I forget what century I'm living in." He smiled. "So who is it you're meeting with?"

"Emma Fielding. Do you know her?"

Alex shook his head.

"Well..." He waved his hand in front of him while laughing. "She runs a hardware store on Culver. That's how I know her. We buy our stuff from the same guy and so we met each other, you know, work stuff. Emma, Sheryl and I are talking about moving into Manhattan, buying up one of those huge apartments in the north end near Yankee Stadium and flipping it. I keep telling Sheryl prices aren't going to get any better the longer we wait. If we don't leave this place now, we are going to be stuck here forever."

"Why are you leaving?"

Jason's eyes said 'you of all people should know.' "It's dangerous here. And every year it gets worse. The Boroughs have always been bad, but where I live…" He shook his head. "I don't want to be around here much longer. I don't have any family here. My mother's in Nebraska, sister's in north Texas. I can still see all my friends, so long as they take the boat out to visit me."

"Where do you live again?" Alex asked. As he did, he knew it had been too long since he had talked to Jason, and it was evident just how bad he was with finding places.

"I live on Court Street, by the docks. That's where it's worst. It always is."

"Crime, you mean?"

"Of course. God, you should know, being a cop! That's where all the illegal contraband comes in—the drugs, the weapons. You want to know where the worst crime is in any city, just go to the harbor. Everywhere around my house are junkies. They break the streetlights and security cameras in the morning, and they take heroin, some of 'em even walk the streets at night strung out. One night a while back, there was a body floating by one of my neighbor's houses. Idiot was massively ODing, fell in the water, didn't even bother swimming; some say he tried going deeper down. Didn't you hear about that?"

"Yeah, that must have been a year ago, though," Alex remarked. "But it's not my turf. I am closer to the center, near the Eye. And as for the drugs coming in at the docks, we have tried searching there numerous times. Never found anything."

"Well, maybe the cops are crooked."

"I've busted a few boats myself."

That stopped Jason. "Sorry. I didn't mean anything. It's just bad there. Maybe the drugs aren't coming from there, but they are making their way there and I don't want any part of it. Sheryl and I are going to leave soon, though, no way we are staying."

"What about jobs?"

"That's what's holding Emma back. But there are jobs everywhere in Manhattan," he said, flustered. "We can land something, or start a business. Maybe run one of those boat cabs. Or one of the fancy ones, like a gondola thing. Maybe sing to people, light candles."

"I remember watching you get drunk and sing a few times at parties. Any couple that signs on to a romantic evening in your boat won't be getting laid that night."

Jason laughed. "I'll take anything, man. But I do have to get out of here."

"Yeah… yeah," Alex agreed. He tapped his wrist and checked the time. It had only been twenty minutes, but he needed to be alone again. "Well, I have to go."

"Off to count flags?"

"Don't tell anyone. Secret police business."

"Sure. Take it easy, man." Jason bumped fists.

"You too, good luck getting out of here."

Jason nodded and walked off to the right.

Alex watched him leave. When he had made a left turn and disappeared behind a houseboat, Alex turned to his right and walked down the opposite road. He looked to his left again and saw the emerald tower a few stories cleaner. He looked forward out to Manhattan. Closer to him, down the street, a familiar icon crowned a liquor store.

Four.

Chapter Eleven

A lex leaned back in his chair and looked up at the maps. As much as he tried to connect the pieces, there didn't seem to be any pattern. Cassidy was right, crime connected the people of the Boroughs together more than anything else, even patriotism, no matter how many new flags went up. His mind registered a few details, intersections, the channels that the drugs took, but there was an inescapable randomness to it. He kept staring at it, hoping to draw reason from the nonsense. But what were the odds that he would unravel the chaos theory of crime that dotted the Boroughs? It didn't matter either way; he was only half-heartedly searching for the root behind all their woes. Alex was just occupying himself before the Manhattan team arrived. Cassidy sat across from him, filling out a form on her computer while watching a telenovela. When Alex had passed by, he saw there were no subtitles, meaning that Cassidy's Spanish was improving or she was riffing it in her head. *Probably the latter.* The sobs of a beautiful Latina to her overly snide-sounding lover made Alex lose his ability to pretend to be busy.

Alex had been told by Captain Hewes that they were partnering up on a hush-hush case for the city. Excitement quickly gave way to worry. *Why is Manhattan sending a team here? I thought they were trying to get rid of any connection to us.* Rumor had it that the current administration was trying to split Manhattan off and become its own city. Pulling up the Boroughs would prove to be a lot trickier and a lot of Manhattanites were thinking, if not saying outright, how much easier it would be if they weren't being weighed down by the slums that fell under their jurisdiction. The last thing the Boroughs needed was for crime to spread from here to Manhattan, giving the people there an excuse to cut off their neighbors.

"Officers Waverly, Kikia?" a voice sounded over the intercom.

"Yes, Jess?" Alex replied.

"Captain Hewes has asked for you and Cassidy in the briefing room."

"Thanks, we'll be up." Alex stood up and straightened his jacket. He looked over at Cassidy, waiting for her to finish the telenovela. After a few seconds, he reached over to turn off her computer.

She slapped his hand away. "I'm coming... Jesus."

The two went up to the top floor and entered a room with a long oval-shaped table. At the end sat Captain Hewes, a worn-looking man with bushy salt and pepper eyebrows and a spotted bald head, though today he kept his cap on. To his right sat two cops who wore new dark-blue cop uniforms with shiny, polished badges, which made Alex feel naked in his plainclothes.

"Alex Waverly, Cassidy Kikia. This is Officer Larry Rothouse," he motioned to the man at his immediate left, a burly officer with short black hair and green eyes, "and Officer Ajay Bhatnager," he motioned to a dark-skinned man with tawny brown hair and mustache.

"Just call me AJ," he said, leaning forward to shake Cassidy's hand.

When the introductions were over, Alex and Cassidy took up a seat on Captain Hewes' right.

"Gentlemen, Cassidy. Make no mistake, you all have a very important assignment and failure cannot be tolerated. For the past four weeks, two high-profile businessmen and one woman, billionaires all, have disappeared. So far, the Manhattan police have not raised the alarm; they're trying to handle this quickly and quietly so as not to disrupt the peace."

Hewes' rehearsed delivery set Alex on edge, as he guessed that the Manhattan PD had given him a script and just as important as revealing the nature of their mission was concealing any sensitive information from himself and Cassidy.

"The Manhattan PD has informed me that it suspects an organized crime unit operating in the Boroughs is abducting high-income people from Manhattan."

"Sir," Alex interrupted. Hewes looked at him gruffly, clearly not finished with his speech, but he relented. "These sudden disappearances of a particular group of people would indicate an organized effort, but why would anyone want to kidnap them? You said this has been happening for a month, and yet I assume that since this hasn't appeared in the news, there isn't any ransom being asked for, so they aren't going after their money. So why kidnap them? And if it's a mystery as you're implying, then how do you know whoever's doing this is from the Boroughs? Manhattan can't have crazies?"

Hewes looked at him solemnly. "It won't take me long to tell what we do know, because it isn't much. What we do know is that whoever did this got sloppy last night." He turned his chair and pulled out a remote from his pocket. He clicked a button and behind him a floating image emerged of a man mid-step, while three youths stood by. Hewes clicked another button. The images moved. The youths chased the man. The perspective changed as it switched to another camera. The man was stabbed and then thrown into the water.

"Mr. Brice Noble, head of Noble Securities, was found dead in the water this morning at the corner of Broome Street and Lafayette. We know very little of the people who murdered him except..." He clicked a button and the camera zoomed in on their shirts. *BlueSea Waste Removal.*

"The logo belongs to a local group of trashmen who were fired by the city government a few days ago. Our cameras caught the boat parked at 5th and Broadway and it sped off to the Boroughs twenty minutes after the murder. It's listed as being in the Northeast Docks, Pier 48. The head of the company is a man named Yiril Zogheib, who, as far as we can tell, didn't take part in the murder itself, though he provided the boat and could have served as the get-away driver. He lives at 358 5th Avenue. Investigate, find the killers, and see who they are working for."

Without any further questions, Alex, Cassidy and their two new partners Larry and Ajay stood up and left the room. Alex led the group of four to the elevator and outside the building.

Was I wrong about the docks? Maybe Jason was right. Maybe crime really is centered around them, or at least the biggest criminals have connections there that we can use to get back to them. And here I spent the day counting flags. Cassidy...

"Be cool and act casual," Alex remarked to the two men behind him. "Your uniforms could scare people."

"Yeah, yeah," Ajay replied. "We'll keep our eyes peeled. This place isn't actually as bad as everyone says it is. Way cheaper than Manhattan, and we haven't had any trouble yet. Hell, I may have to do my shopping out here."

"We've got some cool stuff," Cassidy piped in. "There are shops that sell cameras attached to mini-submarines the size of your hand. You drop 'em in the water and use a remote control and you can explore the old city of Brooklyn and take photos."

"That sounds awesome," Larry replied. "God, you'd think we would have heard of that."

"There are tons of cities that sunk below the water that are a lot prettier than Brooklyn. Amsterdam, Venice, hell, there are a couple Japanese and European castles that have gone underwater. Have you seen any pictures of those?"

The two shook their heads. Cassidy tapped her palm a couple times.

"I just sent you some pictures for later. Most people would rather look at those than Brooklyn, which is just gas stations, restaurants, supermarkets and the like. But every so often, I enjoy dropping it into the water and exploring the city. Once, I took a boat out to Levittown and dropped the cam-sub there and took a video of the 1950s suburbs. That was some freaky stuff."

"Maybe you should take it around the world, drop it over some ruins, take footage."

"I wish. Maybe if I win the lottery I could. I always thought the trippiest thing would be piloting one of the sub-cams and having the underwater ruins of Tamano Castle flashing in front of my eyes while flying in one of those planes with transparent ceilings. Sea all around you and stars above? It's not an impossible thing; the cam's signal could reach to a nearby conduit on land a few hundred feet above it, then that could broadcast to a server, which would link up to a series of satellites that could bounce the info to the plane's internet receiver..."

Cassidy had left no detail to spare in her elaborate fantasy, but a few minutes in and they had already arrived at Pier 48. The boat was there, inconspicuous enough, with the words 'BlueSea Waste Removal' painted on its side in aqua and green. Alex led the team forward. His eyes scanned the lower level of the boat. He turned around. There was a shack behind him in which a Middle Eastern man sat with his eyes closed, feet up and half-open mouth dangling a cigarette. The door to his shack was open.

Alex looked back to the other three. "Cassidy, take Ajay up the side of the boat; if this guy is some sort of thug ringleader, I don't want to have any lackeys of his shooting down on us from above. Stay low and stay out of sight of the shack. Larry, you and I will start interrogating him."

Larry looked at Alex. "Boarding his boat without a warrant would be trespassing."

"You want to potentially face a rain of machine gun fire from the high ground?" Alex asked. He glanced at Ajay. "That's why you stay low, make sure we're not surrounded. There isn't a lot of trust or respect for cops out here and if he sees you on his property, he could react badly. That's why you stay low and cover us until we escort him to HQ; after we turn around the corner, then you step out." Ajay nodded and he and Cassidy quietly got on the boat, looking over to see that Yiril hadn't looked up yet.

As they walked to the shack, Larry rested a hand on his gun.

Sweet Jesus, Alex nearly said out loud. When the other two started climbing the boat, Alex breathed, "Not everyone down here is trying to murder you. Just potentially. Stay calm and don't do anything stupid."

They walked forward. Alex poked his head in the door and knocked. The old man looked over his shoulder. He waved them away, annoyance clear in his jerking motions.

"Sir," Alex addressed him forcefully. He pulled back his jacket to show his badge. The man turned around. The look on his face told Alex that for the first time, he realized just who he was dealing with.

He said something very quickly in what Alex guessed was Arabic and hung up. "What do you want?"

"Mr. Zogheib, my name is Officer Alex Waverly and this is Officer Larry Rothouse. We'd like to ask you a few questions."

Yiril leaned over his desk. Alex didn't like the look of the way he seemed to place his body between them and the far-right drawer, and how his right hand had gone perfectly still.

"What questions? I have done nothing wrong. I am just trying to run a business. Leave."

"Sir, we just have some questions we want to ask you," Larry repeated slowly. "Are you aware that your boat was in Manhattan last night?"

"What?" he asked.

"That's right, Mr. Zogheib," Alex confirmed. "We caught it on the security cams. Did you lend it out to anyone?"

"No, no one. I don't know what you mean, you must be making it up. Leave."

"We aren't accusing you of anything. Maybe someone could have taken it and returned it last night."

"Why would anyone do that? And why do you care? This doesn't make any sense. Why would I have two cops at my door to recover something that isn't lost?"

Larry looked over at Alex. There was no way around it. "Sir, we have video of a group of teenagers taking your boat to midtown Manhattan for illegal activities."

Yiril froze. "Impossible."

"We have video," Larry said calmly. "We're not accusing you of anything, but we do need to take you to the station for questioning."

Yiril looked up, squinting past them. "What the hell are those people doing on my boat?" Alex turned around. He expected Ajay to be leaning over the side like an idiot. Instead, Cassidy had peeked over the railing.

"Drop the weapon!" yelled Larry.

Alex turned. Yiril was pointing a gun at them while Larry held out his.

"You're dirty cops! You're trying to set me up for some shit. Leave!"

"Put your gun down now!" Larry yelled.

Yiril moved the gun from Alex to Larry. "I'm not part of any criminal shit! You're not going to pin anything on me, you dirty cops! Leave now!"

"Calm down," Alex breathed, as much to Larry as to Yiril. "Just listen—"

"Drop your gun—" Yiril's hands shook.

"That's not going to happen." Larry aimed his gun at the center of Yiril's head. Larry took a step forward to stand next to Alex. "Put your gun down now, you don't have to die. Put your gun down."

There was a pause. Yiril's eyes narrowed. Larry jumped to the side. Yiril fired and Larry screamed and fired in response. Alex looked back and saw Larry clutching his bicep in pain. Yiril lay prone with a bullet hole in his head.

Larry put his gun in its holster and screamed. He screamed again, then bit his lip and moaned. Ajay and Cassidy ran in. Cassidy had turned white. She looked at her partner. Alex almost called out, 'I'm all right,' but he wasn't going to say that in front of Larry. *If Larry hadn't been there, or if I hadn't let my guard down...*

"Call the paramedics!" Ajay yelled. Alex tapped his wrist and called a team down. Ajay reached into a small kit in his jacket and bandaged Larry's arm. Larry screamed, but the blood loss sapped the fury from his cry. In minutes, a team of four paramedics showed up. They wrapped up the wounds and put Larry on a gurney.

"You two should escort him," Alex suggested. "I can stay here, call Hewes and see how we should handle this, since it was supposed to be under wraps and all."

Cassidy looked at Ajay, still pale. "Yeah." Her voice cracked. "It's not safe for wounded cops to be out on the streets alone."

The two took off.

Alex looked over at Yiril's corpse and then the giant bloodstain from where Larry had collapsed on the floor. He punched the wall. *Damn it! Why wasn't I ready for this? I should have been ready to tackle him as soon as he reached for a gun. What's happened to me?*

But he knew why. He was still rattled from the last gunfight. He had acted brave when he needed to, but he hadn't stopped shaking the whole night afterward and he still hadn't had a proper night's sleep since. He was so close to death, he didn't want to put himself in that position again. He thought he could handle Yiril with words. He looked down at his corpse. *I was an idiot.* He took some snapshots of the body for the report he would have to write up.

He looked at the desk and opened the drawers. If Yiril was part of any illegal operation, he would have more than just a simple handgun. He would have more powerful weaponry, drugs, illegal hardware, some type of contraband.

Nothing.

He looked in the wardrobe. Nothing.

Had he not been involved in anything? Had the men in the video stolen his boat? Alex turned back to the drawer. He looked at the projection cube on the table and flicked it on. *No password needed, good.* He flicked through Yiril's business records. Yiril only had four employees. Maybe one of them was involved in the murder. He emailed himself all the information in the folder. He would run a search on the names, see if any fit the physical description.

Alex looked down at the dead man. Larry seemed to think that all that cops in the Boroughs did was beat people up and lock them away for anything. Yiril must have believed that too. Alex wondered how widespread that belief was and if he would have to shoot anyone else whose only crime was defending himself.

He paused for a good long minute, then called Captain Hewes, hoping he had stepped out.

Cassidy looked askance at the projected homescreen. She had been streaming an Indonesian sitcom, but had lost interest and stared at the wall. She fell back into the couch, looking out into empty space around the top of her bookshelf, eyes un-focusing, feeling the soft leather on her heels as she stretched out her feet. The apartment was firmly planted in the ground, but she imagined a gentle rocking beneath her.

She put her hands on her face and yelled, "Fuck!"

Everything was going so well. Manhattan rose up out of the sea, for Christ's sake! But now I've screwed everything up. It's my own stupid fault Yiril was killed. I nearly got my partner killed, too.

"Fuck." She breathed the word.

There was a heavy knocking at the door. Cassidy leaned to the right, over the back of the sofa, staring at the flimsy imitation wood door. She stood up and walked to the end of the couch, eyeing her gun on the coffee table.

"Cassidy?" Alex's voice called from the other side.

Cassidy took a deep breath, then ran up to the door, pulled it aside and saw Alex about to knock a second time.

"Hi," was all she could muster. After a second, she asked mechanically, "Would you like to come in?"

"Yeah, privacy never hurts." He stepped past her, into the living room. "It hasn't changed much," he commented. "You've been spending all your money at that gaming bar?"

"Yeah, what else would I spend it on? Gadgets?"

"They're not gadgets, they're tools, ones that have come in handy in quite a few cases, if I recall." He smiled slightly.

As much as she usually enjoyed their sparring matches, she had too much weight on her shoulders to trade barbs with him. "Do you want something to drink?"

"Water, please."

Cassidy nodded, walking into the kitchen, which was only separated from the living room by a thin counter with chipped white paint. He threw her pillow on the floor and took a seat on the far side of the couch. She grabbed two glasses from the top middle cupboard over the sink, poured him a glass of water and herself a soda. She walked back into the living room, sat down beside him and handed him his glass. "Thanks," he said and then proceeded to down half of it before putting it down on the coffee table.

"So what's up?"

He met her eyes and for a long time didn't say anything.

"I was going to ask you if there was something going on in your life that's keeping you from focusing on your work."

Cassidy felt herself tense.

"I wanted to be reassured that you can focus and do your job, because I can't tolerate another mistake like earlier today."

"It was one mistake."

"It was an easy one. I told you to stay out of sight. You know how distrustful of cops these people are, you know how they react when they feel like they're being cornered. Larry and I had gotten him to the point that he was ready to talk, we reassured him that we weren't accusing him of anything and didn't suspect his involvement. But you leapt out, showed him you were searching his boat illegally and he panicked. You could have hid easily, but your head was somewhere else and you couldn't even do something that simple and a cop got shot."

"It was one mistake!" she nearly shouted. She felt herself redden with anger. Alex was speaking in calm, even tones, which unsettled her more, like he was berating a child.

Alex leaned back into the sofa and looked forward. He breathed in slowly, then turned back at her. "Look." He sighed deeply. He shook his head and looked down. "We've had these conversations before. I know you don't like it when I get into your business, because you think I'm acting superior to you." He met her unflinching gaze. "Right, well, if we are going to work together, I need to know that you will have my back, that you won't be off somewhere else and that you won't misstep like you did."

Cassidy looked at her partner, eyes on fire, rage pushing back the exhaustion in her eyes, but she said nothing.

"Are you taking your medication?"

"Excuse me? That is none of your goddamn business."

"It is if it nearly gets us killed."

There was a long silence as Alex looked at her calmly, which only infuriated her more. The silence dragged on until Alex finally said, "You're attacking me as if I am accusing you of something. I care about you. I remember the last time you had an episode, when you were really depressed when you..." He saw the look in her eyes and let the sentence die. "I want you to do well. I didn't want to come over here, I didn't want to get involved in your business, but after today, I knew I needed to make sure you were okay, because I don't want something like that to happen ever again. That's all I have to say."

Alex stood up and walked to the door. He glanced at her over his shoulder. "I hear a lot of cops are transferring to Manhattan, where things are calmer. You should consider it, it's probably for the best."

He opened the door, stepped out and closed it behind him. When Cassidy heard it shut, she instantly stood up, stomped over and locked the door, wishing he had left it open so she could have slammed it shut. She listened to his footsteps go down the stairs, heard the door to the apartment building open and close. She kicked the wall, then again and again.

"Fuck! Fuck! Fuck! Fuck!"

There was a banging from the other wall. She held still, seething. She walked into the living room and started to pace. She reached for his glass so she could clean it, then resisted, knowing she might throw it. She opened the window and looked out, huffing. The salt air rose up to meet her. The cold felt good against her warm skin, calming her down. She looked out at Manhattan.

"Fuck you," she yelled, but by then he was long gone.

Chapter Twelve

A smiling woman in a white suit with an 'Amy Kitzenberg' name tag handed over the tablet to Miles. He typed, wiring the money. After a few seconds, the screen said, 'payment accepted.'

"Congratulations, Mr. Buhari, for the next month you are now the captain of a Hiyamoto Cruiser."

Miles smiled painfully. *This boat has cost me way more than one story. This better pay off.*

He took a key from her, a tiny plastic stub on a keychain with a magnet inside. "Thanks." He turned and stepped onto the boat. It was a sleek, one-story luxury vessel, white with a black triangle rising from its low-riding back until it reached its bow. The top's small deck had a white steering wheel and ship's controls. Beside it, there was a short ladder that led to a bedroom below, with a queen size bed, fridge, and side-drawer with a complimentary bottle of champagne.

Clearly this is a fuck-boat. Miles laughed, wondering how many men had checked out the boat, thought 'this will definitely get me laid,' only to end up downing the bottle alone. Miles gave the room a second look. "I could make this work." As a patrol boat, it wasn't very stealthy, but since the casual observer would look at it and instantly think 'rich snob,' it gave him the excuse to sail around the canals and watch for suspicious activity.

Or maybe I could just bring a few girls back. At least then it would be worth the money.

He went up to the deck and put his key in the slot. Without having to turn it, the engine roared, gently massaging his feet. *Oh, I could get used to this.* He steered it out of its spot. As he pulled up to the end of one line of boats, he saw his turn coming up. If he had one complaint about the boat, it was its length. He was kicking himself, as he knew it would be too long to properly navigate the canals of Manhattan with any reliability. He turned the wheel as far as he could and the boat swung out wide, turning on a dime. Miles shouted as he looked behind him, sure he would hit another luxury boat. He let go of the throttle, bringing it to a slow turn in the water. Mercifully, the boat was just small enough that it didn't collide with the blue speedboat behind it. He pulled his boat out of the harbor and sailed for Manhattan, drifting around buoys as he did, a little too overenthusiastic about how well it handled.

He entered Manhattan's west side and immediately turned south. It was only after he first had to stop at a bridge and saw a swarm of tourists walking across, some stopping on the bridge to take photos of the canals, that he realized how much waiting he would have to do. *I am sitting on a fifteen hundred horsepower love machine waiting for old people to stop admiring centuries-old water-logged buildings.*

A warning bell sounded. The natives rushed to get off the bridge, but the tourists still snapped pictures. "Get off!" Miles yelled up at them. A minute later, the bridge finally rose. Miles headed southeast, where the crowds were thinner. The neighborhood in the southern tip was still a bit slummy in comparison to the blocks just north of it. There were still cleaning crews, as the buildings here hadn't been able to afford the hordes that midtown Manhattan could for their rushed washing. All of the slummy bars and clubs Miles needed to hit would be down here.

Miles kept his eyes sharp for any open spot. He was about to park when he thought, *Do I want to be down here with this boat?* He looked around. There were a few nice boats tied up to the sidewalks, but none as nice as his. He took his first left, then another and headed north. The moment that he spotted a decent boat he turned around and looked for the nearest parking he could find facing south. He saw an open spot and he turned, going forward, then reversing until he was in. He looked around, almost expecting someone to commend his nice piloting, or at least make a comment on his beautiful boat, but everyone's heads were turned back, looking up at the skyscrapers.

Miles pulled the key out of the ignition and put it into his pocket. He checked the time. *7:15 P.M. Still have some time to kill, quite a bit before the clubs open up. Maybe more so for the... main event.*

Miles went downstairs and lay back on the bed. He pulled out his projection cube, laid it on his chest, flicked it on and watched the images hover over him. He started browsing online when he got distracted by the gentle rock of the boat. He closed his eyes and felt the gentle rise and fall. The bed was too comfortable; he felt like he was melting into it, and the gentle rising and falling was like being rocked to sleep. *Forget sex, this is better.* He closed his eyes. But after a minute, he grew bored and returned to his computer.

He typed in 'Manhattan Murder Brice Noble.' News links popped into existence above him. Miles read through one after another.

murdered at the corner of Broome and Lafayette...

Police are on the lookout for a group of youths that committed the murder. They are described as in their late teens, all males, Caucasians...

Miles read through five and got an intense urge to throw the cube. *Shoddy writing, all of it. Poor style, poor hook. How could they all make a murder boring?*

And this was despite the fact that they all lacked substance. All of the stories had descriptions of the boys who committed the murder and none of them said it was from witnesses, but from an official police report. That meant the police must have seen them on the traffic cams. But none of the stories had any pictures or video. That meant that the police were keeping it to themselves. Why? Why not show their faces if it meant they might catch the perpetrators? Maybe they have information about the boat too; why not share that with the public? Because they didn't disclose that information, it most likely meant that the police were covering up, trying to catch the perps themselves without the public getting involved. Why?

None of the stories he read said anything about...

He entered 'Manhattan disappearances.' The news stories were all about mass missing persons cases in countries as far off as Sudan and Ethiopia. Why they appeared, Miles didn't bother to guess. He put quotation marks around 'Manhattan disappearances.' The search only had a few dozen results, most of them about magicians or a serial killer in the 1920s. *How could there be nothing on this? Am I crazy? Seeing things that aren't there?*

He typed in 'Manhattan missing persons.' That led him to the official NYPD listing. There were only twenty listed, but yesterday it was eighteen, a week before, ten. He looked up the two new additions to the list, Lisa Wong and Benjamin Kretz. Lisa was the head of a graphic design firm, one of three left in Manhattan. Benjamin was an unemployed real estate heir. Both were billionaires. That made the official count five billionaires who had suddenly disappeared, alongside a little over a dozen less well-off people in the Bronx. The latter's disappearances were to be expected, and it wasn't a shock to Miles that they didn't make the news. But the billionaires not even getting even slight coverage was interesting, to say the least.

What was more haunting to think about was that there were almost certainly more people who had disappeared but hadn't been reported as missing yet. If Miles was right, there were probably a few more faces sitting on some office junkie's computer, waiting to be added.

Miles looked up through the opening in the boat. The yellow city lights had begun to cut through a dark sky. He set an alarm for midnight, leaned back and slept.

He awoke to the sounds of a man singing a country music song about his wife leaving him, though he still got to keep the dog. He clicked it off. He knew some people who liked to be woken up to their favorite songs, but that only made him hate the music he loved. *Better to play something you hate, start the day with aggression.* He rolled out of bed, ran his hand over his clothes to smooth over any wrinkles. He gave himself a look in the closet mirror.

Time to party.

He bolted up the ladder, closed the hatch, locked the door by inserting the magnetic key into an opening above it, then got off the boat. He walked down the block and tapped his wrist. He opened up a GPS app that showed the nearest clubs. The one with the best reviews was called Twelve Squares. He headed towards it, crossing the nearest bridge. When he turned the corner, he nearly bumped into a group of four women and the men they were hanging onto. There were at least forty people in the slow-moving line.

Miles stepped out of it and paced down the block, looking at the boats around him. He was looking for a ship that was just worn down enough that it wouldn't be noticed in the Boroughs, but at least clean enough that it wouldn't be overly obvious to the people in Manhattan. The boats were all moderately clean, a lot of them older models, but the old ones were expensive in their time, and well kept. He turned the corner. He spotted one dinghy with rust on the sides and paused. *If there are abductions taking place, how are they doing it? Just grabbing people off the street? That's how those three kids were spotted. Are they part of the same group or just copycats? Have people really been abducted by idiots who had no idea what they were doing?*

Miles suspected something bigger. He had no idea what, but his mind wandered all the same. *Maybe rival corporations are hiring gangs to take out their competition?* He would have to check out the employment history of the people who had been abducted. They were of all different races, ages, males and females, their wealth being the one thing they all had in common.

He circled the block, picking two boats on the south side that might be potential targets and three on the western. He returned to the club and got back in line, which was even longer than when he had left it. Half an hour passed when he was finally allowed in. It was one A.M., and Miles wondered if he shouldn't have woken up earlier. The country song came back into his head and he cursed himself. Even with electronic music blaring in the background, he still heard the faint rhythm of a fiddle and guitar.

Miles made his way to the center of the dance floor and lost himself in the crowd. He was grinding on a blonde girl in a low-cut blue dress when he remembered he was supposed to be doing work. He looked around the club for anyone who looked working class and felt a twinge of guilt, feeling like an enormous prick for singling out anyone poorer than him as a potential murderer in the night. The guilt passed in seconds. He searched the dance floor, but with the flashing multi-colored lights and constantly moving and gyrating crowd, it was hard to see. He nearly tripped over himself after stepping on a sticky patch from where some idiot had spilled their drink and worked his way to the wall. He climbed a stairwell and walked up to the second story balcony and looked down. It was nearly as hard to tell who was who up there. His eyes wandered to the ever-present views of cleavage. He was surprisingly fine with his defeat.

Miles turned around, saw a couple getting far too amorous on one of the couches and went back downstairs, taking care to stand on his right, leaning over the railing to watch for any suspicious characters as he descended and approached the bar. He kept scanning the other patrons, waiting for anyone suspicious to appear. A girl started flirting with him whom he shook off, then another tried pulling his arm to get him to dance, but he pulled back. *How can anyone handsome ever go undercover?* He re-thought every spy movie he had ever seen while downing a shot of tequila.

At the far end of the bar, a man in a white shirt with a brown stain underneath the dark green oval logo of Summit, New Jersey's baseball team, and a worn leather jacket was talking to a young, mousy brunette who looked barely old enough to be there. He put a hand on her knee. She visibly tensed, but let him continue. His hand trailed up her dress.

The man locked eyes with Miles and he looked away. Summit turned to the girl and whispered something in her ear. She nodded. They stood up and began to make their way to the exit. Miles looked over his shoulder. He turned back to face the bar just as Summit looked behind him.

Miles slouched down, trying to blend in with the crowd; not an easy thing for a man of his height. He weaved through the opposite side that Summit was taking. Summit exited the door. Miles waited a few seconds, then followed. Outside, he looked left and right. Out of the corner of his eye, he saw Summit turn the right corner. He jogged that way. Miles peered around the corner and saw Summit escorting the girl onto an old boat.

Miles reached into his pocket and pulled out a small, red chrome ball with a lens on one side that made it look like an eyeball without an iris. A light flicked on and it connected to his neural interface and he was seeing through it. He lifted it up, zoomed in and frantically took snapshots of them and the name of the boat, 'Sea Lion.' The two sat on the railing and talked, and held hands. *Any minute now he's going to do something devious.* They kissed. First she pecked him. Then she was throwing herself into him. *Oh, you are good,* Miles thought. *But then... I can see how this man could seduce young rich girls and take them off;* actually, he couldn't, *but how does he get the men, especially the older ones, in his boat? He doesn't seduce them too, does he?*

They were kissing madly when Summit put his arms around her and led her to the lower deck. Miles was unsure how long he was supposed to wait. He pulled up his watch and hit the timer. After fifteen minutes, he cursed himself. *Some conspiracy.* He put the camera back in his pocket and his regular vision returned to him.

He sauntered back towards his sleek cruiser, passing the shorter line of inebriated club-hoppers, walking over the bridge and back. *You idiot, what were you thinking? Go into a seedy club and follow every dodgy-looking guy?* He shook his head, realizing how improbable his plan had been. *It's probably even too late to get lucky.* He looked aside and noticed his ship was close by. He walked towards it, imagining how good it would feel to be rocked to sleep. He stepped next to it and kept walking, driven more by a stubbornness to admit defeat than any sense of purpose for a good cause. He took the next bridge across, then turned left towards the next club.

As Miles turned the corner, he saw a group of four men walking his way. On the left was a brute with pale skin, dark eyes and a thick, sinewy neck. The man on the right was shorter, almost completely covered in a coat, scarf and snow cap. In the middle was a gaunt looking man in his late thirties with a scraggly black goatee and eyes that flew back and forth. Behind him was a giant with a long face wearing a trench coat. They had a quick pace and were coming towards him. Miles' eyes fixed on the terrified soul in the middle. He locked eyes with Miles, his face white and shaking. Miles turned to the man in scarf and snow cap nearest to him. Snowcap looked to his right at the brute, his eyes asking a question Miles thought he wouldn't like the answer to.

As Snowcap came into arm's length, Miles ventured a look at the giant, who grimaced as if he might grab for him, but instead let Miles walk past them. As he did, the man in the middle panted, "Oh god!" and Miles heard him get ribbed hard. Two of the men grabbed him and forced him forward. Miles turned, saw them dragging the middle man forward and followed them. Their pace was slow and Miles was a fast runner. He pulled out his camera.

Just as they passed underneath a streetlight and started across a bridge, he yelled, "Hey, look!"

The three men turned and Miles snapped photos of them. "Hey, what's going on? Giving an old man an escort home, how kind," he yelled, continuing to snap photos as he looked around for anyone to notice the commotion he was trying to cause. There were a few people around, but no cops. He turned back to the four men when he noticed the brutish man drawing a gun on him.

Miles ducked as a *bang* burst through the night. Glass shattered behind him. Another *bang*. Miles jumped to the side, landing in a boat, rolling on its floor until he hit the side. He caught his breath, feeling his heart bursting in his chest. After a few seconds of silence, Miles dared peek over the top. The group was rushing down the street. The gaunt man's near-collapse was slowing their progress, but they made a good pace regardless as the two men on his side dragged him onward. Screams echoed down the canal.

Miles got up and ran after them. As they turned the corner, he sprinted forward. He crossed the bridge and hugged the nearest corner, watching them. As they neared the end of the block, he sprinted forward, following them from cover as they crossed the next bridge. The brutish man saw him running after them and held up his gun. Miles jumped to the side without looking, landing in another boat. He waited a second, then jumped from boat to boat. After the fourth jump, his right leg slipped and his lower half stumbled into the freezing water. He gasped and lifted himself back onto the boat. He saw them continue running straight. He couldn't follow them, there would be no hiding from a straight shot. He waited until they were far down the block and crept after them.

Miles heard a motor rev to life. He gathered his courage, jumped back onto the street, ran to the end of block, and realized he was at the southern end of Manhattan. There were three men on deck, with the brutish man piloting. They sailed off into the dark night towards the dim light of the Boroughs. Miles tapped his wrist and called the police. He pressed CALL.

A voice appeared in his head. "Hello, emergency ser…"

As he listened to the voice at the other end of the line, he reached into his pocket for his mini-cam. He leaned forward into the darkness and lowered the camera, putting his body between the camera and the streetlight, allowing it to adjust to the darkness. He zoomed in as much as he could and started taking photo after photo.

A *bang* erupted in the darkness and blood burst from Miles' stomach. He felt himself being pulled backward like a marionette and he collapsed awkwardly, falling backward, then sideways. The taste of blood in his mouth mixed with the cold salt air while a voice from far away told him to get to cover.

Chapter Thirteen

The sun was directly above the spider web that was Brooklyn. Far outside the writhing whirlpool at its center on its northern fringes, Frederico Vasquez stepped up to a blue shanty house and knocked, three times, then once, then twice. There was a pause and the door opened. Frederico stepped past the armed guard and eyed two seated grisly men inside, wearing tank tops in the midday heat. "El jefe," one of them was called. Frederico nodded at him as he walked across the threshold to a cupboard in the living room, opened the top drawer, pulled out a wetsuit and began putting it on over his clothes. The tight black suit felt awkward and itchy, but more than that, he hated having to put it on in front of his men. He had thought about telling them off while he donned the clown suit, but that might make him seem self-conscious; a small sign of weakness.

"What is it? What's happening?" the man who had opened the door asked.

"I can't say," he coughed while awkwardly putting on the flippers, feeling the eyes of the men behind him.

"Must be something big then," one of the seated men whispered to the other in a hushed tone. "Maybe the revolution is starting."

Frederico paused slightly, trying not to give away his feelings. *Two of my most trusted men believe in this revolution shit? Damn the radicals, spreading that nonsense.* He hefted the oxygen tank onto his back. "This has been re-filled?"

The man at the door nodded. Frederico pulled the straps across his chest and put the mouthpiece against his thick beard. He grabbed a flashlight from the trunk and a harpoon gun from the wall. He walked over to the center of the room and pointed. The two seated men stood up, moved their chairs, rolled up the carpet and pulled back the hatch, revealing a square hole three feet across. Frederico sat down and dipped his legs into the water, disturbing the image of a well-muscled, bearded man with piercing, dark eyes that could intimidate his rivals, despite being half a head shorter than most of his men. *Small, but vicious, like a jackal.* He turned and let himself fall into the cold dark.

The men above him replaced the carpet and darkness re-entered the world. Shafts of dim light broke through the gaps between the streets above, but it did more to obstruct his vision than help. Frederico turned on his flashlight. A small school of fish swam underneath his legs and scattered. He kicked, feeling his flipper brush against a long trail of seaweed as he did.

Frederico swam in the shadows of the streets above, using them as a map. He could hear a steady rumble of the noontime crowd marching across the platforms. Unlike the fish, who had gotten used to the feel of constant motion above them, he hadn't. He aimed his flashlight below him. Concrete streets still stood with sidewalks and even a few post boxes covered in algae. It was almost like looking at history. Frederico imagined kids kicking a ball down the sidewalk, an old couple walking along, all while cars rolled on beside them.

As he neared the southwest corner of the Boroughs, the sound began to soften and more fish appeared. The plastic and steel streets above and the concrete ones below didn't always match, so it was easy to get lost if following the ones above. But Frederico knew the way. He looked down and saw the decrepit black gate of the subway entrance to Bay Ridge Avenue. He kicked downward and descended into the long-abandoned subway station, floating above the stairs like a ghost.

He descended until he was above the tracks that once ran the city like a great motor. He swam down into the pitch black tunnel ahead. His heart began to race. When he was eight years old, his grandmother had given him a picture book about sharks. He loved them, but every time he got in the water, he imagined a shark close by. As he swam down the corridor, a new nightmare came to him and he imagined a light appearing and a train roaring out of the darkness, smashing into him.

After a quarter mile, there was a 'Maintenance Personnel Only' door that had been marked with a giant red 'X.' He swam towards it and pulled the door open. Inside, he turned left and swam, until there was a line of stairs and he turned upward towards a light bright enough to make him squint through his goggles. He swam towards it until his head crested the water and he was in the station's bubble. He stood up and started removing his gear.

Two guards ran over, pointing submachine guns at him.

"Shoot me." Frederico winced, his body braced for the blow.

The guards lowered their gun points to the floor. Frederico hated that password, but it was the last thing anyone would say, and it reminded everyone of how present death was everywhere. *Morbid, but that's how Ezreal is.*

"Go through," one of the guards called as he recognized him. He nearly had to shout over the dual air-filtration system and the water pump. Frederico nodded and walked past them, into the narrow hallway and down to the left. The bright lights from the industrial bulbs hanging from the walls burned his eyes, which had been adjusted to the darkness of the subway. He squinted and walked through a blaze of light until he nearly stumbled into the door at the end of the hallway.

The room was a concrete box that was once the control center for the subway. The linoleum floors had been torn away, having filled with a putrid rot and grime from the flood, which still lingered in the air. The control panels, long useless after their circuit boards had been submerged in water and covered in barnacles, had been torn up and disposed of elsewhere. There were two long steel tables and another horizontal table at the end.

On the right side, nearest the head of the table, was Lloyd Jones, a dark-skinned mammoth of man with a visible scar across the left side of his neck, who was sitting beside his brother Andre, a much leaner man who didn't share his brother's ill-humored look. To Andre's left sat curly gray-haired Ivan Cilic with his thick butcher's hands and dark eyes, and on the near-right, José Martín, who despite being trapped in an air pocket a hundred feet below the water looked as relaxed as if he were drinking a cold beer on a beach.

On his left-hand side, there was an empty chair for him, closest to the table's head. Before that sat Leonid Lebed, looking immovable and uncomfortable, though on the few occasions Frederico had seen him above sea level, he had the same look. Cesare Storace cracked his fat knuckles, looking bored of the whole meeting before it started.

At the head of the assembly sat the deathly pale Ezreal Redding. Green veins bulged out in his face and hands. His wrinkled face and wispy last strands of white hair made him appear wraith-like. Despite his aged body, his eyes had a clear blue sharpness and strong muscles beneath his loose, leathery skin. When Frederico entered, Ezreal smiled, stretching and re-defining a dozen wrinkles on his face. *You've spent far too long under the surface.*

"And now the meeting can start," Ezreal called in a grandfatherly baritone.

Frederico walked to his chair and took his place at Ezreal's right hand.

"Now, we have to discuss the recent events in Manhattan."

"Our cover has been blown," Cilic's gravelly voice broke through Ezreal's calm. "First those idiots kill Brice Noble. Then more idiots capture another person and shot someone else. Now anyone rich enough to hire their own bodyguards will, and before you know it, the stockbrokers will have more guns than we do."

"Yes, it seems that many of the pettier gangsters share our desire to seize the wealth in Manhattan, only they have done it much more clumsily than we have. If it hadn't been for them, we could have abducted half of the rich in Manhattan and they wouldn't have noticed."

"'We' nothing. You mean you could have," Lloyd Jones spat.

A silence overtook the room, broken only by the thrum of the filtration system far beyond them.

Ezreal calmly said, "The wealth should belong to us. To all of us, not just at this table, but everyone in this city."

For half a second, a heavy silence took over as everyone in the room knew what Ezreal was about to pontificate. Lloyd wouldn't give him the chance.

"What the fuck are you talking about? Things are better now than they ever were before. Business in cocaine, heroin, krokodil, all kinds of illegal drugs are pouring into Manhattan. I have made more money in the last month than in the whole year. And you want to stir up trouble that'll make them crack down on us? What for?" His voice rose and the hint of anger at the beginning turned into a snarl as he spoke. "You haven't even asked for a ransom. You have just been cutting off our supply to their money."

Frederico tensed. He had never heard anyone question Ezreal before. He had always seemed like a dark force broiling under the surface, dominating the actions above.

Ezreal waited until he was sure Lloyd had finished. "That's because 'their money' should be 'our money.'"

Lloyd rolled his eyes and flicked his wrist. "Not this shit again."

"It's not shit," Ezreal said, retaining the same calm. "Right now, we are facing a crisis. Manhattan is growing by trillions of dollars every day. The rich in Manhattan are afraid, because finally they have something to lose. I've been reading the journals, the reports. Some are calling for Manhattan to break off and be its own city. Others say that to keep crime out, they should call in the navy and patrol our waters with gunboats as if we were foreign enemies," he spat the last few words with anger. "Whatever happens, they are going to segregate us from them. So we have to prune them. Cut off some of their big players while we buy up, threaten and bully those that we can until we are on top and control Manhattan and all of New York City."

"So?" Lloyd shrugged. "We can always avoid them. Go through the subway. They don't have a clue how we bring the drugs in, they would never suspect that we could put the machines in the stations and make air pockets."

"Now you're using 'we,' when you should be saying 'you.'" Ezreal met Lloyd's eyes, smiling in defiance.

Lloyd didn't budge. "If we just keep dealing, we can be making more money than we ever did. But your plan would take years, even if it would work, which it won't. I say we stop this crazy plan and go back to making money."

There were nods of agreement and murmurs from all around the tables. Only Frederico and Lebed held their peace.

Ezreal waited them out and looked at Lloyd. "How many people did you kill to get to where you are now?" After a pause, he said, "I'm serious. How many deals took a wrong turn? How many people did your crews retaliate against? How many did you have to kill to make it to second place, before I gave you the power to kill your boss and take over? Before I lifted you up and made you a king of your own little realm? All those deaths, all those murders, all that work..." His voice got quiet and he gave Lloyd a sympathetic, almost pleading look. "And all you ever aspired to be was a bottom-feeder?"

Lloyd clenched his hands into fists. He stood up, towering over the aged, shrunken Ezreal.

"My men are waiting outside with machine guns. Touch me and they'll kill you and drag your body down the hallway into the storage unit to feed our guests."

Lloyd's chest heaved and his fists hung at his sides. Frederico saw that Ezreal wanted to taunt him while making a fool of him in front of the table. But he was wise enough not to provoke him past his breaking point and soon, Lloyd sat down. Ezreal turned to the neglected men on his right.

"We don't have to be on the bottom of the social ladder, picking off the scraps that are thrown to us. We will be on top. We will retake Manhattan. We, the lower classes, we were the ones who built it. We mined the ore, forged the steel and raised the buildings for the bankers and creditors. We will take it back.

"My men have been threatening and buying off the aides and

lower-ranking members of the city council. In the next election, we will use our resources and our pull with the local community to put our people into office. In the meantime, those people who blew our cover, who went off killing and capturing the rich, must be punished. Starting with the three kids who killed Brice Noble."

"My men can do the killing," Frederico said. "One of them, Antoni Moretti, has been bragging to some of my men on the street level that he killed a rich guy in Manhattan."

"That still leaves two others," Cesare said.

"I don't know 'em." Frederico shrugged. "He must just be a friend of Antoni's or something. I'll kill him slowly. Wring out the names and have my guys kill the other two."

"Good." The sides of Ezreal's lips turned up while his eyes remained cold and dead. *Happiness isn't a good look for you,* Frederico thought as he turned back to his decrepit boss.

"Now, this leaves the matter of Charles Tanning. The thugs who have captured him last night cannot avoid being found out, sloppy as they were. They shot the journalist Miles Buhari in Manhattan. Even our city's government should be capable enough to find these misguided agitators. We need to find them first. Then—"

"Why?" Martín spoke up. For a moment, the air became tense again as the room expected a second conflict. "Why chase after them? You say the public will have to know soon that rich have been getting picked off, if they don't know already. Why bother finding them if no matter what we do, it won't change things?"

"That is a good point." Ezreal emphasized that there wasn't any animosity between them. "However, this could prove to be a grand opportunity for us. If we want the people of Manhattan to be scared, then let us make them as petrified as possible. I have plans for Charles Tanning. It will be a delicate operation, so my men will take control and make sure that things go badly with them."

"And then?" Lloyd uttered, finally speaking up again. "After the whole city erupts in chaos, what do we do?"

Ezreal turned to face him. "What happens every time there is chaos and bloodshed in the streets? It gets violently repressed."

Eyes darted back and forth as they took in his meaning.

"The mayoral election is in a month. Sophia Ramos will be known as the mayor who let dozens of citizens get captured and then brutally murdered. That'll scare off the conservatives and the old; then she will inevitably crack down on the city when things go bad, which will anger the liberals and young. Meanwhile, I will have support inside and outside the law. I can't possibly lose and with a city council controlled by me, the whole of New York City will be in our pocket."

"Again, why kill the hostages?" Lloyd asked. "She will look just as bad if you let us ransom them and we can make billions."

"I want it to be a landslide," Ezreal said. "I want the old government to be wholly discredited. That way, we can take over the government and the streets and control every facet of the city."

"This is insane," Lloyd said again. "This is a mad scheme, like a cartoon villain's. It can't work."

All eyes darted back to the two as they waited for the first to make a move. Calmly, Ezreal began, "When New York was going under the waves, the biggest companies and firms all fled Manhattan. In retaliation, New York City passed a law that if the companies who owned the skyscrapers didn't use them for any purpose, operate them, or couldn't find anyone to lease them out within a year, they would forfeit their property to the city. The politicians used it as a threat. They thought that the people who owned the skyscrapers would desperately cling onto them even as they sunk under the waves. But even the greedy knew not to stay on a sinking ship just because they had stacks of dollar bills on it. For a while, they cheated the system, some hired one person to sit in the skyscrapers just so they could keep the deed to it. But for decades, they bled money and every skyscraper in Manhattan turned over to the city government. Eventually, they managed to lease out space to apartment buildings and companies which would never pay for the repairs, leaving it to the city. Now the city is above the waves and the big winner is the government and the fat cats who run the city council. This isn't a mad scheme. It's politics. I'm going to put myself in the mayor's office and buy out the people beneath me. When the uprising occurs and the blood spills, those in power will lose their hold on the people. It's happened before. When New York City was going under last time, the rich got on their boats and left the poor to swim. I saw the rage, the riots, the violence. But the movement then was timid, it was focused on correcting the system, rather than breaking it and replacing it with something stronger. The situation now is the same as it was sixty years ago. We just have to stir it up until it reaches a breaking point. We won't fail this time."

Ezreal looked out into the distance, remembering a fight long lost, one that no one else at the table even knew occurred. There was a silence that lasted until Ezreal returned to reality. "Are there any other matters to discuss? No? Then continue dealing as normal. Frederico, kill Antoni and his accomplices and I will handle the rest."

Ezreal remained seated while everyone around him stood up. Lloyd paced to the door, his brother Andre jogging to keep up with him. Martín, Ramirez and Cesare exited in their wake.

Lebed stood in front of Frederico, but waved him forward. "Too cramped," he said gruffly.

Frederico nodded and walked forward into the tight, dank hallway. Frederico had gotten used to the feeling of the cramped conditions of the tunnels when he was walking alone. But in a slow-moving line of people, if any of them stopped, he would be stuck, and their warm breath would make him choke and feel lightheaded. They mercifully turned and were walking down the steps. Frederico waited a long time as each of the gang leaders retrieved their weapons, put their gear on and dove into the water. When it was his turn, Frederico fumbled with the straps and nearly tripped over his flippers. He walked forward and shivered as the cold water on his hot, sweating body paralyzed him. He kept moving forward, feeling the cold roll over him, until it felt refreshing. He let his head sink under the water, turned on his flashlight and kicked downward.

March 13, 2090

Dark clouds covered the sky over New York City, turning noon into night. Countless lights flickered on in the skyscrapers, but the people were in the streets. Tens of thousands of muddy shoes marched across the streets to Bowling Green. Matthew Hammond moved towards the throngs alongside a hundred hard-edged men, with eyes that showed they were steeling for a fight. A thin man in a blue parka stood on a small platform. He held up a megaphone and called, "It seems the police aren't out in the same force as they were yesterday. I guess they thought that a little rain would make us give up the call for justice."

A few scattered laughs broke through the crowd.

"Are we going to let a sprinkling drown our hope?"

"No," the crowd called back half-heartedly.

"Let's try that again. Are we going to give up our call for fairness because of a little rain?"

"No!" the crowd called back a little more forcefully.

"They can't hear you," Matthew called out in a booming voice. Matthew climbed on top of the bull statue and looked out at the crowd. His golden blond hair was muddied and his piercing blue eyes were bloodshot, but his weather-beaten frame gave him a fierceness and determination that silenced the crowd. He wore a coat without hood as he was pelted by the rain, defying it. He raised a megaphone to his lips and called, "They can't hear you in their towers, high above us. And yes, they do think that the rain will wash us away. The hurricane approaching us will make us run back to our homes and hide, and by the time we return to protest, a hundred new companies will have left with our jobs, our wealth, and our only hope of saving what little we have before the water reaches our knees."

Matthew paused as he let the reality sink in to the protestors and watched what little strength they had left wither. In that moment, the desperation came out in their faces. The utter despair of their own situation showed in their sagging shoulders and empty silence.

He grabbed the megaphone from the thin man. "Will you still be a moderate when the water's above your head?" he sneered. He held the megaphone up to his lips and turned to the crowd. "How long are you willing to protest? The corporations that buy out advertisement at Times Square, the stockbrokers, the technocrats have all moved inland to avoid the oncoming tide and they're leaving us on an empty ship and making away with all our lifeboats. To protest is to die a slow death as the sea rises up to wash us away.

"They expect us to give up everything, to walk onto the mainland and beg for scraps. Do you think the government will be there for you? Do you think they will care for ten million hungry mouths? There is your answer." He pointed at the stock market behind him. "We cannot ask for the money and supplies we need to make it off this city. We must take it. You shouldn't be holding signs, you should be holding clubs and guns. March upon the banks and offices and our city government and remind them that we exist and that they cannot leave us behind. They have given us two options: March, or starve and freeze.

"To Wall Street and City Hall!"

Matthew jumped off the bull and headed toward the line of police. Bands of impassioned youths in headscarves and hoodies marched beside him.

There was a momentary pause as the most pacifistic of the crowd held their place. The youths and the desperate led the charge. Within a few tense heartbeats, the whole crowd marched and flattened against the barriers. The police held a line and ordered them to stand back. As the crowd approached, the cops desperately linked up riot shields. Bodies pressed against them and were pressed back. A bottle was thrown, smashing to pieces against a shield. Another object was thrown and a wave of projectiles flew towards the police. One lone canister flew back. Tear gas exploded from the crowd, which stampeded in all directions away from it. Sirens blared as backup forces took up a position on Broadway, cutting off access to the north, pushing the crowd south towards the bridge. Three angry youths brought down a cop and were punching at his helmet. A group of officers rushed over with clubs and beat two of them to the ground. Blood mixed with the rain. Pink water drifted lazily toward the storm drains, creating massive puddles that covered entire streets. All the while, the ocean rose above the edges of the city as the night reached high tide.

The lines of battle blurred between the tear gas and fallen bodies; a few were cops, but most of the wounded were protesters. As the front emerged screaming towards him, Matthew Hammond turned and ran south, merging with the crowd which was retreating across the bridge. All along the bridge, cars honked and drivers screamed as the fleeing protesters brought travel to a standstill. Matthew watched as a kid jumped on a Porsche, his muddy feet cracking the front windshield. Matthew ran through the narrow opening between cars. He panted, but dared not look back at the battle behind him for fear of being trampled.

Finally, at the other side of the bridge, Matthew ran out of the way of the street and leaned over, hands falling to his knees as he panted. He watched as terrified people he had locked eyes with and led just a few minutes ago retreated, back to the homes to weather the hurricane headed their way. Matthew forced himself to keep moving, feeling a sharp pain in his chest as he jogged forward. The crowds began to thin, the sound of car horns, police sirens and helicopters dimming as he walked towards the center of Brooklyn. The streets were empty all around him, stores were boarded up with plywood and half of the streetlights were out. Michael felt a gust of wind buffet his face and roar in his ears. He quickened his pace, hoping to make it home before nightfall.

Headlights appeared behind Matthew. He turned, curious about one of the last cars left on the empty road. He squinted and as he did, the police sirens went off. He jumped and the car's engine revved. It raced towards him. He fell backward and the car stopped right in front of him. Two car doors flew open, two police officers stepped out and one of them shined a flashlight on his face.

"Yeah, that's definitely him, the shitbag who started the riot."

Matthew started to rise, but the cop with the flashlight kicked him in the center of his chest. "Oh, no, buddy, this is it for you. You're not going to run this time." Matthew cried out in pain and rolled halfway over. The officer kicked again and Matthew was on his stomach, face in the curb. The flashlight disappeared and Matthew heard the rattle of handcuffs above him.

"Hey, let him go!"

Three young men, no older than twenty, stepped out of the darkness.

"Back off," the first officer called. He bent down and put Matthew's hands in cuffs, tightening them until the metal bit into his wrists.

"Pigs beating us, forcing us back to die out here."

"I said back off!" The cop reached for his gun.

Gunshots exploded and the first cop fell beside Matthew, his body spasming wildly. The second officer stepped backward and fired. He turned, ducked behind the car door and slammed it shut. Bullets stuck in the glass of the front windshield. The car rolled back down the road as a bullet took out one of its headlights.

The young men ran towards Matthew. "Mr. Hammond, are you all right?" one of them called.

"I haven't been shot," Matthew responded as they helped him to his feet. One of the other boys grabbed the fallen keys and undid his cuffs. Matthew grabbed the boy in front of him. "You let him go! You let him go, you idiot! Do you understand what this means?"

"Let go of me." The boy pushed Matthew back. He raised his gun towards Matthew's chest. The other boys stood beside Matthew and pointed their guns at the first boy.

"Guns down, all of you," Matthew ordered, suddenly realizing that he had to take control of this ragtag group of angry, frightened youths.. "They can't help us now. Now all of New York City will be after us as rioters and cop-killers. That cop is rushing back with a dash-cam with all your faces on it, and mine."

The boy in front of him lowered his gun.

"What do we do?"

Matthew looked back towards Manhattan. "We go back to the safe house. The city should be closing down soon due to the storm. They won't be chasing after us as the hurricane hits." His eyes lingered on Manhattan. He had never seen it so dark before.

"Come on, let's go."

Chapter Fourteen

Rodney bolted upright as the previous night came flashing back to him. He wiped the sleep from his eyes, wishing the memory could be rubbed out just as easily. He rose to his feet, threw on a black t-shirt and a pair of jeans, walked into the kitchen and poured himself a bowl of cereal. His spoon shook and he dropped it into the bowl. He knocked the bowl off the table, grimacing as he heard it break. He took a deep breath and stood up.

What do I do now? He still couldn't find a job and since half of the boats on the docks were idle, he doubted he could find one. *I can't just go back to Sam and continue like life is normal.*

Why not? It's not your fault. You didn't kill him. You didn't really do anything. If you had been in Grease's situation, you would have gotten knocked over by that old guy and possibly drowned. He actually smiled as he thought of getting beaten up by an old man on his first mugging. *First and last,* he thought as his smile faded.

Rodney walked into the other room and picked up his phone. Sam had stopped trying to call him after all her messages had been ignored. He felt an instant pang of guilt, but he knew he couldn't call her. He didn't want to weigh her down or get her involved in anything. He knew she was worrying, and he knew he would have hell to pay later, but he couldn't pretend everything was okay. He had to work his way back to that.

Rodney pocketed the phone and stepped out the front door. He walked away from the docks, toward the Eye. He reached into his pocket and felt the five hundred thousand dollars as he passed an electronics store. He spotted a pastry shop and decided to step in. He instinctively looked at the prices and suddenly realized how little everything cost compared to the money he had on hand, certainly more than he'd ever held in his life. He ordered five jelly rolls and a croissant, figuring he might as well try something sophisticated. The spindly gray-haired woman gave him a look as if she didn't think he could afford it. He whipped out his only bill and handed it to her. She had the same judging look on her face as she suspected that he hadn't acquired the money decently. Still, she handed him an overly large brown sack filled with pastries and his change.

Rodney decided to tour the Eye, looking for any 'Help Wanted' signs. He couldn't find any and soon got distracted by the boutiques. He gazed into a clothes shop window and counted off prices, figuring how much he would have to spend to get the newest trend. He guessed it would be around $420,000 for one outfit. He turned and started looking for the next best thing. He couldn't convince himself to buy it. Even though he would have money to spare, he wasn't sure how long it would last, and it was all he had to rely on.

Rodney spent all morning looking for a job on foot before he decided it was hopeless and he would have to look online. He walked up to a railing, leaned over, pulled out his phone and looked up jobs. Thousands appeared, but when he entered 'High school or less' under 'Education' there were zero results. He felt a weight fall on his shoulders and nearly knock him to his knees. As he exited the web browser, he saw the '5 Missed Calls' notification. He breathed in and called her back. After the second ring, he thought she wouldn't answer him.

"Hello?"

"Hey," he replied, feeling awkward. "Sorry I didn't call you back."

"You know how I worry about you down there, why didn't you call?"

"Sorry, I meant to, it's just, I've been trying to figure things out. I... I got laid off."

"Oh, my God, you missed the boat the other day, didn't you! I told you, you wouldn't make it."

"What? No, I got laid off, that's different from getting fired." He chuckled. "Uh..."

"Well, I'm sorry, I didn't mean to make you feel bad. You still should have called, though."

"Yeah, I know. I've just been wracking my head about this. I have to be honest." He laughed hollowly. "I'm not sure what I'm going to do."

After a sympathetic pause, Sam replied, "Well, if you are saving your money, I can take the ferry out to see you for a change."

"No, don't."

"What, you think the Boroughs is too tough for me? I'm tough.

Probably a lot tougher than you, you softy."

"No, don't, please." He squirmed. "I just have to get things together and focus on getting a job."

"...Okay," Sam replied, hurt.

"It's not that I don't want to spend time with you, it's just that hanging wouldn't be the same. Even if we were together, I would be somewhere else, worrying. But I'll call you tonight, and even if I can't find something, I'll come see you, I've still got some money left."

"I understand. You better call me."

"I will, I will."

"Good luck. Know that I love you."

"Love you too," he replied.

Rodney spent the next five hours looking from shop to shop for a job. He wasn't desperate enough to start asking managers if there were any openings without a sign; he would save that for day two. Around three o'clock, he gave up, headed to the mission for something small to eat and headed back. He called Sam that night and listened to her talk about work and the newest celebrity she saw walking down the street. Her voice calmed him and he actually slept that night.

The next day, he was back to searching. He worked his way northeast until he arrived at the docks. He figured he could stop by the boats asking for work. Maybe even Yiril would have something, though Rodney didn't want to weather his turbulent mood. He stopped in front of BlueSea and looked cautiously into the shack. The door was open and there was a misshapen circle of dried blood on the floor. Rodney froze. *I was just here two days ago. I was standing where that blood is now.* He thought about running, turned around expecting the cops to leap out at him, that this was just a trap they had set for him all along. He looked over his shoulder and saw no one. He heard nothing but the gentle rock of the boats and the call of seagulls.

"Yiril," he tried to shout, but it came out as nothing more than a soft call, as if to someone across the room. He looked in the door. There were two pools of blood on the floor that had spilled into a new one in the middle. Bloody footprints were all around the desk.

Two strong hands grabbed his shoulders and pulled. Rodney yelped and tried to fight them off blindly. He was thrown to the side.

"Knock it off, you idiot!" the throaty voice thundered.

Rodney was lying on the pier, looking up at a man in a dark turtleneck with a long, black beard.

"What the hell are you doing?" Rodney gasped while backing up and rising to his feet.

"There's nothing left to steal. You missed your chance." The man glared.

"I wasn't going to steal anything. I used to work for Yiril, I was seeing if he was all right."

"Oh." The man softened. "Well, I couldn't help but assume. The place got ransacked so quick it disgusted me. Second the police left, someone from Pier 50 charged in and swiped whatever was left. Poor old man. Barely dead and the vultures swooped on him."

Rodney felt as if the ground beneath him was collapsing and he was about to fall into the dark, cold water. Police? They knew. They had to. "What... what happened?"

"A group of cops swarmed the place. Yiril fired on one of them and they shot him. Can't say I know why or how it started. But the cop was being carried away in a stretcher, so they must have thought he was going to live. Yiril wasn't so fortunate."

Overwhelming dread nearly made his knees buckle. Rodney ran off. He heard the man call something behind, but he didn't care, he needed to get away. *They know. They're looking for me. They must know.*

Then why investigate Yiril's? Why not go straight to my house? Maybe Yiril was involved in something illegal and it is a coincidence.

There were flutters of faint hope, only to be choked down again by the memory of the bloodstained office.

It can't be a coincidence. Yiril was an honest man, he never got involved in anything too risky. They're coming for me. They haven't found me yet, but they're coming for me.

Rodney ran until he came upon a red houseboat. He pounded on the door. When there was no response, he pounded again, louder. The door finally opened and Antoni stepped out. He had bags under his eyes and he hadn't shaved for days.

"Now's not a good time. I've had a lot of work to do and I'm in no mood—"

"The cops shot Yiril."

Antoni stopped and looked at him, questioning.

"What does that mean?"

Rodney wasn't sure himself. "The police must know that BlueSea was the ship we used. BlueSea will lead to me. That's why I'm here, you have to hide me, man. I can't go back to my place, the cops could be looking there."

Rodney began to step inside when Antoni pushed him back so hard that he nearly fell over as he stumbled backward. "What the hell? Come on, man, I need a place to hide. I can't go to prison."

"Leave."

Rodney couldn't believe what he was hearing. "What?"

"You heard me. Fuck off. Why should I care if you go to prison?"

Rodney blinked. "We did it together," he growled, biting his teeth.

"Leave before I kill you."

Rodney gave him a look of cold fury. Antoni gave him the same threatening glare. He turned his eyes past Rodney, scanning the walkways for anyone who might have overheard them. He gave Rodney one last look and slowly closed the door.

Rodney turned around, fuming. He ran southward, getting as far away from the docks as he could. After five minutes of running, he stopped, panting.

What do I do now? My list of friends I can count on is nearly up, the police will be after me soon. I'm completely helpless.

He felt the money in his pocket. *Maybe not completely.*

He looked westward at the shoreline city of Summit. The waves had risen up and swallowed much of it, as it had with Manhattan. It was nothing but a skeletal structure, but it was attached to land, true, unmoving land, the kind Rodney had never set foot on. *As long as I'm here in this city, I'm always in danger. But maybe out there...*

The police monitor the ferries. I'll never make it out.

Rodney gave the mainland one last look before he turned and walked in the opposite direction.

Chapter Fifteen

Eyes opened. Bright light. Pain. Eyes shut. Glowing red behind scrunched eyelids. *Don't go towards the light.* It didn't matter. The light wasn't getting any closer. *Just take me.* The world felt like liquid. A cool lightness overtaking. Eyes open.

The world was nothing more than a light above him and the hard, solid bed beneath him. Past his green sheets, there was a blur that would wave and sigh in front of him. After a long moment of watching, the glass doors came into focus, then the people behind them, then the walls behind that. The little signs and words began to take shape, even if he couldn't understand their meaning.

Miles, that's your name. Miles Buhari. I knew that. You're in a... a hospital. You...

What did I do yesterday? What day was yesterday? I can remember a few days clearly but... I rented a cruiser to store my stuff, act as a base and... speed away if I were chased.

But he had been the one doing the chasing.

Miles looked down and saw that he was in a green hospital gown. He looked up to his right and saw a clear bag hooked up to his arm. Whatever it was, it pumped a cold liquid in his arm that made his whole body feel numb. His mind was quickly becoming more lucid, but he felt that every movement he made was wild and clumsy. He groped for the bottom of his gown, then after a while, he realized he would be more capable of finding it if he tried under the sheets. He reached under and lifted. Bandages covered half of his torso. As he looked at them, he felt a stab of pain, or maybe just the memory of it. He pressed on the surface above the bullet wound and felt agonizing heat rise up in his stomach. He put his hand at his side, grimacing.

Miles reached over, fumbling for the assistance button. He pressed it and a minute later, a male nurse with a bald head and a sleeve tattoo with Maori symbols on his left arm walked in. "You're up; how are you feeling, Mr. Buhari?"

"What happened?"

"You were shot."

"I noticed. After that."

"You were rushed here near the dead of night, went through emergency surgery and came out about eight hours ago."

"And where is here?"

"This is Saint Anne's Hospital in Manhattan."

Miles nodded, a colossal effort. "Am I going to live?" *And what uninspired prick will write my obituary?*

"Yes, you'll live, the bullet went clean through your abdomen and the surgery successfully sewed up your lower intestine and the bullet wound. You'll need to stay here and rest for the next week at least, and then you'll have to refrain from any extensive physical activity for two months after that, but you shouldn't have any permanent damage. Try not to move too much; your stitches can bend and flex better than your own skin, but the more you move, the more strain you'll put on your still-healing muscles and organs."

"Thanks," Miles said, as if the nurse had plucked him from the street and healed him himself. Then he remembered why he had called him in. "My camera," he said.

The nurse walked over to a side drawer. "We had to throw away your clothes. They were covered in blood." He pulled out the shiny red orb and handed it to him.

"I could care less," he lied. "The only thing that matters survived."

Miles looked down at it. He flicked his wrist and his internal computer flicked on. He connected to the camera and flipped through the photos. When he finished, he flipped over to his phone app and noticed he had three dozen missed calls, nearly all from his mom and sister. *I hope they don't make the flight out.* He was about to call his mom to tell her not to leave her cozy home in the outskirts of London when a wave of pain and nausea came over him and he dropped his hand to his side. He was too drugged out to deal with his mother's worried cries.

"Are you all right, sir?"

Miles looked up, surprised to see the nurse still there.

"Considering I was just shot? Great."

"Okay, if you need anything, press the button."

"I know how it works."

The nurse gave him a miffed look and walked out.

As the sliding door closed behind him, Miles called out, "Thanks!"

Miles rolled his head, watching the overly bright lights swirl and blur above him. He closed his eyes and the mesmerizing dance continued in his head. He opened them, tapped his wrist and opened a web browser. He checked NYPD's missing persons list. A new face had been added: 'Nara Jung.' He did a general search and found out that she was the CEO of a minor tech company. Not a major player by any means, but her company had generated a few hundred billion dollars in profit last year, so she was among the bigger fish in Manhattan.

In a few days, there's going to be a new name on that list: the kidnapped man I was chasing after.

A flash of recognition appeared on his face. He pulled up his photos. They were all dark and blurry, but he could just make out the name on the back of the ship he had been chasing.

Orca II.

Miles stared at the boat, thinking. He called the police.

"NYPD, what is your emergency?"

"I'd like to report a kidnapping."

"Okay, who was kidnapped?"

"I don't know."

"You don't know."

"No, but last night, around 2 A.M., I was walking around the southern end of Manhattan on Madison Street and these three guys picked up a thirty-year-old white man with brown hair and a goatee. He was wearing a blue turtleneck and jeans and was forcibly taken aboard a fishing ship called *Orca II*, headed to the Boroughs. I have pictures of the ship on my camera, I will send them to you now, I took them just before I got shot." He sent the *Orca II* photos.

"...okay sir, we'll investigate it."

"No, you won't! I know bullshit when I hear it. A half dozen people have gone missing already and it's not being reported. The entire police department needs to get on this."

"Sir, I am just the operator. I do not have the authority to send out the entire police force at my whim."

Miles didn't like being mocked. "Then what have I been doing wasting my time talking to you? Put me on the line with the head of the NYPD."

"Sir, I'm hanging up now."

"My name is Miles Buhari. Do you know who I am?" After a pause, he repeated, "Do you?"

"Sir—"

"If you don't put me on with the head of the NYPD, I am going to publish a story about how your department is letting the citizens of New York City get carried off into the night to never be heard from again."

There was a long pause on the other end of the line. "Please hold."

There was a beep followed by silence and Miles thought she hung up on him. After a few moments of waiting, there was another *click*.

"This is Robert Kerry," a deep voice thundered from the other side of the line. "Is this Mr. Miles Buhari?"

"It is," he replied groggily.

"I see." Kerry stretched the word as if it were something disgusting. "And you have information on a recent kidnapping?"

"I've been keeping up with all the disappearances," Miles shot back. "I just happened to catch one last night."

"And you're threatening to divulge this information to the public."

"I'm a bastard, I know, warning people about realistic danger—"

"Releasing sensitive information about this particular case might jeopardize the life of the man who was abducted. If the men know someone is on their tail, it will put them on high alert and will speed up whatever they designs they already had for the kidnapped man. Any hope they have of making a quiet ransom would be out the door and when their captive has lost his value, then his life will be meaningless to them."

Miles paused. His head swayed back and forth. "You can't outplay me. I have a feeling I know what you're intending to do."

"And what is that?" Kerry said, snorting.

"You want me to sit on this, hold out and not tell the public for as long as possible. It's an almost fair request, considering that any information I divulge *may* endanger the life of the man who was abducted last night. But how many people are going to be pulled down dark corners, thrown into boats and driven off to God-knows-where? What about the rest of them?"

There was a long silence from the other end of the line. "And are you willing to play God with this one person's life?"

"Yes."

"And all the others?"

Miles clenched the sheets with his other hand. He began to feel uncomfortable again, and saw the glass doors in front of him teeter from side to side. "Are you?"

"I have been doing it every day for the past twelve years, kid. By now, I'd figured I was his stand-in here on Earth."

"Well, don't tell the Pope."

Kerry laughed. "You know why the Pope's infallible? Because he never gets his hands dirty."

There was a long pause as Kerry waited for Miles to mock him. The ensuing silence let each of the men know they had come to an understanding. "Don't do anything rash. I will send someone to you for an official interview. Where are you?"

"Saint Anne's. I was shot. Did your secretary not tell you that?"

"I'll send someone over," Kerry said and hung up.

Miles waited a long time. He closed his eyes, trying to sleep, but it wouldn't come to him. He reviewed the missing persons list and saw that it hadn't changed in the last twenty minutes. He debated calling his relatives. He fired off a text to his mom, dad and sister, telling them he was fine, but couldn't talk. Two minutes later, his phone was ringing.

"Mom, I really can't talk—"

"Oh, my God, you're alive!" came his mom's crying voice from the other end of the line. "What happened? Are you hurt? What stupid thing are you doing now that you put yourself in danger like this?"

Miles spent the next half hour trying to tell her he needed his rest and that he was getting a headache from her shrieking until it was finally true. Nothing could sway her, but he finally talked her out of filing for a passport. When she finally let him go, he hung up, let his head fall back into the pillow and tried to let the headache take its course. No amount of rubbing made it hurt any less, but thanks to whatever strong drugs he was on, he felt more nauseated and off-balance than in actual pain.

The sliding doors opened. A short, dark-haired woman wearing a light blue suit stepped into the room. She gave Miles a smile that appeared almost too big for her face. Miles knew he recognized the woman, but he was too addled by the drugs and his own faint headache to pin a solid name on her.

"Mr. Buhari?" the woman said as she approached Miles' right side. "My name is Mayor Sophia Ramos. I assume you know about me, as you have written about me quite extensively."

Miles remembered word for word everything he had typed. The smile on the mayor's face and the steady tone hid any hint of resentment, so much so that Miles thought the hundreds of times he had called her an idiot or corrupt were somehow playful joking. *Now I know how she got the job. That and no one else wanted it three months ago.*

"It's a pleasure to finally meet you."

Damn, I almost believe her. "Same," Miles replied hazily. "I was told by the commissioner that he was sending someone down to interview me. I didn't expect it'd be the mayor."

"There'll be an officer here shortly to gather all the information for the case. I'm here to discuss how we proceed on this delicate matter that you've stumbled upon."

Miles fixated on the words 'stumbled upon.' Even worn down by exhaustion and drugs, Miles could immediately recognize this subtle belittling of his investigative acumen, which she no doubt hoped would make him feel inferior to uniformed detectives.

Miles chose to ignore her subtle jabs and turn the heat back on her. "So you're in on it? For how long?"

"In on it? You make me sound like a conspirator in something. The police have been keeping an eye on the missing persons. Last week, Commissioner Kerry told me that he is certain that these disappearances can't be coincidences. The only problem is that we have had no idea how they've been disappearing."

Miles' eyes narrowed. "What do you mean?"

"Before your story, there's been no trace of the missing people. None at all. No boats or people caught on camera, no witnesses, no gunshots and no signs of struggles in their offices or homes, no break-ins. They just vanish. Except Brice Noble, and a few other murders, but what city doesn't have those? But the missing persons, they are unique."

Miles paused. "So what does this mean?" he asked, realizing he was only asking so because his brain was too wrecked to figure it out himself. He added, "I mean, what have the police concluded?"

"We don't know." Sophia shrugged. For the first time, Miles thought she was being genuine. "We've instructed the businesses of the missing persons and the families to keep a lid on this or declare that they are absent due to health reasons as we searched for some solid clues to their whereabouts, but we couldn't find anything. But we finally have a lead, thanks to you. The name of the ship will unravel whoever is behind this."

"So you want me to keep quiet?"

"If you published the information you had, those men would know they have been compromised. Best let them think that they are getting away with it. That will give the police time to catch them, and maybe find all those missing people."

That was a long shot, and about as hopeless as it was unrealistic. Still, a life was in danger.

"I can't sit on this forever. Maybe your administration and the police can let people get shot and carried off into the night, but unless your men manage to come up with something, then I am publishing everything I know. And I might just mention how you and Commissioner Kerry are complicit in this."

The smile on Ramos' face fell. A look of fear and defiance came on her. She bit her lips. "Thank you for waiting," she forced out. "I will keep you updated on our progress."

You mean you'll monitor me, make sure I don't expose you.

"When we catch these people, I will make sure you are given a medal for bringing us to the first real lead."

The mayor thinks that I'll dance along with everyone else because she's offering an honor that would only dampen my status as an anti-authority figure? And here after finally meeting her, I was beginning to question whether she deserved to be called an idiot.

Sophia stood up and added, "I'll send the detective in. Please tell her everything you know." Miles gave the slightest of nods. The mayor nodded back, turned, opened the sliding door, and walked down the hall. After Miles was sure she was gone, he opened up his blog and clicked 'New Entry.' A small voice told him he shouldn't be writing in his state, but it wouldn't be the first time Miles had written an article while on drugs. When he finished, he clicked the 'Save' button. His finger hovered over 'Publish.'

He clicked 'lock' instead and let the interface disappear just as the door re-opened.

Chapter Sixteen

Sophia wiped the sweat from her brow, threw her shoulders back and walked into City Hall, trying to look as dignified as possible. How "dignified" came to mean "separate from the elements" was beyond her. It was a hot day and Sophia had to book it across town to Saint Anne's to stop Miles from tearing down the whole city, then jump back into another taxi and head to a meeting with the city council. She felt a slight sense of satisfaction from her dedication to duty, but her mind was fixated on collapsing into her black chair in her air-conditioned office with a drink in hand when the meeting was over. She shook her head, trying to wake up. Even though she had hardly slept the last few days, she knew she needed to be on the top of her game.

As Sophia passed through the heart of City Hall towards the elevator, she heard a tenor voice call, "Sophia." She turned and saw a thin, balding man running to catch up to her.

"No need to rush, Jacob, I've got the door," she called as he entered.

He stepped inside, panting slightly. "Sorry, it took longer than I thought to get here—"

"You don't have to make excuses, I'm late too."

"Why are you late?" he asked, genuinely perplexed. "It's your meeting."

Without looking at him, Sophia curtly explained, "I have been doing quite a few very important things. They couldn't wait."

"What things?"

"You'll learn about them soon enough," she replied.

The golden doors opened and they stepped into the long marble hallway. "Robert," Jacob called, reaching out his hand to Kerry, who waited outside the meeting room.

Kerry's chiseled face hardly moved as he grunted, "Hello."

"If you'll excuse us, councilman, Robert and I need to talk."

Jacob nodded and slipped into the meeting room. Noisy chatter echoed out into the hall.

"Are you ready to do this?" Sophia asked.

Robert looked down at her. He didn't give away much, but she caught even the slightest facial movements. He knew he was being probed. "To present my report? Yes."

"Your drastic report."

"It's pretty shocking, yes." After a few seconds, he added, "Almost impossible to solve."

"Almost?" she asked.

"Virtually impossible," he conceded. "If the criminals were a bunch of kids with guns, we could stop 'em if we put cops on every corner, even if they did have connections and safe houses here, but they are too sophisticated. They seem to be able to abduct people without leaving a trace."

Sophia nodded slowly. "Is there any chance that the rich are just absconding to a valley in Colorado to create a capitalist utopia?"

Kerry raised a bushy eyebrow higher than it should have been able to go. "No, I don't think that's likely. A satellite would have picked them out or—"

"Never mind. Let's go inside," she muttered, deciding never to try humor with him again.

Sophia stepped inside a cavernous room with old, polished wood against bleached white walls. She stepped past one of the six tables facing the far wall and walked towards the dais. She took a seat on the left-hand side of Speaker Brown, an older woman with sagging cheeks and round nose who wore a black shirt and pants with gold overcoat to match her long, wispy hair. She waited for Kerry to take his place at her right. When he did, her petite hand reached out and grabbed the gavel, smacking it down with a loud *bang*. Sophia straightened her shoulders and looked out indifferently at no one in particular as various councilmen and women took their seats.

"This meeting of the New York City Council has been called into order," Brown announced. "Police Commissioner Robert Kerry has asked that he be granted time to deliver an urgent update on the crime situation in the city, after which Mayor Ramos will present a measure which she has reserved to disclose until after the presentation by Commissioner Kerry. For Kerry to speak, he needs a second, do I hear a second?" Dozens of hands went up. Speaker Brown waved him forward. "Commissioner Kerry, you have the floor."

Kerry stood up stiffly and nodded at Speaker Brown while turning to face his audience. "Thank you, Madame Speaker. If you don't mind..." He stepped forward and placed a small projection cube on her raised desk. "You'll just see everything in reverse," he said with a small smile.

I suppose that's the closest he comes to humor, Sophia mused.

An empty white screen, almost invisible, appeared behind him. He turned to face the council with a small remote in hand.

"I'm sorry to say this to everyone in the council, but our violent crime problem has not improved, despite forecasts that increased revenue from investment and tourism would cause a drop. Every sociologist working for New York City, centered in Manhattan, hell, anyone with an opinion and a blog, all the experts said that crime would decrease when the money started to pour into New York City. Here are the latest figures."

He pressed a button and a chart appeared.

"Since the Manhattan Miracle, tourism has exploded, with an estimated nine million international tourists pouring into the streets. An additional thirty million domestic tourists have joined them. They are expected to generate over ten trillion dollars for the city. Moreover..." He clicked a button. "Investors have been pooling enormous amounts of capital into New York City, Manhattan, I should say. From buying up space, to investing in companies located in Manhattan, and cruise lines and transportation servicing, the total amount of money that the city has taken in so far is over sixty trillion dollars and climbing.

"So how has this affected the city? Have wages increased?"

There was a palpable silence as dread crept over the members of the council.

"The average is way up," he said, showing a bar graph, under which was the word 'Manhattan.' There was a small, square-shaped gray line entitled 'pre-Miracle,' and a golden rectangle ten times its height entitled 'post-Miracle.' "However, the average for the Boroughs is a different story." There was a tiny gray stub entitled 'OB pre-Miracle.' A gold line lay on top of it, barely a sliver.

"When New York City started to dip below the sea level, the wealth of Brooklyn, Queens and Staten Island, and with them the technical classes and businesses, relocated. While there was an exodus of Manhattan too, not everyone left. I suppose knowing that this city used to be the center of the world, it was hard for the people who owned big chunks of it to let it go." There was silence as he looked out at them. "But what do I know? The point is that Manhattan has been almost a separate city from the rest of New York for a while, arguably for hundreds of years, or so some experts tell me. But the environmental crisis and now this 'Miracle' have exacerbated this great divide between our rich and poor, as the money just isn't trickling outward. More likely, that money will go into the hands of the educated out-of-state Americans, or even foreigners, who are coming into this city in droves, than it will the people of the Boroughs. What makes this situation worse is that because the Boroughs are so filled with crime, employers in Manhattan have turned to hiring people from the mainland who are nearly as close, and because they live on solid ground, they have been less affected by climate change, are less likely to have a criminal record, and are generally more educated. In fact, after an initial spike in employment for the Boroughs, the employment numbers have actually gone down the last few weeks as the Manhattan rich hire out-of-state workers." There was an awkward silence as the rich in the room tried not to look at those council members representing the poorer Boroughs districts, who far outnumbered them.

"So what does this mean for our crime rate?" He clicked a button. He didn't have to look to know how tense the room was becoming. After being a cop for so long, he could feel it. "In the three months just prior to the Manhattan Miracle, there were three hundred twenty-eight homicides in the city, with forty-one occurring within Manhattan. In the three months since the Miracle, that number has jumped to four hundred twelve murders, with eleven occurring in Manhattan."

"That can't be true," a man on Kerry's right said to his neighbor loudly enough for everyone to hear.

Kerry looked at him and said, "It is. The departments of the Boroughs have been fudging the numbers and re-classifying some murders to make things look better, but in light of recent events, I wanted to get a good picture of what's happening to the city, so I put all these cases up for review. I can show you the specifics afterward, but until then, you'll have to take my word for it. The violence in the Boroughs has gotten worse for a number of reasons. Mostly it has to do with gang rivalry; with more money flowing into Manhattan, the gangs of the Boroughs have been fighting each other more so than ever, trying to wipe out their competition to control access to Manhattan's black market demands. They've already made headway; our detectives suspect that including tourists into the numbers, the number of drugs consumed in Manhattan is almost twice as much as before.

"But the most troubling aspect of all this is something which Mayor

Ramos has informed you of, through our department, but which we have been keeping quiet for matters of public safety: the disappearances."

The silence took on a foreboding air. It was like looking out over a calm sea with storm clouds all across the horizon. "Over the last five weeks, there have been six billionaires in Manhattan who have disappeared without a trace, without any message to their families, just gone, with potentially more we are unaware of. Now, we in the police department have tried to keep it out of the press, while at the same time dealing with each case separately, not letting the information go public so that we can solve this problem before a panic breaks out.

"Except that we never will. One of the unique problems of New York City is that since it is floating on water with a deep bay any thug with basic scuba equipment can swim over and appear literally anywhere in Manhattan. We can't have boats covering every canal entrance and we can't have spotters watching every inch of the water, not in the dark, not while it's so deep. We can't use radar because the constant thrum of the machines disturbs the water and makes it useless. Keeping Manhattan safe under the best of conditions is hard, but with all these tourists, criminals, who are much smarter than we gave them credit for, are capable of slipping into the fold undetected."

"Why not use security cameras?" a deep voice from the back called out.

Kerry looked out solemnly, stone-faced. After a few moments, he said, "We are, but we still have no idea how they are abducting people. After the first disappearances, security going in and out of Manhattan was heightened. On three occasions, there were billionaires who vanished one day and the night before, there wasn't a single boat that wasn't checked by officers, either going in or out of Manhattan. Our best bet is that they may have some nest or hideout here in Manhattan, but considering how spread out the abductions seem to be, we can't even be sure of that. We honestly have no idea how people are being abducted."

"We have money now," a blonde-haired woman to his left said. "Why not put out more cops?"

"The only way we could keep the city safe is if we put a cop out on every corner," Sophia called out from the dais. "And even then, we don't know if such extreme measures would work. And in the meantime, with Manhattan known as the world's largest police state, the trillions of dollars in investments would stagnate, if not evaporate, and we would have to lay off the cops almost as soon as we hired them."

"So what do we do?" a woman nearly shouted from the back-middle row.

Kerry turned to Sophia. She stood up and walked forward. Kerry nodded to her, pocketed his projection cube and took a seat.

"I have a proposal. A proposal none of you will like, but one which I think is absolutely necessary."

She reached into her pocket and pulled out her own projection cube and put it on the desk. From inside her pocket, she pressed the button on her clicker and a rotating suspended image of a massive motor appeared. "This is the 'Poseidon' motor which Stanhope Limited's R&D department has been working on. This motor is capable of moving skyscrapers horizontally through the water at a maximum clip of twenty miles per hour while maintaining its stability through compatibility with the Sea Titan motor. This motor," she clicked again and the Carlyle Building appeared, "has been installed on the Carlyle Building. The skyscraper has already been sold to the city of Dover for six trillion dollars." She let the figure sink in. "A skyscraper which was only serving as a den for criminal gangs operating in the Bronx, but it was bought by Dover because many smaller cities, which weren't on the coast until the seas rose, now need skyscrapers. Dover thought they would buy a piece of world history, one of the first skyscrapers ever, and we can ship it to them using the Poseidon Motor."

She looked out at the audience, trying to gauge everyone's feelings. She could see they were frightened. *Good. But are they frightened enough?*

"Council members, we are facing a brink. Once the world finds out about the six billionaires missing and that we cannot protect our people, all of the trillions of dollars this city has gained in investments will evaporate in days and we will be in worse shape than ever. And the world will find out. Very soon. Just this morning I had to make a special trip to Saint Anne's to silence Miles Buhari," the name drew mumbles and curses, "who was about to write a damning op-ed revealing everything that has happened while blaming us. The world will find out. In a few months from now, the world's image of us will have changed from a resurrected Atlantis to a floating slum as the perception of the old New York creeps back into peoples' minds. We risk losing every cent we have gained and more and when that happens, we will be in even worse shape to fight the gangs. I hate to admit it, but it will be difficult to fight them even now that things are going well. Our skyscrapers will be nothing but floating empty relics, a massive floating grave of what was once the greatest city on Earth."

Sophia looked around the room. She could tell they wanted her to stop, that after climbing so high, what she was telling them was so horrible it was hard to imagine.

"But there is a way out. I have been in contact with businessmen and politicians all throughout the Eastern Seaboard. The mid-level cities that were near the coast before the rising sea levels are now on the coast. These places need skyscrapers. We have a huge supply that are unused and we have the means to move them. Furthermore, because all of our businessmen have given up the property rights to the skyscrapers during the crisis period that we have the legal right to authorize the selling off of our skyscrapers. That is the proposal I am putting forward today."

There was silence. A barking laugh from her left broke through the tension. "How are we ever going to explain this to our constituents? How do we explain to the businessmen and the renters that we are selling off their property and apartments to Nowhere, Georgia?"

"We offer them money." Sophia held her ground. "Enough money to make up for the property they will lose through the move and the opportunity to ride along with their skyscraper and take their business or home with them."

"And if they refuse?"

"Then we'll offer them nothing."

"And what about the people in the Boroughs?" asked an elderly woman to Sophia's right. "What will we do for them?"

"Cut them a percentage of the profit. After paying for the cost of installing the motors and the cost of paying off the people in Manhattan, we can pool in trillions to help their police departments and infrastructure."

"You're nuts," a gray-bearded man said in front of her. "Our careers will be over. Who would ever elect the people who sold off New York City for anything?"

"We wouldn't be selling off the whole damn city." Sophia glared at him. "Just enough to make sure that we can finally get our salaries and with the interest for all those times it was late, and guarantee our full pensions."

"That's bribery," the man said, gripping his cane hard. He didn't sound as if he were wholly opposed.

"That's hardly anything," Sophia said. "I sold an old, crumbling building for six trillion. For the Empire State Building, the Chrysler Building, the Freedom Tower, Yankee Stadium; the bidding will start at ten trillion at least. With sixty-one council members, myself, and Commissioner Kerry, that is only six hundred and thirty billion dollars in total."

"Then sell off a few of the old ones, but keep most of them," a large man with sweat beading on his balding head called out.

Sophia turned to the speaker and said, "Everyone wants a piece of Manhattan now, but the second our troubles hit the news, everyone will know we have no choice, and our buildings will plummet in value. After repairs and motor installation, we'll be lucky to break even, which still leaves us buried with debt and an out of control crime problem."

Sophia let out a deep sigh and gave one last look around the room, waiting for any final words, any last questions. There were none.

"None of you are less sad and confused than I am. I have been working non-stop with Commissioner Kerry on this. This is our only solution. I know many of you think that it may be your duty to keep New York City afloat. But what is more important; the city or its people? If we try to keep it going, we will be in a disaster that none of us can fix. But if we go through this plan, as hard as it may be to say 'yes' to, we offer prosperity and wealth to those in Manhattan and over a hundred trillion dollars in much needed aid to the Boroughs, perhaps enough to finally lift them out of poverty and take on the gangs. And our futures will be secure. I know this is a difficult decision. But the measure to give me the authority to make binding contracts to sell off all Manhattan property is one which we must resolve today. By tomorrow, our city might be crashing down. It would already be over if I hadn't stopped Miles a few hours ago. I will do everything I can to keep Manhattan here, where it should be. But I am asking you to give me special powers if that scenario becomes impossible."

Sophia surveyed the crowd and felt the weight of sixty-one pairs of desperate, scared eyes staring back. She took her place beside Speaker Brown and sat down.

"The motion..." Speaker Brown's voice cracked. "The motion is to give Mayor Ramos unchecked authority to broker deals for the selling off of all Manhattan property. All those in favor."

Seven hands went up. Then a few more. After a few seconds, more joined them.

Forty-nine.

"All those opposed."

Twelve.

"Motion passed."

Speaker Brown banged her gavel. To Sophia Ramos, it sounded like a death sentence had just been passed on New York City.

*   *   *

Sophia opened the door to her office, feeling relief and then sudden confusion as she saw Lei Xu sitting in the chair opposite her desk, looking over her shoulder at her.

"Morning," Sophia called bleakly, then realized it was almost noon.

"Morning, Miss Mayor," Lei responded politely, though Sophia could feel the hint of annoyance in her voice. "I have been trying to contact you all morning."

"Yes, well, I've been busy," she snapped, working her way over to her chair.

"I checked out the Carlyle Building."

"Oh, yes. Oh." Sophia started sweating a bit more. "Yes, I imagined it was quite a sight, the renovations and all."

"There was a dead body there."

"So I was informed. I was also informed you didn't take it well."

Lei gave her a shocked look and she realized it was because Sophia didn't look disturbed or put off at all. "As mayor, I've learned that tragedies and even horror strike in the midst of disaster. Whether it's hurricanes or earthquakes, people do terrible things when society falls apart. I think if people knew what had been going on in New York City, they would be revolted beyond reason. Even knowing that these things have been happening in slums in backwater cities all over the world doesn't prepare people when they find out it was happening in their city."

Lei wasn't any less shocked, despite Sophia's efforts to put it into perspective for her. "The police didn't even care to investigate. They said that on your orders, they were removing any 'trash' from the building."

Sophia shrugged. "What could they do?"

"Not throw away the body in a dumpster. They could bury it or cremate it. But that would require a certificate of death and you didn't want anything to get out. If the new CEO found out that there was a cannibal feast on the ninth floor, he might not want to put an office there."

Sophia felt herself tense, but she kept a stern poker face. "There is nothing that anyone could have done and sadly, we can't let people know about how bad things have gotten here. We need to hold up this illusion for the good of New York, for the good of humanity." Sophia saw Lei wince a bit as she said 'humanity' and knew she was stretching herself a bit too far. "Tourists, the investors coming in, they see us as rising from the ashes. If they knew about how bad things had gotten, they might be repulsed and the money would dry up. We need this new money to keep us going, to keep us from going back to what we were: slowly and inevitably dying."

Lei paused. "You've been covering up things like this for a long time, haven't you? Even before the Miracle."

"If you meant I am the one who is saving this city, then yes."

"You didn't. Sverichek did."

"He didn't."

Lei paused. Sophia could see what Lei was thinking by the expressions on her face. Sophia had read all about Lei, but the raw data meant little to her. For Sophia, everything was in the eyes. Lei was thinking, *My hero failed? And this woman, this conniving bureaucrat thinks she is saving the city?* Sophia expected Lei to rebuke her, to deny her work.

"I checked out the plant in Summit that is making my machines. They told me that they are scheduled to make hundreds of them. I couldn't understand why. Stanhope said that my idea for a floating city was impractical. You made no hint that you approved of it. You said you only wanted my motors to sail decrepit skyscrapers away, allowing you to sell them off. But you're making hundreds of them." She laughed and said, "What are you planning to do? Move the whole city?"

Sophia looked her in the eye, watching her expression change as her humor faded away. "People keep comparing Manhattan to Atlantis. It's stupid, and I hated it for the longest time. Venice sunk and no one compared it to Atlantis. Amsterdam, Copenhagen, all of them sank, but no one compared them to Atlantis. That's why I was so glad, among other things, that when the city was raised, people would stop making those comparisons. But recently, I can't help but think about that city. And since it's a myth, I can make up any story I want about it. I couldn't help but think: why did it sink? And my only conclusion was that the ground it was built on must have been bad. So that even if it were lifted up and rebuilt, it would only collapse again." Sophia knew she might have been telling her too much, but Lei was too smart for her to trick her. "Manhattan is surrounded by destitute poor who outnumber us twenty to one. The Boroughs, Long Island, Summit across the inlet. Sverichek could only lift up Manhattan. Surrounding us are the same poor, the same destitute, the same misery, the same lives. They see our towers rise again and expect good times to come to them too. But we can't lift everyone up. And their attempts to make a living for themselves off of our success is like a drowning man pulling someone else down with him."

"So what are you planning?"

Sophia paused. She had been lacking the resolve to go through with this final option. But ever since the Manhattan Miracle, the uncommon had become much more common. "I will try to cut out as much of Manhattan as possible and if enough people invest here, then maybe all of New York City can be saved."

But there are killers out there, roving gangs who take what riches they can with bullets and blood. If they continue to cannibalize the city, then all of Manhattan will be nothing. The Carlyle Building, the Empire State Building, the Chrysler Building, all testaments to human greatness filled with destitute and dead.

"But if we cannot solve our problems, then we will out-sail them."

"And all the people that will be left behind?"

"Will be left behind."

Lei couldn't believe her. Her eyes filled with horror at what Sophia had done, but more from the realization that she had given her that power.

"We will give the Boroughs the lion's share of the profits, after expenses. We are giving all those with leased property in the city the same amount of money that their property is worth and the opportunity to live in those buildings when they are moved, wherever that may be."

"And if I refuse to participate in this?"

"If you mean stop work on the motors, it doesn't matter. We have the fully developed plans and our factory in Summit is mass-producing them as we speak. If you mean you will speak out to the public about this... you won't stop the selling off of New York. All you will be doing is plummeting the prices and impoverishing millions of people. If you mean you won't take the money or move with us, then fine, fall on your ass and swim to shore for all I care."

Tears began to well in Lei's eyes as her ambitions turned to catastrophe. Her tears angered Sophia. She had made her way to this now detestable position because she didn't show that same weakness.

"If you don't have anything else to say, then you can get out of my office. I have to get to work before that idiot Miles Buhari decides to sink us all."

Lei stood up. A small tear began to trickle down her cheek. Without acknowledging Sophia, she turned and left. Sophia looked at her computer screen and clicked the phone app before she could think about what she was doing. Her vision blurred with moisture. She pressed them shut and called the mayor of Brunswick with an offer.

*   *   *

The tears came unbidden despite her efforts to fight them down, but Sophia had kept a stone face, her voice hadn't wavered and by the end of the day, she had sold a fifth of all the buildings in New York City. It was only after she had sold the Chrysler Building that she let her head drop to her desk. She sobbed and slammed her fist down. It was past sunset then, and the tremendous burden of knowing that the downsizing of the Miracle was what she would always be remembered for, combined with her sheer exhaustion, had brought her lower than she ever thought she could go. She might not have cried if only she hadn't been forced to sound cheery and wheedle with the people she was selling Manhattan to. But having to be charming and endearing while doing something that disgusted her was like performing a comedy set with a knife in her stomach. By eight o'clock, she forced herself to call it a day. Most of the wealthy and political elite were off as well. She would have to go at it again tomorrow from dawn until late at night, selling off the city at a breakneck pace. It was the worst thing to look forward to and she balled her hands into fists, knowing she wasn't going to get a good night's sleep just when she needed it most.

On a whim, Sophia decided to see her mother at her retirement community on the way home. Her mother always had a way of soothing her, and she figured she wasn't going to sleep well anyway, so there was no point in falling on a bed only to stare at the ceiling. As she neared the skyscraper containing her mother's retirement community, she realized that it was one of the buildings that she had sold. She pushed that thought aside and entered the building. She took the elevator up to the fifth floor and stepped up to the reception desk. She didn't bother to smile at the lanky young man working it; she had faked being nice too much for today and she needed to do it a lot more tomorrow. After a few seconds during which her ID was checked, she was allowed inside, where she turned down a hallway to her left. She knocked on 134 and waited. "Coming," a strained voice called. Sophia heard her mother's footsteps approach before she opened the door.

"*Mija*," her mother cooed, putting her hand on Sophia's cheek and pulling her down for a kiss.

"*Mamá*." Sophia smiled weakly as she kissed her on the check. Her mother was shorter than Sophia and she hunched forward. Her hair had turned into thin, gray curls. She had deep wrinkles on her face and laugh lines at the side of her mouth that made her look friendly even when she wasn't smiling. She was wearing a purple and black dress with matching peacock pin on her left shoulder. She beamed and embraced her daughter.

"Sophia." Her mother Isabella's thin, shaking arms wrapped around her. "How are you?"

"Good, good, how about we sit down?" Sophia closed the door behind her and led her mother to the small kitchen table, pulling out a chair for her and taking the seat next to her.

"Would you like some tea, Sophia?"

"I'm sorry, I can't have any. I can't stay for long. I just needed to see you, *Mamá*."

"I understand," she said, putting a hand over her daughter's. "Rough day at work?"

"I don't really want to talk about it. I would rather talk about you and how you're doing. So, *Mamá*, how have you been?"

"Oh, good, good, Sophia." She leaned in closer. "I have a new boyfriend."

"Oh?" Sophia gasped in mock shock. "What's his name?"

"Estevan," she said. "He's a good man. He still has his hair; a thick head full of it! That's why I thought he was handsome. Most of the men here have lost theirs."

"Are you sure it's not a wig, Mama? Maybe you should pull it and see if it's real."

"I did."

That made the both of them laugh.

"Do you have a boyfriend?"

Sophia smiled painfully. *I haven't gotten to spend time with him in days, I have been so busy. I wonder how he'll take the news. Will he understand? Will...*

"Yes, Mamá, I do. His name is Charles. I've introduced him to you before, remember?"

Isabella looked confused.

"He has red hair. A goatee."

"Is it serious?"

Sophia put her ringed hand down on her lap. "Maybe. It's too early to tell. Are the staff treating you nicely?"

"Yes. Oh!" Her mother smiled widely and searched for words. "Next week, Saint Patrick's is kicking out all the tourists, blocking off the area, and letting in ticketed members for Mass in the church. I am going with a group of people here. Let me show you my ticket." She reached across the table and grabbed her purse. Sophia looked aside, feeling moisture come to her eyes knowing that she was going to have to try to sell off Patrick's tomorrow. "Ah, here it is." She pulled it out and handed it to Sophia. "I asked them for two, for you, but they only offered one per person."

"It's fine, Mamá. I've been inside the church before. I even had a photo-op there."

"You've been *in* a church, but you haven't been *to* a church in I can't even remember how long."

"Mamá, please don't. It has been a really long day."

"Which is why you should go to Mass. Meet the people, share stories, have an uplifting sermon. You haven't attended Mass since you won the election."

Sophia thought she had been growing numb to pain, but that felt like a needle pressing into her chest.

"All right," she stammered. "Okay, okay, I know. I will go to Mass with you some day. I have just been busy."

"Busy? Too busy for God?"

Sophia had a comeback, something about how God always seemed to take the day off when things got bad, but she held back. She wasn't going to get into an argument with her mother. She remembered the arguments she had with her as a child. Sophia would argue and argue until she couldn't even remember what they were fighting about. Then her mother would get frustrated and yell at her, give her time-outs, a spanking and when she was older, she got a few slaps; only four in her life, but she remembered each one. Sophia could always appear stone-faced and cold, but she still felt every blow.

"Who are you going with?"

"Well," her mother huffed, letting her know she wasn't off the hook, "I am going with Sylvia and Carmen. You remember them."

"Yes," Sophia lied.

"Those are the two gals I know from here that are part of the group. A lot of us will be going, but I don't care for most of the others. Estevan tried to get a ticket, but couldn't. I almost feel guilty going without him, but I can't imagine what it must feel like to step into a cathedral floating on water; it must be spectacular. I have to say, I don't like getting out; these old bones are wearing on me, and I get stiff. The thought of getting up early and moving doesn't sit right with me."

Sophia nodded her head, ignoring what her mother was saying. Her head had an overwhelmingly heavy feeling.

"What is it, Sophia?"

Sophia choked on the words. *How to explain?*

"Mom, how would you like to move somewhere? Somewhere with warmer weather?"

Isabella started shaking her head. "No." She shook her head faster, looking truly upset. "No, I-I-I'm not going anywhere. I like this place very much."

"I didn't mean leave this retirement home. I meant, what if this place was somewhere warmer? Would you like that?"

"What? I don't understand. If this place were somewhere else? What do you mean?"

"I mean, what if there was a retirement home just like this somewhere else?"

"No, we are not talking about it. I like it here and I am not moving."

"I just wanted—"

"Well, this isn't about what you want. I like it here and I'm not moving. Someone my age, packing up and leaving somewhere? I am staying here and that's final."

"All right, okay." Sophia breathed slowly. *My problems were at the door. Why did I bring them in?* "Have you made any new friends?" Sophia sputtered, just to be done with distressing topics.

"Oh, I haven't met anyone new." Isabella waved her hand dismissively. "And if I may say, I for one am glad that all of the people coming into New York are all young people who stay out there and don't bother me in here. I don't care to meet any new people. I have met all the people I care to meet; I don't need to catch up with someone who has eighty years of catching up for me."

Sophia tried not to let her mother see the worried look on her face. She looked down and the flower patterns on the floor began to spin. Her head felt incredibly light. The blurry, dancing flowers rushed up to meet her and then all was black.

Chapter Seventeen

Red light permeated Club Rorschach and illuminated the dance floor. Strobe lights flashed above Lei's head, outlining the bodies around her every half second. Above the revelers, giant floating ink blots stretched out and reformed in different colors, always contrasting with the ceiling lights. The lights turned a soft purple and the floating blots turned a brilliant gold, then red against cyan.

Lei couldn't feel the rhythm. Thirty seconds in, she realized that this was one of her favorite new songs to dance to, but even with that revelation, she still couldn't feel it. Normally, the music soothed her mind, allowing her to lose herself in the rhythm and motion. Now she was trying to force herself to sync with the music and it was giving her a headache. But she pretended she was into it, smiled a little and watched her friends drink.

A group of five men, olive-skinned tourists with gold rings, earring and chains walked up to their group of four. "Ladies," said the man in front, wearing a black over-shirt and speaking in a thick Middle Eastern accent. He danced next to them. Three of the girls laughed, but Olivia, wild hunger in her eyes, smiled, walked up to him, turned her back and danced close to him, letting him grind on her. Julie and Heather were more reserved, but they approached all the same. Lei stood still, letting the last two men, a bald-headed man and someone who looked like his identical twin but with a long ponytail and crooked nose, decide who would have her. The bald man must have won out and he danced next to her. Lei tried to smile, but she knew the look she was giving him must have been awkward. He kept dancing closer to her. She backed up, but bumped into the people behind her.

"I have to go," she was forced to yell over the music. He kept dancing. She wondered whether he couldn't hear her or didn't speak English; most of the tourists who had been invading the club scene didn't. She didn't bother trying to solve the mystery and abruptly walked to the bar. When the bartender finally finished serving those around her, she yelled, "A mojito." Somehow, the bartender heard her through the booming electronic drum, nodded, and turned. Lei waited until her drink came out and downed a third of it before she got her credit card back. Another one of her favorite songs came on. The lights dimmed and the dancing was slower. Then the bass kicked in and her head started pounding. *I should leave before all my favorite songs are ruined.*

Her friends walked towards her with their newly acquired men, crowding around her seat awkwardly, or at least it felt so to her. Mercifully, the other two men had taken the hint and were looking for someone else to go home with.

"Lei, what's wrong? Aren't you having fun?"

"Yes, I'm just tired."

"I'll bet," Heather piped in, "with all the work that you've been doing."

"What do you do?" her date asked, over-pronouncing each word just slightly.

"She lifts up skyscrapers," Olivia said.

"You made the... 'Manhattan Miracle'?" another one of the men asked, wide-eyed with fascination. Julie gave an annoyed look that her date was paying more attention to Lei than her.

"No, that was Marko Sverichek. I could never do that." She looked down, the words hitting her more than she expected they would.

"She's doing something better." Olivia beamed. "She's going to turn Manhattan into a moving city."

"What are you talking about, beautiful?" the man with his arm wrapped around Olivia said coyly.

"Tell him," Olivia waved at Lei.

"It's complicated," she breathed.

"No, no, tell us," Julie's date pleaded, still not noticing the aggravated look on Julie's face.

"I'll tell you," Olivia stepped in. "She's told me all about it, numerous times, usually while drunk, claiming she'll be the next Sverichek, because she's obsessed with him. Anyway..."

Lei had finished her mojito and, against her better judgment, ordered another when she heard Olivia say, "Like the inside of a giant clock."

"That's amazing."

"You do this? That's incredible."

"And the best part is that we're all going to be rich, thanks to her." Heather said. "I've invested all my money in tourist companies that work here."

"You mean the unlicensed cabs?" Olivia laughed.

"Shut up, nothing like that. All legitimate stuff. I put my money there for a week and I've already made a killing, and it can only go up."

"Sell it," Lei said, looking serious. She caught a confused look on Heather's face before the world blurred again, lights flashed and she teetered on her seat.

"What?"

"Sell it, don't invest in New York."

"What are you talking about?" Julie laughed. "Lei, are you drunk?"

"Are you okay?" Olivia asked, sounding more serious.

Lei saw Olivia's serious look a moment before her eyes watered up. "I have to go to the bathroom," she said while turning, trying not to let them see her face.

Lei stumbled down the length of the bar, feeling their eyes on her. She turned into the restroom and realized just how drunk she was. She felt a wave of self-loathing roll over her, then nausea. The stalls were all occupied. She turned to the mirror, breathed in deep and tried to compose herself. She let it out and the world spun. *I can't have drunk this much,* she argued with her body.

"Lei." Olivia stepped beside Lei and put an arm around her. "Hey, what's the matter?"

Lei tried to say 'nothing', but the word came out as a slurred sob.

"Don't say 'nothing' if you can't even pronounce the word." She pushed her towards the door. "Here, I am going to take you home, don't try to argue because I'm not going to be able to understand what you're saying anyway." Olivia pushed against Lei's back and they stumbled out of the bathroom together. "Come on, that's a big girl. We're going to go outside, get some fresh air." She was nearly yelling in Lei's ears as the music blasted over them. "And then we're getting a cab back home. Doesn't that sound fun? A nice, romantic night cruise through Manhattan."

Lei could feel the boat rocking in her mind and felt sick. She covered her mouth and turned from Olivia. They stepped outside the bar and onto the street and were immediately hit with the cold night air. "It got cold fast, didn't it? It was sweltering earlier." Olivia remarked.

"Don't invest in Manhattan," Lei said.

"I'll be sure to tell Heather that; more coherently of course," Olivia replied as they walked down the block, looking for a taxi boat. "There'll be a taxi any minute. They all crowd around the clubs at this time."

"You have to leave Manhattan as soon as you can," Lei pleaded.

Olivia ignored Lei and looked out at the canals. With one hand, she held her drunken friend up while waving for a ride with the other.

"It's all going to be gone soon. The whole city."

"Calm down, Lei, it'll be there in the morning."

"It will. I worked on it. I made the machines. The whole city is going to disappear and it's my fault." The tears flew freely.

"Sweetie, you're drunk."

"No, you have to leave Manhattan before it's all gone."

Lei retched and vomited on the street. She heard laughter behind her.

Chapter Eighteen

As they walked down the pier, Cassidy noticed how uncomfortable her partner looked as he seemed to lean away from the boats. His brow was furrowed and he hadn't said a word to her since they left. Cassidy knew he didn't want to be the first person to say anything since their fight. He wanted her to address him, granting him a minor forgiveness to put their disagreement on hold.

"Don't think about it. We're off the case anyway, for now," she said, completely misreading his current mood.

Since that morning, they and half the cops not on patrol had been assigned to seek out information on the ship *Orca II*. There were five roving SWAT teams from Manhattan ready to appear at any location in the Boroughs within fifteen minutes once they had any information on where last night's newly kidnapped Charles Tanning might be. Captain Hewes had explained the reassignment from the Brice Noble case by saying they needed to 'focus on the living, not the dead.' Alex didn't seem to be taking that to heart.

"We all make mistakes."

"Cassidy."

Cassidy bit her lip, waiting for a reprimand.

"If we get in another situation like that, if we ever think there might be danger ahead, I want you to take point."

"What?" she breathed, startled. "Why?"

Alex coughed. He struggled to say, "I saw it coming. At Yiril's. I could have drawn, but I didn't. Yes, you made a mistake, but I did too."

"Why?"

"That gunfight we had last week at Warner rattled me. That, and I knew the old man wasn't guilty of the murder. He wasn't in the surveillance video from Manhattan, the one where Brice Noble was killed. And police hardly arrest smugglers, unless they are big time, and he didn't look the part. I didn't expect anything. He must have just gotten spooked by having so many cops there, acting like real cops."

Cassidy nodded.

"I didn't think that it would come to guns. I thought we could have sorted everything out by talking."

Cassidy nodded, taking it as the closest to an apology she was going to get.

After looking at a hundred ships, they spotted the *Orca II* at the western dock 27. It was a nasty ship, its hull ringed by green grime. Cassidy stepped forward, scanned the immediate vicinity, pulled out her gun and heard Alex do the same behind her. Cassidy stepped down from the dock and into the boat. She walked forward, toward the cabin. She didn't see or hear anyone, so she turned the door handle, only to discover it was locked. Cassidy reached into her belt and pulled out a rectangular silver object with a small handle. She clicked a button on the end and a tiny silver pole extended forward. After a second, a red light scanned the keyhole. When the light went out, the tiny silver extension formed grooves and indents. When it took on a definite shape, Cassidy inserted the newly formed key into the hole and turned. A familiar *click* sounded and she opened the door, walking inside.

"And people think you have no break-ins on file because you're a good cop."

Cassidy smiled. "Best there is."

The universal key had sold like crazy for a year before it was banned. Then, as time went on, people realized how irrelevant it had been, as nearly all keys, for cars, boats, houses and apartment complexes, were electronic. But the Boroughs relied on the cheap and with hacking electronic signals becoming more widespread, metal locks and keys came back in vogue. Getting her hands on the contraband key was well worth its outrageous price.

The room was vacant, but cluttered. The controls were cheap plastic and looked as if they had never been washed. The speedometer and most of the dashboard was covered in dust. There was a toolbox in one corner with a coil of rope on top of it. Alex put away his gun and scanned for prints. There were hundreds scattered throughout the room, many on top of the others.

After a few seconds, the prints ran through the police database and a list of names and faces appeared alongside a thumbnail displaying how many of the fingerprints were theirs. Alex clicked on the top name, 'Harry Carmine.' A panoramic image of the boat's interior appeared, with his fingerprints in glowing green while the others were all dark purple. Carmine's were the only ones on the steering wheel.

It checks out. Not only was the boat licensed under his name, he's the only one who seems to have piloted it. That was good, Alex didn't want another complicated case like with Yiril. He picked the other three top names and sent them to the police HQ network for a background check. Carmine's house had already been checked as a witness's description matched his, so if the kidnappers were hiding out somewhere else, it was probably one of his accomplices' homes.

Alex slipped on a pair of gloves and looked for any other potential clues. There was nothing overtly damning; no drugs, though there was a trace of powder he thought might be cocaine. *There's no valuables, weapons or drugs here; they must have preferred to leave them at home.* Alex wasn't surprised. He didn't expect shoddy kidnappers to have any serious contraband, especially in their getaway vehicle. He removed his gloves and stepped outside, Cassidy in tow.

"Come on, let's call a crew out to tow the boat."

Cassidy nodded and they hopped off.

"So do you think he's still alive?" Alex asked Cassidy.

Cassidy paused, not sure she believed Alex could ask a question like that. "You mean Charles Tanning? Of course he's alive, why wouldn't he be? Whoever it was that kidnapped him kept him alive at least until he was out of Manhattan, and how else could they get a ransom if they killed him off? He has to be alive."

Alex didn't appear convinced. "I suppose you're right. Why else would anyone capture someone? Unless they have personal history, but I doubt a bunch of poor brutes from the Boroughs would know some rich guy from across the strait."

After waiting for twenty minutes, a tugboat with a faded NYPD logo pulled into view. Alex waved at it and pointed at the *Orca II*. Cassidy undid the line tying it to the dock and let the tugboat pull it out.

"Now what?" she asked.

"Patrol, keep the peace until we get word of a lead."

She nodded.

"About the Noble case, after searching Zogheib's records, we know Rodney Maxwell was on his payroll and must have been one of the boys present at the killing. We should get to work on tracking him down."

Cassidy nodded slowly. "You know, it's not your fault he's dead."

"I know."

"Then who do you blame?"

"What?" Alex gave her an astonished look. "Nobody."

"Nobody? You can't blame nobody. Someone died, there has to be a reason. You must blame someone. Larry, since he shot Mr. Zogheib, or Mr. Zogheib for pulling a gun on a cop," *Me*. "You can't just blame no one, no one does that."

"People die. It happens. Some die in a storm, some get cancer, others get shot. In the end, they're all dead."

Cassidy looked at her partner as if she didn't recognize him. "But what about justice?"

"What about justice?"

Cassidy felt a flush of anger. "What's the point of being a cop if you don't care about justice?"

"I do," Alex said with more emotion than he usually gave for their arguments, "but justice is for the living. There's no justice in death, no meaning."

Cassidy was about to retort, but she bit her tongue. They had passed the morning in silence; she wasn't going to press him now that he had finally gotten off her back.

Half a block down, Alex got a call. "All right. On our way." He turned to Cassidy. "We have to get to 493 Gardener Avenue now."

"They found Charles Tanning?"

"Possibly. HQ received an anonymous tip from someone earlier today, saying he knew that Carmine was using the abandoned house for his illegal drug operations. SWAT showed up and there's a stand-off."

The two sprinted down the streets. Gardener Avenue was near the northern edge of the city, but they weren't too far away. They arrived panting and ran up to a team of eight black-clad SWAT units with bulletproof shields held up, facing a faded green house that had wooden boards over the windows.

"Hold up!" one of the men called, seeing Alex and Cassidy. "Stay back."

Alex held up his badge. "NYPD." They ran over, taking cover behind the closest shields. "We were called over."

"Not very much organization down here, is there?" muttered a sergeant holding a megaphone at his side. Another man held a shield up to cover him, and Alex assumed he was in charge.

"What's the situation?"

The sergeant looked at Alex, annoyed, but said, "We have the four suspects in there with Mr. Tanning. We IDed him before the blinds were closed. Shots were fired from their end, but we held back because we couldn't take them all out. In my experience, it's better to have them all alive or dead; anything in between and you never know what they might do."

"Are there any boats out behind them to cut off escape? Helicopters?"

"Our guys left a boat behind the house. I have been trying to tell the gunmen to take it and leave Mr. Tanning."

"Does the boat have a tracking device?"

"Of course."

With no more questions to ask, the crew waited, listening to the dead silence around them. People began to poke their heads out all around them. Alex wanted to yell at them to get inside, but he didn't want to be the one to scare the kidnappers.

With a creak, the front door opened. A terrified man with a black goatee and bloodshot eyes stepped outside. Behind him were two men, a pale giant and a beady-eyed man wearing a snow cap. Both had guns pointed at the back of the terrified man's head. A third man came out behind them. They walked toward the police officers.

"Stay back!" the SWAT leader called with the megaphone. The four moved forward from the house. The SWAT leader cursed. As they neared, he turned to his men, put the megaphone down and called, "Give them a wide berth, but keep your guns on them." The SWAT team, along with Alex, Cassidy, and a third police officer, who had been leveling her gun at the men along with the others, took to the edge of the walkway. It was hardly a 'wide' berth; the walkways were only six feet across on the city's edge. The gunmen stepped forward onto the walkway. The SWAT team leveled their guns at them.

Tanning's arms were up. He looked out at the police with a pleading look amidst his terror. He looked as if he couldn't understand why they weren't helping him as they outnumbered the kidnappers and they had assault rifles. Alex looked into the eyes of the kidnappers and saw fear, too. This was a move of desperation.

"What are you going to do?" Alex called.

That made them stop. Tension rose in the air. All eyes turned to him.

"Fuck him. Keep moving." One of the men put a hand on Tanning's shoulder and pushed him forward.

The sound of barely muffled gunfire exploded in the air. Snowcap tensed and his gun fired, leaving nothing left of the left side of Tanning's head but the spine and sinewy strings of unattached muscle. Alex saw a look of horror from Snowcap as he looked at the place where Mr. Tanning's head had been. Then a hail of gunfire exploded all around him. The kidnappers and the house behind them were riddled with bullets. Even after they fell, the SWAT team continued to shoot. Blood trickled down both sides of the pier.

"Damn it, who was that? Who fired that first shot?" The squad leader walked toward Alex. "What the hell did you do?"

"He didn't shoot, captain," a woman in black gear said behind him. "I didn't see a blast from his gun."

The captain turned around and looked at his squad. "Are you sure?" he asked, confirming, though he knew the truth. The men behind him nodded.

The captain grimaced. He got down on his knees and leaned down, pointing his gun down at the water while flicking on a flashlight. He scanned, then looked back up. "It sounded like..." He shook the thought from his head and looked back at Alex and Cassidy, growling. "Section this area off; bring in the forensic teams to do the cleanup work."

Alex was still stunned by the carnage. The captain mistook his shock for pride and anger at having been ordered by someone who had no authority over him. "Or are you just going to leave these bodies out in the open?"

"I'm on it," Cassidy intervened, stepping in front of Alex. While Cassidy took the verbal beating, Alex taped off the walkway with the third cop. A forensic team arrived by the time the SWAT team had cleared out. Among the three forensics experts, a heavily-tanned woman with a blue baseball cap, an NYPD navy blue jacket, and carrying a silver briefcase whistled in disbelief at the gory sight, set the case down and got to work.

Alex tapped his palm and brought up his video cam. He rewound fifteen minutes. Half of his vision was the house, perfectly peaceful, the only movement being the gentle waves, and in real time, he saw the shack torn apart by gunfire. He watched the peaceful image until the familiar sound burst inside of him again, but there was no flash of light from anywhere around. Once again, the police retaliated, bullets rained, and the two houses became one bloody mess.

Alex turned off his camera, walked over to the side of the walkway, got on his stomach, and peered down into the water. He pulled out his flashlight and scanned the pillars, looking for anything. When he found nothing, he stood back up.

"No one saw the blast of gunfire. No one was hit by that first shot. I could have sworn the sound came from just below us."

Cassidy looked down in the water and felt cold and threatened.

Goosebumps appeared on her skin. She was about to say something about how sometimes freak accidents occur, how the older streets, made with cheap concrete, accumulated cracks from the ocean waves and sometimes burst suddenly and made a loud cracking sound... but she knew it was bullshit. *There's a reason for everything, even a reason for Mr. Tanning's death. Perhaps not a good reason, but a reason.*

Chapter Nineteen

Smoking warmth entered Antoni's lungs as he sucked at the end of his cigar. He let the fumes trail out of his mouth into the cold air. The night was monotonous waiting as Antoni stood outside a boarded-up houseboat, looking out at dark nothing. He felt the metal frame of his black pistol in the inside of his right jacket pocket every time he inhaled. He looked down the streets to his left and right, daring anyone to come down his way. *Empty down either direction.* All of the houseboats around him had their lights off. They all knew some gang controlled the house he guarded and weren't looking to draw any attention to themselves.

Antoni wished that some rival gang would appear that he could shoot at. He wished that he could prove himself. Anything to move from outside in the cold, waiting and doing nothing. When Antoni, or at least his partner in crime Grease, killed Brice Noble, it had been outside the orders of the gang. He couldn't take any credit for it, at least not with people who mattered. He told other night guards and the few friends he had outside that group that were in the gang, but not anyone who mattered. *At least not yet,* he thought. *The other guards will talk and word will make its way up that I am a killer, that I got away with murder. Then I'll get promoted and start bossing around my own crew.* The thought warmed Antoni.

There was a sudden loud series of footfalls to his left that caused Antoni to jump and turn. Seven men in dark coats walked towards him. Antoni reached for his gun.

"Don't you start!" a high-pitched yell broke through the cold night air.

Antoni pulled out his cheap cigar and tossed it into the water. "Dominic?" he called to the caporegime. As they approached, he said,

"I'm sorry, you can't be too careful."

Dominic looked down at Antoni and said, "Do you know who this is?" gesturing to the brutish man standing in the center of the group. Antoni immediately realized by how he held himself that he was important. He shook his head nervously.

"This is the Don Frederico Vasquez."

"Don," Antoni breathed lamely. He didn't know how he was supposed to greet him, so he saluted. The men around him burst out laughing.

"This kid." Frederico smiled, turning to Dominic.

"Put your hands down," Dominic ordered. "Open the door for us and get the guard on break out to replace you."

Antoni nodded lamely. "Yes," he said. He looked at Frederico, frightened.

"Nice watch." Frederico chuckled.

"Th-thanks—"

"Now!"

Antoni jogged to the door. He knocked three times, then five, then a tap, then twice. The door opened and the man behind it kept his shotgun lowered to the floor. He peered out, saw the men behind Antoni and immediately flung it out wide. Antoni walked in, stepped into the kitchen and found James sitting in a chair, eyes closed. Antoni shook him and said, "Get out, it's your turn."

James opened his eyes, looking at his cheap watch with worn leather straps. "You liar, my shift isn't for another thirty minutes."

"It's now, orders of the Don."

James' eyes opened wide, then narrowed. "You shithead, I'm not going to fall for that."

"Get up." Antoni grabbed the back of James' coat and pulled him up. James shrugged him off. He pulled back his fists as if he were about to punch Antoni when he saw the succession of men walk into the houseboat.

"Well? Get going," Antoni said.

James scowled, waited for them to pass, and stepped outside.

"Antoni," Frederico called from the other room. Antoni nearly jumped. *He knows my name?* Antoni ran into the other room, forced himself not to salute and said, "Yes, Don?"

"We need three more chairs. If there are any in the kitchen or the bedroom, pull 'em out."

Eight chairs? He wants to talk to me.

"Sure thing," Antoni said, feeling important even as he gathered up the chairs. When he walked back in, the men had formed a circle with an open spot left at the right hand of the Don near the far wall. Frederico saw him stall and waved toward the empty space. Antoni put the chair down and sat next to him, looking straight forward at a space in between Dominic and a capo he didn't know. He could feel the weight of Frederico's eyes upon him at his side. It was heavier than anything he had ever felt before.

"Antoni Marino," Frederico recited, drawing Antoni's eyes towards him. "I've heard a lot of talk about you recently."

Antoni felt a flush of pride mix with his unease. "I've run things pretty well down here."

"And you've been active in other places," Frederico remarked.

Antoni paused. "I wasn't looking to move into anyone else's territory, but there are a few neighborhoods that aren't ours that don't get a good supply of anything. I don't go there, you understand, that would break the truce, they come to me." Antoni read the silence as an implication to continue and added, "But if you're looking for someone to bash some heads and start taking territory, I know my crew could do it."

Frederico smiled. "You're a little bruiser, are you?" The men around the circle laughed and Antoni tried not to flush with embarrassment. "Have you ever killed anyone before?"

Antoni froze. "Yes…" he breathed, hoping there wasn't a follow-up.

"Who?" Frederico asked.

"There was some kid who tried to jump me a few months ago. I fought him off, tied weights to his legs and let him sink, like in the old days." Antoni grinned at his own lie.

"And since then, have you killed anyone else?"

"No."

"What about Brice Noble in Manhattan?

Antoni shook. "I didn't kill no one in Manhattan."

"Are you lying to the Don?" one of the men shouted from across the room. Antoni's eyes were fixed on the calm face of Frederico.

"Antoni," he almost cooed. "It's not a bad thing that you killed this man. What is bad is that everyone knows it. We know you killed Brice Noble. All of our associates know you killed him. When you kill someone, the whole point is that no one finds out. But you're on camera doing it."

Antoni felt his insides melt. "Wha—"

Antoni was slapped hard from his right. "You don't speak unless he asks you a question."

"You killed him," Frederico said calmly.

"I killed him," Antoni heard himself say.

"And this is the last time you will ever speak of Brice Noble, or killing anybody ever, do you understand?"

Antoni nodded.

"Good," Frederico continued. "Brice Noble was an important man, a rich man. His death won't go unnoticed and the police, so I hear, are very interested in finding his killers."

Antoni looked at him, unblinking.

"We need to cover our tracks, make sure that the police find a cold trail. You had two associates."

There was heavy silence in the room. "What are you going to do with them?"

"Give me their names, Antoni."

Antoni was about to speak when Frederico slowly lifted his hand and put it on Antoni's shoulder. The meaty palm weighed down on Antoni's bony frame. "The next words out of your mouth will be the two names... or I'm going to kill you."

The house gently rocked beneath them as high tide rose against its creaky frame. Antoni felt a chill from the cold run up his spine and he tried not to shake, but knew Frederico could feel it. "Darren Toohey, he's called Grease by most of his friends."

Frederico nodded.

"Rodney Maxwell."

"Good."

With his left hand, Frederico reached to his side and pulled out a black revolver. He brought it up to Antoni's face. Antoni squirmed frantically, but Frederico held him down. Frederico pulled the trigger and Antoni's brain splattered on the wall behind him.

"Hey, kid!" Frederico called. "Get in here."

Silence met Frederico. After a second, James slowly opened the door, his face pale white. He looked at the bloody hole in Antoni's head.

"What's your name?"

"James. James Yates." He forced the words.

"James Yates," Frederico said, as if tasting the words. "I'll remember that. Have you ever disposed of a body before?"

"No."

"No, sir," the man closest to him corrected.

"No, sir."

Frederico nodded at Dominic. "Teach him." Frederico stepped over the blood that had begun to pool at Antoni's feet. James side-stepped, allowing for Frederico to pass him. As he did, Frederico turned to him and said, loud enough for everyone to hear, "Don't take the watch.

Make sure it gets disposed of."

James nodded stiffly.

"You never take trophies from the dead. And you sure as hell never wear them around in public. It's disrespectful. You understand?"

James nodded again. "Yes, I understand... I understand, *sir*."

Frederico gave him a long look and said, "Good boy." He waved a finger in his face. "I'll remember you."

Chapter Twenty

Anxiety spread over Manhattan when Charles Tanning's death hit the evening news. There was a general feeling of worry that spread over Manhattan, but no one could pin down exactly why it was they should be afraid; they just felt an ominous shadow at the edge of their vision. People preferred to travel in groups and those who walked alone looked over their shoulders with suspicion. The news reports hinted at dark happenings, but wouldn't speculate on the whereabouts of some of the missing. The foreboding silence of those in power sounded out a silent alarm among many.

Miles put terror into words and put the disparate images together to make a monster.

Manhattan has been under an illusion; the illusion that just because the ship has been set upright means that all its people are safe. You are not. Only your danger doesn't come from the sea or the elements, or the wrath of God. Congratulations, you have beaten them all. Your doom comes from those you have left behind.

Manhattan has risen again and it only has enough money for itself. It has left the rest of the city behind. Now those left behind are coming back. While Manhattan has managed to keep itself afloat, the rest of New York is pulling it under like a drowning man. Last Thursday, Brice Noble, president of Noble Securities, was stabbed to death on Broome and Lafayette after attempting to flee from three poor teenagers who stole off in a boat owned by 'BlueSea Waste Removal.' The perpetrators are still at large while the owner of the company and getaway boat, Yiril Zogheib, was gunned down by police the following day during a fatal police interrogation.

After Brice, there was Charles Tanning, head of Tanning Industrial

Supplies. He was successfully abducted from lower Manhattan and taken to the Boroughs. I saw the man abducted myself, as it seems it was my duty to chase the men down due to the lack of cops on the streets. I took a bullet in the process and currently write to you from St. Anne's. I doubt I will receive a medal for my heroism, though, at least not from Mayor Ramos, who instructed me not to speak to the public on the abduction. After being abducted, Tanning was held out in a house, where a SWAT team engaged in a stand-off with the criminals, which resulted in the deaths of the kidnappers and Mr. Tanning, as yet again the curious habit of the police to shoot anyone on sight shockingly failed to ease tensions and bring about a peaceful solution.

But more terrifying is what is currently going unreported. Six CEOs, VPs, and other expensive acronyms from Manhattan have simply vanished without a trace (that we know of). And meanwhile, Mayor Sophia Ramos and Police Commissioner Robert Kerry have been covering up the recent abductions in order to maintain a veneer of calm. But now that the bodies have begun to pile up, that calm must be stripped away.

So why should Manhattan be afraid? Why are we any different than Detroit, or Boston, or any other city that is sinking beneath the waves? Because despite all that's happened to it, Manhattan still has an enormous reserve of concentrated wealth. It was almost as if the bankers and the financiers couldn't believe that Manhattan would go under, even while the famous bull statue started sprouting sea anemones. Yet, just across the water, there are millions of people living in destitution. New York is one of the most striking examples of a city where millions of miserablés live in the towering shadow of the few rich. Practically none of the money that is pouring into Manhattan has made it to the Boroughs, and now some of them have decided to reach out and take it.

I know it's hard to believe, but Manhattan was better off when it was sinking.

Within hours of publication, news agencies opened their broadcasts with, "Are roving gangs of marauders streaming into Manhattan from the Boroughs?" The cameras then cut to City Hall shining serenely in the midday sun with nicely dressed people trying to dodge the throng of reporters. It wasn't as apocalyptic as the networks must have wanted, because they turned to the average person on the street and asked for their terrified, uninformed opinion.

Chapter Twenty-One

"What a pity." Ezreal Redding stared at the dozens of screens that covered the wall. Every screen was turned to a news channel, where interchangeable groups of talking heads discussed Miles Buhari's article and how the apocalypse had already happened without their notice. He turned to face Frederico, who met Ezreal's gaze with difficulty. Ezreal's long tenure underwater had given him a marble-white, almost ghostly look that terrified Frederico more than a little. "I was hoping for subtlety. I could have kidnapped half of them before they started to panic."

"Of course," Frederico's deep voice echoed in the chamber.

"It's just like before. Except now we're striking first." Ezreal nodded at his own statement. He turned to the screen again, watching the two reporters argue in silence. Ezreal laughed. Frederico choked back a cough. It infuriated him how Ezreal would laugh at nothing, mutter to himself, rub his chin and occasionally look off at some object, seeing a hidden value which Frederico couldn't pinpoint, all without explaining himself. It was as if he were in a whole other world and made no attempt to invite his second-in-command in. Frederico tried to retain his composure, but he was growing annoyed at how the old man seemed to gain a new life as he recounted some past defeat long ago that he could redeem with a bloody victory now.

Maybe I have come down here too many times recently. Has the salty air done more than just given me a cough? What time is it on the surface? Frederico looked around for a clock, found none and realized there weren't any calendars either. His own men brought down files with video footage of news reports to keep Ezreal informed of what was happening; it was too cumbersome to run down a direct cable. Ezreal had no idea what was truly happening beyond the tapes that they gave him. *He could spend the rest of his life down here and never know what was really happening just above his head; if his men exchanged the videos with conspiracy videos or espionage thrillers, would he even know the difference?* He pushed back the thoughts.

"What should we do now, Ezreal?"

Ezreal looked off over Frederico's shoulder. Frederico thought of looking over, but knew he wouldn't see whatever ghost Ezreal must have been gazing at. He clenched his teeth.

Ezreal looked back to him and said, "They are already filled with fear. All we have to do is set it off."

"Then why not start the revolution?" Frederico asked, sarcasm thick in his voice.

"No," Ezreal replied with a soft finality like a death sentence. For a long while, he remained silent and stared directly into Frederico's eyes until Frederico caught himself looking at his own reflection. He felt a nervous awkwardness, like he was being stared down. For a second, he thought of apologizing for his tone. Then anger rose in him. *Does he think I am a child? I am one of the most powerful men in New York! And he toys with me like this!* With effort, he kept his hands from clenching into fists.

He summoned the courage to ask, "Why not?

"They have the energy for revolt and the fear to get them off their asses to act. But they still have hope, hope that their leaders can solve their problems. Rather than marching and protesting, they will merely shuffle out their old two-faced empty-suits for new ones and they won't be ready for an unknown, not me. They'll choose some other lifelong politician that can give them lies that they know to be lies, but are just charming enough that they'll buy them. Then they will become complacent again. Oh yes, even the poor. No country in the world has more completely duped its poor into fighting for the right to wear their shackles."

Frederico waited in silence. The people on the monitors were mouthing nonsense to his right. The maddening echo of the television was weighing on Frederico as he waited for Ezreal to speak. *Why can't he say something? Hasn't he grown tired of living down here in solitude and darkness? Has it drained his will, his sanity, his soul? Doesn't he need to speak to someone, to have them understand, respond and verify that he is human?* Frederico didn't ask him, wouldn't ask him for the next part of his plan. He would let him speak or wait in silence, but he would not ask him for enlightenment.

He didn't have to ask. Frederico nearly missed the softly spoken word from the old man.

"Direction. That's all they need. We need to give the people an enemy, a hate figure to rally around."

Frederico paused this time, registering the word. "How do we do that?"

"I will do it," Ezreal said. He turned and walked toward the exit of the room that Frederico had never seen him outside of in all the time he had known him.

"It is time that I returned to the surface."

Chapter Twenty-Two

Even though he had barely slept, Rodney still woke up before everyone else at the mission. He stood up quietly and looked around in the near darkness as light was just beginning to creep through the window slits in the giant house. It was so sturdy he couldn't even feel the gentle waves beneath his feet. He gently kicked aside the sleeping bag and awkwardly stepped over and between the bodies around him, wincing with every creak. There were thirty or so people lying on the floor and from how each of them seemed to sleep soundly, he knew that they had accepted their hard-luck life. He had suspected it when he first arrived the previous night; there was a dead look in most of their eyes and even though the older people had learned to smile behind that, he could see the same tired resignation. Rodney didn't want to accept living in a giant room, sleeping side to side with thirty people, but he wasn't sure what he could do with the cops chasing after him and a lack of money. *Well, I'm not completely shit out of luck yet,* he tried to perk himself up. *I still have nearly five hundred k in my pocket.*

He stepped outside the main room, then walked out the bare entryway and exited the building. The sun was sitting just above the waves and the day was already starting to heat up. There was hardly any wind at all and Rodney felt himself starting to sweat in his uncomfortable clothes. A gull drifted lazily overhead, cawing. Rodney looked up at it, following its slow trail, and caught himself wondering why he would. He had never bothered to pay any attention to the gulls since he chased after them as a young boy; they had just been a part of life. His head turned, watching it slowly drift down, then settle on a roof, then fly off a few moments later.

Rodney pulled out his cell phone and called Sam.

Ring.
Ring.
Ring...

Nothing. Rodney felt a weight in his stomach. *Why isn't she responding? Is it something I did? No, she probably picked up a shift since you told her you weren't going to see her. Just call later,* he thought while pocketing his phone.

His stomach rumbled. Rodney looked northwest, toward the Eye. He didn't want to walk any closer to the center of town, since he knew there would be cops there. But that was the only place with food shops nearby and he had done a good enough job of blending in. With a sigh and a heavy first step, Rodney trudged toward the Eye. As he neared it, he saw two cops and nearly froze. He thought about walking in another direction, but instead kept moving forward. They passed him. He had to force himself not to look over his shoulder as he shook.

Rodney saw the bakery which he had been in the habit of visiting. He nearly stepped in, but caught himself when he saw the long line. He didn't mind the wait, but he had taken to avoiding places where there were lots of people; except the mission, of course, where everyone was anonymous. He kept walking forward until he noticed a bar called the Old Pike on his left. He was old enough to go in, but just young enough that he worried he might have to pull out an ID. *A bartender is going to be carding you, not a cop. Relax.*

The bar was dark, and there were only two other people there, both older men sitting down at a table. Rodney convinced himself it was a good idea to be here; it seemed like one of the only empty places in the Eye. He walked up to the counter, sat down and grabbed a menu.

A thirty-something mousy woman with wrinkles about her eyes but a nice enough look to her asked, "What can I get you?"

"Dog's Head beer, a large, and do you serve food yet?"

"Sure," she said.

"Can I get a burger and fries?"

"'Course."

She stepped back, poured out a glass for him, handed it back with a 'cheers' and retreated into the back room. Rodney downed his beer a little too quickly. When the food came out, he asked for another beer and managed to keep himself from chugging it down. He was hardly starving. He had been eating convenience store food outside in addition to the meals at the mission, though he hadn't had anything as filling as a burger in ages. The burger he had wasn't even very good, but he devoured it greedily. When he had finished, he still had half a glass of beer he was determined to finish. He took a gulp, then sat back. The bar was just as empty when he had entered. He soaked in the atmosphere when he noticed a TV against the far corner. A dark man in a fine suit and red bowtie was saying something, but the TV was on mute. Underneath him were the words 'Massacre in the Boroughs.'

"Excuse me, ma'am," he said, realizing how much he sounded like a child. "Can you turn the sound on for the television?"

She looked over and said, "The TV's broken. No one's minded before, though, nobody asks to turn it on." She looked up at the news. "Haven't you heard what's been going on?"

Rodney shook his head.

"There was a police shootout. Four people dead up north a ways. It was supposed to be a rescue mission, can you believe that? The cops slaughter four people in a rescue mission and meanwhile, none of them were hurt. It's unbelievable."

Rodney's heart nearly stopped. An image came to his mind of the empty shack that was once Yiril's workplace. First him, now four more dead?

"What's going on? What happened?"

"Retaliation, I suppose. Same as any gang war."

Rodney was confused. "What do you mean?"

"Do you live under a rock or something? This story's been all over the news. People have been getting abducted from Manhattan by kidnappers here. Now the police are trying to get them back the only way they know how: by shooting anyone they think might be involved."

Rodney felt as if he might fall over in his seat.

"Unbelievable," she remarked and turned around. Rodney looked behind him. When he saw that no one was paying him any attention, he pocketed the steak knife on the table. He stood up, took a step back, wiped his forehead, turned around, left a twenty thousand dollar bill on the counter and walked out. He felt a shortness of breath as he stepped outside, panting.

Rodney pulled out his phone and called Antoni. No response. He called again, then a third time. He gave up after a fourth time. Rodney called Grease. No response. Rodney felt as if he might fall over. He called Grease again, then accidentally called Antoni again to no response. Rodney's hand dropped at his side.

Rodney pocketed the phone and took an unsteady step. He kept walking, looking for a place to sit down or lean against, but there was nothing. The gathering crowds of early morning shoppers kept walking by, thronging the walkways and bumping into him. Rodney suddenly knew where he had to go. He walked forward, turned left at the third street, then another left. A gull screeched above him. He opened the door into a gun and gold store and heard the tinkling of a small bell over his head.

"What can I do for you?" a grey-bearded, pink-faced man called from behind the far counter as he entered, sounding cautious and stern all at once. Rodney stepped forward and put his hands on the counter.

"How much for a cheap handgun? For self-defense?"

The man raised a bushy eyebrow. "Not much for small talk," he muttered. All the same, he reached down under the glass case and pulled out a black handgun. "This is the cheapest we got, but don't be fooled, it's reliable. Selling price is two hundred k."

"All right," Rodney said, reaching into his pocket and handing over two hundred thousand dollar bills. The man eyed Rodney, but didn't look too perturbed. *He must have done this before, with people just like me.*

"Your name and identification."

"What?"

"Your name and an ID. For the waiting period."

"What?"

"Son," the man said, stowing the gun back underneath the glass. "I need an ID which I can give to the DOJ to run a background check on you. Then, if it clears, there's a waiting period up to six months."

Rodney put a hand up to his forehead and looked down. After a moment, he said, "Is there any way around that?"

"Which part?"

Rodney caught his eye. Somehow, through the terror and the booze, he knew a law-abiding gun dealer wouldn't ask that question. "Three hundred. It's all I have."

"Bullshit."

"Three fifty."

"Fifty thousand dollar bills are rarer than hundreds. Four hundred thousand."

Rodney bit his lip. If he bought the gun, he would only have twenty-three thousand left. "All right, but it has to come with bullets, I honestly can't afford them if you're taking my four hundred."

"Would six be enough?" The man smiled.

Rodney nodded, ignoring the man's dark sense of humor.

The dealer pulled out the gun. "Insert the magazine like this. The safety is on, press here to remove it." He released the magazine and handed the two parts to Rodney. "Be sure to do this someplace else, all right?"

Rodney nodded again. He put the four hundred thousand on the table and grabbed the gun, stuffing it into the back of his pants. He snatched up the magazine and put it in his front pocket.

"You have a fine day now," the dealer called after him.

Chapter Twenty-Three

Sophia Ramos was attempting to tie her silver tie while fuming. Somehow, her pure, overpowering rage had made it impossible to tie it and she only ended up undoing the knot. After the third attempt, she threw it at the dresser. It fell lazily to the ground next to a cracked projection cube that had just been covering Miles' op-ed on the incompetence and cover up of the kidnappings. Sophia could handle hypocrisy, she just couldn't stand seeing anyone being praised for it. She balled her hands into fists and walked to the dresser, eyeing the mirror. She stopped herself. *No, you can't lose it. Losing it now would only make everything even worse than it already is.*

Sophia tried to console herself by telling herself for the hundredth time that even though everyone read his column, most people didn't believe Miles Buhari was a credible news source. More so, Miles attacked her Police Commissioner along with her. *The more people that fingers are wagged at, the less people pay attention. People like one big, evil figure they can blame for everything. I should know.* But Robert Kerry was well-respected, one of the few people in the city who were. She took a calming breath and looked at herself in the mirror, paying special attention to the bump on her head. She hoped that she had applied just enough makeup to cover it up, but even she couldn't know what the cameras would pick up. She grabbed her tie and finally succeeded. She put on her black heels, gave herself one more look-over in the mirror, making sure there were no stray strings on her light blue suit, and walked out of her apartment.

She took the elevator down, thankful not to run into anyone. Outside, there were reporters who had already begun to take photos of her. She smiled, almost laughing. She was going to have to make a graceful run through the gauntlet. There were screams all around her and people waving their microphones. She waved and called, "I'm going to be late, thank you." At the end of the block, a police boat with two officers standing beside it waited for her. She jumped onto the boat and they took off for the Grace Hotel.

Sophia gazed out at the people as she passed. There was an anxious fear hanging in the air. Most of the people stopped to stare at the large boat as it flew by them. She wondered if they knew it was her. *What do they think of me? Do they think I am a monster?* As they arrived at City Hall, the mayor put her thoughts aside and put on a smile. She stepped out, waving at the reporters. She laughed and grinned ear to ear. The thought that kept her smiling was, *The idiot reporters stalking me at my house should have been here. That'll teach them.* It was a small victory, but she had beaten a few people. The reporters called out questions to her, mostly about the murders. But when she heard one that was about something else, she jumped forward and answered the question, then moved on before they could ask anything else. *Keep them calm. Everything changes tonight.*

Sophia stepped inside, headed into the conference room and gazed around at the gathered crowd as everyone took their seats. All of the powerful people in the room, the sheer precipice the city stood on, it all reminded her of the night atop the Empire State Building, when Sverichek had raised up Manhattan. She had been worried, but that day it had fallen on Sverichek's shoulders to raise the city. Now it was on hers. The major difference between that night and this was that the room was filled not just with Manhattan's elite, but the richest people all down the Eastern Seaboard and their representatives.

Sophia walked toward the nearest table. The seated people rose and shook her hand, smiled and shared pleasantries. *Good, at least I still get respect from the powerful. When I lose that, I'll worry.* She walked on to the next table, going past each one until her fingers were numb. Finally, she made it to her table, where there was a place open to her between Robert Kerry in his full police attire and Lei Xu. She shook hands with them both and sat down.

"Big night. Ready to take center stage?" she asked Lei. Lei smiled, but Sophia could tell it was forced. "Don't worry, you'll be fine, I'll do all the talking. I'll point you out, you stand up, smile and wave, and take a minute to give a super dumbed down version of the dumbed down version of what you told me. You can't screw that up. And even if you do, I'll prattle on and people will forget all about you." Sophia laughed while Lei tried to smile before lifting the champagne glass to her lips. Sophia glanced at her reddening cheeks and wondered how much Lei had already taken before deciding she should start drinking, too.

Mediterranean salad was followed by the main course of smoked salmon, followed by a mixed kiwi and strawberry topped dark chocolate cake. When the meal was done, the master of ceremonies announced Sophia. The mayor walked up to the podium, foregoing her usual jogging pace after such a big meal. As the spotlights hit her, she was sure to keep her smile overly wide; anything smaller didn't pick up as well with the cameras.

"Good evening," she said. "I hope you all have enjoyed the finest that New York City has to offer." There was a general murmur of approval. "It seems like so many years ago, New York was just one of thousands of cities that were sinking beneath the rising sea level. All over the world, countries were losing their largest cities as the coast was pushed back. But then... Marko Sverichek..." The name alone drew cheers. "Marko Sverichek, who is a bit of a recluse, and deigned not to be here tonight, came up with a crazy plan. An insane scheme to raise New York City out of the sea. And it worked. The Miracle lifted the city out of the ocean and our skyscrapers rose again, the only thing like it in the world.

"But Sverichek was not the only genius and his Miracle was not the only miracle that Ma—New York, could produce," Sophia licked her lips and paused for a second. "I would like to introduce Miss Lei Xu, head of R&D at Stanhope Limited, who will explain to everyone her own miracle."

There was polite applause as Lei stood up and took the podium. She cleared her throat, took the clicker from Sophia and pressed the button. A heavily detailed model of her motor appeared on the screen, with hundreds of tiny black tags pointing to various parts of it. "This is what I have developed over the past few months with Stanhope Limited." She clicked the button again. "And this is what it did." A video appeared on the screen. "This was taken from a helicopter three days ago and below, it shows the two hundred year-old Carlyle Building, one of the first skyscrapers ever made. The press has been busy the past few days, so it didn't notice our brief trial."

The muscles in Sophia's neck tensed at that and her smile turned rigid. On the screen, the Carlyle Building broke from the line of skyscrapers and went out into the harbor. It made a tight circle, then returned to its place. There was complete silence in the building. Lei waited, expecting applause. When it didn't come, she blushed and continued. "With a very small amount of reusable energy, this motor has made it possible to move skyscrapers. But it's not just the Carlyle Building. This motor, if adapted, could move even the Empire State

Building. Thank you."

She stepped down awkwardly, almost running to avoid the spotlight, and received a tenuous clapping.

Mayor Ramos hastily retook the podium and said, "Thank you, Miss Xu. Now the question is: what does this mean for New York City and for all of you? Well, that is very simple. As we all know, Manhattan's population has been severely depleted in the days when it was being liquidated." She heard three people laugh. "What this means is that we have an excess of two hundred skyscrapers without occupants. These skyscrapers, while previously privately owned, have been turned over to the city. Meaning, Manhattan has all these buildings without occupants and there are cities along the coast, like Dover, Norfolk, North Charleston, Jacksonville and others that have become the new port cities of the east coast of America. All of these places need office buildings, they need skyscrapers in particular. But those are expensive to build, costing trillions of dollars. I intend to sell off Manhattan's excess skyscrapers. The money received will be put into hiring a larger police force, educating our young, rebuilding infrastructure and benefitting every New Yorker, not just those in Manhattan."

There was a wild applause. Sophia basked in it; it had been a long time since she had gotten applause and she had never gotten any this enthusiastic. When they had finished, she said, "Before any new buyers emerge, let me announce that the Carlyle Building will be the first to leave Manhattan, as it has already been sold to the city of Dover. The building will leave Manhattan tomorrow at noon through the strait between Staten Island and Queens and is expected to arrive there within two weeks of its departure. I hope all of you will join me in watching it leave the city; I promise you there will be nothing like it." She broke with her script and added, "And this will solve every problem we have."

There was more uproarious applause. Sophia wanted to stay on stage, but she forced herself to smile gracefully and return to her table. As the event winded down and people began to leave, Kerry turned to her and said, "I was worried. People had told me you could spin anything, but that was quite the speech."

Sophia knew Kerry well enough to know he was trying to give her a genuine compliment, but his use of the word 'spin' irked her. She chose to ignore the poor phrasing. "The story of the murders will linger, but all the same, the tourists will flock like never before to see a sailing skyscraper. We can't erase the past, but this will buy you enough time to get the serious criminals off the streets. Don't fail, the city depends on you catching these dangerous people."

"Then the city depends on blind luck."

Sophia watched as he took another gulp of champagne and was reminded why no one had promoted Kerry before her.

Chapter Twenty-Four

The entire east side of Manhattan all the way up to the southern tip was packed with people. Reporters had to fight with tourists for a spot to film as the hot noonday sun beat down on the gathering legions. The crowds became agitated at the delay as they bumped into each other and stood on tip-toes to look over those who had gotten a better view. As afternoon passed and the fringes of the Atlantic began to darken, a red-brick ten-story skyscraper glided across the water, one hundred feet out from the coast. People watched in silent amazement that was only broken by the calls of children. "Look, Mommy, that building's sailing!"

The Carlyle Building cut through the water at a clip of ten miles per hour. An observer might have said that was slow, but no one had seen a building sail past them before. As it did, its shadow reached out toward the people in Manhattan. People stared into the building, not sure what to expect. The windows were shined to perfection, but the inside was bare, save for a few people, who waved as they passed. Two Coast Guard boats trailed on each side of the Carlyle. Their crew looked upward, as if not believing what it was they were doing.

After an hour, the building was clearing the southern tip of Manhattan. The exits of the canals had been roped off for security, leaving only a few police vehicles and the private yachts of the rich investors from the south to watch as the skyscraper's wake gently rocked their boats.

A champagne glass in one hand, sitting on a white chair alongside her brilliant engineer and members of her administration, Sophia turned to Lei and smiled. Sophia wanted to tell Lei that she had done this, then she saw that Lei wasn't looking at the skyscraper, but the horizon beyond it and she had already finished her champagne. *She hasn't learned to hide her feelings yet.*

Lei couldn't bear to watch that beautiful building sail away. She felt like crying, or throwing something. *I thought I was going to make something brilliant. Something that would revitalize Manhattan and bring wonder to the people. Instead, I made the machine that is going to sell it off, piece by piece, to CEOs and venture capitalists who just found out something better to show off than rare paintings and aboriginal artifacts. I wanted to save this city, but I just bottled it and sold it off. Well, I guess I'm not the one selling it.*

Lei looked at Sophia, who smiled widely back at her. She didn't hate her as much as she hated herself. Still, she felt an intense urge to throw the glass in the mayor's face.

"Champagne, Miss Xu?"

"Yes," she said and replaced her glass. She took a gulp and watched bleary-eyed as the skyscraper cut through the water, reaching the midpoint of the bay, in between Manhattan, the Boroughs, and Staten Island. Her eye fell from the skyscraper to the piers of the Boroughs. Just barely, she could see people crowding the boardwalk's length.

In a matter of minutes, the skyscraper was in the strait between Staten Island and the Boroughs. Ezreal and Frederico watched it, along with a bustling, noisy crowd along the southwestern edge of the spider-web city. Ezreal balled his hands into fists. A vein popped out on his temple, visible underneath his thin hair. He clenched his yellowing teeth.

Frederico followed the skyscraper's trail until it passed the strait. After twenty minutes, the Coast Guard boats faded from sight, but he knew the skyscraper would take much longer. As it trailed off, Frederico turned from Ezreal and the skyscraper and looked at the crowd. *What are they feeling? What are they thinking?* He looked into the eyes of an old woman who stood with her husband. He turned to a group of children led by an older boy, who had wandered away from their parents. They all seemed to have the same look in their eyes: amazement and confusion. Amazement because it was a sight no one would have ever thought they would see, and confusion at what this might mean for them and the city. He looked back at Ezreal. He was so pale that his skin looked a light green from the tint of his veins. *You should probably put on some sunscreen before you burst into flames, you strange ghost.*

Ezreal laughed and shook his head. "It's all the same," he said wistfully. "Just like before, when the rich left New York back when it was first sinking under the waves, when every hurricane would wash out a slum, to be replaced by shanty houses." Ezreal looked around at the houseboats strung out as far as the eye could see. "All that's changed is that our enemies have gotten cleverer. This technology could mark the end of us... no. The people will be stirred up to take back the city they forgot belonged to them." Frederico watched the skyscraper in wonder, hardly hearing what Ezreal had said.

Ezreal let his fists fall open. He stopped gritting his teeth and closed cracked lips. His visage changed from hatred to resolution. As the skyscraper trailed off into the distance, Frederico turned to Ezreal and guessed that after living for years under what was once the capital of the world, he didn't expect his first sight above ground would be the city he had dreamed of sailing away.

"The haves are afraid. A few idiots, or perhaps visionaries ahead of their time, showed them that whatever ill they can do to us, we can repay back. Now they seek to abandon us. To literally pack up and take away our city, which we built." He turned to Frederico. "Do you think any of them built those buildings? Do you think any of them forged the steel or laid the beams?"

"No." Frederico had to stop himself from saying 'sir.' In the past week, he had to put up with more rants from Ezreal than ever before, as the subtle references to re-taking power had become the maddened beginnings of raved speeches for empty rooms, rehearsed and delivered to ghosts long dead. Frederico hated being lectured to, especially by someone who was talking to memories more than to him.

"No, they didn't. But now they want to leave and take our city with them."

He glared off into the distance. His palms were open, his breathing steady, but Frederico could still feel Ezreal's rage in his cold eyes. It was as if all his hatred had condensed into those grey orbs.

"So what is our plan?" Frederico dared, hoping that he sounded like a co-conspirator and not a subordinate. "We have to do something quickly; hundreds of buildings are on schedule to leave before the election. There's no way we can stop this..." He let the sentence trail off. The Carlyle Building had become a dot on the horizon.

After a pause, Ezreal said, "The masses will be stirred to action."

"Half the city may be gone by then."

"Then we will grease the wheels with blood."

"But how? Every rich person in Manhattan has hired bodyguards and the police are in full force, monitoring any boats and ferries coming in and out of Manhattan. They have the Coast Guard following the skyscrapers and word has it the navy might even join the larger, more iconic buildings. Your enemies are untouchable."

"Which is why we will kill some of our own."

Frederico fell silent, stunned. Frederico thought he had become accustomed to Ezreal's odd mannerisms, his mad rants. As odd as Frederico thought he was, he never questioned his mad devotion to revolution. But killing the people he sought to lead?

"But, why?" was all he could manage.

"Every movement needs martyrs."

Alex sat at his desk. Projected in front of him were the official Brice Noble murder files, the report on the Yiril Zogheib killing and his own notes on Rodney Maxwell, his sole lead. He had an urge to look at the giant map behind him, but according to the records, Rodney hadn't been arrested for anything else and wouldn't appear in any crime database. Alex looked to the side screen, which played a muted live feed of the Carlyle Building slowly cruising down the coast. He hadn't watched it since turning it on. He was looking past it, at Cassidy's desk. Like nearly every cop on the force, she had found an excuse to patrol the coast and watch a piece of the Miracle float away.

He couldn't tear his eyes from the empty desk. There was hardly a time when he was in the office and she wasn't sitting there watching an anime or telenovela while filling out a report or a file. He would pace and think and she would fire something off, sometimes an insult, other times an insightful idea, other times an almost intelligent point that would lead him on a train of thought where he would solve whatever problem they faced. More often than not, his trains of thought just led to another mark on his map, which led to nowhere. But Cassidy was somewhere else, pretending to control the crowds while watching history head south. He pulled his eyes away and wondered how long he had been staring, thinking.

"I need to be more like Cassidy," he remarked to himself. *She has a life outside of this job. For me, it is everything. It is a way to make a living, protect myself.* Alex thought back to two years ago. It had been a rough year; he had been shot in his left side and gotten three months off. Back then, he had thought about leaving the Boroughs. He had even filed for a transfer without telling Cassidy. But hardly any police force in America would take cops from the Boroughs; they had a notoriously high rate of corruption, and even though he had a perfect record, he couldn't get a break.

Alex closed the web browser with the feed of the Carlyle Building. He clicked on a personal folder and opened up a picture of himself seated, holding up a model sailing ship, complete with miniature masts, ship's wheel, working rudder, everything a miniature figure needed to sail off into the sunset. Leaning over him and hugging him around his neck was a doe-eyed young woman with rose-colored hair and a too-excited smile.

Alex chuckled. He leaned back in his chair and laughed until his sides hurt. He had taken up the hobby of making model ships and had gotten so good at it that he had thoughts of using it to get out of the Boroughs. Building them, selling them to collectors, maybe even opening up a shop. He put a hand over his face and laughed softly. He looked back at the photo and thought, *What an idiot.*

Alex's eyes fell to the girl in the photo. He knew she didn't want to work in that model store, but she had gotten stuck with it since there weren't any jobs left in the Boroughs. He couldn't remember what her ambitions were. At one point, he had asked her if she wanted to leave the Boroughs with him. It hadn't been a straight proposal or a question. It was more of a *what if?* slipped in the middle of a bigger conversation. Then he had recovered from his injury, went back to work, and hadn't spoken to her since.

Alex looked at her for a long moment. He double-tapped his wrist and flipped through his contacts.

Ring... ring... ring...

"Hello?" a honey-sweet excited voice asked from the other end. A dozen calls and gasps of amazement sounded in the background.

"Oh, hey, Haley."

"Hey, who is this? Sorry, this isn't a good time, we're watching the skyscraper, can you call me back sometime?"

"It's Alex, Alex Waverly, and yeah, uhm, I understand. I will—"

"Alex? Oh, my God, I didn't expect a call from you. How have you been? I haven't heard from you in... a while. Did you find another hobby shop? You know there's no better than Morgan's Hobby and Crafts." Haley laughed.

"Oh, no, no, I stopped making those when I got better. I-I was wondering if you wanted to meet up sometime."

"Yeah, sure. Wow. Hey, are you not watching this?"

"You mean the skyscraper?"

"Duh!" she shrieked. Alex smiled from ear to ear. Somehow she was in a permanent state of perkiness, even if it was exhausted sarcastic pep. "You aren't watching this? Get out and see this! What's wrong

with you? Look, it's great that you called, I'd still love to see you, but—
yes, I am getting off now—hold on. I would love to keep chatting, but
can we do this at a time when there isn't a giant skyscraper floating
by?"

"Oh, yeah, sure."

"All right, bye, Alex."

"Bye," he said after the line had gone dead.

Alex sighed and closed his eyes. When he opened them, his eyes
were drawn to a floating speck in the window. In the far distance, a
skyscraper appeared over the hovels.

He pulled his chair up closer to his desk and re-opened the Brice
Noble case file.

Cassidy was watching the Carlyle Building from a raised platform at
the western edge of Brooklyn. Along with two other cops, she kept
people from untying the boats they were clamoring into. They had
clear orders not to let anyone sail out to where the Coast Guard
patrols were. God forbid there be yet another incident for the city
government to deal with while the whole world was watching.

The patrol boats were trailing behind the building now. After a few
minutes of riding the huge wake, they had learned to hang back as the
building cut a deep gash in the water. Dark water rolled toward the
docks and Cassidy heard a few cries from the boats around her as the
first waves tossed them up. They were large enough to make the boats
rise and bump against the docks, but there was no real danger and the
people inside were safe from falling in. *Good. I don't want to get
soaked, especially in front of everyone else.*

Then the building was right in front of her. She remembered the
tiny blot on the horizon and couldn't believe that dot was the colossal
structure towering over her. She looked down. She was so close that
she could see clearly through the windows out to the mainland. Then
it passed by, obscuring part of Staten Island as it skirted the strait.
There were gasps and excited talking behind her. Cassidy looked
down at the wake left by the building. There was a massive clear-blue
path from Manhattan out toward the horizon.

And I'm still here.

Cassidy heard Dennis call out to a group of people beside her, "All
right, show's over, out of the boats. I know those aren't yours. Oh, it
is? Registration or get out."

Cassidy heard a thousand footsteps, heavy, thudding, small,
pattering, shuffling, skipping, behind her as all of the Boroughs

cleared and dispersed, back to their old lives. She didn't want to join them. She didn't want to go back. She stepped out to the edge of the dock, feeling her toes clear the landing.

If I jumped out and swam to one of the ships, they would have to pick me up. They wouldn't bring me back, they couldn't change their course and they couldn't leave the building unprotected, even for a second. Her eyes followed the sky-blue wake cutting a clear path through the dark, dirty water of Manhattan, a clear trail, an almost angelic path away from New York City, away, somewhere warmer, where the land beneath her feet would be solid. There was a gust of wind behind her. She lurched forward and saw the dark water lunge up toward her, reaching up in a crashing wave as it splashed against the docks. She teetered back, reeling on the edge. She found her footing and stepped back, breathing heavily.

"Cassidy, are you okay?"

She heard footsteps rush up behind her.

"I'm fine," she called over her shoulder, holding up a hand behind her. "I'm fine, thanks."

She heard a group of teenage boys laugh behind her and one called out, "Stupid bitch."

She ignored them and turned back to the building. It had passed Staten Island and become another small object somewhere far off. The wake began to soften as the white foam gave way to dark blue. She watched it for another ten seconds, capturing the image of that proud building disappearing into the distance. She turned around and walked back toward the city.

March 14, 2090

Harsh winds tore at the thin walls. Heavy raindrops spattered against the windows so loudly Matthew looked up more than once to see if it was hail. His right fist clenched on his thigh. *The hurricane is just two days away; will these walls hold when it comes?* Matthew's other hand thrummed on the table. The other men, half in their teens, eyed Matthew nervously. He smiled slightly, knowing they were more anxious than he was. Sirens blared from outside. Matthew waited for them to come to a stop outside the house. The sirens came closer, closer... then passed. Then a host of sirens blared all around them. The men grabbed their guns and stood up. Matthew felt the gun in his belt, a black 9mm pistol. *Against what they're carrying, I might as well shoot myself.* What sounded like a dozen sirens approached the house until they deafened even the sound of the pounding rain. All the sirens rolled past the house in turn, dispersing in all directions until there was nothing but an all-encompassing howl from far away.

"They don't know where you are." One of the boys smiled, stupidly.

"They wouldn't send the entire police force after him," one of the other men said. "Something has happened."

Matthew nodded. He pulled up a laptop and placed it on the table. "No connection," he said and turned to look out the window as if the storm could provide him with answers.

"They won't be chasing after you." One of the boys addressed Matthew, his thumb nervously rubbing his pistol. "There's a hurricane coming on and the city is in upheaval. You can slip between the cracks. You can sneak away, disappear..."

Matthew ground his teeth. He was tired of how panic loosened untrained boys' tongues. "They won't forget. What's worse is that Save New York City," he spat the name, "turned on me. They never wanted their movement to accomplish anything and now the government and the pacifists have both turned on me. Officially, I am accused of inciting a riot and killing two officers."

"That's bullshit!" The boy at the door gawked as if Matthew didn't know.

"Frightened people do stupid things." Matthew knew the boy wouldn't catch the insult.

A heavy bang at the front door made them all jump. The banging continued, frantically. Matthew stood up. "Get the door, damn it!"

One of the men stood up and opened up the door to the unholy roar of the emerging storm. A lanky man with platinum-blond hair and a trench coat ran wildly through the entryway and into the kitchen. One of the boys screamed and tackled the man.

"Get off of him," Matthew roared to be heard against the wind, sirens and chaos in the room.

The trench-coated man pushed the boy off, cursing him. Matthew stepped aside, pushing the stunned boy away. He offered his hand to the cursing man on the ground. "Ignore the green boys, Jon. What's so important that you came running in to tell us?"

Jon looked at him as if he had just remembered what it was he was here to say. Fury drained from his face and he went ghostly white. "The subway has flooded."

Matthew heard the words, but couldn't attach any meaning to them. "Which stations? Which lines?"

"The whole damn thing," Jon said. "All of it. The storm's come faster than anyone predicted. The water started seeping into the tunnels, one of them must have burst and the ocean flooded the whole thing."

Matthew looked at his men. The same boy was running his fingers over his pistol madly. Matthew grabbed the pistol from him and waved it in his face. "It's not your cock. If you're not going to use it, put it away." He pressed it against the boy's chest. The stunned boy awkwardly grabbed for it. Matthew threw it against the far wall, smacked the boy across the head and turned back to Jon. "Were there many people in the tunnels?"

"Most people avoided them," Jon replied. "But there were still thousands on the lines. Now the subway's completely destroyed. Word is the navy is coming in to occupy the city and start evacuating people, starting with those closest to the sea."

Matthew lowered his eyes to the floor. He clenched his fist. A gust of wind pounded the wall.

"We could run," Drew offered. "Steal a boat. There's nothing left for us here."

"He's right. Half of us have arrest warrants. We need to leave."

Matthew thrummed his fingers on the table. "No. This is ours. We will not leave it."

"What we have will be underwater before long. The coast line has already moved in fifty feet, any storm would flood our houses, wash away a few, even—"

Matthew slammed his fist on the table. He let his head droop until it hung an inch above the table. He raised himself up and looked at Jon, mad determination in his eyes. "Jon, do you know if the police are pulling up bodies yet?"

Jon stuttered. "I-I'm sure they're not. It's too dangerous in this storm, and some of the cars stopped halfway between stations."

Matthew nodded his head. "Good. Then we can do it ourselves without being bothered."

The other men were too stunned to talk.

"Come on," Matthew ordered grimly. "Let's grab some scuba gear. None of you fellow revolutionaries are opposed to stealing, now, are you?" He smiled alone.

Jon kicked madly downward as he tried to push away the thought of what he was doing from his mind. His puny flashlight offered the smallest ray of light directly in front of him while the rest of the world in his periphery was absolute darkness. The tunnels were so filled with dirt particles that he couldn't see more than a foot in front of him. The thought that he had lost all direction and could get stranded in the tunnels never left his mind.

The dirty brown water turned a light pink. Jon reached forward and saw the water grow redder around his fingers. He gave a little kick forward and let himself drift downward. In front of him was a subway car filled with bodies. He drifted towards the top, but the car was filled to capacity and the faces of those trapped inside pressed against the glass. Jon gasped madly, looking around, seeing blood and bodies. He felt his legs hit the twisted metal of the rails. He thought he would pass out. He felt a hand grab him and press his face down. Jon jerked and looked up. Drew swam beside him and put himself between the car and Jon. Jon looked down, breathing slowly. When he had recovered, he looked back up and nodded at Drew. Drew swam towards the car and noticed that one of the windows had been cracked. He punched it until the glass shattered. He pulled out one of the bodies. He looked at the face and then threw it to the ground. Jon stood up, swam to the car, grabbed the first body he could and without looking at it, he swam backwards.

Jon struggled the entire way back as he kicked madly toward the subway station where Matthew and his men waited. His head breached the surface. He pulled his mask off and gasped for air. Matthew walked over and grabbed the body. "No." He shook his head. "This doesn't work. Go back down there."

"This is insanity," Jon spat back. "That is hell down there. Cars full of bodies, some I knew since I was a kid. There is no other way to describe it."

Matthew stood up looked down at Jon. "You know... you look a lot like me."

Jon withered under Matthew's hateful gaze. He looked at the men behind Matthew. He put his mask back on and went back underwater.

Jon was so exhausted he could barely bring back the fifth body. He threw off his mask and heard it clatter against the tiled floor of the station. The overwhelming stench of the piled bodies in the corner hit Jon and he vomited in the water. Jon looked at the corner of the decrepit subway. A host of wet rats that had rushed out of the oncoming waters were waiting on the edges of the group, staring at the pile of corpses hungrily. One of them eased forward, lifted itself onto its back feet and sniffed the air, showing its long teeth.

"This is it," he heard Matthew say as he stood over one particular corpse. "Ezreal Redding," he read off the man's driver's license. "It's an almost perfect match. Ryan," he called over one of the boys. "Drew, we need to carry this body back. Dispose of it. No trace of the real Ezreal Redding can be left, not even his teeth."

Matthew walked over to Jon. "Good work." He grabbed his head and thrust it into the water. Jon tried to rise, his aching body struggling madly. He felt his nostrils fill up with his own vomit and blood from a half-dozen corpses. Jon gasped for air and cold death entered his lungs. His body relaxed and he lay facedown in the water.

Matthew took a step into the water, avoiding the pool of vomit. He turned Jon over. Matthew pulled his wallet out of his pants and stuffed it into Jon's inner coat pocket. "Drew, Ryan," he called. "Strip off Jon's scuba suit, take this body, and all the others except Ezreal Redding's back down into the car." He turned back to see them looking at him. Ryan held his gun at his side. "They won't be taking DNA off of anyone that has ID on them. They'll know Matthew Hammond died."

The two stood fixed in place. Drew looked down. He walked

towards Jon and began to strip the scuba suit off. He threw the suit at Ryan. He donned his mask, grabbed Jon's body and swam downward.

After they left, Matthew returned to his examination of Ezreal Redding's body. Matthew squinted. He grabbed the man's wrist and held it up. He pulled out a knife and pressed it against the middle of the palm. "He has one of those internal computers inside of him. It'll have an ID and all his personal information, bank accounts, passwords, family photos, favorite videos, music and pictures, if my guess is correct. If I'm lucky, he'll have put his whole life in it." He started cutting.

Chapter Twenty-Five

The sun hovered above the distant mainland, painting the sky an orange-red by the time Ezreal Redding's men quietly assembled a small platform for their leader near the Eye. Ezreal waited until rush hour came and crowds began to circle when he took the stage.

"Citizens of New York!" he cried. It was enough to cause everyone around to stop, even if they couldn't hear his exact words over the chatter. Ezreal looked out, catching the eyes of the supporters he had placed throughout the crowd. "You have been cheated and lied to by a government which is wholly against you."

Most of the crowd moved on in their rotation around the Eye, but Ezreal noticed that a few more people than just his own followers stayed to listen. "Do you think that any of the money from the buildings this corrupt government sells will make it to you? When those in power could keep it for themselves?" There was some small laughing; Ezreal hoped it wasn't just being feigned by his own men. "This same government which has massacred its people numerous times?"

That got the circle to stop turning. More heads turned. Now those who wanted to go on shopping had to weave through the crowd like an obstacle course as people peppered throughout the crowd stopped and listened. Some trying to escape grew frustrated and turned to look at Ezreal.

"Surely you've heard about the slaughter which our police call justice. Two days ago, four men were executed, even though not a single one of them fired a shot at the police. Mr. Yiril Zogheib gunned down in his own establishment even though he wasn't even accused of anything. And there have been six cases of cops killing squatters in the last month. This corrupt government hosts lavish parties in the grandest buildings on Earth, yet they send in their dogs to shoot anyone who tries to put a roof over their heads."

There was clapping and heated calls, but it was almost wholly from his own men. The other people around them looked frightened by their cheers, wondering what this mad man was saying. *I don't need applause so long as they're paying attention, so long as I can plant a seed.*

"People of New York City, the bureaucrats and the politicians in Manhattan are leaving us behind! They have stolen all our wealth for themselves, but have found no way to detach themselves from us. Like a leech, they've fed on us, bleeding us of our last few dollars and our own livelihood to feed their greed. Now that we have nothing left to steal, they fear us. They've made demons out of those people who tried to steal from the rich just so they could have some food to eat, while meanwhile, the news calls the cops who slaughter us heroes!"

That drew more outrage, still mostly his own men, but the Eye had come to a near stand-still.

"But now a miracle has happened for them: they now have the machines they need to leave us behind and take with them Manhattan, and they will. Don't believe Mayor Ramos when she tells you that the money will trickle down to us. We won't get a drop. They will leave us behind in their floating palaces."

"Crackpot!" someone shouted from the crowd. It was met with boos and hisses from his men as people turned to the sound.

"What was that?" Ezreal called. "What did you say?"

"Forgot to take your pills today, you crazy old fuck?"

A few tepid laughs broke out.

Ezreal called for calm. "You don't think that the government in Manhattan fears you, hates you and wants to remove the people who live outside of it from everything that is happening? Then why did our city's government choose to build the motors in Summit, New Jersey, away from our shores, providing hundreds of jobs for people outside our city?"

A silence overtook the crowd. Even the waves seemed to still.

"You didn't know about that, did you? I bet you also didn't know that they were staffing the factories exclusively with non-New Yorker workers."

That drew another pause as people looked at each other, as if the person next to them could confirm whether what he was saying were true.

"They hide their intentions, they use outside labor, they have removed all of us in the Boroughs from their doings because the men above us are con men! Con men who are trying to pull off the biggest heist in history; they are stealing a whole city from us! But they can't do that. It isn't theirs to take. It belongs to us! It doesn't belong to the people who bought it. It belongs to the people who built it!

"Open your eyes! Who do you people think own the buildings in Manhattan? A few bankers and corporate leaders? All because they have a few pieces of paper they wrote themselves saying it's theirs? They don't have the right to take away our city, our only hope for a living wage. This city is ours. We can take it back by throwing a wrench into their machine. If we shut down the factory that makes the motor, we can keep them from taking our city from us. Don't let them take what's yours away. The city belongs to you."

At that, Ezreal stepped down. The eyes of the crowd seemed to linger, though he got no applause, except a few hollers from his followers. He could see that the people didn't trust him, didn't love him, or agree with him. But they were filled with fear; he could see it in their eyes.

Good. All I have to do is wait for Ramos and the city government to panic. Then they will overreact and confirm our every fear. Knowing them, I won't have long to wait.

Chapter Twenty-Six

Sophia straightened her tie, feeling as if it were a noose. *Why couldn't the victory last longer than a day?*

Sophia had tried everything she could to keep people's minds on the wonder of the Carlyle Building. She had commissioned a website that would track the skyscraper from space so that people could watch it every second until it arrived, with interviews of the onboard staff and clips from reporters as they passed various landmarks on their way south. But an increasing number of people were taking to the streets to protest the silence over the kidnappings. She told everyone from press secretaries to every officer on the force to respond to reporters and grieving family members alike that it was for their own security, but they were hardly placated.

Sophia looked at herself in the mirror, wondering whether she could get out of this. No. Not appearing would make her look like she was dodging the issue. But if she made a speech, it could reassure at least some people that everything was fine. She figured she would always have the families of the missing people as enemies, but she was sure that as long as she looked leader-like, she could get a free pass on the blame with the rest of Manhattan and the Boroughs. They might not like her, but who could they trust to replace her?

Sophia smoothed back her hair, turned from the mirror and walked out of her office. She walked down the hall, giving a small smile to her secretary as she passed and took the marble stairs down to the second floor. As she did, a security guard stepped forward and escorted her to the press room, where a dozen reporters sat waiting. She stepped up to the stage just as she was announced by Kerry and greeted by light applause from the audience of twenty. She stepped up to the podium and tried not to squint from the bright lights.

"Thank you for being here today. I am sorry I couldn't answer your
questions earlier, as I was caught up overseeing the transfer of the
Carlyle Building to Dover. But now I am here to speak a little bit about
a more somber matter, specifically the high-profile disappearances.
The police have been monitoring these disappearances and we have
been tracking down potential leads. Due to the delicate nature of this
operation, we cannot release any information, but..." Sophia raised
her voice and right hand as a man with a bow tie started to shout out
a question. "Let me be clear, those bloggers and so-called journalists
who have said that we have been unaware or inactive are saying so
not based on any fact, but pure sensationalism. We have been
pursuing every lead and using every available resource to track down
these missing people. Unfortunately, whoever is abducting these rich
citizens of Manhattan is very sophisticated. Manhattan has not seen
this level of organized crime since the Mafia died out. Whoever these
people are, they will be brought to justice and punished in the
harshest means possible. To that end, I am declaring a state of
emergency as of six P.M. tonight. The National Guard will be brought
in to monitor incoming vessels around the southern tip of Manhattan.
Furthermore, the ferries going back and forth from between the
Boroughs will have National Guard who will conduct weapons
searches on any incoming people to Manhattan. Finally, I have spoken
to Summit's Mayor Kreutzer and there will be National Guard posted
outside the factory which makes the Poseidon motors.

"Rest assured," she tried to finish on a strong note even while
people began to speak over her, "we will find these criminals and
bring justice to New York. First question, you." She pointed to a
woman in a black top.

"Mary Daschle, *Midtown Examiner*. Do you have any leads on the
kidnappers?"

"Yes, we do," Ramos lied, though in fairness a lead could be nothing
more than a guess, and she was sure her department wasn't without a
few of those. "However, we cannot reveal what those are for obvious
reasons. Yes, you." She pointed to a bald gentleman with deep
wrinkles and a scowl on his face.

"Bernard Waters, the *Lower Manhattan Reporter*. Miss Mayor, how
is it possible that thirty-five people can go missing when there are
cameras posted all throughout the city?"

"Obviously, surveillance cannot end all crime. Cities around the
world have been installing cameras and it hasn't eliminated crime.
Manhattan is a city which has changed entirely since the Miracle and
our police force is still adjusting to the different landscape. Another

problem that we are facing is the problem of understaffing in our police, which is why I have contacted the governor and acquired the aid of the National Guard. What we are seeing happen is that an enormous influx of money has entered into New York City and with any great wealth comes the criminals who want to take it. What makes this situation unique, aside from a terrain which police have never had to work in before, is that the criminal response has been highly organized and has unfortunately caught our officers off-guard. But that ends now. With the help of the National Guard, Manhattan will be made safe until these criminals can be brought to justice."

Sophia wished she could have ended it on that note, but two questions were hardly enough. She pointed to a pale, long-faced woman with too-wide green eyes.

"Amanda Schultz, *Queens Business Examiner*. Why was the plant that makes the Poseidon Motor placed in Summit and kept secret until the installation of the Carlyle Building?"

"We kept it secret for security reasons."

She pointed to an old man with bushy eyebrows when Ms. Schultz added, "And you couldn't have hired New York workers?"

"No. The development of the motors needed to be kept a secret due to potential threats."

"Potential threats? Like what?"

"In light of the recent kidnappings, I think keeping this endeavor under wraps was justified," Ramos shot back.

Ms. Schultz gave off a shocked 'ah!' sound. "Miss Mayor, half of the people who had been kidnapped had been so since before the motors went into development. And even so, how could that have been a threat to the motors?"

"Ms. Schultz," Ramos interrupted and scrambled for something to say. She wasn't given the opportunity.

"Was this not a bold-faced use of executive privilege to keep secrets from the citizens you were sworn to serve?"

"Ma'am—"

"Your administration hides the development of the motor, doesn't give those much-needed jobs to the workers in the Boroughs, and now you are bringing in the army to keep them out, to keep out the rest of New York City while Manhattan scavenges whatever profits it can." Ramos began to raise her voice, but Ms. Schultz shouted above her, "Miss Mayor, you have engaged in a hostile takeover of this city and have sold it to the vultures that are picking it off!"

Ramos raised her hand. As bad as this looked, a shouting match would only be worse. When Schultz had quieted down, Sophia said, "It is this sort of hysteria which puts our city at risk." Schultz continued her shouting, but Sophia talked over her. "The reason why this was done in secret was because New York City had an excess of buildings and a large amount of debt. The idea of rising cities, moving buildings, this is all new and scary and anything new can lead people to panic. But my administration has overseen the smooth transition of massive amounts of capital into the city in order to reach solvency and grow our economy. I didn't hire five hundred New Yorkers today so that I could hire five hundred thousand tomorrow."

Schultz scoffed and began to protest, but Sophia continued all the same.

"Yes, our city has a problem with overly sophisticated criminals. We always have, but the Mafia was beaten eventually and these criminals will as well. Over the last few decades, we have been sinking, but our ingenuity lifted this city up, unlike any other city in the world. Whatever problem we have, we can face it so long as our people don't give in to these insane fears and conspiracy theories. That is all—no more questions."

As she walked out of the room and back towards her office to pour a drink and wait for a new disaster to appear on her desk, she contemplated the headlines and quotes the papers would use in their reports. She had tried to make everything inspiring, something that JFK might have said, without firing off any easily malleable quotes. She knew they wouldn't make her look good in their reports, but far worse politicians than her had emerged from scandals clean by appearing to have been caught in the middle of corrupt forces rather than being at the center of them.

Chapter Twenty-Seven

Ezreal's angry speech had gone viral. All over the internet, it was shared by conspiracy theorists, anti-establishment sites, activist networks, income inequality groups and a host of other left and right-wing groups that somehow resonated with Ezreal's impassioned disillusionment with the 'powers-that-be.' People stopped walking and watched even as the stage was being set up. A few camera crews that had been waiting around the Eye had begun to take positions; whether to mock him or to spread his message, it was hard to tell. By the time Ezreal slowly took the stage, the circle had stopped rotating; the great axle had ground to a near-standstill and in that moment, Ezreal felt as if he had stopped the whole machine from running. But he knew that Manhattan still roared across the bay. He wasn't here to slow down the machine that was the Boroughs; he was there to fire it up until it overheated and burst.

"Now you have the proof!" he thundered. "Noon today, your mayor announced that the National Guard have arrived in Manhattan. Their orders? To keep us out of our own city! They've arrived at the ferries and the docks with machine guns and if they act anything like our police, they will shoot anyone who demands their common rights. There is no conspiracy, people of New York; they aren't trying to hide their malicious intent!"

All through the crowd, a solemn quiet held sway. He knew what it meant: they didn't want him to be right, they wished so much that the strange, pale incarnation of death was wrong.

"What's more, they've posted National Guard at the Poseidon plant in Summit. Well, I say we don't stand for it!" He paused and let that last statement echo in their minds. "The haves may be able to keep us have-nots from setting foot in Manhattan, but they can't stop us from docking near the plant. I say that tomorrow, we sail out to Summit, march on the factory, and stop the production of these machines before they take away our whole city with them, what say you?"

There were roars and angered cheers from the crowd; some from his men, a few from anarchists and rabble-rousers, but the real force came from one section of about three hundred men and women who stood in a block together. Ezreal knew they were from the Boroughs Metalworkers Union, as he had made sure to bring them there. His men used the connections they had to coerce them and Ezreal had promised that he had a scheme to give them jobs. It was enough for half of them to appear in support. Ezreal could see the sense of betrayal in their eyes: they were the stuff revolutions were made of.

"Tomorrow, let us all sail out to Summit and protest the plant and ensure that not one more motor comes out of there! This corrupt government is trying to pay outside workers, sell off our city and gun down anyone who disagrees with them. But we can stop them and we will stop them; tomorrow, when we break their machines!"

That drew another roar, but just from that one block of people, the random thugs, his own men and unaffiliated troublemakers.

"What say you, Mr. Worthington?" Ezreal stretched out his hand, which had burned in his short time in the sun, palm upward, gesturing towards the head of the Boroughs Metalworkers Union, a dark man in jeans and a collared shirt who seemed to tower over the people around him. He looked strong and vital, but his face was haggard. It was the face of someone fatigued, not from being overburdened, but for having nothing to do. For a moment, he stood stock still. Then he stepped forward towards Ezreal, who motioned for him to stand on the stage. Worthington stepped up to the platform. He looked out at the people around him slowly.

Finally, he said in a deep voice that carried throughout the Eye, "When I was a younger man, everyone around me was filled with doom and gloom that the world was coming to an end, or at least our corner of it. They all told me not to go to school, that it wouldn't lead to anything. They told me to get a job and just work. But I wanted to do something meaningful, to build something meaningful. I thought maybe if we had the spirit that the people who built those buildings had, then maybe we could get ourselves out of this mess. So I became a metalworker. I was employed for five years and helped build the motors that lifted up Manhattan, before the last plant out here closed. Then I ended up taking the jobs I had been avoiding my whole life. For these last few months, I've worked as an unlicensed taxi-man in Manhattan. I thought so long as I'm not picking up rich peoples' garbage, I can live with this. But then they kicked out all the unlicensed taxis from the Boroughs. Then they kicked out the garbage men. They replaced the garbage men with professional, *licensed*," he said the word as if it were a punchline, "workers from upstate. They replaced the taxi service exclusively with Manhattan workers too. And now they've replaced the metalworkers with workers from New Jersey." He bit his lip, filling with palpable rage.

He looked at Manhattan and pointed. "I did that!" he yelled. "I lifted those buildings up!" There were angry roars from the metalworkers, followed by solemn silence. "Now that they don't need me, they have replaced me with people who take orders quietly and politely. Let's replace them." He got cheers from more people now as garbage men, taxi drivers, and a host of unlicensed food vendors, street performers and other workers who had previously shown up in Manhattan pining for their money, voiced their anger.

"Your solidarity gives me hope," Ezreal called to the crowd. "Let us remind them we exist."

Miles shouted as pain shot up his spine. His hands gripped the parallel bars on either side of him. He groaned until the pain eased out of him as he lifted himself off his legs, which still felt like wet noodles from the week in bed.

"Oh, quit crying, you baby," Mylie called. She was sitting down in a chair against the far side of the room to his left, watching the television projection on the wall.

Miles looked over at her. He had recently been taken off his pain meds and his wit hadn't quite returned to him.

"You're doing fine, Mr. Buhari," cheered a mousy, almond-haired woman in nurse's uniform standing at the end of the bars. "Can you reach the end or do you need help?"

Miles looked back at her and waved a hand quickly before grabbing onto the bar and grunted, "No, I'm fine." He planted his feet firmly into the mat and took another step. His knee wobbled for a second, but he pushed down with his arms on the bars and took another step, then another. One more and he was at the end.

"Very good, Mr. Buhari, you should be back to 100% in no time."

"How long is no time?"

"Miles, don't be snippy to the nurses!"

"She's not a nurse, she's a physical therapist, and I have a right to know when I can get around without training wheels. So, how much longer, Susan?"

"Another week should see you walking out of here, though you should take it easy after that, no exercise, aside from therapy, and nothing strenuous."

"What about dancing?"

Susan scrunched her thin lips. "That depends on what kind of dancing you want to do."

"Do I look like the kind of person who does ballroom dancing?" He smiled charmingly at her.

"Not many people's first thought after getting shot is 'how long until I can dance again.'"

"No, my first thought was, 'how can I bring down the city government.' Dancing came after."

Susan gave him a disapproving look. Miles smiled wide, showing a row of pearly white. She turned around, pulled up his wheelchair and helped him into it.

"That's it for the day, would you like me to wheel you to your room?"

"No, we'll be fine," Miles said.

Susan nodded and walked out of the room while Miles wheeled himself over to where Mylie was sitting. She watched the screen above him. He tried turning himself around, but nearly ran into the wall.

"Are you trying to parallel park that?"

He grimaced as a warm pain pulsed from his stomach. He finally managed to turn it so he was facing the screen. Through a pained grimace, he said, "You'd think you'd be nicer to someone who's just been shot."

"You'd think." She didn't tear her eyes from the screen.

Miles looked up and saw Ezreal speaking in the middle of the Eye. His speech was muted while a reporter talked over it, calling him wild and dangerous.

"The reporters are summarizing what he's saying instead of actually broadcasting his speech. Why do you think that is?" Miles asked, already knowing the answer.

"Because he's trying to take down the government."

Miles looked up. He wanted to sympathize with Ezreal, with anyone that was being silenced, but even though he was a contrarian, he didn't like the look of Ezreal, didn't like his name, didn't like anything about him. *One week after I get shot and the world goes to hell.*

"He looks insane. Never trust an angry man who stands on a soapbox, waves their fist and rails against the government."

For the first time, Mylie looked away from the screen and turned to Miles.

"What?"

She bowed her head and raised an eyebrow.

"What?"

"You cannot be that thick," she said. "You do the same thing he does."

Miles laughed. "You must be joking. When have I ever gone on a soapbox and given a speech like that?"

"You might not stand on a stage and yell at people, but you do pretty much the same thing in your articles."

"I do not."

"You rant against certain people, painting them as hate figures." She held out one finger and waved it at him. "And you tell your readers that the truth is hidden from them by shady government officials and a corrupt press."

"And that isn't the truth?"

"You're a conspiracy theorist just like him."

"No, I was a conspiracy theorist before him. I'm original." Miles laughed, but Mylie just stared, stone-faced. She sighed and shook her head disapprovingly.

"The one difference between him and you is that he actually offers solutions to our problems." She turned to Miles, looking him square in his tired face, rising indignation in her eyes. "I guess that's the difference between a cynic and a 'crazy person.' You travel to ritzy cities like Paris, Moscow, Berlin, you get a place in the nicest part of the city, travel out to the periphery of the danger areas for a few hours, and then write a piece about how everything is falling apart and it's all the government's fault."

Mylie turned and looked back to the screen. The story had changed to an update on the financial impact on stockholder fears over whether the companies they invested in would exist if they were relocated a thousand miles down the coast. She couldn't have been less interested in it.

"Hey," Miles said. "Hey, look at me." He kicked at her closest chair leg.

She turned, looking as if she were preparing for another weak blow.

"Is that what you think of me?"

She didn't respond.

Miles pursed his lips. "Why do you think I'm here? I was shot." He opened up his shirt and showed her the scar.

"You're here because the story was more important than his life."

Furrows appeared on Miles' face. "What? Mylie, what the hell are you talking about? Are you pissed at me for something? Do I owe you money that I forgot about? I don't understand what you're saying."

"You could have called the police the second you thought Charles Tanning was in danger, but you didn't. You chased after them taking photos; you never even tried to get him help. You let him get kidnapped because that made for the better story. And now that he's dead, you look like a hero because you took a bullet following his killers and blamed the government for his death, taking away from your own culpability."

Miles' brow furrowed and he felt himself grow hot. He looked up at the television. "He's ugly as all hell. Anyone that ghoulish who thinks he can be a populist leader must have some sort of complex."

"Really? You're attacking his looks now?"

"I can smell the dumpster he's been sleeping in just from looking at the screen. The man's nuts." After a second, he added, "You don't have to believe me now, just remember that I said it so I don't have to say 'I told you so' later."

Mylie sighed and stood up. "I should go. Do you want me to take you back to your room?"

He waved her off. "Go ahead."

Mylie left, leaving Miles to watch the screen. After a moment, he wheeled himself to the exit.

Chapter Twenty-Eight

It was a cool morning on the mainland. The salty sea air mixed with the scent of pines and firs. As the Atlantic rose up to tear away civilization, the forests approached from the other side and there were green trees on what open turf wasn't paved over by concrete. Grass and weeds shot up from between the cracks in the sidewalks.

"It's gonna be hot." Mackey looked over to one of his fellow guards.

"It's already hot in all this gear," James retorted. "Why the hell are we wearing these? This isn't a war zone; this is Jersey!"

"Newbie's already sweating? It'll be a long day then." Sergeant Hastings laughed.

"I'm just saying, why do we have to wear bulletproof vests when we are a mile down the road from a McDonald's?"

"Newbie, do you know what the Romans used to do?" McElroy looked at James incredulously, though he always looked that way with his bristly grey eyebrows. The rest of the squad would have interrupted with some mocking insult, but McElroy had earned the right to blather. "Roman soldiers used to march twenty miles a day in full metal armor with forty-five pound packs on their backs. Then when they finished marching, they would make a giant fort, with palisades and a trench, and they wouldn't even take off their armor while digging, cutting wood and building it. Then, come morning, they would burn it down so no one else could use it and then keep marching. Every day. Meanwhile, what Herculean task do you have to do?"

"Listen to you."

As they continued to talk, Private Miguel Sanchez got up and walked forward, away from the plant. He understood their frustration; they were trained soldiers and yet they were acting as bodyguards. They didn't even wave the numerous trucks into the factory; there were security guards who handled that. Instead, they set up camp near the gate and tried to fight off the ennui, mostly by talking. It just gave Miguel a headache. That, and the pounding of the massive machines from inside the factory, the beeping of trucks backing up to load motors, and the occasional piercing shriek of metal.

He stepped forward over a small rising hill and looked out at the coast. When he looked over, he did a double take. For a second, he thought an invading fleet had landed on the shore. There were hundreds of boats that had docked, some crashed, onto the beach with even more following behind the armada. After a second, Miguel wondered if there was some catastrophe happening in New York that was causing them all to flee for the mainland. He looked out to the Boroughs and Manhattan; everything seemed normal. He looked back down and saw people get out of their boats and start marching towards the factory.

Miguel turned and ran back to the factory's gates. The rest of the men were still arguing. "Sir." Miguel quickly saluted Sergeant Hastings. "There seems to be a situation developing."

The men beside the gate burst out laughing.

The sergeant smiled and asked, "Seagulls?" which drew more laughs.

"Sir, hundreds of civilian boats have landed on the coast five hundred meters from here. They seem to be marching towards us."

Hastings looked like he couldn't believe what he was hearing. After a moment's pause, he said, "Show me." Then, turning back, he roared, "At attention, men!" There was some scattered grumbling, but each man lined up against the tall fence, guns in hand, looking outward. Hastings ran forward, outpacing Miguel to the shore. What looked like five hundred people had formed a solid mass and were marching up toward the factory. Hastings nodded at Miguel and the two ran back to the factory.

"Hold formation in front of the gate" Hastings boomed, "we have civilian protesters approaching." The twenty men ran in front of the gate, their line extending past the opening. Hastings flicked his wrist nervously and called the governor. "Sir, there are hundreds of protesters marching on the Poseidon factory. We only have twenty men and not enough tear gas to subdue all of them. We'll need back up if we want to hold... sir, we'll try, but they outnumber... Yes, I understand, sir. Yes, sir."

Hastings hung up and held a grave look on his face. He turned back to his men. "Men, grab your riot shields. Sanchez, get me the megaphone." The soldiers lined up in front of the gate, riot shields acting like a second fence in front of the entrance. Behind them, workers in the yard looked on in fear and the soft whisper of worried voices turned into a loud buzzing, only matched by the thrumming of footsteps that marched towards them. His men held the shields in one hand and rifles in the other, save Hastings, who held his shield in one and a megaphone in the other with his rifle slung over his back, praying he could avert the worst from occurring as the protesters closed in around them. To his dismay, Hastings saw many carrying wrenches, hammers and other tools. But no guns, unless they were hiding them.

Hastings lifted his megaphone and called, "Stay back! You are not authorized to be here."

They continued to march forward within fifty meters.

"Stay back!" he called again. "Or my men will be forced to use tear gas."

They only quickened their pace.

Hastings looked to his right. "Use the gas!" he yelled. The fifth and tenth man on his right and the fifth and tenth man on his left threw canisters of tear gas at the protesters. The ones in front began to cry out in pain and stopped, but the wave of protesters from behind pushed them forward and a canister was kicked back towards the guards. Hastings was about to order another round of gas canisters, but there were protesters spilling out from the sides and sprinting towards the gate.

"Hold!" Hastings yelled to his men. They braced themselves.

Hastings lifted the megaphone and yelled. "Turn back! Go back to your homes, you are not authorized to be here." He dropped the megaphone with a curse as the first of the protesters ran into the shields. Hastings knocked a young man back, throwing him to the ground. But then the wave approached and people were trampling each other to push the guards back. Hastings strained, biting his teeth, feeling with every second as if his muscles would give out, but he held on. From out of the corner of his eye, he saw a tall man raising himself above James' shield and hit him with a wrench on his helmet. Hastings felt himself moving back and couldn't let his man be beaten down. He reached for his pistol and fired it into the air. That got a moment's reprieve as the crowd froze. The wrench slammed against James, knocking him to the ground. Mackey aimed his rifle at the man who was assaulting James. His head exploded into mist just as Hastings screamed, "No!"

Screams. Chaos erupted. Some ran. A few were emboldened. Filled with bloodlust, they started attacking Mackey and the man next to him until they were lying on the ground. Hastings cursed, leveled his pistol and fired rubber bullets at the three men who stood over his own guard. The rest of the crowd had dispersed at that point. When the crowd had cleared, Hastings walked over to his men and helped them get to their feet. James was bleeding and Hastings turned him over to Private Kim for medical attention. Kim escorted him past the terrified onlookers and into the factory, where there was a medical wing for onsite injuries.

"Hold the line in case any come back," Hastings yelled. With his men in place and the protestors in retreat, he called the governor. "Sergeant Hastings. Yes, sir, we held it... your boys are late, sir. No, don't send them back. There was a full-blown riot and one rioter was killed, but the rest were driven back with tear gas and rubber bullets. I thought you would like to hear it from me first... well, I'm not a political man, sir, but I think most of the shit won't fall on your head. Thank you, sir."

Chapter Twenty-Nine

Alex drummed his fingers on the table. His foot was tapping out of rhythm with the blues rock playing over the speakers. He looked out the window at the walkway, observing the people as they passed. Rain had just started to fall, gently pattering the window as it left a million little ripples in the water between the buildings. People ran by, covering their heads with their hands as they rushed to escape the downpour. There was a woman with deep red hair barely visible under an umbrella. She peered through the diner's windows and met Alex's eyes. *Haley?* She looked a bit different, but then, he hadn't seen her in a year. The split-second passed and she kept walking down the street. *That was her. She just bailed on me! No, that couldn't be her, her nose wasn't as big. Or it wasn't as small. Or it was shaped different. It wasn't her.*

"Sir, would you like something to drink?"

Alex turned to the smiling woman who stood over him. "Yeah, sure. Coffee."

"Alright, I'll bring that right up."

"And a water. For my date."

"Coming right up."

Alex turned to look out the window again. He sighed. *When was the last time I was out enjoying myself, doing something fun?* Alex laughed. *Oh yeah, I was counting flags.*

The coffee arrived and Alex's thoughts were briefly halted. *I should learn to get better at putting work aside and take up distractions. Cassidy doesn't have a problem with these things. She is vid-gaming, or watching TV or something. Her whole life is distractions. I bet she doesn't re-evaluate her life in the silent moments of anticipation.* Once he started thinking about Cassidy, he felt a pang of guilt.

"Hey!"

Alex looked up and saw Haley smiling down at him, her pink lips stretching from ear to ear, eyes sparkling, red hair draping over a cream white coat, dripping blue umbrella at her side.

Alex grinned and stood up. "Hey." He stood up and gave her a hug. As they sat down, he said, "You haven't changed."

"Should I have?"

"Well, no, I just meant—"

Haley laughed. "You have. You haven't shaved!"

Shit, I knew I forgot something.

"I was going for the mountain man look. Thought you would like it."

"Yeah, I dig it. You look like you've put on muscle too. You've been working out?"

"Eating," he said. "The last time you saw me, I had just been shot and was going through surgeries and treatments."

She nodded her head. "Right. Getting shot is bad for your health."

"I swear, we need to put out a PSA or something, I bet it would do a lot of good."

"Yeah, you'd be surprised how many people around here don't know bullets aren't good for you." Haley laughed. "So what's new with you?"

"I..." *Don't say nothing.* "Quite a lot. It has been a while."

"It has!"

"I've been transitioning to more of a detective role recently. I'm still a cop, but I helped solve some complicated cases and now I've been doing that."

"Wow," she said, sounding genuinely impressed. "Any good cases? Any psychopaths? Don't tell me if they are too bloody or are anywhere near Prospect."

"No, no, I haven't met any psychopaths, not the kind you see in movies. I did get shot at two weeks ago."

"Anywhere near Prospect?" Her eyes went wide.

"No, no, all the way over on the other side of town."

"Okay, good."

"Yay, I got shot at somewhere else!"

"Oh, you'll be fine, you've been shot before."

The waitress stepped up to their table. "Are you two ready to order?"

"The vegetarian salad, with vinegar."

The waitress nodded.

"Burger, medium-rare, with fries," Alex replied.

The waitress smiled and said, "That'll be right up."

"So, yeah. How have you been?" Alex turned back to Haley.

"Good. Same ol', same ol'. I had a job as a tour guide for a while."

"Legal?"

Haley paused. "Oh, right, you're a cop."

Alex whispered, "I'll let you off this time."

"Yes, it was legal, the boats all had permits and everything. I was pulling in twice as much as I made in the hobby shop. It was a great job, I was even thinking of quitting my regular job and getting a place in Manhattan. A cheap place, you know. I figured there's no way I could lose this job. Then, three weeks ago, I was laid off alongside a bunch of other people."

"You're just all kinds of bad luck."

"Yeah, no kidding. But I guess now it's..."

"Back to the hobby shop?"

"For a bit," she said and sipped her water.

Alex furrowed his brow. "What? You taking off somewhere?"

"I was thinking of it."

"Thinking of it? You have a plan?"

"Nope."

"Well, do you have friends somewhere who will give you a place to stay until you get on your feet?"

"Around Reno, yeah."

"That's quite a ways away. Can you afford the transportation?"

"I don't know."

Alex started to chuckle. "Well..." He laughed.

"I know, I know," she said, smiling. "But, those buildings leaving, it feels like a sign; like I should be taking off, too. You don't think so?"

"I don't think New York packing up and leaving is a personal sign to me, no."

"You don't think God, the universe, sends up signals every now and then?"

"I believe in God; I don't think that sailing buildings are his way of talking to me."

"Then how does God talk to you?"

"I don't know; he's always been short on words." Alex laughed. Haley smiled, cheery as always, but she seemed more serious than he was and wasn't going to let him laugh away the conversation.

"Okay, well, then what do you think it means when a big part of your city up and leaves where you live? A city, one that used to be pretty important too, just up and leaves. That's a sign."

Alex wanted to argue that there was a difference between common sense and divine revelation, but that would be splitting hairs and he knew how that always turned out with Cassidy. Granted, Haley was better-tempered than Cassidy, but Alex had learned through experience that people were never impressed by his ability to beat them in arguments.

"Okay." He put his hands on the table. "You have your sign. You have a bit of money in your pocket. Where is the universe telling you to go?"

Haley thought about that for a moment. "India."

"That's pretty far away, and takes you even farther from Reno."

"I think that's where I'm supposed to be."

"Well, you know the universe is pretty big, it might not realize how far away it is for you. To the universe, America and India are right next door; it can't quite see everything in between."

"Ah!" She gasped in mock outrage. "Fine. But don't tell me that you have never thought about getting out of here, leaving the Boroughs."

"Yeah, I used to all the time, especially after I got shot. I thought to myself, 'I am getting out of here, somewhere far away from the sea. Anywhere. And even if I get a job that hardly pays to feed me, it's better than this.'"

"Why didn't you leave?"

"I just..."

I had this crazy idea that I could take you with me. And by the time I got better and fell into routine, I still hadn't won you.

"I got better. Recovered from the wound, got back on my feet. I enjoyed my work—"

"Aside from getting shot."

"Yeah, thanks, that needed to be stated."

They both laughed.

"Yeah." He shrugged. "Leaving here, becoming a farmer out in Oklahoma or something. It was a great dream when I was lying in a hospital bed and pissing through a catheter, but when I got back to the job, it just faded to the back of my mind, you know? And being a cop, you have to always be there. You have to be focused one hundred percent. So having niggling doubts about anything, it can distract, make things dangerous. Get you killed." Yiril Zogheib holding a gun to his face appeared in his mind. *I was closest to him. If I hadn't been distracted, if I had kept my eyes on him, I could have gotten the gun out of his hand. No one needed to die. Rodney Maxwell and the two other kids don't need to die. If I can find them, I won't be off, I can take them in—*

Haley nodded slowly. "It must be tough."

Alex shrugged. "Nah, easiest thing in the world." He sipped his coffee.

Their food came and conversation took a lighter turn. Mostly, Haley couldn't believe how good it was for being a 'cheap diner at the end of the universe.'

"There are tons of great diners scattered throughout the Boroughs," Alex said. "I just know this one because it's close by. I'm not great with directions, so usually it's my partner who finds the best places. I can't even find half of the holes in the wall that she does."

"The Boroughs are nothing but holes in the wall. You can't find places here when you've lived here all your life? And you're a cop?"

Every time Alex said he was bad with directions, invariably that was the response. Somehow, he hadn't come up with a good comeback yet, so he just took a giant bite of his burger. They finished the meal and, after a few more minutes of light conversation, made to leave.

"Hey, can I walk you home? I'm a cop, no one safer to walk with."

"Do you have a gun on you?" Haley asked.

He nodded.

"That makes two of us," she replied. "But sure, it'll give us a bit longer to talk."

Alex opened the door. Haley opened her umbrella and the pair walked close together as the rain started to pour. After a few minutes of walking, the buildings got taller and the wind flung rainwater at them from the open spaces between them. They broke into a near-run. Left turn, right, a straight run down a near-empty neighborhood that had so many boats converted into houses it looked like a pier, then a right. Houses started appearing, not houseboats but proper houses with concrete stilts deep into the ground below. Somehow, Alex remembered which one she lived in with her father. They stopped at the door and she turned to him, blue eyes breaking through the world's grey gloom.

"Thanks for seeing me, Alex," she called to be heard over the rising storm.

"Yeah, it was good," he said. "I really want—"

"You don't have an umbrella, do you? Just a coat?"

"Oh, no, I don't. But listen, I'm fine."

"Take this." She pressed the umbrella into his hand.

"I can't," he said lamely.

"Yes, you can. Take it."

"All right, thanks."

She reached for the doorknob when he blurted out, "Hey, maybe we can meet up again sometime. We can grab Indian food. And I can give you your umbrella back."

"Sure, sounds great," she said, smiling her wide smile, eyes shining, tiny raindrops on her cheeks.

"Okay... I'll see you around."

"See you, Alex," she said and reached out a hand for a quick, wet, side-hug. She opened the front door, stepped out of the rain, turned, waved one last time and closed the door.

Alex took a deep breath. He let his head fall back, closed his eyes and thought of all the things he should have said. He turned around and walked to the police station. As he entered, he shook the umbrella and felt a twinge of sympathy for all the cops left out in the rain. Criminals might be less active when it stormed, but cops couldn't be deterred by the weather. One guard sat in the waiting room reading a magazine, but aside from him, a receptionist and one woman who quickly ducked into an office, HQ was eerily quiet.

Alex took the elevator and flicked water off of his coat. He entered the office and turned on the light. Habitually, he looked over to Cassidy's seat. He grimaced and tore off his overcoat, pushing away the unwanted thoughts from his mind. He draped his coat on his spinning chair and leaned the umbrella against his desk. He turned on his computer and pulled up the Brice Noble file.

He flipped through the pages of the report, skipping past the autopsy photos of Mr. Noble and Yiril Zogheib. There was a single page on Rodney Maxwell, identification and a home address. It seemed obvious what was supposed to come next: check the house and go from there. No mystery to it, no detective work needed. Alex looked out his window just as a crack of thunder somewhere shook the walls. *I'm off the clock and I don't have my partner to back me up. Maybe I should stay inside tonight.* Alex minimized the file and pulled up his own notes and pictures taken from the Charles Tanning incident.

493 Gardener Avenue. I wonder if there has been any other gang activity there.

Alex stood up and walked over to his map of New York City. It was so filled up with pins that he couldn't find Gardener Avenue. He tapped his wrist and pulled up a GPS.

Searching for satellites.

He tried connecting to the wifi and an error popped up.

"Cheap piece of shit." *Never skimp on neural implants.*

He leaned in close to the map, squinting, looking up each individual street. *This'll take forever, there must be thousands of streets in the*

Boroughs.

As he searched, Alex started tracking each pin. *Black for drug incidents, grey for weapons, red for violence, purple for misdemeanors—why would I track misdemeanors across the whole city? No, these were just particularly suspicious cases.* Yellow tracked big name criminals, but the pins on the map were worthless, as they didn't tell him which criminals they were; those were on the map in his computer. *Pink? What the fuck was that again?*

He pulled up the garbage can and placed it under the map. As dexterously as he could, he tore the map off with its pins still embedded and threw it in the garbage. Loose pins of half a dozen colors fell to the floor. He fell to his knees and started picking them up, cursing as the first one drew blood. When he had finished, he put the trash can back in its place, sat down at his computer and typed in 'New York City' in an image search. The screen filled with pictures of floating skyscrapers. When he scrolled down, there were pictures of the city before it had flooded. Alex typed in 'New York City Map.' This time, the screen filled with varied maps of the city. He was about to click on one when he realized it couldn't have been New York City; at least, not his. His cursor hovered over a map of New York City before it went underwater. Most of the streets were the same, though some had disappeared and new ones formed. He leaned in and saw that dotting the entire map of New York City, from the Bronx to Queens and Staten Island, were little square 'M's.' He clicked on one and it read 'Metro.'

Alex clicked the save button. He opened up his map program, the one he had used to keep track of all the crimes, suspicious activity, and other random indicators he had completely forgotten about. By now, this map was even more cluttered than the one that had just been on his wall a few minutes ago, without a single inch of the Boroughs visible underneath the electronic pins. Alex edited the parameters, saving just 'drugs' and 'weapons.' Now the pinpoints were scattered across the Boroughs, concentrating in a few areas, but with no real pattern. It looked like Brooklyn had acne. Alex pulled up the New York City subway map, opened his map program and overlaid the subway map over his map of the Boroughs. He scaled for height, lining everything up as best he could. When the two images roughly corresponded, all of the 'drug' and 'weapons' hot spots centered around the metro stations while the space in between metros was mostly devoid of the pins, save for smaller-scale busts. Alex examined every individual station. He had to be crazy; there couldn't have been a connection. Then he took a closer look and saw that the highest rates of violence and drug busts in the city were all centered around half of the metros, while the rest of the city, including the other metros, were much less active.

Could the gangs be storing drugs and weapons inside the metro stations somehow? How is that possible? That seems too sophisticated. No matter how many of their low-level lackeys were caught, the drugs and weapons flow was never interrupted. That would explain why after nearly a decade, the police had never managed to catch the source of the drugs or the high level gang leaders.

Alex pulled out his projection cube from his desk and e-mailed the maps from his computer to it. He bolted upright, pocketed the cube and ran out the door. He took the elevator to the tenth floor and ran down to the end of the hallway. He stepped past the empty reception booth and knocked hard on the door. Normally, Captain Hewes was gone by now, but the light was still on and his frame cast a shadow on the door.

"Go away," he called.

Alex opened the door and stepped in.

Hewes look up from his desk and barked, "I said 'go away.' I have enough work to do on these disappearances and I don't need any distractions."

"It's about the disappearances," Alex lied. Recently, the department had been divided between tracking down the kidnapped rich or everything else, which had been unofficially labeled 'trivial.' No large undertakings had been issued, nothing controversial had been approved. Alex knew his only way to get the time of day was to say he had a lead on the disappearances. Alex walked around to the side of the desk and placed his cube in front of Hewes. He turned it on and pulled up the map of the Boroughs.

"Here is a map of the Boroughs with black pinpricks for major drug busts and grey for weapons busts. See how they are seemingly random, but the drugs and weapons are in the same area?"

"They are always like that. Drugs and weapons, you use one to get the other."

"Yes, but notice how the occurrences of these are completely random. They aren't near any ports or in particularly populated areas and no one major ethnic group or single gang controls the drugs and weapons. They are spread out everywhere, seemingly at random?"

"Seemingly." Hewes urged him onward.

Alex clicked a button that overlaid the old map of Brooklyn and Queens over the Boroughs. Alex saw his boss' tired eyes sharpen as he looked at it. "What am I looking at?" he said, scanning the image.

"I overlaid a map of New York City from before the flood. Now all the major drug and violence centers are concentrated around select metro stations."

He let Hewes look at it for a minute. He turned to Alex and said, "But the metro stations are underwater. What are you getting at?"

"Not every metro has gang activity around it, but every large center of major organized criminal activity in the city, at least based on the research I've done, is around a metro. Not only that, but the centers of drug and weapons activity just happens to fall in lines corresponding to the metro lines G, M, R and 7, connecting the Boroughs and Manhattan. This can't be a coincidence."

"So what are you saying? You have to say more than, 'this can't be a coincidence'."

"I think that the criminal organizations in the Boroughs are storing their drugs in the old metro stations. I don't know how, but something is going—"

"This sounds like a load of horse shit."

"A few months ago, hundreds of skyscrapers just rose out of the ocean, so nothing is impossible if you have money and balls, both of which Boroughs' criminals have. I think that some gang with a lot of foresight must have realized that the subway stations were the perfect place to store things. They are beyond any eyes, well below any, the subways can let up discreetly into storehouses so their routes are completely safe; it would be the easiest way to transport weapons and drugs."

"That would take a hell of a mind."

"If there's one thing New York City has never wanted for, it's inventive gangsters. This is the city where Frank Lucas and the Mafia changed the face of crime all over the world."

Hewes gave him a long look and Alex waited for the reprimand. After a moment, Hewes calmly said, "Interesting idea, Alex, but I can't act on a hunch. Not with resources strained as it is." He rubbed his forehead and chuckled. "I'm willing to try anything at this point, but there's no way I could get anything cleared without good evidence that it'll lead to something."

"What else do you have?"

He waited for Hewes to respond, but they both knew the answer.

"How long have you been captain? How long have you seen drugs and weapons appear out of thin air? How many times have you seen thugs and bruisers get thrown in prison or shot? Have you ever seen a true boss, a capo, a don, get locked up? Somehow, the big gangs in this city have managed to set aside their differences, hardly ever engage in gang-on-gang violence for reasons which we never knew, and they have more power now than they've ever had. I think I found out why. It's a hunch, but it's the answer to a hunch you've had for twenty goddamn years: that there's no way all the major criminal organizations can live in harmony unless there is something larger controlling them and forcing them to work together. If the kidnapped people are anywhere..." Alex looked at the map. "There's no better place I know of to look. I'm guessing you can't think of any either."

"Police Commissioner Kerry, City Council and the Mayor would never let me take one SWAT member or special investigator away from the kidnappings cases, especially if it revealed a more terrifying, sinister organization to terrify the public."

Alex stared him down and saw he wasn't going to flinch. He rolled his eyes and walked away. He heard metal chair legs scratch against the floor and he turned to see Hewes standing up. "Give me something, Alex. Anything. Until then, show some goddamn respect to a superior officer."

Alex stopped at the door. After a second, he nodded deferentially and left. The door closed behind him and he stood stock still, biting his lower lip. His mind was racing; images of a whole underwater network just under their feet flew past his mind. *To think that they're getting away with it when they're right there!* The more he thought about it, the more sense it made. *Radar can't catch them. There are so many machines operating just above the water. Hell, Manhattan alone is like one thrumming, roaring noisemaker on top of the bay; no radar or wi-fi can cut through it. If their scheme wasn't perfect before, it is now.*

Alex put his hand on the doorknob. He was about to throw it open when he got another idea. He let it go and walked away. He double-tapped his wrist and brought up his phone app. *Please be in a good mood...*

"Alex?"

"Hey, Cassidy, I had a question. You know those mini sub-cameras that you use to take pics of the undercity with? Are they expensive?"

"Starting prices are pretty high; maybe a month's salary for us. The good ones are a lot more. Why?"

"I was hoping to use one for a while."

"Well, you can use mine if you want. I haven't used it since March."

"You're the best."

"I know. I'll bring it in tomorrow."

"Thanks."

Chapter Thirty

Faint sunlight cut through the dark clouds and a gentle golden ray filtered through the thin windowpane of Frederico's safe house, illuminating the dust as it rose gently and danced in the light. Frederico looked out toward the horizon and saw a rainbow and was reminded of the joke New Yorkers told every time they saw a rainbow: that it was God's promise not to flood New York again. Frederico raised a cold glass of water to his lips and drank, savoring the chill feeling. For the past three weeks, he had been diving down and back up, meeting with Ezreal. Once, he thought he saw a shark, but he couldn't tell. The water was so dark that there could be a submarine just fifteen feet away and he wouldn't see it. Frederico had been filled with worry over Ezreal's rise to the surface, this conflict on the mainland, the Feds and SWAT teams marching down the streets, the Coast Guard patrolling the waters and the rumor of the Marines coming in to execute suspected gang leaders. *But if there's one thing I won't have to worry about anymore, it's fucking sharks.*

There was a knock on the door.

"Enter."

A man with a shaved head and tattoos all over his arms stepped inside. "Boss, there's something big happening outside."

"Speak up, Gustavo."

"A group of blacks are camped out on the other side of the street. Looks like they are all packing. Lloyd Jones is with them. He says he needs to meet with you personally."

"Let him in."

"He wants you to come out."

Frederico picked up his drink and gulped down the last of the water. He stood up and walked past him. From behind, he heard

Gustavo say, "We'll all be watching from the windows with AKs."

Don't bother, Frederico thought as he stepped down the rickety staircase. He knew what Lloyd was coming to discuss. He couldn't put it off any longer, as much as he tried.

Frederico stepped down into the entryway, where his worried soldiers looked on, guns in hand. "Relax." He passed by nonchalantly. "Don't you know I'm unkillable?"

He opened the front door. Directly across from him were ten black men, most of them taller than Frederico. They wore baggy coats, obviously concealing weapons. Not that Frederico expected anything else, as ten non-Hispanic men standing outside his safehouse, let alone in his neighborhood, would be insane not to carry heavy firepower. As Frederico walked across the landing towards them, the men parted and Lloyd stepped forward.

Frederico put his hands at his side and called, "*¡Mi hermano!*"

Lloyd wasn't amused. Frederico stepped inside the circle of Lloyd's posse. He could just imagine the guns lining up in the window. The men surrounding him must be thinking the same thing, as they were looking at the windows behind him.

"You couldn't talk over the phone?"

"It wasn't one of those conversations," Lloyd growled. "Let's walk."

"I'm not walking with a whole gang of your boys around me, truce or not."

"They're not coming." Slowly, eyes on Frederico's safe house, Lloyd's men walked down the opposite way.

"Just to the Petty Dock. We can speak there."

Frederico nodded. The walk was slow and he was on edge. At an intersection, they were passed by two men in suits with trench coats over them. Frederico guessed that they were FBI. They hadn't shown up in force, but their presence alone was troubling. He had never seen one in the Boroughs before the Miracle, yet he had seen six in the last week.

A minute later, they arrived at the Petty Dock, a small inlet that cut off 'Brooklyn' and 'Queens' northern docks.

"You are pretty trusting," Lloyd remarked. "This could have been a trap."

"I had a feeling you weren't looking to kill *me.*"

Lloyd gave him a cold look. "So you understand we have to kill Ezreal."

"Have to?"

"Yes, have to, did I—" He stopped himself from yelling at Frederico and took a second to calm down. After regaining his calm, he said,

"We don't need him. He had us all by the balls before. When he hid down there, we had to kiss his ass or else he cut off our supply and one of the other gangs took over. Hell, that's why you and I are on top. But now he's on the surface. When we see him tomorrow night for the next meeting of the bosses, we kill him."

Frederico cracked his knuckles and considered it. "It'll be dangerous. He'll have men around him."

"And I'll have mine around the house. That's my whole point; we don't need him. Our men outnumber his. He has a few loyal men, but no real army, not anything like ours. He has no following on land, hell, who knows if he even grew up here? Not many are loyal to him, he is just everyone's middleman. Tomorrow night, I'll blow his brains out and the second he stops breathing, his men will be ours."

Frederico looked at him warily. "You're betting with our lives."

"No one is loyal to a corpse. So you're in?"

"I didn't say that," Frederico shot back. There was an air of new menace mixed with the cold salt spray.

"You're either in or you're dead," Lloyd said. "I'm not showing up to that meeting knowing that you've been snitching in his ear."

"Who else have you talked to?"

"Every other boss. They're all in."

"I'm supposed to believe that?" Frederico laughed. "That you got all of them in on your conspiracy."

"I came to you last because you're his puppet on the surface. But you don't have to be. They all agreed because they know that without Ezreal, we don't have to pay a middleman for weapons or guns, all that money goes straight in our pockets. Then all this shit that's been going down in New York City goes away."

"Does it?" Frederico asked.

"Yes, it does. Why wouldn't it? Give it time. Things will go back to normal."

"And what about the hostages?"

Lloyd paused. "They know about how we move our drugs and weapons. If we let them go, one of them will talk. They have to be killed."

Frederico nodded. He knew it was unavoidable.

"You in?"

He nodded. "You're not giving me a choice."

"No, I'm not."

Frederico laughed heartily.

"What's so funny?" Lloyd grimaced.

"My men were so worried when I walked out the door and followed you alone. They were sure you were trying to kill me. But I know you; you want money, not war. There's only one person you want to kill."

"More than one, but he's the only one I need to right now."

"So much bark," Frederico chided.

"I can back it up."

"I know. That's why I'm saying 'yes.' All that time breathing in the salt water has messed with his brain. Now he's chasing ghosts."

"Well then, I'll put a bullet through his head and make it that much easier for him." Lloyd smiled at his own dark humor.

"It'd be a favor to us all," Frederico agreed and walked away.

Chapter Thirty-One

A lex bypassed Captain Hewes' secretary and knocked on the door.
"Come in."

Alex stepped through and, without a word, put a projection cube on his desk. He tapped his wrist twice, connecting his neural interface to the cube. He pulled up a video and Hewes watched as Alex dropped a mini-sub into the bay. The sub dove until it hovered just above the broken concrete sidewalk of the old city. A block in front of it was the opening to a subway station marked 'Marcy Avenue.' Alex fast-forwarded the video. After thirty minutes, two figures swam out of the station with a large waterproof case held between them, harpoons attached to their backs. They swam out past the view of the camera and the video ended.

Alex looked back at Hewes.

"You didn't follow them?"

"No point," Alex replied. "There are thousands of weapons storehouses, coke dens... the only thing that matters is down there. Just give me a team. You got your evidence, now give me a shot."

"What?"

"Let me form a team. We can do a dive."

Hewes glanced at the video screen as if it could give him the right decision.

"I'm quitting," Alex began slowly. "I'm leaving the city. I want to finish the Brice Noble case and wrap up a few other things, but I am doing what I should have done two years ago and getting the hell out of this shit hole. Give me some of your people that have nothing better to do and we can all go on this goose chase together. Or you can shoot me down, say 'no,' and keep stalling until you've exhausted everything else. Either way, I'll leave New York and never look back, but at least

I'll know I gave it a shot, and maybe when people do the autopsy of this city, I'll watch it on the news from an apartment in Kansas and know I was right."

Hewes put a hand on his chin. The fire in his eyes was nearly snuffed out. He looked exhausted and Alex suspected his hair was thinner than it was the last time they spoke.

"No," he grunted.

Alex looked down at his superior. He grabbed his projection cube and made for the exit. From behind him, he heard Hewes laughing just as he had opened the door.

"Maybe I was wrong," Hewes called.

Alex turned, angry and confused.

"I was going to say, 'no, you couldn't leave here, not without knowing.' But now you're leaving without putting up a fight? Just like that?"

Alex's eyes lit up. "Don't jerk me around, Captain."

"Would you be content? Leaving with unfinished business?"

"Which answer gets me the green light?"

"You have it. Now answer the question."

Alex took a second to think it over, but his mind was too distracted by his own mad scheme. "I would be content. Every second here is one less second of a 'what if' fantasy I have been playing over in my head for a long time."

Beneath his stern demeanor, Alex thought he saw disappointment in Hewes' eyes. *Of what? Is he disappointed I am not the dutiful cop he is? Or is he disappointed that I am leaving to start a new life while it's too late for him? Or maybe I am just seeing sadness where there is none.*

"It closes."

"What?"

"The door, what do you think?"

Alex smirked and stepped out, victorious.

The strike team had holed up two blocks north of Broadway in a decaying townhouse that had once been a small apartment a decade ago. It had since been taken over by squatters until just that morning, when a surprise raid had cleaned out the building. Alex sat on one of three trunks' worth of equipment against the far wall of the bare living room. Four other cops were milling about around him. Darcy and Chance were telling a story about a bust gone bad. Chance was smiling his boyish grin, but Alex could tell how nervous he was. Eddie and Jacob appeared on edge too, and had taken to looking out the cracks in the boarded off windows, occupying themselves with as much of the surface world as they could before they dove under. Alex was scared, too, but he was more excited than afraid. He knew there would be danger involved; he had heard a few rumors of sharks, octopi, even alligators, though he thought the water was too cold for the latter. He pushed those thoughts from his mind and tried to focus.

There was a knock at the door and the tiny pinpricks of light in the holes around it went dark. All eyes flew to it. Alex lifted his head up and called, "Enter if you want, but just know we're all cops in here."

There were chuckles all around as the door opened and Jim walked in. He looked them over and said, "You sure don't look the part."

"Maybe I'm undercover."

"You'll be underwater soon. Apparently, all the drugs in the city have been under our feet the whole time..." Jim sounded skeptical, which irritated Alex. "So what's going to happen when we go down there? The fish are going to see a bunch of cops and think, 'oh shit, hide the coke!'"

"You know, this is Brooklyn, I wouldn't be surprised," Chance called to laughs.

Jim smiled and the temporary tension between him and Alex diffused. "Oh shit, that must be it! That's how they keep getting away! The fish have been behind it all along."

"Yeah, why do you think they taste so bad?" Chance added.

"All right, all right, everyone awake now?" Alex called.

Chance turned to Darcy and whispered loud enough for the room to hear, "Meth."

Alex lifted himself off the trunk and looked at his team. "Okay, I think we all know of each other vaguely, but we might as well get formal introductions out of the way." He waved at Jim.

"Jim Peterson, I work the northern docks."

"Darcy Prager, south side!"

Alex motioned toward Chance before the meeting descended into chaos again. "Chance Williams. I work with Eddie, monitoring the ferries between Manhattan and the Queens station."

"I'm Jacob Nickelson and I do none of that, I'm just here to keep a lookout."

"And I'm Alex Waverly, I patrol near the center of Brooklyn. Obviously, you can see why you're all here." Alex stepped forward. "You all deal with crime in and around the docks, you probably have a little experience in the water too—"

"Especially if you fall in." Chance ended Alex's speech. "So why are you here?"

"Because I'm the guy who came up with the idea." He turned around and opened the trunk he had been sitting on. "We have wetsuits for five. Jacob is going to stay behind and watch this place for us. Each of these has small head lights, but let's keep their use to a minimum so as not to attract any attention. The rest of you can suit up in a second." Alex walked over to the second trunk, opened it and pulled out a titanium harpoon gun with a second harpoon attached to it. "Each of you will get one of these. If you see anyone else down there, do not shoot, even if they have a harpoon gun. Stay with the group and avoid them. If we do shoot them, that will attract sharks."

For the first time, there was a chill silence as his team finally realized the danger of the mission, except Jacob, who quietly said to no one in particular, "Good luck with that."

"Finally..." Alex walked over to the last trunk, opening it. "We have an assortment of tools to take with us. Bolt-cutters, a small vial of acid that I've been told can cut through any lock; don't worry, it is in an extremely durable seal, it won't just break on you if you bump into something; tear gas and guns in plastic bags to protect against water clogging them, one for each of us. Jim, Darcy and Eddie can divvy up the items. Chance is taking point with me." Alex took a look around the room. "Any questions?"

Jim raised a hand. "What do you expect us to run into down there?"

"No idea," Alex replied. "But at the end of it, I think we're going to find lots of drugs and weapons."

Jim and Eddie shared a look. Before they could say anything, Alex said, "There shouldn't be much security at all down there, if I am right. They have been relying on secrecy and moving large groups of people would be cumbersome." There was another momentary silence. "No other questions? Alright, suit up."

Darcy stepped forward, grabbed her wetsuit and walked into the next room. When she left, Eddie muttered, "Damn it," and disrobed. When they had finished, they each put on a thin plastic belt and hooked on the sealed guns. Alex hefted a harpoon gun just as Darcy walked back into the room. When they had doled out the equipment, Alex looked at his group, turned, and walked into the next room, trying not to feel stupid as his giant flippers slapped down against the floor with every step. There was a large square-shaped opening in the floor that the strike team had cut for them before leaving.

Alex sat on the edge, put his mask on, clicked on the light, and fell into the darkness. He swam out of the way and in a few seconds, Chance joined him, then Jim, Darcy and Eddie. Alex nodded at them and looked at his wristwatch. There was a map on its screen, but it couldn't connect to the GPS underwater, so he had to guess where he was going. He let himself sink a little and looked up to his left. Broadway ran above him, long, wide, cutting through the smaller streets. He followed it, looking downward. Beneath him were the concrete remains of New York City, which seemed somehow whole, unlike the stitched-together upper world. There were streets, the foundations of buildings, and even a mini-mart that had been left untouched, its glass doors covered in algae. There were steel cages that once housed trash bins and fire hydrants that connected to the long unused sewer system. Alex couldn't help but be distracted by what he was seeing. He felt as if he were rediscovering a lost city. Fish darted out of the way of the light as he dove deeper.

Then he saw it. He nearly missed the small opening, the manufactured crack in the sidewalk with a sign over it that read 'Marcy Avenue,' covered in grime, its letters faded.

"There," Alex said while turning on the short-range radio and dove down. They descended as one down the stairs, past the escalator. They swam down to the platform, into the all-pervading darkness. One of the subway cars was still there, covered in decades-old grime.

"Think we'll find something here?" Alex heard Chance's voice in his comm.

Alex swam near the middle car and tried to peer through the grime. "Doubt it…" he said, but all the same, he tried to pull on one of the doors. After a few seconds, he gave up and said, "No, stick to the plan, let's go to the maintenance and control rooms. They should be higher up, elevation-wise, and harder to find, not so much in the open like these."

The group pivoted and swam down the long tunnel Alex guessed was heading to Manhattan. He pushed himself forward, his head turning left and right, looking for any door.

"Do you hear that?" Jim asked.

"What?"

"Quiet."

The five of them stopped and listened. "I don't hear anything," Darcy said.

"I hear it," Chance interrupted. "Like a low rumble, just ahead."

Alex couldn't hear it, but he would follow any lead at this point. He kicked forward and raced down the tunnel. As he did, he heard the rumble get louder and louder. Pretty soon, he didn't even have to look for the door. The group turned. Alex's heart pounded and between the two sounds, he felt as if he would go deaf. He pulled on the handle of the rusty metal door in front of him. It swung open and a diluted light raced down to them. Alex looked at Chance, turned off his suit's light, lifted his harpoon gun and nodded. He began to swim up the shaft, his fins kicking against the stairs below him.

Alex's head crested the top of the water. At first, he didn't register it, he was so confused. Part of his brain tried to comprehend how there was air inside the stairwell. The other part of him was focused on the two men just in front of him, who were holding guns. In a second, he fell backward and desperately kicked back as fast as he could. Above him, he saw a bright flash and heard a deafening crash. He looked just in front of him where a bullet appeared, shining above his mask. Another one appeared, then another. The bullets cut into the water and slowed just in front of him. Then the explosions stopped. Alex watched, panting in horror as a dozen bullets stopped, suspended in water. Slowly, lazily, they fell down onto his chest. Alex shivered as they bounced off him.

Alex let his feet drop to a submerged step beneath him and planted his feet. He lifted the harpoon gun until its end was out of the water and fired at the man on his right, catching him in the chest. The man's body jerked backward awkwardly, his muscles spasming. The second man let the empty magazine in his gun drop to the ground as he replaced it with a new one. Alex dropped the harpoon gun, kicked until he came to the edge of the water, placed a foot on the lowest step and lunged. He instantly cursed himself, realizing how sluggish he was in his gear. Just as the man fitted the magazine into the gun, Alex leapt forward, desperately throwing himself on the man. The two tumbled and the man was caught awkwardly leaning against the far wall. Alex reached out, desperately grabbing for his right wrist. He slammed it against the wall, but his hands kept slipping and he was kneed hard in the stomach. Alex gasped in pain and fell to his knees. Through his fogging mask, he saw the man lower the gun to his face.

Blood exploded across his mask. Alex jumped back, patting his wetsuit, feeling for a wound. He ripped off the mask and looked at the fallen corpse of the man who had just been standing over him. A harpoon had cut clean through his skull, exiting out the other side of his head, resting on the stairs.

Alex looked over at the half-submerged Chance. He lifted his mask. "Holy shit."

"Just what I was thinking," Alex agreed, still stunned. "Nice shot."

"How is there air here?" Chance panted, clearly more concerned about the environment they were in, choosing to ignore the fact that he had just harpooned a man.

"I don't know…"

"Aren't we underwater? I mean, we aren't in here, but above this concrete there's… that's where we came from."

Alex nodded. "Oh, shit!" He pulled down his mask with one hand and said, "Come up, it's safe." In a moment, his crew surfaced. Before questions could be asked, Alex barked out orders. "Flippers off. There's a hallway up ahead, I'm going to need you to cover me, Chance. You three, carry the bodies up the stairs behind you. We don't want our entryway murking up with blood."

Alex retrieved the plastic bag with his gun, pulled it out and hugged the wall. Chance nodded and they stepped into the hallway, back-to-back, guns pointing in both directions.

"This is pretty damn narrow," Chance said over his shoulder.

"Yeah, run to your end, make sure there's no one waiting for us." Alex took off toward the door at the end of the hallway, hearing the faint wet patter of Chance's feet mirroring his own, barely audible above the thrum of the machine Alex assumed kept air in the station. At the end of the station, there was a metal door with rust coating every inch of it. Suspended on the old door was a brand new padlock. Alex lowered his mask. "Whoever has the bolt cutters, get over here now."

In a few seconds, Darcy ran up beside him, panting. She pulled off the bolt cutters from her back and Alex noticed that her hands were covered in blood. She gripped the padlock and snapped. As the lock fell to the ground, Alex kicked open the door and lifted his gun.

Nine wide-eyed people in soiled business suits and fine linen clothes cowered before him. Alex lowered his gun to his side. His heart beat wildly and he could hardly breathe. The people inside looked out at him with terror in their eyes, waiting; for death, for orders, for something horrific. Alex stepped forward. They cringed, but they didn't look away.

"It's all right," he said in a loud voice to be heard above the mystery machine's horrific rumble. "NYPD. I'm going to get you all out of here." Alex lowered his mask to his face and said, "Chance, find anything?"

"No more guards, but holy shit, the stash here! AKs, krokodil, heroin, meth, painkillers, tons of other bottled shit I don't even know! You won't believe what I have here."

A gray-haired woman lifted herself to her knees. Alex stepped forward, reached out a hand and helped her to her feet. "Whatever you have, I am pretty sure I can top it."

*   *   *

Until sunrise, the broken-down townhouse had been a squatter's den for cocaine addicts. By noon, it was the new Boroughs Police HQ, overseen by Captain Elba, who had brought with him over a dozen officers. Cops with shotguns stood outside the building, standing guard while nurses and EMTs stepped in and cared for the victims who were being pulled out of the tunnels by a new squad of police with more diving training than anyone on Alex's team had. By the time the sun was starting to set, all the hostages were up and receiving medical attention. There was hardly any room to keep the drugs and one of the newly rescued was forced to sit on a stack of cocaine bags as he was examined by a nurse.

"Waverly," Captain Elba called as he walked towards him. The floorboards creaked underneath his feet and Alex worried that the old building might not support all their weight. Elba stuck out his hand to him. "Well done. Well done."

Alex shook it. "Thanks, I had a hunch."

"Quite a good one. I'm sure you're going to be the hero of New York by tomorrow. I'm jealous. For now, though, you can head back to the station."

Alex looked around and couldn't see anything useful for him to do, but he didn't want to leave; he needed to be a part of this in some way. "Isn't there something I can do? I can keep watch."

"No," Elba ordered. "I have enough people doing that. Besides," he chuckled, "it should get a lot more crowded soon. I hear the mayor is even coming out here, press and all. There's going to be more bodies than I can manage."

Alex looked around the room and a strange sense of overpowering hope overcame him. Now that the root had been pulled out, the worst of the chaos and strife on the surface would die out. Alex looked around at the people he had helped rescue. *This is the real miracle here. Those machines just rescued the buildings from the sea. We rescued the people. But then again, I don't want to be here when the mayor's entourage arrives and the building collapses and everyone goes underwater.* Alex nodded at Elba, turned and walked out the door. He had a small smile that refused to go away plastered across his face as he walked back.

He entered the police station to cheers and smiled at how fast 'confidential' information spread as a crowd of people surged around him. He shook hands until his wrist went numb. He was slapped on the shoulders, pictures flashed and there was so much noise he could hardly hear anything, but he didn't care. After ten minutes of cheers,

Lieutenant Daniels calmed everyone down just long enough to say, "All right, remember, you are professionals," to some laughs. "Our orders are to keep everything as hush-hush as possible. No commenting to reporters, no posting about this on your blog or a video message, nothing about anything, especially the identity of the young police officer who figured this all out. It would be hell on the streets for him if the criminals knew who he was, so we aren't going to reveal his identity until he is living out in the mountains in Utah pumping out a shitty crime thriller about this."

After that, the party died down a bit and Alex could actually hear what people were saying. He answered questions and at one point stood on top of a desk and dramatically acted out when he and Chance each harpooned a guard. A few minutes after he had finished, Daniels clapped his hands and called out, "Don't tell them any more kid, otherwise they will never buy your book when it comes out. Back to work."

Alex jumped down from the desk and shared a last few smart remarks before his fellow officers dispersed. Most of them clocked out, though a few remained to fill out some last paperwork. As everyone filtered out, the main lobby suddenly became vacant. Alex sighed, looked up at the clock in the entryway, wondering if she would even still be here. *Better to get this over with sooner than later,* he thought, though he didn't believe himself and his foot felt heavy even as he took the first step toward the elevator. His pace had slowed to a crawl by the time he entered the hallway of the ninth floor. He grabbed the handle and opened the door.

Cassidy sat in the chair, looking blankly at her computer screen. The news was on and the blonde woman on the screen was reporting that some of the missing people had been found.

"Hey," Alex called to her.

Silence.

Alex was considering what he should say next. He looked at Cassidy, who still stared blankly at the screen. He knew she was waiting for whatever he had to say. He could dodge, try to make small talk, or come out with it. He couldn't decide, so he let the silence hang.

The story changed to a news flash about recalled peas. Cassidy still didn't look up. Alex knew she could outwait him, so he finally spoke.

"You can be a good cop."

She looked up. Her eyes were wide, almost feral.

"You can be a good cop, but I couldn't have taken you down there. The risks were too high."

Cassidy's mouth opened, but she didn't say anything. She tried again and managed, "You fucking bastard."

"Cassidy—"

"No. No, just don't. Don't 'Cassidy' me. Don't act like my friend. I'm your partner and you lied to me, used me and side-lined me. For one mistake!"

"I couldn't trust you. Not down there. I nearly died. Chance kept a calm head and had steady aim and he saved me at the last second. I'm not sure you would have."

"I make one mistake. One goddamn mistake and you use that as an excuse to act superior to me every fucking time we see each other."

"I nearly died because you screwed up; I couldn't have a repeat. And..." He waved his hands in front of him as if surrendering. "And it wasn't even just you. It was me too. If I went on a mission with you, I wouldn't be focused, I would always be looking over my shoulder."

Cassidy had begun to turn red. "So it wasn't me? It wasn't me, it was just that I am such a fuck-up you would be distracted by how much of a fuck-up I am?"

"That's not what I said."

"That is what you goddamn said!" Cassidy shouted and stood up. "We are a team. Do you know what that means? That means we stick with each other no matter what. We don't abandon each other or look for a way out or the next best thing. You don't fly solo, you trust your teammate and they trust you. But you chose not to work with me. You just come over to my place and you criticize me and without even giving me a chance, you turn me out and go on this all by yourself."

"This just came up. I couldn't wait for how long it would take for me to trust you again. But we can still be a team. We can work back up to where we used to be."

Cassidy shook her head. She bit her lip and her eyes watered. "No. No, we can't be a team. Not after this. I deserved it, when you came to my place and told me I fucked up. Maybe not the way you said it, but I deserved it. Then you started acting like you weren't my partner, like you were my boss. And now this. Now you run off, be the big hero, 'save New York City,' and you cut me out. We're done, I can't trust you."

There was a heavy silence between the two that seemed to last forever, before Cassidy finally said, "I filed for a transfer this afternoon. I am looking to do the same thing with a different partner. You still have to write me up, give me a recommendation. Or fuck me over. God knows, you are some big hero now; tell them that I can't be trusted in a tense situation out here and I will be lucky to work as a mall cop."

Alex sighed. "Cassidy..."

"No." She shook her head and pointed at him. "Don't." She stepped past him and walked out.

Everything seemed so perfect just a few minutes ago. Everything. He imagined a city where the drug houses and gangs could be dealt with rather than being accepted as inevitable. He imagined American flags, clean windows and stores, and people who could walk the streets at night without fear. It was a crazy dream, but it seemed like New York City was becoming the place for those sorts of things.

He opened up his neural interface and saw that Cassidy's recommendation papers had been e-mailed to him and were waiting to be filled out. *Fuck. Did I make the right call? Should I have brought her along?* The second he thought that, he pushed it from his mind, forcing it down. *Yes. Yes, I made the right call.* His stomach clenched and he felt a new weight on him. But he could weather any pressure now. He had changed in the last few days. He was a man with conviction. *I did the right thing today. Besides, this isn't going to matter for long anyway. I am getting out of here. Daniels was right; they won't let me stay in New York, not with a name as famous as mine. I can get a transfer out of here to somewhere far away. Somewhere with solid ground. Maybe I could even write a book.* He gave off a chuckle as he thought about it.

Things are going to be settled for me. Now, if I could convince Haley to come with me, then things will be perfect. He smiled, but then his eyes wandered to the empty chair across from him.

How did I push Cassidy away? I didn't mean to that night when I berated her. I tried not to think how much I would hurt her, just so I could get the necessary out of the way. Then we drifted apart more, and now I am trying to leave New York...

His head bowed. The triumph of the morning had been washed away. He looked at the blank report papers in front of him. He wanted to throw them out. He wanted his partner back, he wanted things to be the way they were before he left, everything else, every single, improbable and impossible thing had gone his way that day; was it so much to ask that a friendship that had lasted for years might hold on for another month before he left?

It's not too late, Alex. You can run down the stairs, catch her on the way out. If she is already out, then run down after her on the streets, and if she isn't there, run to her home. And then...

All she wants is an apology.

Alex pulled out his projection cube, opened up her recommendation file and began to write.

Chapter Thirty-Two

It was the first time Sophia had visited the Boroughs since the election. Her police escort cut its way slowly through a press so tightly packed Sophia was afraid they would start falling into the water. Her officers met the squad from the Boroughs and she squeezed her way into the building. She took a moment to talk to each of the rescued, reassuring them and hearing their stories while Captain Elba followed her throughout the building. At first glance, the scene appeared chaotic with medical supplies and drugs put up seemingly haphazardly throughout the building, but after a few minutes, Sophia grasped the strange, organized anarchy of it all. Elba ran a tight ship and he had trained those under him to the point where they were coordinating perfectly in the odd circumstances, as if they had one mind. Sophia broke away from the throngs of people and walked to a tiny alcove where no one was being cared for and turned to Elba.

"So you've found the source?"

"It's too early to tell," Elba replied, but the light in his eyes and the sound of his voice betrayed to Sophia an unshakable optimism. "But if you make some calls and cut through the red tape to bring me some trained teams, maybe bring in some Navy Seals, I think we could clear out the old subway stations in a matter of a few weeks, maybe even faster."

"You'll have everything you need," she replied with relief. An officer walked up to Elba and he turned to address a new concern. Without waiting for a formal 'goodbye,' Sophia delicately stepped over a tube, waved to a nurse whom she had been chatting with ten minutes ago and walked to the door. A guard grabbed the handle and opened it for her. Instantly, she was greeted by a flash of lights and microphones being pressed her way. She smiled and put her hands up, quieting them.

"Today, we have one of the most uplifting stories in a long time. Thanks to the brave work of the men and women in uniform, nine of the missing business leaders from Manhattan have been found and freed from their capture by criminal groups. So far, little is known, as we are just finding new information, but just know that what has happened here tonight is the best news that we have had in a long time and it is much appreciated."

A flurry of questions broke out. Sophia loved the chaos of breaking news on the street. It was something she could control. In a press room, individual people spoke and were heard; on the street, everyone was shouting and she could ignore the hard questions and answer the simplest, least informative ones. After a few questions, she heard one reporter through the tumult ask, "Since the root of the organized criminals' plan has been discovered, does that mean Manhattan will be staying?"

It was too long a question, Sophia was sure no one heard it but herself. Instead, she answered a question about who the brave cop was and she said, "I can't release that information just yet, but when it is revealed, we'll be sure to make a hero out of him or her. No more questions."

Her own group of four police broke through the pack of reporters and she was whisked away to the docks, where a police cruiser waited for her. She got into it eagerly; the Boroughs were never safe and she hadn't made many friends there. "To the City Chambers," she called to the captain. "Don't stop at the harbor, get there as fast as you can." The boat's captain nodded. A low purr resonated from the engine and the deck thrummed with the power of the boat. It cut through the water gracefully, hardly bobbing at all, even as it kicked up spray. Sophia looked forward and felt an intense pain as she gazed at beautiful Manhattan shining under the stars. She wanted to glance away, but forced herself to keep looking. *I am going to be strong. I need to be strong. I can't pass out again. Especially now that I have to stop a handful of idiots from ruining everything.*

At the City Chambers, she hurried to the elevator, not bothering to look dignified for the few people left there. On the third floor, she rushed to the City Council assembly room, where everyone was already seated and waiting. As she entered and saw the heads turn, she felt the strangest sensation that she was the enemy; despite her recent victory, she knew varied factions were conspiring against her. Proudly, she walked forward to the front of the room, taking her place opposite the council.

"This meeting of the New York City Council has been called into order," Speaker Brown called out, bringing down her gavel purely out of ceremony, as the room was as silent as a graveyard. "Councilman Chavez has asked to speak."

At the front of the room, directly across from Sophia, a towering man with leathery brown skin and a perfectly pressed blue suit stood up and folded his arms in front of him. He stepped forward, eyes locked on Sophia. He turned and faced the council.

"The best news that we could have ever received just came from the Boroughs today. Nine high profile missing people were found just hours ago. Since their disappearance and the security issue in Manhattan was the reason that we have sold off our skyscrapers, many of us have been talking and have decided that since the crisis is being resolved, we should keep our buildings here rather than sell them off to different cities."

"Except that's impossible," Sophia interrupted from behind him. "Most of the buildings have already been sold off."

"We can unsell them. Declare an emergency, call in the Governor, he could even order in the National Guard, declare martial law. We can keep our city if we have the strength and courage to save it."

That kind of speech was the kind someone running for office would make. Too bad the city will be gone before he gets the chance to run for mayor.

"No, we can't unsell them. Even if we kept the buildings themselves, the companies here in Manhattan have already started moving and relocating; some in anticipation of keeping their leases in the buildings, others abandoning them. If we kept the skyscrapers, then Manhattan would be a ghost town."

"Then we can rebuild."

"Yes!" a councilman cheered in agreement.

"No, we can't!" Sophia slapped her palm down on her desk. "I know you all want to live in this happy world where we can reclaim everything we have lost, but we can't. Even if our buildings have risen out of the sea, we are drowning in debt. So many companies and professionals have left due to the hostage crisis. In between paying off all the expenses of maintaining our city, I'm not sure that we could afford to keep it afloat another year."

A cold doom had taken hold of the chamber.

"Yes, one day, if we could manage to keep things running, then we could recover enough to start rebuilding. But we won't even make it to the recovery period. Even though a brave team of police officers from the Boroughs managed to free some of the hostages, they think that the organized crime in our city, mostly across the bay, is capable of more activity, and it would take months to break their hold on the city. We can't fight a crime war with all of our wealth gone. Meanwhile, the costs that we have had to pay to build that factory in Summit and build the new motors, combined with all our other debt, has us in a guaranteed state of bankruptcy, which is bad enough for any city, but when you have to pay through the nose for engineers and parts to keep us floating, bankruptcy means death. That's where we're headed." She looked at Chavez, then out to the council members and said, "I know we were all filled with hope when the skyscrapers first rose up. We don't want to think that we can't do anything, not after reclaiming our city. But what Chavez said was wrong. You can vote for his ludicrous plan to seize en masse private property in the absurd hope that it'll win back investors." She rolled her eyes. "But you'd be a fool to." As she finished, she could see the rage on Chavez's face and knew she had crossed a line of decency. Like I care. I'm not running for re-election anytime soon.

Sophia stepped down from her place onto the level floor and walked out to the first table, putting her hands on it and looking out towards everyone assembled. "I know this seems grim. It is grim. But even though we can't have the future that we want, we can have a brighter future than we thought we were going to have. The money that the city will be receiving is enough for each of us to live on for decades."

"And what about those of us left behind?" a woman from the Boroughs called out.

"There will be trillions that the Boroughs can use to hire enough cops to root out the criminals that have taken it over. You know, New York City used to be one of the safest cities in the world." She laughed. "I read about it a long time ago in a history book. With trillions going to infrastructure, education and a police force that knows the weak point of crime in the Boroughs, they can recover. I know you all don't like to be told that this is your only choice. I don't like being backed into a corner, least of anyone. But this is our only choice and it's still a good choice."

She looked at Chavez. He held her glance, hatred in his eyes. He looked as if he wanted to stare her down, but she was in no mood. She turned back to the council and said, "I'm not sure what we're voting on; there isn't really anything that can be done at this point. But whatever it is, please, don't support it. Don't throw our city into chaos when it needs leadership more than ever before, even if it doesn't understand what we're doing." She stayed at the table, looking out at the council.

Chavez wouldn't be beaten so easily. "I propose a motion to rescind the selling of every one of our skyscrapers. To achieve this, we will seek every means possible, including state and federal procedures."

There was a dead silence that followed.

From behind, Speaker Brown called, "Do I hear a second?"

Chavez looked to his table at those members closest to him. One of them shook his head.

"Motion fails." The gavel came down again. "If there is no other business to be settled, I suggest we all head home. Any other calls to attention?" After a second, Brown called, "Meeting adjourned."

Sophia didn't bother to stick around or make small talk. She walked past the rows of tables. Thankfully, the rest of the council members didn't seem to want to chit-chat either. As she walked out, she felt a strange sense of triumph come over her, one that she hadn't felt in a long time. How many times have I saved this city in the last few days? First Buhari threatening to blow it up, then he did and I had to do damage control, now Chavez tries to drown us with his good intentions. But history won't remember me for any of this. She put the thought aside. She didn't want to think about what people had or would say about her. She preferred her own opinion of herself, and ever since she realized she would never run for office ever again, she had stopped caring at all for anyone else's opinion of her.

Except one person.

She walked down from the City Chambers to the canal. There were a handful of police officers walking in front of it, checking the cabs that stopped for licenses. She got into one of the boats, told the driver her address and they took off. As the boat hummed through the canals of Manhattan, she looked up at the stars and remembered the night she got engaged to Charlie. As she did, she saw the nearest skyscrapers turn deep red, and at their base were palm trees and white sand. As the boat turned, she saw the skyscraper to her right towering above a small town with a few historic cobblestone roads, gas lamps and Victorian townhouses. She didn't know if she was assigning the right skyscrapers to the places they would arrive in, but the images still came to her mind, unbidden. A wave of calm rolled over her as her city was no longer decaying; it was just splitting up and moving on.

When they arrived, she was in such a strangely whimsical mood that she gave the cab driver a twenty thousand dollar tip. She turned into her apartment building and took the elevator up to the twenty-eighth floor. She knocked on 47. She heard Charlie's heavy footsteps from behind the door. He opened it and looked down at her.

"Hi." He sounded a little shocked and not quite pleased. "I didn't expect you."

Sophia wrapped her arms around his neck, stood on her tiptoes and kissed him passionately. He put his hands on her sides and looked down, a twinge of a smile on his face.

"Hi," he tried again.

He closed the door behind her.

"I'm sorry. I'm so sorry, I really am. I kept trying to get away from work to see you, but I really couldn't," she begged.

"No, no, it's all right." Charlie suddenly felt bad for being so stand-offish to his fiancée. "I understand. I see you every time the news is on anyway. Sounds like a lot has been happening. I hear some good news finally crossed your path." He perked up a bit.

Sophia put a finger on his lips. "That's out there. I just want to be with you now."

He smiled, leaned down and they shared a long kiss.

Sophia looked back up into his eyes and said, "I'm never going to disappear like that again. Pretty soon, Manhattan will split up and you and I will ride this apartment like a giant ship all the way to Washington and we'll have enough money to retire. We can stay there, or we can move inland. Or across the world."

"Where do you want to go?"

She laughed and lowered her head against his chest. "You pick. I never want to make another decision again. I have had to think for this whole city. I just got back from a meeting; this idiot, Alberto Chavez, tried to sink all of Manhattan."

"Oh, did he now?" Charlie laughed. "And you rushed in and saved us?"

"Yes, I did," she stated confidently.

Charlie kissed her on the top of the head. "Well, thank you. This city's been a pretty scary place lately. I know I can sleep at night knowing that you are out there, fighting crime, swimming the canals and talking to fish. Where would New York City be without its great protector?"

She lifted her head and looked up into his eyes. "You don't want to know."

"I probably don't." He kissed her again.

Chapter Thirty-Three

The news that there had been a raid on one of the subway stations had reached Frederico an hour before the meeting was supposed to take place. He walked toward the edge of what was once the Queens-Brooklyn border, along with a posse of two other members of his crew, feeling an immense weight in his stomach. Ezreal's floating mansion was in a nicer part of town, with two-story or higher buildings more common than one-story shanties or houseboats, and most of these had open windows and lights on. Frederico glanced aside at the houses as he passed, knowing that on all sides of the three-story mansion, Lloyd's men had moved in, taking up spots in the apartments and houseboats around it.

Frederico knew Lloyd had been planning to take down Ezreal for a long time. His spies told him that he had once hoped to cut him off on solid ground and then starve him from below, something which he never successfully sold to the other crime bosses due to the cost. Now that Ezreal had moved to the surface, Jones could take him and his organization out in one fell swoop.

There were two men standing outside the door to Ezreal's mansion. Normally it would have seemed suspicious, but with all the violent activity in the last month, every rich person had started hiring bodyguards. Frederico walked up to them with his crew as a lightness in his chest decided to join his queasiness.

"Frederico Vasquez." One of the men held up a hand. "You can go inside, but your men can't." Frederico nodded and stepped forward. The bodyguard held out a hand and said, "They can't hang around here. They would draw attention."

He turned around. "Go home, boys."

"But—" one of them started to say until he saw Frederico's *do not question me in front of anyone else* look. He nodded and the two turned and walked away.

"Please, step inside," the bodyguard intoned, opening the door for him. *No pat down? Ezreal must think he's invincible. The irony will make this all the better.*

The brightly lit mansion showcased all the glamor that was lacking in Ezreal's subterranean lair. There was a polished oak staircase leading up to the second floor and Persian carpets of all different colors and patterns were laid down in the entryway. Deep purple wallpaper with a golden crown design covered the hallway and a grandfather clock with dials for days, months and years rested against the wall. *Not the sort of house I would expect a sociopath to live in.*

"Frederico," a voice called from his right as he stepped into the massive living room. Ezreal and the rest of the company stood around a faux fireplace, sofas and chairs left vacant. Frederico looked around the room and realized there were no photos anywhere, no childhood trophies, nothing that would indicate that a feeling being lived there. *That's closer to what I expected.*

"Now we're all here." Ezreal looked aside, his tone as grim as death. Frederico joined the group, stepping into the half oval that had formed around Ezreal. Lloyd shot a look at him. Frederico saw him, but kept his eyes straight at Ezreal. Lloyd looked at the rest of the group, who met him with a similar response.

"I am sure you all have heard by now," Ezreal said. "Our plot has been found out, it seems."

There was a calm silence. Ezreal opened his mouth to speak again, but before he could, Lloyd chimed in, "I guess you were wrong."

Ezreal looked up at him. "Wrong? About what? I was wrong about nothing. Blood has started spilling, the people grow more militant. They want this fight, they think they can win this fight. Ramos' crumbling government can't beat us down forever, even if they are hitting our seedier operations."

"They found people captured, starving down there," Frederico interrupted. He had looked worried before, but when confronted, Frederico showed no fear. "How else can they see whoever did that and view them as anything but enemies? They can't pin this on any of us, but the cops know who the big bosses are, and now they know that the guns and drugs have been shuffled through the subway. They will put two and two together and bring us down."

"They have nothing to link what is done underground to us, I made sure of that. I was careful, I was professional. If you go down, it is your own fault."

"They don't need proof!" Frederico bellowed at Ezreal. Everyone in the room visibly stiffened. Even Lloyd was shocked. As much as he and probably more than a few people in the room hated Ezreal, he had always seemed like a mysterious creature that lived under the waves and held a stranglehold on all of them, like some ageless kraken. Now that he stood on the surface, surrounded and reprimanded by an underling, he seemed much less godlike than before and more like the sad, defeated man standing beside the empty fireplace. "They have the National Guard at the plant in New Jersey and word is they are going to be all over here too, up until Manhattan is gone. With whatever is left of New York under the army's control, at best, we will lose our hold on the streets and have to hide away until they're gone; at worst, martial law is going to be imposed and they are going to bring us down. With New York turning into a military base, it is the end for us. You've made us lose everything as part of this mad scheme."

A deep silence followed. Ezreal arched his back, raising himself to his full height, though he was still a head shorter than Frederico. "Well, then," Ezreal said with an easy calm that made Lloyd tense up. "You should be my strongest supporter. You know what will happen when the army rolls in. We will need a strong man with a vision, someone who can take them on. If we just sit on our hands, we lose everything."

"And you think that's you?" Lloyd spat. "You failed to start a revolution back then, all you did was cause a few riots and get a lot of people killed, mostly your own. And now you've done the same. Look at you, you pathetic freak." Even though the room was fast turning on Ezreal, the open mockery caused a shiver to run through Frederico. "Can you take a guess why people don't follow you? You're an angry little bitch that dreams he's a king, but everybody can see the truth but you." Lloyd turned to the rest of the group. "The army will leave once Manhattan is gone. We can rebuild then, take back everything we lost. We just have one thing to do before then." Lloyd's hand shot into the inside of his jacket and grabbed his gun.

"Stop." His brother Andre breathed quietly from behind. Lloyd looked over his shoulder. Andre had pointed a gun at his head.

"What the fuck are you doing?"

"I went to Ezreal," Andre explained, "once you started meeting up with the other bosses, plotting to kill him and put yourself in his place."

Lloyd felt the gun in his hand and Frederico saw that he was clearly questioning his options.

"I'm your blood, Andre."

"So was our uncle. But you struck a deal with Ezreal. You killed him and took over in his place. I asked Ezreal if he would still accept the same deal for me and he said yes." Andre looked past Lloyd to Ezreal. "But it's not enough."

Lloyd felt a twinge of hope, but the gun was still pointed at his head. He looked over at the rest of the bosses; they were frozen stiff.

"What do you want, Andre?" Ezreal asked calmly.

"Make me an offer."

"Goddamnit, what the fuck are you doing?"

"The Freedom Tower. It'll be ironic, at least." Ezreal smiled.

"No deal. I want the Empire State Building."

"That is where I intend to move the city council to, once I am elected mayor, of course," Ezreal said calmly.

"You can rule from anywhere." He smirked. "You did it from tunnels underground and underwater. But symbols have power. If I had the Empire State Building, no one would fuck with me. I want it."

Ezreal paused. "Done."

"Come to your senses, Andre, he's—"

Lloyd's brain splattered across the wall and the windows. Andre turned, gun aimed at the other bosses.

"No, no, Andre, no," Ezreal said. "Put your gun down, but not away." Ezreal turned to the rest of them. He breathed calmly and looked at them invitingly. He began to smile. "Whoever shoots Frederico first wins his way back into my good graces."

Frederico backed up and reached inside his jacket for his gun. Cesare already had a hand on his. Just as Frederico leveled his gun at Ezreal, Cesare whipped out his own and shot Frederico in the chest once, then again and again, until his clip was empty. Frederico fell to the ground in a bloody heap, twitched for a few seconds, then fell still.

"Guns away, please," Ezreal intoned like a father chiding his children. "I knew there was a plot, but I chose to face it. I am not afraid, not this time. I have faced death before." He waved his hands out. "And here I stand!" He laughed. He waved at Lloyd and Frederico's corpses. "And my enemies lay dead while I didn't so much as lift a finger." He gazed at the remaining bosses. "It is true; the army is coming and Manhattan is leaving. But there is something in our favor. Once I heard that they had found one of our hiding places, I ordered my men to pull up all our weapons they could. We will need them for our fallback plan. It is not the plan I wanted. This plan will see a lot more bodies piling up, but we will win the battle for Manhattan. We will not walk away with nothing. When the time comes, we will sail back with everything."

Chapter Thirty-Four

When morning came, the people of the Boroughs were woken up by the blaring of ships and the sound of heavy boots pounding in unison on the boardwalk, first many on the docks, then fewer as they neared the center, then two by two, marching. Rodney had been dozing as peacefully as he ever did in the past week, the gentle rocking of the stray row boat he had been crammed into lulling him to sleep. When he looked up, two National Guardsmen looked down at him with suspicion. Rodney leaned back, panicking. His mind told him to grab the gun he had stowed in the back of his jeans, but he was too afraid to move. The troops walked on, leaving Rodney to stare after them.

"I had heard I was going to see some strange things in New York City, but nothing could have prepared me for this."

"It's a wonder people still live out here. Get on dry ground, people!"

Rodney's muscles still tensed even after the two turned down the road, their heavy thudding echoing in the light morning air. Rodney lay back down uncomfortably against the crossing board on the small boat. He tried to close his eyes and let his mind rouse, but the pain in his back forced him to shakily stand up and climb back onto the walkway.

He started walking, but didn't know where he was walking to. He felt a hollow weight in the pit of his stomach. *I don't have much money left, certainly none which will last me. Maybe I should steal a boat? No, the waters are being watched by the freaking Navy now, there's no way out of the Boroughs without them catching me and when they find out the boat is stolen, then I'll be brought into a station.* He passed by another patrol and saw a third down another street, walking at the edges of the gathering morning crowds, and thought better of it.

Rodney walked down a side street and a waft of warm, fresh baked bread escaped through a window. He put his hand on the door and was about to walk inside. He passed it and hoped that the soup kitchens were serving breakfast. If they were, it would be a good way to save some money, at least for a little while, while he figured out a plan.

What's the plan? How long can I keep hiding? It's not like the police are never going to find me. They'll get me eventually, won't they? His heart began to pound and his eyes were on the ground. He nearly ran into someone as he passed the narrow walkways on the edge of town. Rodney saw Sam's worried face and he suddenly felt panicked. *How long can I avoid her? There's no way I can get to her, and if she comes to me, I'd be putting her in danger... but I have to get away. I have to see her, before Manhattan sails off...*

Rodney pulled out his phone and called Sam.

"Hey, Rodney." He could tell she was tired.

"Hey, baby." He smiled and looked around, making sure no one was nearby. "God, I've missed you."

"Me, too. How's the job searching going?"

"Heh..." He paused. "I haven't given it much thought, really."

"Oh. I'm sorry, baby. You should come see me. I could cook us something nice and we could just relax at my place for a while. What do you say?"

"I wish I could, I really do. There's nothing more I could possibly want than to see you. But I can't."

"Why not?"

He grimaced and looked over his shoulder. "I'm not even sure I can say it over the phone, they might be listening."

"Who?"

"The police. Everything is on lockdown here, it's like a giant floating prison."

"Why would the police be listening to your phone? What's going on?"

"I... I can't say exactly, but when I was hanging out with Antoni and Grease—"

"Oh, those two? You know I never liked them."

"Well, you were right." Rodney laughed hollowly. "I was desperate, I just wanted to make money and see you. But I ended up seeing something, being somewhere I shouldn't have been. I don't think it would be safe for me to try to take the ferry."

"Oh god, do you have money? Do you need some? Let me help you.

I can come out there—"

"No, no, no, don't. Stay there. I have a plan. It's not perfect, but... I hear Manhattan is taking off in a week. When it leaves, the National Guard, the Navy, all that will be gone. When they are, I am going to take a boat and hit land. Then I can just follow you wherever you end up and we can be together."

"Can you make it? Do you have money?"

"I have some. I can hitch a ride, or, hell, I could even walk. There's nothing else I have going for me except you. If you're willing to wait for me, that is."

"You idiot. Of course." She laughed. "Well... okay, I can wait. Just stay safe for the next week. And when you hit land, be sure to call me every day, tell me all the crazy stuff you see on the way."

Rodney genuinely smiled. "Thanks. By the way, do you know where your building is headed?"

"Yeah, Augusta, Georgia."

"Damn... that's a long way to walk."

"It'll be good for you. And I'll be waiting at the end with some sweet tea and grits."

"Can't wait to be somewhere warm. I'll see you as soon as I can, I promise."

"Okay. Be safe."

"I will. Love you."

"Love you too."

It was a long time before Rodney hung up. He felt a heavy weight return to his stomach. He knew his situation was dire, but he had a reason to go on.

Now I have to survive until then. He turned and looked back. *Where to? The mission?* He didn't like the thought of that; too public. He started walking to his house. *The police must have searched my house by now. Maybe if my house has already been searched, they won't be looking there again.*

As he walked, a newfound hunger came to him. He nearly knocked into another pair of guard troops as he passed through the busier districts en route to his house. The streets were deserted and he arrived back at the little blue-painted houseboat with its drawn white curtains. The sun was setting and the lights were off. *That's a good sign.*

Rodney looked around, stepped up to the door and turned the handle. *Locked. Another good sign. The cops wouldn't have the key and probably wouldn't bother locking it if they did.*

Rodney reached into his pocket and pulled out the metal key. The door opened with a loud creak and he stepped inside. As he did, he saw a dark flash at the corner of his eye and felt cold metal press against his neck. His heart began to beat fast as his warm skin kissed the cold opening of the gun.

"Rodney?"

"Grease?"

He felt the gun lower.

"Jesus, man, what the fuck was that?" Grease yelled, closing the door. He locked it and peered through the closest window.

After recovering from the shock, Rodney breathed, "What are you doing here? This is my house!"

Grease looked up at him. "And yet you've been gone two days."

"You've been living here two days?"

"Yeah." He suddenly became defensive. "Only going out for food. You haven't been here, what do you care?"

Rodney shook his head. "I went on the run. I saw Yiril got shot by the cops and figured they were after us. I tried calling Antoni, but he didn't pick up."

Grease looked down.

"What is it?"

"He's dead. Word is he was executed by his own gang."

"What for?" Rodney went numb.

"It has to be because we killed that rich guy in Manhattan. I can't think of anything else, Antoni and I were always involved in stuff, but nothing big, nothing that would make anyone want to kill us. Three days ago, these thugs came out of nowhere and started shooting at me. I dove into the water, swam as far away as I could, nearly died of the cold. I have been running and hiding ever since. I figured if they were coming for all of us, then maybe if they already killed you, I would hide in your place."

"Thanks for looking out for me."

"Hey, if I had known, I would have warned you, but you split and I didn't want to use a phone."

"Well, now I'm here." Rodney didn't mean for that to sound like a threat, but Grease seemed to take it that way.

"So here you are," he repeated, sizing him up. Rodney looked down at the gun in Grease's hand, knowing he could never get to his in time, or if he could ever pull the trigger.

"Look, since we are both here and in the same boat, so to speak, we might as well look out for each other. Same enemies, same problems." Rodney looked around and saw that what little he had had moved and there was a broken cup in the corner of the room. "Did you make this mess?"

"No." Grease sounded too defensive, but Rodney couldn't be sure.

"Yeah? If you're not lying, then that means this place was searched by the police, or by the people trying to kill us; maybe both. If so, then maybe they will pass us by for a while. We can camp out here, take turns going out for food."

Grease nodded jerkily. "Yeah, yeah, yeah…" He stared off with a gaunt look in his eyes and Rodney wondered how long it had been since he had food. *He better have some money. I might not have enough for the both of us for a week.*

"Then what?" Grease asked.

Rodney looked off. "Let's figure that out when we get there. Can you put your gun away?"

Grease looked down as if he just realized he had it out. "Yeah, yeah, yeah, yeah…" he said, putting it into the back of his pants. He scratched his head. Rodney felt a pang of guilt. Antoni's death sank in and Rodney realized Grease was the closest thing he had to a friend. *And I'm going to leave him behind? With people who are going to kill him? Maybe I can convince Sam to take him with me.* An image of Grease stabbing the old man came back to him.

You did this to yourself, Rodney thought, and repeated that thought to himself over and over in his head. Rodney had already picked out which door he was going to slip out of when the time came. *Just survive one week.*

Chapter Thirty-Five

Trepidation hung in the air thicker than salt throughout the Boroughs. Nowhere were the people more nervous than in the Eye. Ezreal's podium had been left in its center, waiting to be filled. Even empty, it had betrayed an unspoken fear and excitement to the people who circled the Eye. When Miles stepped off the side street and into the massive crowd, he began to assimilate to the comfortable rage the crowd felt. Ezreal hit all the right notes that night. He was vague enough in his outrage that he appealed to the youthful need to rebel and the elderly fear of losing what they cherished to the new. He would ask questions where the answer was a roaring 'NO!' It wasn't hard when you had such an obvious hate figure: corrupt politicians and elitist rich. And of course, Manhattan was so close that the crowd could look over and see what was 'theirs,' which the corrupt politicians and capitalists were trying to take away.

I could do that. I do do that, Miles thought.

This time, though, Ezreal ended his speech with a direct call to action. "Find your representatives and demand that they hold a special election for everyone in New York City. They think that they can get away with this?"

"NO!" the crowd roared.

"Yes," Miles said under his breath.

Miles looked over his shoulder. There were pairs of National Guard staged at every street entrance. They gripped their guns and watched the crowd rather than the speaker, looking tense.

But Ezreal isn't attacking the whole government, or asking for violence. He is using violent rhetoric, sure, the type that leads whackos on the extreme to go on shooting sprees while he can deny he ever called for violence. Ezreal seems a lot smarter than the kook he is portrayed as in the media.

Ezreal ended the speech just as the sun was setting. When he stepped down from the podium, the crowd clamored around him. Miles tried to push his way through, but the calls of adoration and questions were drowning him out. Ezreal answered a few while walking, appearing for all the world like some wizened sage, minus the massive brutes who shadowed him wearing trench coats. As cold as it was, Miles couldn't help but think they were covering up gang tattoos. *Or maybe I am just a prejudiced fuck who thinks every poor person is out to murder me. Get out of my head, Mylie!*

Ezreal's trail started to dwindle the farther he got away from the Eye. Eventually, it was just Ezreal and his men, who looked over their shoulders with glares that told him to stay away.

"Ezreal!"

"I'm done answering questions," he called back in a surprisingly harsh tone.

"How would you like to get your message out?" Miles called after him.

He kept walking. The two goons behind him started to approach Miles.

"I'm Miles Buhari," he shouted. "Ambassador of the whole fucking planet."

The two men were towering over him when Ezreal turned and ordered, "Wait." He walked over to Miles and looked him over. "These are dangerous streets. I wouldn't advise shouting your name. I can think of a lot of people who'd want to kill you."

"Care to give me a list?"

Ezreal cracked a genuine smile that wasn't any less creepy for its authenticity. "How about everyone in New York City? The have-nots for your money, the haves because you say everyone except you doesn't deserve wealth."

"Like you?"

"I don't annoy them. I terrify them."

"Ah, well, in that case, maybe you can teach me. The whole world is watching what is happening in New York City right now. Everywhere on Earth, people care more about what's happening here than in their own back yard. You give me an interview and I can put you in the center of it."

"I already am at the center of it."

"A boogeyman that's thrusting the city into chaos is at the center of it. I can give you a face; a human one."

Ezreal chuckled. "That's just what I wanted to hear. You can never trust media people. They're in their job for scandal, all because it sells. The only truth that ever gets out is when something really awful happens."

Miles nodded. It took a colossal amount of effort for him, the man who called out more bullshit than any other human on the planet, not to laugh at the irony. "So when can I interview you?"

"Tomorrow evening. Six P.M."

"Sounds good. Where shall we meet?"

"Tell me where you're staying here. I will send my men to escort you to my house. You can't be too careful nowadays."

Miles felt uneasy at the thought of the people staring him down as his personal escort. "The Seaside on Broadway," he said truthfully. "I'll be waiting in the lobby a half hour before."

Ezreal nodded. "My men will be there, Mr. Buhari. I look forward to getting the truth out."

As the entourage walked off, Miles was about to say something to himself, but grimaced in pain. There was a dull ache in his stomach. His insides had healed and the hole had patched up, but he still felt sore. For a second, his clothes were incredibly heavy and he felt a horrible wave of nausea. The feeling passed slowly and though he felt light-headed, he managed to keep steady.

"Well, that's a good sign."

Miles walked into the Brooklyn police station HQ, passing through security and into the main lobby, where there was an unusually relaxed atmosphere. Two officers were conversing in a doorway and the receptionist in the center of the room was talking quietly into a small black bar. Miles had to do a double-take; it'd been so long since he'd seen a physical cell phone. *To think there are some people in America that can't afford to be wired and have a permanent link to all technology 24/7.* Miles couldn't imagine how boring that must be.

Miles walked up to the counter, where a woman was talking absentmindedly. After a few seconds, she finished her conversation, said a command word and the invisible bullet-proof glass shield dropped.

"Hello, how can I help you?"

"I'm looking for Alex Waverly."

"For what purpose?"

"To report a crime."

"Sir," she said with a hint of annoyance, "you can report the crime to me and I will have an officer meet with you."

"No," he said, "it has to be Alex Waverly. Tell him I have something bigger for him."

The receptionist gave him a suspicious look. "Your name?"

"Miles Buhari."

"Hang on. Command: raise." The shield raised again. The receptionist started talking, though Miles couldn't hear a word of it. He began to worry, as he remembered some of the columns he had written about the Boroughs police force. After a brief moment of panic, the receptionist turned to him, lowering the shield. "He's out, but his partner Cassidy Kikia said she would talk to you."

"Thanks." *I like this girl; she must not know who I am.*

He waited a few minutes when a short woman with long, dark hair stepped out of an elevator. Her piercing eyes spotted him and walked across the lobby to meet him.

"Mr. Buhari?"

"Call me Miles. I was looking for Alex Waverly, but I was told you're his partner?"

"Currently. I'm Cassidy Kikia." She uttered the name with pride. "And in a few weeks, I will be with someone else."

"Well, if you're as bold as he is, then maybe I can share some information with you."

"About what?"

"About how I can help you make the biggest bust in the Boroughs history. Even bigger than the one you two went on in the subway."

Cassidy tried not to show any emotion. "How do you know Alex was involved in the subway bust? We've been trying to keep it under wraps, especially the names of the people involved. I wouldn't think civilians would have much information, assuming you are a civilian, which you appear to be."

"I am, and proud of it, no offense to those who work in the public sector," he said, smiling, though his charm didn't work on her. "Well, sorry if I broke through some privacy walls. Actually, your name didn't come up, Officer Kikia. Nor any of the other squad members. Just Alex Waverly's. Word spreads among journalists and we have our contacts within the police department. They say he is going to be America's new hero, replacing Marko Sverichek. 'The hero who dove down and saved all of New York City.' They're probably going to put him on the front of every news site in America when the city feels safe enough to release his identity to the public."

Cassidy was fuming, her eyes narrowing, her face turning red, her fingers stiffening. She looked like she would explode.

"Good for him." She tried to sound pleased, but instead sounded as if she were hacking up bile. After a few seconds of heavy breathing, she began, "You said that you had information that could lead to a bust bigger than the one he was in."

"Maybe," he replied. "It's a possibility."

"What is it?" she demanded.

Miles leaned in. "What do you know about Ezreal Redding?"

Cassidy furrowed her eyebrows. "The un-medicated lunatic who gives a speech every other day calling for the overthrow of the government, blocking up the walkways near all the best shops?"

"He's not a lunatic," Miles intoned gravely. "I've listened to a few of his speeches before television stations stopped broadcasting them. I came in today and heard another. He is a brilliant man, sounds like he has experience rallying up crowds. He has quite a lot of power, though I suspect he won't use it well. Remember the attack on the motor plant in New Jersey?"

Cassidy nodded.

"The media, the government, everyone involved started panicking about a broad lower class movement, that it might disrupt the selling off of Manhattan. I heard you and even the police in Manhattan were planning for riots, and yet while everyone was panicking and losing their heads, no one bothered to ask the simple question... who owned the boats that took them to shore?"

Cassidy paused.

"About four dozen boats showed up carrying angry people to that shore. Yet the Boroughs is a poor place and Ezreal's message appealed to the poorest people. So how could a riot realistically take place when the people most likely to be angry are mostly without transport? I went over the footage from the riot, the little security footage that had been released to the public, and amateur videos of the event, getting the licenses of the boats. It was fucking frustrating, let me tell you, trying to zoom in on shitty footage and pick out the names and identifying numbers of all these boats on low quality, far away, shaky cam footage, but I was in the hospital recovering from a gunshot wound, so I didn't have anything else to do. Anyway. It turns out that all of the boats couldn't be found in a government database and are unlicensed."

"The Boroughs has had that problem for as long as I have worked here. Lots of boats go unregistered."

There was a pause as Miles looked at Cassidy.

"Okay," she said. "Yeah, it is suspicious."

"He can organize, and that kind of organization doesn't seem to come up out of nowhere. I would be surprised if most of the people were honest rioters even; more likely, he paid them."

"That's just a guess," Cassidy intoned.

"But a damn good one," he riposted. "The media is brushing him off as a whackjob and maybe something is wrong with him, but he is more dangerous than people realize, I am sure. He's ambitious, he is calling for the overthrow of the government, he can organize violence, even against National Guard troops, and what's creepiest is that he appeared out of nowhere. According to the official records, Ezreal Redding was a divorce lawyer with no criminal record or even a history of advocacy fifty years ago, back when the Boroughs were flooding over. Then he disappears for fifty years and suddenly he comes back leading a revolution against the powers that be? Don't tell me that isn't suspicious as all hell."

"Call some of his family members, maybe they can give you the info."

"I did. His only living relations are an ex-wife and a daughter who live out in the California mountains. I managed to get into contact with her, but when I asked her about her husband, she hung up on me. I managed to talk to the daughter, she says she was just a baby when her mother left him. I swear this guy's a ghost. The one person in the world who might know why he's doing all this isn't talking. Well... there is one other person."

Miles leaned in. "I landed an interview with Ezreal Redding for tomorrow." He let that sink in for a moment. "I am going to check out his house, find some proof and take him down. I came here because I was looking for a good cop to help me bag him after I prove that I'm right. I was looking for Alex because I heard he was the best cop in the city."

"Well, you found his better half, Mr. Buhari."

"Miles," he replied.

Cassidy looked at him in stunned realization. "Wait... not—"

"Yes, that one. Hate me all you want for the things I've said about cops in the past, but I'm hardly ever wrong. And assuming I'm right, this'll bag the person behind the subway conspiracy. Maybe the biggest crime boss ever."

"*If* you're right." She enunciated her doubts. "And no, I will only hate you if you're wrong. All right, let me give you my information so you can reach me directly. I'll tell Alex what you told me."

Miles nodded and Cassidy gave him her email and phone number.

"I'll call you tomorrow night."

"You better find something," Cassidy said and watched him step out.

*   *   *

"A harpoon gun?" Haley asked, putting her coffee cup back down on the table.

"It worked." Alex couldn't help but laugh at himself.

"If I were being told that my job involved a harpoon gun, I wouldn't take it."

Alex took another bite of his turkey sandwich and said, "That's why you're not a hero." Between mouthfuls, he said, "You know, you shouldn't be so mean to me. I just told you my daring tale of heroism and adventure. Everyone else is going to have to buy my book or wait a few years and see the movie."

"Oh, they're going to make a movie about you!" She raised her eyebrows.

"Damn right. Only in the movie, I'll have the harpoon jam and fight off a shark with my fists."

"So when do I see your face on the news?" Haley asked. "How long are they going to keep this under wraps?"

"I was told a week. It would be dangerous for someone who dealt the biggest blow to organized crime in New York history to be walking the streets at night, so they are processing me for a transfer to somewhere on land."

"That's awesome. In a week, you'll never have to pay for a drink again. Try to soak this up while you can." She waved her finger around at the normality that surrounded them.

"Thanks."

"Are you really going to write a book?" Haley asked.

"No, no, I'll have someone else write it for me, like all celebrities do."

"You lazy bastard."

"Indeed. Shall we clear out?"

"This isn't a war zone, we can just leave."

Alex left forty thousand dollars on the table and they walked out. "Here, it's getting dark, I'll walk you back to your place."

"I thought you had to get back to work?"

"I'm out in a week, I don't even have to show up. Come on, don't you want to get as much of me as you can before I leave here and never come back?"

"Do you have to make it sound so dramatic?" she asked.

"Yeah, I do, it's a big deal!" He leaned in and talked quieter. "I grew up here, spent my whole life in this city. In a week from now, I won't be able to set foot here without getting shot. I am making out like a bandit. I make it dramatic because it is."

"Yes," she said softly, musing.

"'Yes'?"

"Well, I'll miss you," she blurted out. "I missed you the first time you went away. When you were recovering from that bullet wound and dropped by the shop looking to relax and kill time. I had a really good time getting to know you. Then you never called again, never showed up, and I thought I was just a distraction for you until you were up on your feet. Now you're leaving again, and I'll never see you... again. I guess this time you have a good excuse, though."

There was a long moment of silence until Haley said, "I'm sorry, I didn't mean to sound harsh, it's just... I thought I had gotten over it. I was angry when you left..."

"Come with me."

"What?"

"I have to get out. Not just because of the danger, but this place, it weighs on you. Living here amidst all the misery, the poverty, the lack of hope. When Manhattan rose up, it felt like that weight was lifting, but now that it's leaving, that weight is crashing down on my shoulders again, on everyone's. You said it, it's a sign. Hell, the whole city's moving and so should we."

Haley paused, fixating on his last word. "We? Where are we going? Do you even know?"

"No." Alex smiled.

"Do... do you have any idea? Like where they are stationing you, what city needs the most cops."

"Not a fucking clue," he said, liking how each of the words sounded.

Haley couldn't help but smile, but he could see the reservation in her eyes. "You left me the last time. You couldn't even tell I liked you, you dope. What if things don't work out between us?"

"I'm not asking for a relationship. I like you, too. I like you a lot. A whole lot. Very very much and a lot." He made her laugh. "But if you want to take it slow and cautious, I understand. Maybe I deserve it. But I'm not asking you to be my girl, I'm asking you to leave with me. To go on an adventure. To put this place behind and see the world. I can't say where, but I'll have some money, some fame, and something tells me that anywhere but here is the best start to an adventure. I think that's how all good adventures start."

Haley stopped walking. She looked aside, out past the buildings to somewhere off on the horizon. He tried to follow her gaze, but couldn't. Left with his own thoughts, he breathed in deep, tasting the cold salt air again, feeling regret turn into determination.

Haley looked up at him, put her hands on his shoulders and kissed him. Alex kissed her back and put a hand on her hip, another behind the small of her back, feeling her soft hair between his fingers. She broke the kiss and leaned back, looking up into his eyes.

"I know better than to wait for you to tell me you care about me, Alex. I just needed to know that you do."

Alex blushed, embarrassed as he thought. *I can't believe it took me two years to come to this point.* He nodded. "I do."

"I'll have everything packed for next week," she said. "Don't forget me."

Again. The unsaid word pounded into his gut like a fist.

"Never again," he said, and enjoyed the shortest, longest and happiest walk of his life.

Chapter Thirty-Six

Miles feared that the steady hum and every-three-second *clank* of the heater in the Seaside Hotel's lobby would be stuck in his brain forever, replaying in every dream and nightmare. It was too rattling; a machine that roared as it worked, then coughed and wheezed in a way that made one think that it would gutter, spurt and die, but no matter how many times it sounded as if something were breaking inside, it continued to push foul-tasting warm air into the lobby, which made Miles sweat and started to give him a headache. He had long ago given up on trying to read anything to pass the time. All the news was shit except what he put out and he hadn't written an article since he exposed the government complicity in the Manhattan disappearances. He stewed and sweated and wished that this night would be over. All the while, he felt the heat getting to him. *You must be a crazy daredevil. Marching into danger like this, about to poke and prod a man who is probably the hired hand-puppet of the Boroughs' demons.*

You're a coward. You wouldn't come down to a place where millions of people already live until you had the U.S. Army occupying it for you.

The two sides blasted away their points in his head, neither side arguing or addressing the other. His head lolled and he let his eyes close.

What felt like a second but simultaneously an eternity later, the door opened to the sound of bells tinkling and heavy feet stopped just in front of his chair. Miles looked up, feeling drool at the side of his mouth. There was a gray-haired man with calm blue eyes and a scar over the left side of his lip, dressed in a black winter coat and cap, looking down at him.

"Mr. Buhari, are you ready to go?"

"Ye-yeah." He nodded, but that only made his head hurt.

"My name is Mr. Smith. Follow me." The man turned and walked past the teenage girl sitting behind the lobby's counter, who watched with a smile and a cheery wave as Miles followed the worst decision he had ever made. Outside, the cold hit him like a slap across his exposed face. His headache abated and the chill bite actually felt good on his skin. After a few paces, three men who had been standing underneath a lamppost saw the two of them, nodded at Mr. Smith, and stepped in line beside him. Miles was about to ask about them, but he decided not to. There was nothing he could do, so he figured he may as well not annoy them.

So much for bravery.

After walking for at least a mile, they arrived in a neighborhood filled with three story mansions. As stealthily as Miles could, he tapped his wrist and checked the GPS, saving the location before switching it off. He felt nervous, but no one seemed to notice. That gave him some comfort, but not much. *At least it'll be easier for the police to find my body.* They walked up to the largest mansion and Mr. Smith opened the door and ushered the four of them inside.

It was not anything Miles had expected. *No torture devices or corpses. Pleasant surprise.* There was a grand entryway with an oak stairway, but all around him, the room was completely bare of anything. Vases, paintings, photographs. Aside from two antique chairs and matching sofa, only the purple and gold wallpaper offered anything by means of decoration.

"Mr. Buhari." Smith waved to his right. Miles stepped into the living room. The room was immensely long and reminded him of a French chateau's reception hall. But just like the previous room, it was completely bare, save for a faux fireplace that had been turned on, and two plush chairs and a side table with glasses of water and a bottle of something golden brown. One of the chairs was occupied by Ezreal, who eyed him from across the room.

Ezreal waited for Miles to walk over and take the seat next to him before he said, "Thank you for coming to my home."

"It's a lovely home," Miles remarked as he felt the gentle warmth of the fire.

"I was never so fond of it, but it will do."

"I would expect a big family to live here, but you live here alone? I assume, because there aren't any pictures."

"I lost a lot in the flood," Ezreal said in a voice that felt so unnaturally calm that it set Miles on edge. "Nearly everything of value

I had was lost..." He sighed. "No... everything I had. But my will. That's all I had after the New York City that I knew disappeared."

Miles nodded. "I bet that's an interesting story. Well, I suppose we can skip pleasantries and get straight to the interview."

"I can be pleasant and still talk business."

After a second, Miles realized it was supposed to be a joke, and he forced out a chuckle. "But why not talk about it? Because that's where this thing started?"

Ezreal said nothing.

"All right," Miles improvised, "tell me about the Flood. How did it impact you, make you who you are? But first, I'll have to record it." Ezreal nodded and Miles pulled out a small recorder. He pressed the red button and placed it down on the side table.

Ezreal looked past Miles. "It was a desperate time. The rich had everything; they had for the longest time. Even my grandfather told me that in his time, the city and the country was divided between the haves and have-nots; the ludicrously wealthy and the struggling poor. There had been movements by those on the bottom in his time, since time immemorial, I suppose. But now it was different. We weren't protesting for fairness, but for survival. The climate was changing, the polar caps were melting, and the sins of civilization and worldwide greed were catching up to us. Well, at least those of us near the coast. The storms grew worse, horrible they were. Not like now, with the government firing ice pellets into the clouds to stop them before they reach us. Our hurricanes were harsh, like the wrath of God threatening to drown the planet. There was a movement called Save New York City; it was the bastard grandchild of every failed social movement we've had: Occupy Wall Street, Fairness in America, you name it. I watched on the sidelines back then. Then Hurricane Florence hit, killing tens of thousands and any hope we had of starting new lives with any dignity. Some fled, some swam back. Me, I lost my home, my job. Then one morning, while I was out getting food from the FEMA stations, I came back to our ruined hovel and found my wife had left me with our infant child."

Miles waited in silence. "So why didn't you leave?"

Ezreal looked aside. A small flicker appeared in his eyes, then it died. "I had nothing left at that point. I suppose I was trapped. But now I look out and I see the same thing that happened then is happening now. The rich were packing up and leaving then, while millions were left at the mercy of the storm without the money to survive. Now the advancement of technology has enabled the rich to sail away with the whole damn city. This time I won't be on the sidelines."

"So this is a continuation of an old movement. When did you decide to start this movement?"

"I didn't start the movement."

"Really?" Miles poured himself a shot of the golden-brown scotch. "There are others here who stand on street corners and do what you do?"

"Yes, and they organize people into political parties and groups."

"I haven't heard of them."

"With the media silencing all truth, I am not surprised that you haven't."

Complete bullshit, let's continue. "What would you characterize as your central message?"

"The have-nots will not allow the haves to steal what is ours. We built the skyscrapers they live in and the machines that keep them up. We will not watch them sail away."

We? And you live in a mansion. You can't believe this. "How do you intend on achieving this?"

Ezreal cleared his throat. "The people are already calling for a special election to be held, one that will replace the politicians who have voted to allow Manhattan to sail away."

"But that's not going to happen. The governor declared martial law, put troops and the Coast Guard all around the city, occupied it. He doesn't say he supports Manhattan's decision to break up because he fears that might hurt his popularity, but he knows that revenue from the sales will flow his way and he'll use that for re-election. Every politician in New York City and the state supports this, even if they say they don't."

"Then we will replace them."

"Replace all the politicians in the state in less than two weeks? That seems highly unlikely."

Miles hoped to get a rise out of Ezreal, he was waiting for him to scream propaganda at him. His response sounded somehow calmer than before. "The people of New York City will not allow Manhattan to leave."

"What do you mean? What will they do?"

"They will not allow Manhattan to leave. The people of New York City are stronger than the politicians and their owners. They think that we are tired from all the work we do on their behalf, but we are not. We will fight them and we will win."

"Right." Miles groaned and he took a drink of the scotch, feeling the warmth flow through him. "Are you not drinking?"

"Only water," Ezreal declared.

"The one drink I can't stomach," Miles noted.

This time, it was Ezreal's turn not to laugh at a joke.

Miles put the drink down and continued. "I have seen a lot of turnout at your events. But where is the organization? Is there a central party or group that coordinates all this?"

"No. We are not an organization, a party or a lobby. We are the people."

"I don't understand."

Ezreal laughed heartily. "A strange concept in today's world, wouldn't you say? But I see you still have your doubts. You don't think that the people can organize themselves, that they can voice their concerns and direct themselves?"

"Not for a second. I have been all around the world. People are like spiritualistic cavemen. A rare few among them, ultranationalists, utopianists, those who claim divinity, rock stars... in my travels around the world, I have seen them all... these rare people are fixated on a central point beyond anything that anyone else can see, and the rest of humanity, wanting something bigger, better, brighter, shinier, follow these men anywhere, even off a cliff."

"You have no faith in people?"

Miles realized that he was letting Ezreal question him when he had come here to scope out the man, uncover him. But Ezreal was too smooth, dodging every question with his rambling while never rising to Miles' mocking challenge, and now this old man was dictating to him.

"Why do you?" Miles tried to get things back on track.

"I believe in people because they are the only thing to believe in. Humanity has waited for God for an awfully long time. He didn't save us from war and disease. Now we have a new worldwide flood and you would think He might have showed up to this one. But every rainbow is a broken promise. It is in us to solve our problems and we can. Humans have created most every problem, so it follows that humans can solve them."

"Some humans. You say that the working classes are the ones which make everything and the rich take everything."

"Because they do," Ezreal stated. Miles thought something else was following, but apparently what he pronounced was so evidently true it didn't need to be elaborated on.

"What do you think about the captured billionaires? Those that had been held hostage, some for months, inside the abandoned subway stations?"

"That was unfortunate."

When Ezreal didn't follow up, Miles asked, "Unfortunate how?"

Ezreal paused. "It was unfortunate that some people decided to take out their rage against the haves through violence. It sullies the rest of—"

"How do you know that the people who kidnapped the billionaires did so as part of a class war?"

That made Ezreal stop. After a few seconds, he said, "I assumed that was it."

"Why?"

"Because what other reason did the kidnappers have? I heard there was no ransom, so what else could it have been but revenge?"

Miles replied, "They could have been other rich trying to take over their adversaries' companies, or foreign terrorism. Why assume it was part of class warfare?"

Ezreal stared unblinking at Miles, his pale white face a perfect canvas for the shadows that danced across it from the fireplace. "I suppose. I guess we will know when the captors are caught."

"We can only hope," Miles said. "What is one message that you would like everyone to hear, one that the media hasn't reported?"

After the shortest of pauses in which Ezreal recomposed himself, he replied, "Our economic woes will be rectified. You cannot stand against the majority of the people. You can either join us or oppose us, but justice is inevitable."

The next few minutes jumped from a diatribe on how dire the plight of the poor in the Boroughs were to Ezreal praising the new Commune of Tajikistan. Miles tried to pose questions to him, but Ezreal would start to answer and then proceed to talk about whatever he felt like. After a few minutes, he simply ignored the questions altogether in an uninterrupted diatribe. When Miles thought he couldn't take any more, he waited for a pause, said, "Thank you for that," picked up the recorder, clicked, 'end,' and put it in his pocket. Miles and Ezreal stood up and shook hands.

"My pleasure," Ezreal said curtly. "Be sure to put that interview up shortly. Time is pressing."

"I'm always on the cutting edge," he replied.

Ezreal smiled, but his eyes didn't look pleased. "Good evening, Mr. Buhari."

Miles nodded and turned his back on Ezreal. He walked past the guards, smiling at each in turn. None of them reciprocated as Mr. Smith opened the door and nearly pushed him out. Miles walked off, looking up at the windows of the mansions he passed. He doubted any of them were as spartan as Ezreal's, nor their occupants as suspicious. He went over in his head all the suspicions that he had. A small voice that sounded a lot like Mylie asked if he too wasn't becoming paranoid and insane. He shrugged it off. He realized he had no solid evidence to go on, but that wasn't the point. He hardly expected to break Ezreal down to tears, have him confess to everything, and open up a closet filled with corpses.

In all his travels, he had found that the poorer the people and the stronger the gangs, the more likely it was that any given individual was connected to organized crime. There were few places in America as poor and with gangs as powerful, and with Ezreal literally screaming for attention, he seemed to be the obvious link. Miles couldn't find anything to prove his suspicions there, only reinforce them. But he had an address to a mansion, a cop who wanted desperately to make a name for herself in the eleventh hour of New York City, and a hunch that an unannounced sweep of the place might reveal something bigger.

It's perfect. If I can direct Officer Kikia to a lead that will unravel the gangs, then I can claim credit for taking on some of the most hardened criminal organizations in the world, all while sailing a skyscraper down the East Coast and sipping whiskey.

Miles was so enraptured in the fantasy that he hardly noticed as the streets grew dirtier, the mansions gave way to houseboats and the air took on a menacing feel as the only people out were National Guard with rifles. He glanced at pair of angry-looking uniformed men with assault rifles, smiled and waved.

I think I like America.

Chapter Thirty-Seven

Cassidy had fallen off the cliff. She lay in bed watching the clock. *5:00 P.M.* She had been lying in bed all day, only getting up to drink some water and go to the bathroom. She hadn't touched her meds for the second day in a row. Sometime around noon, she had begun to panic. Her heartbeat was too fast and her breathing was shallow and she was frightened, but couldn't understand why. She fell asleep, she didn't know when, and now lay looking at the clock. She had to go to work at six. *What if I don't show up? What if I just lie here?*

She looked at the clock again. *5:30 P.M.*

Just a second ago it was 5:00, I know it. How did it change so fast?

Slowly, Cassidy rolled her body until her legs slid out on the side of the bed awkwardly. Feet hit floor and a sense of vertigo overcame her. The hazy world tilted left, then right. Her head felt light and hot. She closed her eyes, looked at the clock and stood up.

Alex glanced over at Cassidy as she entered the office. She knew what he was thinking: that she was late, that she was doing it just to spite him. *Fuck you, it's five minutes.* He didn't say anything and Cassidy walked over to her desk, putting down some of her personal items.

"Ready to go?"

Cassidy made sure to nod quickly, trying not to look off balance or lethargic. She didn't want to get in another fight about how she felt.

"Okay." Alex said the word slowly and stood up. "So far, with all our attention focused on Manhattan's problems, there hasn't been any work done on the Brice Noble case. We know that Rodney Maxwell was involved, but there's barely been any work done to find him. His house was checked, but there were no suspicious items. Still, I want to

go check it out, see if anything might lead us to him. It's at 9236
Giuliani Avenue. Don't worry, I think I can find it without getting us
lost this time." He smiled as he said it.

Cassidy's expression didn't change in the slightest.

"Okay." He nodded, looking aside. "I don't expect this kid to be
anything that we can't handle. There's no evidence to suggest that he's
armed, but we should proceed as if he is. Let's bring him in alive if
possible. He is the only one who can give us any information on the
other two who were involved. And he is just a kid after all."

Cassidy looked at him blankly, or at least she thought she did. As
she looked at her partner, she felt an immense sense of sadness, but at
what, she couldn't tell. *Because you betrayed me? Or because you are
leaving me behind, for some place with solid ground and a bright
future, while I'm stuck here? Or because you're not my friend
anymore?* Her melancholy could be caused by anything or nothing.
She had to look away, letting her long, dark hair fall in front of her
face.

Alex stepped out the door with Cassidy following.

*Talk to him, say something. Tell him you're sorry. No, yell at him,
tell him how much you hate him. Fight, then make up.*

They didn't say a word to each other. The sun had already set and
most people had turned in for the night. Many of those who didn't
retire to their cozy interiors looked suspicious, but she paid them no
mind. She remembered what their patrols across town had been like
before: the eternal battle between her optimism and his determination
to be depressed. *You idiot, don't you realize that maybe I need to be
told that things are going to be all right once? That maybe instead of
chastising me when I'm down, you can tell me things are going to be
all right like I have with you?*

But it wasn't the same. He had said time after time that their work
didn't dent crime, but he continued to fight as hard as ever anyway.
Alex was like a force that never slowed down, no matter how much
resistance was placed on it. Hell, he even seemed to enjoy the
challenge that problems brought. It was amazing how determined he
could be without conviction and how little she could be with it.

The house was on the far western side of the Boroughs and it took
half an hour to get there. It was a large, blue houseboat and judging
by the older, cheaper model, it had the living room and kitchen in the
middle, one room to the west side, another to the east side. All the
shutters were drawn closed.

"Okay, we're going to do this like we did the last raid. I knock on
the front door. You go around back, you hear any shit, you break in

and back me up. Got it?"

Cassidy nodded, realizing that she hadn't said a word to him since work started.

"Okay, go, get into position."

Cassidy stalked forward. She drew her gun, which felt awkward and heavy in her hands. It shook and she felt light-headed, realizing she hadn't eaten all day and hardly at all the day before. She walked around the house, ducking under the windows, which also had their curtains drawn. She stood by the back door, waiting. She heard a loud, hard knock from the other side. Cassidy instinctively counted down. *Someone answer the door, now.* She knew the drill; she knew there wouldn't be a second knock. After ten seconds, she kicked in the door and saw the shadowy figure of her partner in the opposite doorframe. The room was unlit, almost pitch black. Her partner had leveled his gun to her right. She looked over and squinted against the darkness and saw the dark silhouette of Rodney staring white-faced at Alex, gun leveled at her partner.

"It's all right, kid, listen to me—"

"Get the fuck out, I will shoot!" Rodney yelled, trying to sound menacing, but instead sounding terrified, something which scared Cassidy a lot more.

"Rodney," Alex said calmly. He held his gun steadily towards Rodney's chest. Rodney's shook in his hands, but at this distance, he couldn't miss. "It's going to be all right."

"You two are pointing guns at me, don't tell me it's going to be all right!" He looked over at Cassidy. She saw a sense of dread in his eyes. *Leave him,* she thought. *Alex can handle him. Make sure there aren't any guns pointed at his back.*

She tried to move as little as possible, glancing to her left. There was an open window between the living room and kitchen area. There was a lamppost from the street behind her that was ruining her night vision and she couldn't see into the kitchen area. She risked it, taking a step forward, putting her back against the house.

"Rodney, if I wanted to kill you, my partner could have done that already. But we're not here to hurt you. We want to help you."

"Help me how?"

Cassidy closed her eyes just for a second. When she opened them, she could just barely see into the dark kitchen. *Empty.* She looked back to Rodney, but kept one eye to her left.

"You and two others were involved in an incident in Manhattan. You three were part of a mugging that went wrong when one of your friends killed Brice Noble. If you can help us find the other two, then we can reduce any prison sentence you might have, because now the charge is second-degree murder. You don't have to die or spend the rest of your life in prison."

"Oh, God," Rodney gasped. He looked down, but he still held his gun out towards Alex's chest.

"Please don't do anything stupid," Alex pleaded. "Your life isn't over. We can solve this. I want to help you."

"How am I supposed to trust you?" Rodney shouted. He was angry, but it sounded like he wanted to believe Alex.

"We're not here to hurt you, Rodney, we're here to help. Put the gun down."

Rodney's hands were shaking. Cassidy's eyes went wide. She aimed at his shaking hands, expecting at any moment that the gun would fire.

"Put the gun down," Alex said more forcefully.

There was a flash of light and a deafening bang. Two guns hit the ground, then a body. Cassidy turned to her left and saw a shadow take aim at her. She fired, but it ducked just in time. Cassidy stepped into the kitchen. The shadow leapt out of the window, glass breaking everywhere, shutters banging against the walls. She turned back to the living room. Rodney's hands were up. Alex was holding his chest and gasping for air as blood poured down his shirt.

"I didn't do it. I-I..."

Cassidy leveled her gun at him. Rodney looked down at the floor. Cassidy crossed the distance and kicked him in the stomach. She hit him over the head with the butt of her gun, sending him to the floor. She kicked him once, twice, until his gasps of pain came out as a low grimace. She looked out the door frame to see if anyone was there. Seeing no one, she put her gun away, pulled out her handcuffs and cuffed Rodney. She slapped her wrist until the neural interface appeared, brought up the phone app, and looked down at Alex. "I need backup, Cassidy..." She looked down at her partner. "Oh, God, no." Her voice cracked and she looked away. "Backup. EMT at 9236 Giuliani Avenue, right now! Officer down!"

She picked up Rodney's fallen gun, stowing it. She was about to pick up Alex's when her gaze fell to his closed eyes.

"Oh, God, Alex, stay with me, stay with me. N.I. wifi link-up activate." A line appeared in her vision that read *Enter password.*

"Hollow399."

His interface came up in her vision.

"Display vitals."

She saw his temperature drop from 98.2 to 98.1, then 98.0. A line shot up, then went flat, then shot up, then went flat and she held her breath as she watched his heartbeat, thinking each time that the line would stop rising. She wrapped his chest with her stomach and pressed down as blood covered her hands. "Hold on, Alex, hold on."

Five minutes passed of Cassidy feeling his warm blood grow cold as she stared at his unconscious face while watching his heart rate monitor. An eternity passed before she heard boots from outside. She raised her gun.

"Stand down, Cassidy," a voice called as two officers stepped in. One of them waved over two pairs of EMTs, one of whom approached Cassidy while the other tended to Alex. Flashlights waved in front of her vision.

"Who is this person you have in cuffs?" an officer asked Cassidy as another cop lifted the beaten and bloody Rodney to his feet.

"Here, help me stop the bleeding. Scissors," an EMT ordered his partner.

"Cassidy, talk to me."

"Rodney Maxwell," she choked. "He is a suspect in the murder of Brice Noble."

The officer nodded. He turned around and the two of them escorted the shaking kid outside.

"Miss Kikia, come with me," an EMT ordered, placing a hand around her and walking her outside. "You're going to be all right. Where are you hurt?"

Cassidy looked over her shoulder and saw the EMTs leaning over Alex's prone body. She kept watching his heartbeat until a notification appeared that read *Connection Lost*.

Chapter Thirty-Eight

L ei had been waiting for the mayor to return to her office when she heard the news that every building in Manhattan had been sold off. She was reading off quotes from a press conference the mayor had been to that morning in which she exclaimed with 'enthusiasm and cheer' that despite crime and scandal, the buildings managed to sell off at a competitive price. According to the article, she had emphasized over and over that trillions of dollars would be left over for the Boroughs after Manhattan departed.

I suppose it's good that they all sold. It would be weird if when all the other skyscrapers sail off, there are a half dozen scattered around the bay, old reminders of a city that once was.

The article stated that within two days, a website would be up that would detail where each skyscraper was going, and 'The Maiden Voyage of New York City' could be live-streamed, with satellites following the skyscrapers in real time. Lei glanced to the door just in time to see Sophia step through. She eyed Lei and gave a wan smile. Apparently, she thought they were co-conspirators, that she could let Lei know exactly how she felt. Lei pined for the days when she was fed optimistic lies while the grim truth was kept from her.

"Miss Xu, please step inside my office," she beckoned while ushering her in. Sophia grabbed a bottle of water from the side table and walked to the seat behind her desk. Lei sat down, looking at Sophia. "So, are you pleased with your building's re-assignment? Laurel, Mississippi. It's a booming city now. I'm sure you'll be able to find a good job there."

"I haven't really given much thought to my employment recently. I figured I would stay on with Stanhope."

Sophia chuckled. "Of course. But after this, I am sure you could get a job at any tech company on Earth. When the world sees these giant skyscrapers sailing down the coast, they'll know it was because of you."

Lei clenched up. "I didn't think history will remember me like this."

"Ah," Sophia said, realizing how badly she missed the mark. "Politics and human nature. They ruin the best of intentions. I'm sure the world will be able to distinguish between what you built and what others did. Hell, I'm pretty sure I'll go down as the villain in all of this."

It was meant as a joke, but neither of them laughed.

"This is actually why I wanted to talk to you. I was hoping that you would take charge of the operations and lead this whole fleet. It wouldn't be a very demanding job; just oversee the operations from the Empire State Building, manage the skyscrapers, make sure they don't bump into each other."

Lei felt a sickening feeling in her stomach, one that she had every time she met with the mayor since the sell-off of the Carlyle Building was announced. "How long do I have to make a decision?"

"I assumed you would just say yes!" Sophia balked. It was then that Lei noticed the bags under her eyes and the way her shoulders sagged. Sophia wasn't in the mood for questions and didn't even consider that someone might disagree with her. "Fine, take your time. Can I just go over the plans with you before you leave?"

Lei nodded. For the next ten minutes, Sophia showed her the plans for the control room, situated on top of the Empire State Building. There was a central computer hub with six holo-screens and behind the 'captain's' chair were two other navigators with similar setups and over a dozen pilots who would be controlling the skyscrapers directly. Sophia explained slowly because she didn't understand it very well, but Lei had it figured out just from the schematics. Lei was just directing the pilots; easy work.

"So will you take the job?"

"I'm not sure." Lei hesitated.

It wasn't what Sophia wanted to hear. She sat down. "Tell me by the end of the day. Here is my personal number." She passed Lei a piece of paper.

Lei pocketed it and stood up. "I'll call you before then."

"Be sure to say 'yes.'"

Lei turned and left Sophia to her business.

Lei stepped out and looked at her watch. She decided to spend the day out. After being consoled by her friends and vowing never to drink alcohol after a second night of vomiting, she had come to accept her role in the fate of New York City. It depressed her, but she knew she had to appear resolute. *Who else could have moved these buildings? Who else could have done what I have?* Ramos was right: as much as it made her cringe to think how she would be remembered, she knew that she would be respected by the scientific community, at least. *My journey isn't over. I have too much to offer. One day, I will blot out the stain that is the break-up of New York.*

She hailed a cab.

"Where to, ma'am?"

"Give me a tour of the whole city."

The cab driver laughed nervously. "That would cost a bit."

"I can pay," she reassured him.

He looked at her, disbelieving, then looked behind her at City Hall. From the changing look on his face, he must have just assumed that she was an important person. "Hop in," he said, stopping just short of asking her if she was one of the people buying the buildings.

Lei took her place in the boat and as she sat down, she realized that this would be one in a series of 'lasts' she would have to endure. *Calling floating cabbies to bustle through busy canals to get from one historic skyscraper to the next will seem like a fantasy in ten years. No one but the historians will believe we did it.* Strangely, the thought gave her a sense of joy. The feeling birthed bewilderment until she realized that it was the joy of uniqueness she was feeling. Even in her despair, she felt a sense that what she did would never be repeated.

"You came at the right time to tour the city," the skipper said behind her. "Everyone's cleared out, canals are empty, but meanwhile the place is all prettied up. You should have seen it before."

Lei nodded, realizing where he was taking her. Saint Patrick's Cathedral loomed over them, its age leaving a longer shadow than the highest skyscrapers around it. "There used to be a big houseboat that they converted into a floating church, before St. Paddy's rose up again. I used to pray there, back before it was packed with tourists," the driver said reverently. "I got saved there."

"Did you?"

"Yes, I did. Me and a few of the altar boys snuck some of the communion wine, I got piss drunk, fell into the water and Father Moore jumped in and saved me."

Lei grinned mischievously.

"How about you? Any good memories of New York you've been reliving?"

"Well... I nearly got married to the man who owned that café."

"Nearly? Oh, this has got to be a good story. What happened?

Couldn't have been another woman; you're far too beautiful for any guy to take his eyes off long enough to check out other women."

"It was another coffee shop. I just need my space to work and I would come into his coffee shop and he chatted me up once and it was cute. But then things got really serious between us and then every time I came there, he just walked up to me and started talking to me. So one day I just needed some space and I went to another café that had a lot better coffee. I just kept going there for a week. Well, one day, he walked through the door, yelled, 'Lei, what are you doing here? How could you?'" She put a hand on her face. "God, I was trying to forget that. Maybe I should have just bought a boat and become a taxi driver. It seems so peaceful," she mused as she watched the shops and the people pass by.

"It's not so bad. I'm just a simple man. Didn't get a good education, never had much family support. But I do have a boat and here is one of the few places a dinghy like mine matters. So I prayed every other week for God to send me a miracle."

Lei turned to face him.

He smiled, shrugging. "It worked for a while. I finally had a business. At least I get to walk away with some savings. And I have a place in Manhattan, a small apartment. Two days ago, I got a notice saying the apartment was shipping off to Beeville, Texas. Can you imagine?"

Lei grinned. "So is this a win for you?"

"It's a new beginning, that's all. I can't bring my boat with me."

"Why not?"

The man burst out laughing. "Why not? I'm not even going to bother asking the city if they can tie my dinghy to the back of a skyscraper and haul it down to Texas! Maybe if I get married, they will..."

Lei laughed along with him and said, "Maybe someone in your building will have a wedding and you can all tie your boats on as noise-makers."

"That would be a sight." He smirked. "And this is a city that has given the world some sights."

He urged the boat forward, and it hacked and spurted past the cathedral down another row of past glory. Lei looked at each building in turn. She imagined one in the humid marshlands of southern Texas, another on the rocky coasts of Massachusetts, another emerging from a seaside forest in Maine, a fourth sailing over sunken Mobile, Alabama, travelling up the flooded lowlands and following the new inlet all the way to Montgomery. As she did, she had an incredibly calming sense that the city was not lost. *New York will have a better fate now than it did before. Without my machines, the city would be a graveyard of Old America waiting for the engines to stop running, a titanic Detroit that when its machines failed, would fall into the sea. Now New York City will be saved and given to the entire country.*

"That's enough," Lei said. "Can you take me to the corner of 9th Street and 2nd Avenue?"

"What else is this boat for?" The cabbie slowed the boat, and a violent sputter of water churned out of its motor. As they turned, Lei pulled out Sophia's number and called her.

"Yes?" Sophia answered after the third ring.

"This is Lei Xu, Miss Mayor."

"Oh, Lei." She seemed to perk up, but was clearly still exhausted. "Have you accepted the position?"

"I can't. You should be just fine without me, though."

The line went dead. Lei smiled, finally learning not to care.

Chapter Thirty-Nine

Cassidy's emotions had gone haywire, even with the meds. One day she told herself she was all right, but then immediately felt guilty for ever thinking she could be all right again. Vomiting and bouts of vertigo made her head swim even as she lay still. She would eventually fall asleep, only to have her sickness break through the depression. After the second day, her nerves were on end, but the vomiting and nightmares had stopped.

On the third day, she went outside, feeling the loneliness of walking the streets by herself, knowing that even if Alex recovered, things would never be the same. The weight of the thought nearly brought her to her knees twice. When she was finally back in her apartment, she fell to the floor, trying to feel the hard, solid foundation, hoping it would steady her. She whimpered and felt the tears well up in her eyes. She pressed her right wrist. The digital interface appeared before her eyes and she clicked on the phone icon. She had thirty-two missed calls. Two from Sarah yesterday, Jessica, Jonathan. Cassidy brought up her mom from her contacts list and called her.

Ring... ring... ring... ring... ring...

"Hello, you've reached Alicia Kikia's number—"

Cassidy hung up and gasped. She clicked 'call' again.

Ring... ring... ring... ring... ring...

"Hello, you've reached Alicia Kikia's number—"

Cassidy called again. And again. And again. And again...

After the fifth time, she gave up and brought up her voicemail.

"Hey, Cass-cass, it's your mother... I've been calling, texting and IMing you since Wednesday now, hoping you'd say something to me. I've been worried ever since you stopped keeping up with me. I just want to know everything's okay and you're getting along all right.

Please call back, I love you very much."

Cassidy clicked on her mother's number and was about to call it again. She looked at the name. After a minute of inactivity, the interface shut off and she was left to her empty room. She rolled over, feeling another pang of vertigo. She gagged, but her stomach was empty. *I need to call someone, but who? Someone at the police department? No, they must all think it was my fault Alex got shot.*

It must be my fault. The thought flashed in her head and echoed through her mind.

Was it? her subconscious replied back.

He would be okay if it weren't for me.

It's your fault.

Her brain was on auto-pilot, one part of her damning her, the other defending her, but she felt nothing from the words. The struggle taking place in her mind was just the newest form that her depression had taken and by now, she was numb to it.

She brought up her phone application and brought up Alex's name.

"Hi, Alex," she said without calling. The dam burst and the tears cascaded down her face. She felt her nose stuffing up. "I'm proud of you. I really am. You did so much good for all of us. I wanted you gone before... Before..." She sniffled and looked down towards the floor, barely visible in the faint streetlight that shone through her window.

"I wish you were here. I hated you so much. I'm sorry."

Cassidy was terrified of every step forward she took. She watched as if from far away as she walked toward the hospital reception desk.

"Ma'am, are you feeling all right? You're pale and shaking."

Cassidy put a heavily shaking hand on the desk. She was about to say 'no' when she realized what would happen if she did. "It's just the cold from outside." She tried to keep an even voice. "I'm here to see my partner, Alex—" She gulped. "Alex Waverly. He was shot on duty, but I was informed he had stabilized."

In the time it took her to say that, the receptionist pulled up an image on her computer. "Ah, yes, he's here and accepting visitors, though he will probably be quite out of it with all the painkillers he's on. Be patient with him." The receptionist smiled. "Room 323. Elevators to the right just past this desk."

Cassidy lurched past the desk. She savored the brief solitude and quiet of the elevator for the few seconds it lasted. The doors opened and she headed right, towards room 323. She knocked.

"Come in," a young woman's voice replied from the other side.

Cassidy didn't move. *This can't be the right room...?* She opened the door. Alex was lying in bed with his eyes closed. There were wires hooked up to his arm and his shirt was open, revealing his heavily bandaged chest. A woman with bright red hair sat in a chair on Alex's left.

"Hello," she called.

Cassidy stared at Alex's wound.

"He's all right," the woman announced. "The doctor says he's stabilized, he just needs rest. They say in a couple of days, he could even check out with a wheelchair. That's what I'm hoping for; I hate to see him like this."

Cassidy looked over at the girl. "Who are you?"

"Hi." She smiled. "I'm Haley Williams. I'm Alex's... well, we're friends, I guess you could say. And you are..."

"Cassidy Kikia. I'm his partner."

"Oh, I see."

"I was there," she breathed softly.

"I'm sorry." Haley immediately softened. "He should wake in an hour or so. He goes in and out, but he's never asleep for long. I'm sure he would be happy to see you."

Cassidy's eyes fell to his wound. She cast her eyes back down the hall to the elevator.

"No," she murmured. "I can't..."

The world started to spin. She felt her head grow faint and a ringing noise rose in her ears, growing until it deafened her. She lurched forward and ran to the elevator. She pressed the button. It opened and mercifully it was empty. She waited for the door to close and she let herself fall to the floor. She kicked her feet into the air and let them rest against the elevator wall. *Breathe, long and deep, breathe. Keep your legs up, let the blood flow back to your head. Breathe, breathe, long and deep. Eyes closed, breathe.*

The ringing subsided, replaced by the sound of her madly thumping heart. Her vision cleared. She thought she was good enough to stand up, but decided it would be safer if she gave it another minute. The elevator doors opened and a man and woman in scrubs were standing over her.

"Ma'am, are you okay?"

"Yes, I just had a panic attack," Cassidy said quickly.

"Do you feel well enough to stand?"

"Yes."

"Okay, let us help you up. That's it, we're just going to have you sit down for a minute before we let you go. Do you want some water?"

The two scrubs flanked her and led her forward. Cassidy counted the numbers of the rooms as they proceeded.

313. 315. 317. 319. 321.

They helped her into a chair in the hallway just before room 323.

"I'm going to come back with a cup of water, just relax and breathe in for me, okay?"

Cassidy nodded and closed her eyes.

Cassidy returned to work on the fourth day. Hewes ordered her to stick to office work for the next few weeks and she chose not to argue with him. The boredom got to her within minutes. By mid-afternoon, she had watched a Bollywood love story and three Honduran dramas. It was out of this unending tedium that caused her to say 'yes, send him up' when the front desk told her, "Miles Buhari wants to talk to you, he's says it's top secret."

Miles' tall frame barely fit through the door. "Hello, Cass."

"Officer Kikia."

"Ah, professional. Fine." Miles walked over to Alex's desk.

"Don't sit there!" Sudden venom came into her.

Miles stopped and calmly took a step away from the chair. "I understand. How is he doing?"

Cassidy looked out the window. "He's recovering. The doctor says he can leave in a wheelchair in a couple of days."

"And how long before he's back on the force?"

Cassidy looked back at him with a glance that said *are you trying to get on my every nerve?*

"Well, I wish him well and thank God he made it through. But now back to business. I've uncovered something big and I've been trying to contact you, but you weren't returning my calls. I understand why, but this… this is huge, Miss Kikia."

"You didn't think to get anyone else?" she replied.

"There is no one else."

"Why? Did you kill your reputation with every cop in the city?"

"Yeah," Miles admitted. "After you checked out, I tried talking to some other cops in the station. They decided to kick me out of HQ; I had to drop your name just to be let back in the building. If you're still talking to me, I am guessing they didn't put me on any official blacklist, but they might as well have. You're the only authority I can turn to if we want to investigate Ezreal."

"Why should I?"

That made Miles pause. She wasn't asking for proof of anything related to the crime, she was focusing solely on herself. *She must be in bad shape.* He grimaced.

"Because it's the right thing to do."

Cassidy waved a shaking finger in front of his face. "Don't you feed me that bullshit! I know you. You go to day spas in the same cities as 'danger-zones' but never set foot anywhere you might actually be under fire and leave. I have lived here my whole life and I won't be lectured to about what's right. So fuck you."

"How about a way out?"

Cassidy stopped and Miles knew he had his chance.

"When Manhattan sails off, I can let you ride in my apartment and I can even let you off with a pretty big sum of money."

Cassidy stopped and turned to look at him, eyes cold. "Why would you do that?"

"Because if I'm right and I unravel a huge conspiracy, I will be even more famous and credible than I already am."

"Credible." She laughed.

"Ouch. So, you help me chase down a hunch and I let you get a ride out of here and leave you with some cash."

"How much?"

"A billion."

That put Cassidy back. "Dollars?"

"Jelly rolls. Of course dollars!"

Cassidy nodded slowly. That was a lot of money, more than twenty years' salary for the best of officers.

"Where is your building headed to?"

Miles shrugged. "Don't know, don't care. I am flying back to England afterwards anyway."

Cassidy looked aside. "I suppose I don't care either," she breathed to the wind.

"So is that a 'yes'?"

Cassidy looked back. "All right." She stuck out a hand. Miles didn't shake it.

"You have to understand one thing: as much money as I have, a billion dollars is a large amount and I never gamble."

Cassidy's eyes narrowed. "What does that mean?"

"It means if you can help me prove that there's a conspiracy, you get the money and the ride."

"Otherwise nothing?"

"Bingo."

After feeling numb for so long, Cassidy felt white-hot hate boiling up inside her. "What do you have to go on?"

"Ezreal Redding is creepy."

Cassidy waited for a second part. None came. "That's it?"

"He also lives in a three-story building in one of the nicest parts of town, which there aren't many out in this floating toilet, despite not existing for fifty years. Oh, and the house isn't officially held in his name."

"There's lots of undocumented people. Lots of records got lost in the floods, he could have been doing odd jobs all around the Boroughs for fifty years, maybe some petty crime and there'd be no record."

"Are there lots of rich people who have never held a job, never been photographed, never mentioned on a social media site? I didn't land on an undiscovered island of grass-skirt-wearing tribesmen, did I? He comes out of nowhere preaching the overthrow of the government, there are no records of his existence and he lives in a three-story house and can hire 'bodyguards' who don't have any visible tattoos, but I swear they must be in some gang."

"Well, if you swear it," Cassidy bit back.

"Well, excuse me for doing investigative research; your job, if I remember correctly. I am convinced he must be the mouthpiece for these gangs, must have some connection. He has the motive. He keeps trying to get people to revolt against the government, to keep Manhattan from leaving."

"Lots of people here don't want Manhattan to leave," Cassidy stated condescendingly. "There's lots of money there and some of it makes it this way."

"But it's how he is doing it, you see. He is calling for Manhattan and its people to stay, even while calling the people who live there evil tyrants and demonizing them as much as possible. Why do you think that is? Why do you think he demonizes the same people who he is asking to stay?"

Cassidy paused for the answer, but Miles was waiting for her to guess. Finally, he uttered, "I don't know. I don't know what he intends, but I know the result: chaos. And who is chaos good for? Criminals.

"All right, so all you have is motive, what about proof?"

"I interviewed him at his mansion. I only got to check out the first floor of his house, but I am sure if we checked the upper floors, we will find some serious shit. Maybe it's a safehouse, maybe the gangs are even moving their drugs and guns back from the subway up into the mansion to avoid the raids."

"And what am I supposed to go on? How can I get a warrant with just your suspicions?"

"I hear you cops don't use warrants out here."

Cassidy felt the hot anger pulse through her again. "I'm a good cop."

"Then you wouldn't be opposed to catching bad people. Come up with some excuse."

"If it turns out he's clean, I will be the asshole cop who took down a local icon, even if he is a kook. I'd lose my job and might even get killed by some radical sympathizers."

"Yeah, how's your life going now?"

Cassidy felt paralyzed. After a few seconds, she wasn't breathing. The world grew fuzzy.

"These are the best cookies I've ever had," Alex said with a mouthful, an uncharacteristic breach in his austere posture. He had long hair and a goatee back then, as well as a haggard look in his eyes. He was thinner than he was before the shooting that took him off the force for months that seemed like years as Cassidy was left in an office and on patrol alone.

"You didn't have to make them for me."

"Yes, I did, just look at you! Did they not serve any food at the hospital?"

"No, the food was amazing."

"Bullshit, all hospital food is terrible. You are just saying you like it because you don't cook."

"You would think you'd be nicer to me, seeing how I was shot."

"I am being nice! I made you cookies, how much nicer can I be?"

Alex looked down into Cassidy's smiling face. He wrapped his arms around her in a hug. His arms felt so heavy and warm against her small back. "Thank you. I appreciate it."

"I'm glad you're back, Alex. I was really worried for you. I thought—" She stopped herself from saying it, but the look on Alex's face told her he knew.

"Miss Kikia?"

Cassidy looked up into Miles' face. The world had been so warm and fluid, but now she felt the cold air on her as reality flooded back into her vision.

"I thought I could go up there, knock on the door and when he comes out and you see him, that'll be the legal proof you need to arrest him, for squatting. Do we have a plan?"

"That's actually not too bad," she breathed. "That's at least a legal precedent. But you better stick to your end of the bargain."

Miles nodded. "When shall we do it? Soon would be best."

"An hour," Cassidy said. "Meet you there, go through with the plan just like you said we should."

"Okay, I'm going to send you the address." Miles tapped his wrist until a notification appeared at the edge of Cassidy's vision. Miles stood up and walked to the door. "See you there."

"See you there."

"Cassidy."

"What?..."

Alex sighed. "I wish you had other people you could depend on."

"It's your first day back after being shot! Don't do that thing you do when you ignore your own glaring problems and try to fix other people." She tried to sound like she was joking, but Alex wasn't taking it that way. He looked too deeply into her eyes. Something about Alex's kind nature made meeting his gaze easy. As she looked back at him, she could see everything he was feeling, the ebb and flow of different emotions as he decided what he was going to say.

"Just promise me that you'll always be fine. That you'll have someone to see you through if you ever have another episode or forget to take your meds."

There was a silence as Cassidy looked up into Alex's calming, gentle eyes. After a few seconds in which he said nothing, he looked aside, then back at her. "All right, what's the first thing on the agenda?"

"Nothing. We are patrolling the north shopping district."

"You've got to be kidding me. Are we investigating a disturbance or a break-in, or maybe a murder?"

"Nope. Captain Hewes wants you to get back into the swing of things slowly."

"Damn. I've been sitting on my ass for months. I was hoping for something interesting."

Cassidy saw his boyish grin and smiled through teary eyes.

Cassidy waited down the block for Miles to appear. Her eyes flew from house to house, looking for anyone suspicious. She couldn't trust a civilian to know he had been followed and of all people, Miles was a high-risk target. It was a huge gamble; there could be a sniper anywhere, or even armed gangsters behind the doors. She waited, hand on her gun. She was still shaking, but not as badly as at the hospital. She heard Miles knock loudly on the door.

"Hello? A few more questions, if you please?"

Cassidy eyed the windows for any movement or shadow in the curtains.

Miles banged on the door. No response. Miles looked off behind him to where Cassidy was peering out behind the street corner. Cassidy came out of hiding and jogged up to his side. She ran up to the window. It was almost completely bare. She ran around to the next window. She ran around the whole house, checking each window. There was no one inside and hardly any decorations or furniture at all. She pounded on the front door. *No response.*

"Shit," Cassidy said under her breath.

"Do we come back later?" Miles asked.

Cassidy's eyes flashed back and forth. *Maybe he's still in there hiding. Maybe he has cameras installed and caught me somehow. If he's in there, this might be my only chance; Miles might renege on the deal if someone else catches him.*

"You can testify that Ezreal Redding was here when you met him, correct?"

"Yeah, I thought we went over this—"

"There doesn't seem to be any sign of anyone else living here that might have invited him. Your testimony will have to be good enough."

Cassidy looked down at the lock. It was hard steel, like most of the older buildings around the block. She pulled out her universal key. After a second of recalibrating, there was a *clink.*

"Stand back," she whispered as she pocketed the key and drew her gun.

Cassidy pushed the door open and thrust her gun forward. The hallway and grand stairs were empty aside from two chairs and a sofa. She turned to her left and leaned into the room. *Empty.* She turned to her right and walked into the overly long reception room. *Empty. And not just of people, but pictures and decorations; it is all bare except for a few chairs.*

"It was always empty."

Cassidy spun around, gun swinging to face Miles.

"Easy!"

"Get back outside!" she commanded.

Miles gave her an angry look, but backed out. Cassidy closed and locked the door. She turned and vaulted up the stairs two at a time. On the second floor landing, she leaned in. There were eight doors. She checked the closest middle one. *Empty.* What should have been a bedroom was completely empty. She checked the next room, a bathroom, and was surprised to find a sink, toilet and shower, but no toothbrush or hair comb or anything personal. She checked the next few rooms, finding nothing. She even jumped up and down and pounded on a few of the walls, feeling for anything unnatural.

Cassidy walked up to the third floor and opened the first door. She nearly jumped as she caught in the dim light a giant pile of bags and dark metallic objects. She walked to the other side of the room and opened the window. Sunlight shone on what must have been a hundred pounds of cocaine and heroin and a pile of submachine guns. Cassidy walked into the next room. More guns, more drugs. She walked into a third and found even more piled at random on the floor.

"Holy shit."

After checking all the rooms and finding more guns and drugs than she had ever seen in her life, Cassidy put her gun in her pocket and walked down the flights of steps. She opened the door and nearly knocked into Miles.

"Well?"

"Mr. Buhari, you need to clear out, this is going to be swarming with cops any moment."

"I knew it!" He pumped his fist. "What did you find?"

"Promise this isn't going to be in any upcoming articles?"

Miles nodded.

"Everything but a dead hooker."

"This is fantastic! But wait, why was there no one there to guard it? I don't even hear an alarm system... something's not right. Where's the crazy old man?"

Cassidy looked down the street. Nothing appeared out of the ordinary, but her hair stood on end and she couldn't tell if it was cop instincts or a chemical imbalance.

"There was no one up there? No one at all?"

Cassidy nodded. "No one. They must have cleared out."

Miles looked worried. "Cleared out? What do you mean?"

"You don't have any proof that you spoke with Ezreal here, do you?"

"I have an interview—"

"Specifically here? Is there anything at all that you can use to prove that you interviewed him here?"

"His men took me here, that's how I know where it was."

"Do you have anything aside from your own testimony," she pronounced slowly.

"...No."

Cassidy looked aside. "You said there were others. Can you ID them?"

"No."

"Well, then that means we just confirmed our suspicions, but proved it to no one."

"But what if you find some DNA or hair or something from Ezreal?"

"That will definitely get us an arrest warrant; any ideas where he might be in the meantime?"

Miles grimaced. "That's your job."

"In that case, we'll just have to wait until a team comes by to search for DNA putting Ezreal Redding at this location. Then maybe we can get more people after him and catch him soon."

Miles gave her a cold look. "I'll take off. I wouldn't want to halt a police investigation." Without looking back, he said, "I would hurry if I were you."

No evidence was found beyond the drugs and weapons. There were fingerprints, but all of them couldn't be identified, except one person: Matthew Hammond. Cassidy accused Ezreal of illegal activities including drug-running, conspiracy and the lesser offense of squatting. An arrest warrant was sent out, but he couldn't be found. He had disappeared from New York City, never to deliver a crazed speech again. The raids underwater continued and a few more stores were found, pockets of air, but the weapons and drugs had disappeared. Whether the thugs who had set up the caches were leaving New York City or just retreating and trying to find other ways to disseminate their product once Manhattan left, and by extension the National Guard, no one knew.

"You got your story! Matthew Hammond, old-school militant revolutionary from antediluvian New York City poses as a dead man and returns to win a battle he lost six decades ago."

"What would I write? New York crime briefly had a utopian mouthpiece? I hired you to catch a top tier member of the organization controlling the crime in New York, not to indict someone who *might* be involved that you can't find."

Miles hung up on her before she could call him an asshole. Just like that, another avenue of her life, something short but which looked so promising, had abruptly ended, leaving her stranded and lost. Cassidy had tried tracking Ezreal Redding, Matthew Hammond, whoever he was; she had tried to come up with some plan to find him, but there was no trace. She was so desperate that one night she walked over to Alex's side of the office and pulled his maps out of the trash bin, looking for anything that might point out where Ezreal was. She hung the maps on the wall and stared at them. Every time she focused on a particular point, trying to connect it to a crime, she could only think of memories with Alex. Her eyes fell on Pier 48, then 9236 Giuliani Avenue. She tried to look at a different part of the map, but she couldn't concentrate. She finally tore her eyes from the maps in disgust. She turned back and tore them off the wall and threw them into the corner, huffing.

Ezreal is gone, disappeared into the aether. Even if he turns up in the next week, it will only be because of sheer dumb luck, not good police work. She looked at the crumpled maps in the corner. A white-hot pain shot through her and she forgot how to breathe as her mind played out a similar conversation she had with Alex, about how his maps were completely random. Looking at them now, she realized they were a star-chart of coincidences.

Cassidy couldn't stand to be in the room anymore. She walked out, seeing the blackness creeping at the edges of her vision as she did. She let herself fall back against the door and breathed, concentrating on what she could see. The darkness receded.

There's only one thing I can do now.

She went downstairs and filed a request to interview Rodney Maxwell. After spending five minutes reassuring the supervisor on duty, then another ten for them to retrieve the boy, she walked into the interrogation room where Rodney Maxwell sat cuffed to the table. Bruises still covered his face and his left eye was swollen shut. When he saw Cassidy sit down opposite him, his eyes went wide like an animal caught in the light.

"Rodney Luther Maxwell," she enunciated. She knew she didn't look menacing, especially since she was half a foot shorter than he was, but after catching glimpses of her disheveled face in the mirror over the last few days, she knew she looked half-insane. The fact that she had just recently beat him into the ground must have helped.

"You are accused of being an accessory in the murder of Mr. Brice Noble on May 2nd, and attempted murder of policeman Alex Waverly on August 23rd. My partner."

"That wasn't me!" His voice cracked. "It was Grease!"

"Grease killed them?" Her voice piqued.

"Darren Toohey. He's my friend, or was. He killed them both. He stabbed Noble, and he shot..." He couldn't finish.

"And you were completely innocent in all this?" Cassidy asked. She could feel herself being watched by the camera over her right shoulder. The police wanted the murderer and cop killer and Rodney looked like he was going to spill his guts to her. But she wanted to make him squirm. She needed to thrust her anger on someone.

"I..." Rodney looked down. "I never killed anyone."

"You were present at two murders."

"I didn't do anything! I didn't stab or shoot anyone."

"What were you doing in Manhattan, then? We have video of you and two other boys chasing down Brice Noble." Cassidy didn't bother asking who the third member was and she knew her superior must have noticed. She didn't care.

"My friend Antoni Marino, he had this idea that we should go rob some rich person. He had heard that was what everyone was doing. So I—"

"What do you mean, 'that's what everyone was doing'?"

"Antoni was a gangster. A real one. I was never part of any gang, but he was a low-level thug, I don't know who he was working for, only that he was selling drugs, everyone knew. He told me that people from the Boroughs were sailing over and assaulting people from Manhattan or something like that."

Cassidy's heart raced as she sensed her chance to find a link that would unravel the conspiracy again. *Could it be? Could he be part of the gang that was abducting people?* "Where is Antoni Marino?"

"He's dead. At least, that's what Grease told me."

"Did he have any known affiliates?"

"I don't know! I never got involved in that stuff."

Cassidy slammed a fist on the table. Rodney jumped at the sound.

"What about your other friend?"

"The one who shot your partner?" Rodney immediately looked away as Cassidy's eyes shot daggers at him. He took in a deep breath. "No. He tried getting into that stuff, but he was kind of a junkie. He couldn't be trusted."

"Where is he now?"

"I don't know. He heard about Antoni getting killed, he said some people were after him too, but he got away. He snuck into my home as a place to hide, two nights before you two showed up."

"And you have no idea where he could be?" Cassidy was practically begging for a lead.

Rodney shook his head. Cassidy's shoulders sagged and her eyes fell to her closed fists. A minute of silence passed as Cassidy leaned back in her chair, breathing, while Rodney looked on.

"I'm sorry your partner got killed."

Cassidy looked up.

"I didn't mean for any of it to go down. I was just trying to get out. My girlfriend from Manhattan promised to let me ride out of the city with her. I was going to go with her, leave everything behind. But then this all happened."

"You're sorry?" Cassidy seethed. "Sorry?" She stood up and placed her palms down on the table. She could hear footsteps behind her. The door opened.

"Officer Kikia," Captain Hewes' deep voice commanded her. "That'll be all."

Cassidy spun around and walked past him, feeling his eyes follow her. *I have the name of a kid who's a lot less likely to disappear than Ezreal. Darren Toohey. A kid who might be connected to a dead kid, who is connected to people who might know something.* She looked out on the streets in front of her and imagined them flattening and filled with color until they looked like Alex's maps. Random markings and scratches appeared. Cassidy looked beyond the Boroughs to Manhattan. The city looked as if it were a thousand miles away and moving away from her. Cassidy didn't know where she was going, but she made sure her first step was towards it as she re-entered the labyrinth of the Boroughs, looking for her way out.

Chapter Forty

"Three blocks away, a highly paid engineer who's been sitting at a desk his whole life is training himself to sail Manhattan, the largest sea-faring vessel ever made. He must feel like an astronaut, a voyager readying to captain this new colossal vehicle... I wonder what was weirder for the first astronauts who landed on the moon: the strange new world they appeared on, or the cramped, flaming metal tube they were trapped in?" Lei took another sip of her mojito.

"I'm not interested in why a nameless pencil pusher gets promoted to the job of 'Captain of Manhattan.' I want to know why you turned it down." Miles reached for his golden-brown shot-glass. "Funny thing..."

"What?"

Miles held up his glass and downed it. He raised a finger and called, "Another," to the bartender. He turned to Lei. "The Old World has been refining alcohol for ten thousand years, even creating religions around it, and they still can't make anything better than Kentucky bourbon. Does it make you proud to be an American?"

Lei gave him a half-smile. "I guess I never considered it," she said, disinterested. "So what does alcohol tell you about us?"

"That Americans aren't afraid to have a good time and love to drink their problems away. See, British alcohol," he said with a hint of disgust, "it was all controlled by aristocrats who could afford the vineyards and distilleries. Still is today. One hundred million people on an island the size of Michigan, no one can afford to buy land, especially not enough to make good booze, except the rich."

"What's wrong with that?"

"Well, ignoring the obvious social problems—"

"Oh, my God, you're one of those people! You're one of the rioters and crazies who are trying to overthrow the government!"

"I'm a rebel and a partier. I just hit important people with a stick for fun and if a mob gathers when I'm done, all the better." He downed another shot. "Back to alcohol—"

"Back to alcohol? I'd rather talk about how you're trying to be a revolutionary while wearing nice clothes and hitting up expensive bars."

Miles paused. He looked over his shoulder slowly, then leaned in close and whispered, "I'm sabotaging the system from within." Miles grinned and Lei laughed. "I swear alcohol relates in this case, it always does, let me tell you why our alcohol sucks and why you should be proud to be from the States."

"Okay." Lei took another drink, this time genuinely interested in how he was going to tie it together.

"In Britain, it's all alcohol handed down to us from those few people rich enough to own the plants. It's not that our alcohol tastes awful, it's that it lacks any soul, or spirit. It's market tested, sent to laboratories to make it as tasty and addictive as possible. Britain and the 'wet-ankled' countries of Europe are doing with beer what fast-food did for food. Ironically enough, this isn't happening in America. See, our alcohol isn't genuine. It tastes good at first, but there is no substance to it. You can't learn to like it, like with rich food, there's no refinement of taste. You either drink it or you don't. That's why in Britain, everyone drinks imported American liquor and Polish vodka.

"Meanwhile, in the States, hundreds of years ago, your liquor was made by hillbillies, prospectors and half-insane people, a tradition that has continued to this day." He lifted his glass. Lei lifted hers in turn and clinked it against his and drank. "To this day, anyone with a passion for inebriation can run off into the boonies, buy up a bunch of unused land in the Ozarks and make his own liquor, one that conveys all the sorrow and struggle of whoever made it."

"I think you've had too much to drink," Lei said. "If you think you can taste class struggle in your alcohol..."

Miles turned and waved over the bartender. "Glass of Tennessee whiskey." The bartender handed it to Miles, who passed it to Lei. "Take a big gulp, let it roll down your throat like syrup."

Lei did as she was told, squinting a little from the burn. Miles waited a second before saying, "Feel that? Feel the warmth in your nostrils."

Lei half-nodded, half-swayed.

"Describe the taste to me. First words that come to your mind."

"Rich. Very rich, I would say."

"Yet that drink is probably the cheapest in this uppity bar. Rich is a good word. The first bottle of this particular brand was made by a man who failed at gold-panning in North Dakota and decided not to try his luck again in California. A poor man serving other poor men, but the taste is rich because it is literally a taste of something they could never have."

"Hmm."

"People create luxury where they can. And that little flair, that little oddity or aftertaste, is where you find their beliefs, their goals. That's why most true southern alcohol tastes so rich; because they're poor man's drinks."

"Why doesn't vodka taste as rich then, if it's made by poor people, too?"

"Because they're crazy Russians, what do you expect?"

Lei chuckled and sipped at her mojito to wash down the taste. "I think we found a flaw in your theory."

"Yes, well, I can ignore that. Besides, it's not why I'm here. I'm here for you."

"Are you?" she said coyly, then remembered he was supposed to be interviewing her. She felt stupid for a moment and put down her drink. "Do you interview everyone like this, in a loud public place without any recording equipment?"

"Only when I want to have a good time. So, tell me, why did you turn down the job of sailing Manhattan out?"

Lei thought it over. "Because..." She realized that it had disgusted her in so many ways she couldn't pin one down. "Because I couldn't bear the thought of my work, which was meant to save Manhattan, ending Manhattan."

"Tragic. What does that feel like?"

Lei took another drink and he had his answer. "I'm coming to terms with it," she forced out. "I did what I could. It's not my fault if half the city is revolting and the other half is too scared to stick around and work out their problems."

"So who do you think is responsible for the break-up of the city? The mayor, the government?"

"The anarchists, probably."

"The anarchists? I don't think I've heard about any anarchists."

"They're all over the news."

"Is that what the news is calling them?" Miles muttered.

"I don't really care. I'm not going to stick around."

"You're not going to ride down the coast with the rest of Manhattan? I think you're the only one who'll be turning that down."

"I don't care," she said slowly.

"You don't want to see what your invention can really do? I thought that's what techies live for."

"Watching the city use my machines to sell off Manhattan piece by piece, it would be like Oppenheimer seeing the A-bomb go off."

"That's pretty harsh." He eyed her empty drink. "You know, you might be disgusted with what your machines are doing now, but I bet they're going to change the world for the better, and you'll go down in history as a hero."

"You're just saying that to flatter me." She leaned forward and Miles smelled the low-class whiskey mixing with the overpriced mojito in an unholy manner.

"I'm serious. Imagine all the good these machines could do for a city once they really start to get developed and put into place. If there's a massive hurricane warning, the people won't have to board up their windows with duct tape and a wish; they can just move the city and return it to its natural place when the storm passes. Hell, no one would even have to take work off. Or imagine that you have a small city-state, like Singapore, or the Free East Indian Cities. Imagine that a nation tries to invade them. They could just leave, stay out on the water, maybe float to someplace more hospitable. I swear, the sailing off of Manhattan could just be the first speed bump on the way to history-changing progress, and you will always be remembered for making it, Miss Lei Xu."

Lei felt a smile work its way across her face. She let the words sink in and remembered the way she felt when Ramos first hired her to work on the motors. She felt like the world was so open, that anything could be accomplished. If what Miles said was right, then what she had done was better than anything she could have imagined. "I won't be remembered," she said meekly, though her smile held. "Marko Sverichek will."

"Oh, Sverichek, the hermit who doesn't even show his face after lifting up the city? Doesn't appear on talk shows, or write a book? No, no. He'll go down in history the same way Antonio Meucci did."

"Who?"

"Exactly. He's the man who originally invented the telephone. Then Alexander Graham Bell made it a household item, so everyone just says Bell invented it. Makes the history textbooks shorter, and you Americans are shit at history to begin with."

She smirked and he added, "I'm sorry, your alcohol is great, your education not so much. Maybe the two are related. All I'm saying is you have a marketable face. People know your name, people like you.

You're young, sophisticated, attractive, everything that most scientists are not. All the credit for the machines from here until the end of time is going to be yours."

Lei couldn't keep down her smile. "Thank you. I appreciate it, I mean it. I never really thought about it that way. I don't think it will be that grand, but maybe history will justify my work."

"Oh, dream a little," Miles groaned. "The future hasn't happened, which means every good thing that could happen will until proven otherwise." He waved the bartender over. "Two more glasses of Tennessee whiskey." The bartender gave them each a glass. Miles leaned in and said, "Tonight, you will drink the way you should have always been drinking: like a poor man destined to be king." She raised her glass to her lips, watching as Miles downed the liquor in one gulp. She did the same, clenching her teeth and forcing the burning liquid down her throat. Her eyes went wide and she gave a little cough as it went down. The warmth spread through her, followed by an immediate sense of pride as Miles called, "See, I knew you had it in you!"

Two drinks later and the warmth was replaced by an overwhelming confidence that everything was going to be all right. She completely forgot about the interview.

It was nearly midnight by the time they stepped out of the bar. "My apartment is only four blocks away, I can walk."

"No, I'll get us a cab, I insist. It's dangerous to walk around at night."

Miles turned and saw that there were already cabs waiting outside the bar. He realized he was drunker than he thought. He chuckled to himself and helped her descend into the nearest cab. Lei gave the man her address and the boat took off. Lei leaned against Miles, pressing into him with each wild turn. When they finally arrived, Miles handed the skipper a handful of bills, helped Lei up and walked her to her door.

"Did you get all the questions you needed? I mean, did I answer your questions—"

"I know what you mean. That depends, do you have more to share?"

"Maybe..." She smiled widely.

"Well then, how about we continue where we left off in your apartment?"

Lei opened the lobby door and led him to the elevator. Once the doors shut, she threw herself on him. She grabbed onto his jacket and pulled him close as she kissed him, her tongue working its way around his, her lipstick and alcohol mixing in her mouth. Miles placed his hands around her and pulled her close to him.

The elevator *dinged* and Lei fell back. She grabbed his hand and stumbled forward to her door. She nearly dropped her keys as she felt his lips against her neck. She opened the door, pulled him inside and kicked off her high heels. Miles grabbed for her, but she stepped out of reach, snatched his hands and walked backward towards the bedroom, eyes wild. She pulled his hands and stepped towards him like a dancer. She placed his arms on her top. She leaned in for another kiss before he pulled off her dress.

Chapter Forty-One

Sophia held Charlie's arm across her breasts. Her every curve sank into the bed and was absorbed by the warm foam mattress. The feeling made her eyelids leaden. She tried to chain her mind to the bed, let herself be absorbed by the sensual pleasure, but all she could think about was what she was going to say that evening during her 'last spin.' Sophia opened her eyes and gently lifted Charlie's hand. She started to get up when the hand came back around her. "Charlie, I have to get up."

"No, you don't." He pulled her closer. "You can stay here forever."

Sophia laughed and looked over at Charlie. Half his face was sunk in the pillow. His one eye fixated on her and he smiled mischievously.

She stroked the side of his face, feeling the stubble prickle against her hand. "Soon."

"It's always 'soon.'"

"I mean it this time, though. I will never be able to run for political office again and my pride won't let me take anything below a mid-level managing job, so after we arrive in Texas, I'm going to be out of things to do for quite a while." Sophia tried to smile, though she could tell by the way he looked at her that she couldn't hide it from him.

Charlie repositioned himself so he could look at her with both eyes. "No, you won't. I know you. You're stubborn enough that you'll be running for governor the moment we land. But that's okay, because I will always be here waiting for you." He kissed her hand.

Sophia flushed. She leaned over and kissed him. They broke apart and she pivoted and got out of bed. She headed straight for the shower and spent the next hour getting her hair and face perfect. *These are the photos they're going to use for the history books; they should be good ones.*

By the time she stepped back into the bedroom, Charlie had gone back to sleep. She couldn't blame him; after all the long nights he had put in working on the transition for his company, he deserved it. She dressed as quietly as possible, donning a light grey dress suit. Her escort waited at the bottom of the stairs. Sophia took the middle seat in the covered police boat as it made a decent clip towards City Hall. She had seen enough of the city that she didn't care to look again, but her eye caught the reflection of Saint Patrick's Cathedral in the water. *How wonderful it would have been to have been married there.* But the cathedral was headed north to Vermont's new coast and a flight there wouldn't give her the same dream wedding she had imagined.

For the first time in months, there was a steady thrum of planes overhead. Reporters flocking in, tourists cramming the streets trying to see Manhattan one last time before it broke apart, and the relatives and friends of people who resided in Manhattan who wanted to hitch a ride with them across the coast.

Cameras flashed as Sophia descended from the boat. She smiled instinctively and hoped they caught her good side as she walked up the steps to the assembled podium at the top steps of City Hall. Poking out amongst the journalists was a handful of the billionaires who had been kidnapped, surrounded by their families. Sophia smiled at them, grateful for the ones who had turned out. She took the podium and looked out at the crowd. It was almost beautiful. The sun was shining brightly with just a few puffy clouds wafting across the sky. The water was a clear blue, the months of litter crews working morning to night having picked it clean. As she looked straight out, she saw the reflection of the massive skyscrapers in the water. The crowd was waiting for her to deliver Manhattan's farewell speech, and meanwhile, she was being hit with a vision of a paradise that almost was. An awkward silence passed as they began to stir. *Just get out the first word. That's what you used to do when you were afraid to speak in public. Just say the first word and everything will flow from there.*

"Thank you all for coming." She heard the rise and fall of her own voice as she gave New York its last farewell. But she was somewhere far away. She was walking through the revived Central Park with its floating Buddhist monastery. She was sitting just above the dugout of Yankee stadium, watching the President throw out the first pitch of its re-inauguration. She was at the Metropolitan, watching a ballet with foreign dignitaries.

"New York City could not hope to survive as an island that watches the slowly rising tide push the continent farther away from us. Literally hundreds of trillions of dollars have been pumped into the city due to the selling off of the skyscrapers, which will be relocated to prosperous cities, where they will never fear sinking into the ocean again. As for those left behind, nearly all of the money will go directly to the new city government for the rest of New York City. With all the money they will be receiving, it will be more than enough to fund police efforts to finally end organized crime, keep up repairs on the city and keep it floating for another hundred years.

"It was a difficult decision to make, and one I did not make alone. I and the rest of the city council are convinced that this was the right thing to do. It might not have been the most glamorous course, and it was certainly not what we hoped for when the skyscrapers first rose up and we were all filled with so much hope. But what we have done was best for the people who live here. This gives me hope, and the confidence that I did what was right."

Sophia looked up at the vision of the perfect city rising from the waves again. She looked down at the people, catching the eyes of a woman who had been cringing in terror underground just a few weeks before. She held her daughter in front of her, smiling, her green eyes outshone only by the little girl's.

"Paradise won't be handed to us from above or by any great man with a brilliant idea. We'll just have to make it ourselves."

Sophia waved her hand, and after a few seconds of smiling at the crowd, she turned and entered City Hall for the last time.

Chapter Forty-Two

Cassidy stared curiously at the blood trickling from her hand. *The pain isn't so bad.* She looked down at the shattered cup she had dropped and caught her reflection in the glass. She reached down. Her finger stopped on a protruding edge. She pressed down and watched blood leak onto the glass fragment. She pressed harder. The edge sank beneath her skin. Her finger began to shake as she imagined the glass nearing her bone. The shard cracked. Cassidy saw her pill lying on the floor in the corner of her eye. She pulled her finger up, wincing at the pain. She grabbed the pill, forced it down, and walked into the bathroom, looking for the Band-Aids. She walked out the door, leaving the blood-stained glass still strewn across the kitchen floor.

Cassidy walked the streets alone. She imagined people coming out with menacing looks, with hands in jackets, but when she turned, it was only a mother with her child. Cassidy was afraid; now she had the mantle of 'Alex's successor,' hunting down the criminal organizations in his place, as everyone assumed she would finish what her partner had started. The title had been secret, whispered by other cops, but it still weighed on her. She stared at his maps and tried to think up something.

But there was nothing. Crime had plummeted. Murder, theft and drug abuse were barely reported. The great criminal masterminds had disappeared. Cassidy kept expecting them to be found one day, but she couldn't wait for that day to come, not when she needed to find a way out. She started to resign herself to the idea that she would be stuck in the Boroughs, left with nothing but the search for Alex's assailant and chasing the wind until her hair turned gray.

Two days before Manhattan was set to sail away and there hadn't been a trace of even mid-level drug lords. For a week, Cassidy had been struggling to maintain calm, to not let her stress give her a panic attack that would have her lose her vision or asphyxiate in the middle of a gunfight. She had been trying breathing exercises and focusing her mind on the search. But two days to go and she still felt as if something horrible was about to happen and she convinced herself it couldn't have just been her depression speaking.

Cassidy had been knocking heads all morning when she finally got the police captain of Manhattan on the line. "Captain Dreyer, this is Cassidy Kikia, I am one of the officers leading the recent busts in the Boroughs. I wanted to warn you, I suspect something bad is going to happen before Manhattan sets sail."

"You suspect? Are you telling me I should be looking for a report to come in, or any specific targets...?"

"No. But you have to understand, all the criminal organizations we have been tracking in the Boroughs have been disappearing, lessening their activities, the drug supplies have all but vanished."

"That might have something to do with all the raids..."

"But whenever there is a raid, there is blowback, there's bloodshed. But there's been nothing so far, crime has just evaporated."

"So we've done your job for you?"

Cassidy bit her lip. "Look, there has been a lot of anger out here; I and a lot of others think there is a conspiracy going on to keep Manhattan here by force. You have to keep them—"

"Ma'am, I have listened this far, but unless you hadn't noticed, Manhattan is one giant steel cage. The Coast Guard patrols the waters and the National Guard and more bodyguards than I care to count are on every block. We even have radar on the edges of the city to make sure no one comes up from the water on the off chance the criminals have submarines. Waste of taxpayer dollars if you ask me..."

"Where are they all going to be when the ships sail?" Cassidy retorted. "The bodyguards won't be riding with the skyscrapers, neither will the National Guard, there is no place to stay, all the living quarters will be packed."

"There will be a Coast Guard escort."

"How many boats?"

Cassidy heard Captain Dreyer sigh from the other end of the line. "I can't disclose that information, but I can tell you it's practically an armada. Does that alleviate your fears?"

Oddly, it did, but Cassidy didn't want to admit he was right. "Yes, I understand. I just wanted to make sure we were remaining vigilant," she finished lamely.

"Well, thank you for your concern. Good day."

Cassidy had hoped to sound more convincing, but she was having a hard time convincing herself. She pressed her thumb against her temple and grimaced. *This is hopeless. There are Navy Seals diving down into the subways, National Guard walking the piers, and I have no leads.* She looked out at Manhattan. *Why can't I sail away? I ruined everything. I got an innocent man killed, Alex is lying in a hospital bed because of me. Why can't I just...*

Her eyes widened. She ran to police headquarters as an idea started to form in her mind. Without knocking, she burst into Captain Hewes' office.

"Captain Hewes, I'm sorry."

"I'll forgive you this time, Cassidy, but only because you caught me in an off moment. I'm amazed you did, I've had government officials and military personnel in and out of my office for weeks; it's a miracle you didn't barge in while I was shaking hands with the President." When she didn't laugh, he scowled. "All right, what is it?"

"I want Rodney Maxwell to be pardoned."

"You're going to have to explain this at least once."

"Sir, he was only an innocent bystander. Alex's shooter was Darren Toohey; Rodney was just a friend who was resting in his own house at the time."

"According to your report, Rodney pointed an unregistered firearm at you."

"Which he immediately dropped when we announced we were police officers and which was probably also Darren Toohey's."

Hewes fell uncharacteristically silent. His eyes focused and Cassidy felt she was being examined. "You better give me a good reason."

"Well—"

"Not that I'm going to let him go, I mean you better give me a goddamn great reason so that I don't give you a few more days' leave to get your head back together."

Cassidy steeled herself. "I want to follow him to Alex's real shooter."

That caught Hewes off guard.

"He's innocent," she continued. "He was in his own house, hiding from gangsters and thugs who were threatening to kill him. We burst through the door and he panicked, but he dropped the gun the second we announced ourselves. I don't think he's dangerous, but his friend is. Rodney said that the gangs killed his only other friend, Antoni, so Toohey is all he has left. Let Rodney go and I can follow him and we can find the real shooter."

"He stole a boat and assisted in the murder of Brice Noble."

"That was Darren Toohey again. Toohey is the dangerous one, he is a killer and he shot a cop. Rodney was just in the wrong place at the wrong time."

"He's done that twice now."

"And I think he'll do it a third time and when he does, I will be there."

Hewes met her gaze. She didn't flinch. "He had an illegally purchased firearm."

He's grasping, he wants me to convince him. "Who the hell doesn't out here? Even cops. You want to protect your family? I'm guessing you *at least* have a shotgun at your house, probably more."

"I don't like your tone," he spat. He thrummed his fingers on his chair and looked aside. "I don't want you going alone."

"I'm going alone," she said and before he could start, she continued, "at first. There are so many cops out here, Guard, Navy, he's going to be constantly looking over his shoulder like a frightened rabbit. It'll be hard to track him. If a bunch of cops follow him, he only has to spot one to get away. Let me track him alone; if he goes in a building, then I'll call for backup, and if anything bad happens, there will literally be soldiers on every block."

Hewes didn't have a response and Cassidy knew she had him. "I'll put in the order," he said without looking up. "You follow him, but if you lose it, or god forbid you try some revenge bullshit—"

"I won't."

"I will end you." He enunciated every word.

Cassidy nodded, knowing that was the closest to a 'yes' Hewes would ever say.

Rodney waited in his cell, looking up at the ceiling. *I was so close. I was so close.* The thought had nearly driven him mad. He was looking right at the ferry, Sam was standing right beside him.

There was an electronic *click* and then the cell opened. A guard stepped in and Rodney expected to be interrogated again. "Get up and follow me," the guard intoned. Rodney got to his feet and did as he was told. They walked down the long hall toward the exit instead of back to the interrogation rooms. *This is it. I'm going to be transferred to a prison on the mainland. Either the other inmates are going to kill me or the guards will if they think I'm a cop-killer.* His knees began to shake. They stepped into the processing room. On a cold metal table were Rodney's clothes, wallet and cell phone.

"Change," one of the guards commanded. Rodney eyed him

suspiciously. "You're leaving today."

"Where to?"

"Hell, preferably," he grumbled. "The accessory murder charge against Brice Noble and the assault charge against an officer with a deadly weapon have been dropped and all the blame has been placed on your accomplice; your testimony and time served has been deemed sufficient to let you leave. God only knows when the criminals took over the NYPD. You're free to go."

Rodney's heart began to pound in his chest. *Is that true? How much power do the gangs have? Are they only letting me out so they can kill me?* "How many more days before Manhattan leaves?"

The guard gave him an odd look. "You looking to kill again? Don't bother, the Guards have everything sealed up, you little shit."

It's still here? I didn't miss it! Rodney's heart pounded faster. He disrobed down to his underwear and put on his old clothes. The guard escorted him out of the floating prison, shoving him out the last door. Rodney looked up at the sky and saw a pack of seagulls flying overhead. He looked down at his phone. *Battery's dead. No surprise.* He started running, a small glimmer of hope seeping into him. As he started to enter more populated areas, he slowed down. He stopped for a second and looked into his pocket and pulled out his wallet. *Empty. What the fuck? It wasn't empty when I was arrested.* He began to feel an immense sense of dread overcome him as he realized he was without any money, any food, friends, family and now he didn't even have a gun to protect himself in a city where there were still people trying to kill him. He tried to calm himself. *It's okay. You can go into a tech store, tell them your phone died and you were looking for help fixing it. They will recharge it, you walk out, thank them, and get the hell out. And no one's going to try to kill you if you stay where there are Guardsmen.* He nodded to himself, liking the plan, but it didn't ease his nerves.

He trekked towards the center of town, then turned down a side street to get to the off-brand tech stores. A hand grabbed his left shoulder and he felt the cold steel of a gun press against his neck, digging into his spine.

"Rodney Maxwell."

Rodney shivered violently as he recognized the voice of the female officer from that night.

"Please don't kill me. I didn't do anything. I wasn't going to shoot."

"Shut up. Listen, you said you were riding out on a skyscraper, you said you had a contact, a girlfriend. Who?"

Rodney paused.

"Who?" Cassidy demanded, pressing the gun down into his neck.

"Samantha Harding."

"Good, you didn't just make her up. So the question is: can you get me a ride, too?"

Rodney paused. "What?"

"Could you get a place for me on the skyscrapers too?"

"I..."

Cassidy pressed the gun down again.

"We're going to try," she asserted. "I'll get you to her and you get me out of New York. Deal?"

"Yes," Rodney croaked. "Okay. I have her number on my phone, but it's dead."

"Give it to me," she ordered.

Rodney reached into his pocket and handed her his phone.

"Old model, but I have a charger for this. We'll go back to my apartment and charge it. If I don't have one, we can go to a store for the right one."

Cassidy lifted the gun from his neck and released her hand from his shoulder. Rodney turned just in time to see her pocket the phone and the gun. Cassidy was shorter than him and had a small frame, but she looked wild, like a cornered animal.

"You first." She nodded forward.

They walked in silence. Rodney tried not to let her see he was afraid. After ten minutes of walking in silence, they entered the apartment complex and marched up to the second story. Cassidy took her eyes off of him as she fumbled with the lock, messing up the code once, then twice.

You can hit her right now. Do it. Knock her out as the lock flashes green, take the phone and run.

The door clicked green. Cassidy looked at him and waved forward. The door shut behind him with a loud *bang* and he winced as he heard it lock. "Watch for glass shards, I dropped a cup earlier," she said as she walked into the next room. Rodney was too nervous to sit down and remained standing in the middle of the room. A few awkward minutes passed as he eyed the door while listening to her rummaging through electronics boxes, occasionally throwing wires and parts on the floor.

Leave! Run away. She's not looking! Go!

And do what? With no money, no food, no way to contact Sam? Your friends have been dropping like flies, who's to say you won't be next?

Cassidy returned and handed him the phone. "My name is Cassidy

Kikia. Repeat it."

"Cassidy Kikia."

"Mention me to Samantha Harding. Tell her I am an exemplary cop who helped in the subway raids that needs a ride out and that you can't get out of here without my help. Tell her you're too poor to buy a ticket," Cassidy emphasized. "I saw you had no money in your wallet and we didn't see any bank records. I'm guessing it's true anyway. Mention nothing else."

Rodney flicked through his contacts and called Sam.

"Rodney! Oh, my God, I haven't heard from you in so long! Where the hell have you been, the city's leaving tomorrow!"

"Hey, Sam. Listen, it's hard to explain, I'm sorry I haven't called. Everything is still good? I can come stay with you, right?" Rodney looked down at Cassidy, who eyed him with contempt.

"Of course! Oh, my God, you had me so worried, don't ever do that again. I have called so many times."

"Baby... I'm sorry. I really am. You have no idea how much I want to put all this behind us. Seriously, the sooner we get the hell out of here, the better. But... how do I put this... would you mind if someone else came with us?"

"Someone else? Who?"

"A police officer; Cassidy Kikia."

Sam paused. "What's going on? Are you in trouble?"

"No, no, it's not that. Just the opposite. Cassidy got me out of trouble. There were some guys looking to get me and Cassidy helped me out. But she told me she wants out of New York. She wants a ride, she says she'll leave the second we hit land. In exchange, she says she'll buy my ticket for the ferry. Look, I am so sorry for asking you, babe, I—"

"Rodney, it's okay. Just get here, all right? I've heard you tell me everything will be okay over the phone so many times, and I don't want to hear it anymore, I just want to see you here."

Rodney bit his lip. "Okay. I'm sor..." He looked over at Cassidy. "We'll be over with the next ferry."

"Okay, see you soon."

Rodney hung up.

"Nice girl." Cassidy chuckled. "I have nothing to pack except a few clothes. You?"

Rodney shook his head. "I've got some at her place... we were looking to move in together."

"Okay, wait here." Cassidy walked into the next room. A few minutes later, she came out with a grey suitcase. Without a word, the two of them stepped out.

It was a short walk to the ferry. As the guards scanned Rodney's face, Cassidy worried that he would be taken back in, but apparently the release orders had been received and they let him pass. Soon, they were in Manhattan and another short walk led them to an imitation brick apartment building. They stepped in and made their way to the fifth floor. Rodney went up to room 514 and knocked. The door flew open and a girl with curly, dark hair jumped into Rodney's arms.

"Finally! You had me worried sick!" She kissed him passionately.

"Okay," Cassidy interrupted loudly.

Sam turned on the spot. "Oh, hello. You must be..."

"Officer..." She sighed. "Just Cassidy."

"All right, Cassidy, well, come on in."

The three stepped into the small living room. There was a couch and an old recliner that had seen better days. On the floor against the far wall sat a projection cube that was far out of date.

"Make yourselves at home," Sam offered kindly. Cassidy put her suitcase against the end of the couch before collapsing onto it.

"Hey, babe," Rodney whispered. "I was hoping I could get a shower real quick? We sort of had to run to the ferry and I'm sweaty."

"Oh, right. Here, let me..."

Cassidy could guess that Sam was looking over at her. Cassidy closed her eyes. She opened her neural interface and decided to watch her new Mexican drama film, 'Noches de Pasión Interminables.' She thought she heard two pairs of feet stamp on a shower floor that was far too close to the living room to easily ignore. She turned the volume up.

Halfway through the movie, she felt footsteps approach. She minimized the movie until it appeared as a small square at the bottom-right corner of her vision. Rodney was standing awkwardly in the kitchen area, glancing between Cassidy and the floor, while Sam stood over her.

"Come on, Cassidy, help me make dinner!"

"I don't cook," she replied.

"Then I can teach, come on."

Cassidy glared at her.

"Look." Sam met her gaze. "This ride is going to last a while and it's going to get mighty awkward if you're just the loner that hangs around here. If we're stuck together, we might as well enjoy it."

Cassidy sighed loudly.

"Oh, don't give me that, come on!" Sam grabbed her arm and helped her to her feet, leading her into the small but homey kitchen.

Cassidy mindlessly stirred the spaghetti as Hector Plasio Francisco Santiago Jesus José Juan Carlos Alberto y Garcia de Barajas and his lover Carmen danced under a Spanish moon. When Carmen let her red dress drop to the marble floor, Cassidy poured the tomato sauce into the pot. Hector removed his pants and revealed his enormous uncircumcised penis just as she set the bowl of noodles down on the table.

The three sat down and started helping themselves to rolls, spaghetti and steamed vegetables.

"I can't believe I made it out," Rodney said to Sam as he bit into a roll. "Part of me wants to go back just for the book."

"Was it that good?" Sam asked.

"No." Rodney laughed. "I doubt it sold many copies. Maybe the guy who wrote it just kept one of the few for himself. But there was just something special about finding something that had been lost. Every time I turned the page, it was like I was diving deeper into something."

"Did you finish it?"

"I got to an ending point," he replied. "Peponi spends five years in an off-the-books max security prison, doing nothing but practicing the piano every day. His love, Jenna, gets killed in a terrorist attack. Peponi convinces the government that enough people died that they should intervene. They agree, he turns back time, and everyone comes back to life. One late night at the bar where Jenna works, he walks in. It's completely empty, everyone in the city has turned to God, trying to find a reason why they miraculously came back from the dead. He walks in and tries talking to her. She thanks him for saving her, but she still hates him for disappearing. He puts his arm around her and they're both half-laughing and half-crying. Peponi looks past her because he knows that there are government agents waiting to take him back once he's done talking to her. Peponi asks Jenna, 'Do you want to go back, to when we were carefree and young?' She says, 'Aren't we now?'"

Cassidy watched sweat fall off Hector's brow and onto Carmen's naked buttocks.

Sam waited for him to finish. "And? Does he use his powers to take them back, or does he just let her go, and accept that no matter what, he can't escape his bad choices?"

Rodney annoyed Sam by taking a giant bite of spaghetti before saying, "I don't know. That's as far as I got. I can't help but think he should let her go, but probably didn't. Despite having the power to turn back time, he always carries some baggage with him."

"Hmmm." Sam nodded. She turned to Cassidy, as if realizing for the first time that they hadn't spoken since they sat down. "So you're a police officer, Cassidy? That must be exciting."

"I'm done. Just tired of it."

"Want to try something new, eh?" Rodney asked. When she didn't respond, he added, "I don't blame you. It's bad enough living out there, but being a cop, you must have had a target on your back. It would drive me crazy."

¡Oh, Hector! ¡Oh, Hector! ¡Mi guapo gigante!

"Does he always talk this much?" Cassidy shot.

"Hey, no need to be rude." Sam frowned. "He's just trying to make conversation. You've hardly said a thing. It's impolite. And here I still don't even know how you two met up. How did that happen anyway?" She turned to Rodney.

Rodney looked down. After a long moment, he said, "I was desperate. I didn't know what else to do. Antoni and Grease suggested we mug some rich guy and take his money. But Grease pulled out a knife and accidentally killed the poor guy."

Sam gasped.

"It was awful. I couldn't believe it. Then all the chaos started when people figured out gangs from the Boroughs were doing the same thing; targeting rich people in Manhattan. I thought either the gangs would kill me for being part of the headlines that uncovered what they were doing or the police for being involved with Antoni and Grease. It was so stupid, dumbest thing I've ever done, I wish I could take it back."

¡Mas, mas, mas!

"Oh, my God. I told you not to get involved with them, they are nothing but trouble." She pushed against his shoulder.

"Not a day goes by that I don't regret it. That's why I can't wait for Manhattan to get moving. I just want to leave it all behind. All of it. Start fresh. I don't even want to remember it." He looked at Cassidy. "How about you? That must be what you're doing, right? Running away from life back there."

"Why are you two together?" Cassidy asked between a mouthful of spaghetti. "He must be amazing in bed, right? What else has he got going for him?"

Sam glared at her, but Cassidy wouldn't stop. "He's an idiot. I mean, he's young, he's a man, and like most people in the Boroughs, he didn't get a good education, so it's not a surprise he ended up tied to gangs, but that's no excuse to think, 'Oh hey, I'll just rob someone at knife-point, what could possibly go wrong?'" She turned to Rodney and said, "You must be godly in the sack."

"He's a great man." Sam tried to keep her voice level. "You don't know what we've been through together. How hard it's been. My family all moved out of New York years ago penniless, begging for food. I haven't even heard from most of them in a while." She had to fight to keep her voice from wavering. "But I stayed because I was the only one lucky enough to get a job. Rodney was a lot like me, except... he never knew his father, and his mom got sick and passed away years ago. But Rodney never gave up. He worked hard and kept out of the crime scene. Not an easy thing to do out there." She leaned in towards Cassidy in a *you should know* that look. "And one day when he was picking up trash in Manhattan, he saw me waitressing; the next night, he came in and spent all the money he had on an ice cream sundae and when I brought it out, he asked me to share it with him."

Sam looked at Cassidy defiantly. "Every man has his faults. If you can't accept one who does, then I'm not surprised you don't have one."

¡Mi querido, mi amor, estoy casi allí!

Cassidy tapped her plate with her fork. "I'm sorry. You're right. I just want to start over. I didn't mean to bring any bitterness with me. I am trying to start anew too."

Sam and Rodney watched her. "That's okay," Sam replied, easing up. "It sounds like you've all been through a lot."

Cassidy nodded. "Anyway, I saw you have a projection cube. It looks old, but can it run any games made in the last year or so?"

"It's broken," Rodney answered.

"What?" Cassidy shot up. "Do you have another?"

Sam laughed. "I'm a waitress and he's an unemployed garbage man. What did you expect?"

"Well..." Cassidy thought. "At least we can connect to each other's neural interfaces and play some basic games."

This time, Rodney joined Sam in laughing. "We don't have any internal comps," Rodney explained.

Cassidy's eyes widened as she thought of the next two weeks. "Then what are we going to do?"

"Talk. Play old board games. Look out and watch the coastline fly by as we sail away."

Cassidy blanched. "That sounds so boring."

"Why?" Sam asked. "Do you have to constantly be fiddling with something? Why not live in the moment? I always hate those things. At the restaurant, everyone who comes in has those and they always watch comedy videos or look at stocks, or read the news. They're always laughing or moaning or crying to themselves, even when there are other people there. It's like an insane asylum cafeteria. A few times, I think I've even caught a few people watching porn while they were eating."

Cassidy stopped the movie.

"Okay." She sighed, defeated. "But I'm beat, so we can start that tomorrow. I take it I'm collapsing on the couch?"

"Help me clean the dishes first." Sam stood up and the three cleared the table.

Cassidy had her hands in the sink when she asked, "So, how did you know they were watching porn?"

"Because their eyes were huge right when they walked in."

Cassidy smiled.

"They were salivating before the food even came."

She chuckled.

"And afterwards, they gave me a huge tip."

Chapter Forty-Three

"**D**on't strain yourself," Haley chided Alex as she tried to push him back into his wheelchair.

"My legs will fall off if I sit any longer," he grunted as he rose to his feet. Miraculously, his legs held, but his chest warmed with a heavy, dull ache. He leaned in for a kiss.

"You could spend another day resting up before we leave."

"No." Alex shook his head. "Pack up your stuff. I'll come by your house in a few hours. I just want to turn in my badge, head over to my place and pack up. We can catch the first ferry we can."

Haley beamed at him. "I'm excited. Once we hit land, where do you want to go?"

"Forward. And when we hit the Pacific, we can wave and turn back."

Haley pecked him on the lips. "I can't wait." She added quickly, "But no rush if you're not feeling well."

Haley and Alex parted ways outside the hospital doors. Alex had gotten twenty feet when he had to slow down. He couldn't feel the stitches; they were so thin and flexible the doctors had told him that he would sooner pull a muscle than stretch one of the near-invisible wires. But even still, every step forward started to wear on him. What should have been a twenty minute walk took twice as long. As Alex stepped into police headquarters, he kept his head down, hoping he would be left alone. Mercifully, most of the staff was on duty or out to lunch. He nodded to security and headed towards Hewes' office.

This time he remembered to knock.

"Go away."

Alex stepped in.

Hewes looked up at him, shocked. "My God, kid, you're the last person I thought was going to come through that door."

"Surprise. By the way, you should get a lock."

"Oh hell no, I live for moments like this. Are you coming back to tell me you have an unstoppable thirst for justice, or are you still sticking to your plan to quit?"

Alex sauntered to Hewes' desk. He pulled out his badge and put it on the table. "You already have my gun."

"Well, it was good to have you." It was as close as Hewes came to being sentimental.

"When you see Cassidy next, could you tell her I wish her the best and I'm sorry?"

"Cassidy? She hasn't come in for a few days now."

Alex tilted his head to the side. "What?"

"I've called her. She didn't respond, but she sent me a message, said she was taking all her sick days. Last we talked, she asked for permission to track down your shooter using Rodney Maxwell as bait."

"What? How can she do that?"

"We released him. As far as I know, she's been shadowing him ever since."

Alex tried to process that information. "Do you have any idea where she is?"

"With the raids still going on and the force preparing for the move out of Manhattan, I've been far too busy to micromanage one murder case. Should I be worried about her?"

Alex paused, going over the words that might kill whatever friendship he had left with Cassidy. He gave a long look at his badge before he turned and walked out the door. He jogged out of the office, stopped in the hallway and pulled up his neural interface. He blinked in confusion before realizing that the replacement the hospital gave him was an updated, sleeker version. After spending a minute getting used to the new layout, he called Cassidy.

"Alex?"

"Cassidy." He grimaced and pressed the bottom of his palm against his chest. "Hey."

There was silence from the other end.

"I..." Alex didn't know what to say. He closed his eyes and took a deep breath. "I'm okay."

"Yeah, me too."

"That's good. I'm leaving the city."

"Me too," Cassidy replied.

"I heard different. Captain Hewes just told me you were tracking the guy who shot me."

"I'm not. That was just the excuse I gave him. I'm in Manhattan, waiting for it to leave. You're not going to tell him, are you? Don't you dare, it's taking off in a few hours, by then I'll be long gone."

"Wait, you snuck into Manhattan? You're riding it off? How?"

"Does it matter?" she shot back.

"Yeah, it does. I'm worried about you, Cassidy. I'm worried you're not in a right state of mind right now. Have you been taking your meds? Have you talked this over with anyone? From what Hewes mentioned, it seems like you are going rogue and you've got no one there to help you back up if your plan goes bust."

"What do you care?" she nearly shouted. "You didn't trust me to help you, you berated me, and you weren't there when I needed you."

"I'm sorry." Alex choked against the rising pain in his chest. "I didn't mean to knock you down. Everything I did just made you angry and I thought I would give you space, I didn't mean to make it worse. Look, can we just talk in person? Can I come see you, please? I won't try to stop you, but if I could have fifteen minutes with you, at least to say goodbye—"

Call ended.

Dammit.

Alex paused and took a stabilizing breath as he waited for the pain to subside. He looked out a nearby window at Manhattan. *God, Cass... is that night really going to be the last time I ever see you?*

He called Haley.

"Alex, I was thinking maybe you shouldn't push yourself. Don't come to my place. How about we meet each other at the ferry? Or I could drop by your place and help you carry your things?"

"I'm going to be late."

"Why, what's going on?"

"I have to make a stop into Manhattan. It's my partner, Cassidy, I have to see her."

"What's happening...?"

"I don't think she's in a good place right now. I think she's having a major depressive episode. She just took off, left the force, didn't tell anyone what she was doing and is riding a skyscraper to I don't even think she knows where."

"Oh..."

"Look, I'll be back by evening, okay? Call you later, love you, bye."

Alex ran back into Hewes' office. He grabbed the badge from the table and turned around.

"You can't keep that as a souvenir."

"You'll get it back," Alex called over his shoulder.

"Leave it with the secretary and stop barging in, you obnoxious bastard!"

Alex logged into the police communications network and called up a patrol boat to take him to Manhattan. He ran towards the edge of the city, grimacing in pain from the rising fire in his chest. He got into a police cruiser, shook a few hands and promised to sign autographs if they took him out. The boat raced across the water towards Manhattan and Alex prayed he could get his feet on solid ground before it sailed away.

Sophia rode the elevator to the top floor of the Empire State Building for the first time since the Miracle. The observation deck, a tourist center a hundred years ago, then briefly a tourist center again recently, had been reconverted into a control deck. Sophia looked towards the 'helm,' where an older man with a ridiculous salt and pepper mustache looked back at her through glasses so thin she barely noticed them.

"Is the pomp and circumstance finished?"

Sophia nodded. "Take us out, Captain."

The man turned back to the floating projection of Manhattan. The forty-five degree tilt made the city look as if it were one giant ship that had just hit an iceberg. On his right, there was another screen devoid of the pretty images, replaced by numbers, meters and gauges. Sophia watched him press projected buttons for a moment before leaving him to his work. She turned and walked to the edges of the room and looked out. In the distance, the skyscrapers on the periphery started to move, then the next row, then the next. After a few minutes of breathless anticipation, Sophia felt a tugging at her back. They were moving forward, south, out towards the inlet between what was once Staten Island and Brooklyn.

Cassidy felt the world lurch and woke with a start. She had been half-asleep and trying to go back to her dream when she heard a girl's voice cry, "Oh, my God!"

She opened her eyes and sat up. Cassidy looked past Samantha and Rodney, out the window. The next line of skyscrapers was waving and rolling in a way that was giving her nausea. She looked aside, but it felt as if the building they were in had lost its center of gravity. She stood up, finding it surprisingly easy to do so, and joined them at the window. She looked down and saw the building moving in the water, creating a massive wake behind it.

"I can't believe it," Rodney gawked. "I can't believe I'm getting out."

Me too. Cassidy smiled as she imagined all the socialites and powerful people who had flown in to be part of this. They no doubt expected the greatest show humanity had ever seen, but unless they were in apartments looking outward on the edges of the city or were in one of the biggest skyscrapers, all they would see is other skyscrapers on all sides keeping pace with theirs.

She lay back down and closed her eyes.

I didn't come for a carnival show. I'm leaving it.

Monsoon rains poured over northern India. A trickling wave of mud sloshed over onto the streets. Sub-zero temperatures in Moscow made the slightest puff of wind seem like a death chill. A sandstorm rolled across the dunes east of Dubai, rising like a giant dark golden cloud in the distance. But everyone was inside, watching the satellite feed as Manhattan sailed south. The first row of skyscrapers passed the inlet between sunken Staten Island and the Boroughs. After the last row went through, bright lights began to appear all over the southern half of the Boroughs as fires erupted, first burning the reserve Coast Guard and police cruisers, then all the commercial boats.

"Now is our time," Ezreal's voice echoed in a hundred ship radios and over a dark web feed. "There is your city, being dragged away from you. Take it back."

The roar of a hundred motors cut through the morning air. From the shore of New Jersey, Ezreal and his men tore towards the moving Manhattan. As they approached, five Coast Guard cruisers sailed to intercept them.

Over a booming speaker, they announced, "Turn back or be fired upon."

The approaching boats sped up and without warning, machine guns and assault rifles fired on the Coast Guard with deafening sound. Three boats caught fire, a fourth sank. The farthest south retreated into the shifting canals of fleeing Manhattan. Glass shards cascaded into the water from the buildings, shimmering as they descended into the dark water.

*   *   *

Cassidy looked out to her left down the length of skyscrapers. She could hardly see anything but a few bright flashes, accompanied by the unmistakable sound of gunfire. She raced towards the door.

"Where are you going?" Sam followed her with scared eyes.

"Lock the doors, don't step out unless you have to," Cassidy called back while slamming the door in her face. She ran to the elevator and pressed the button. There was no response. She pressed it again, and a third time. Nothing. She walked over to the emergency stairs. Locked. *Shit!*

Cassidy tapped her wrist and called Miles. "Miles, listen to me, I need your help."

"Now's not a good time. You know those crazy bastards you were supposed to catch? They're attacking the city. News says they've burned all the reserve Coast Guard and police boats in the Boroughs, too, so there's nothing but a handful of leftover cops between them and us. I take back everything good I ever said about America."

"Miles, calm down, shut up. I'm here, in Manhattan. I'm in the Bellevue, but the whole place is on lockdown, I can't even get off this floor. I expect all the skyscrapers must have some emergency safety protocols enacted. You have powerful friends on the underground, hackers and such, help me out."

"The fuck am I supposed to do? You're the cop!"

"Okay, I'll just shoot my way to ground floor. Come on, think!"

There was a brief pause. "I may have someone. I'm adding her to this convo."

"Hello, this is Lei Xu, I invented the motors and the interface the city is using to control the skyscrapers. I think I can open a backdoor into the system using the info the mayor gave me and get you out of there."

"Awesome. Do it."

Cassidy waited impatiently, holding her gun at her side. She started to pace when the elevator doors opened.

"You're a miracle worker," Cassidy said as she stepped into the elevator. "Do you guys know what's going on?"

"The Second Amendment on water."

"Shut up, Miles."

"Wherever these guys are going, they can't make it to the Empire State Building," Lei interrupted.

"Why?"

"Because that's where the main building control hub is. If they get there, they would control Manhattan." Lei's voice shook. "You can't let them get there."

"How many are there?" she asked. The elevator doors opened and she stepped into the lobby.

"A fuckload. AKA, too many for the cops here."

Just as he said that, a boat flew by and a stream of bullets tore into the lobby. Cassidy fell to the floor as glass crashed all around her.

"I'll try to call the main control hub," Lei said. "If they rotated every other building, then the canals would be too narrow for the boats. They would be crushed against the skyscrapers and that could buy enough time for the Navy to get here. In the meantime, I'll try to lower some bridges for you."

"You do that," Cassidy grunted, rising. She took a cautious step outside, looked westward and saw ships coming her way. She bolted in the other direction, stopping at the corner. There was a vast gulf in between her and the next skyscraper. A sudden loud creak sounded as the blue bridge began to lower. She looked back, seeing the ships careening down the canal. As soon as the bridge began to level, she raced across it, down the block toward the next one. As she did, she could feel the city still moving southward. White spray kicked up as she crossed the bridge.

Cassidy ran down the next block, seeing another bridge lower as she ran. She placed her foot on it when a boat careened through. With a sickening metallic screech, the bridge's hinges burst and it was knocked into the water. The ship stalled and slowly sank. A few members of the crew poked their heads up. They were covered in blood from the impact. Cassidy didn't wait around for them to get back up and bolted to the right. The bridge on the next corner was lowering. She heard splashes behind her as the crew abandoned ship.

A phone icon flashed in front of her. She tapped her wrist. "Make it quick!"

"The control team says they can't do it," Lei said. "They're afraid they will topple the buildings if they do."

"Did you tell them that will happen if they don't?"

"The pilot is my replacement and only trained for about a week. He's basically auto-piloting my plan while dropping bridges to slow them down."

Cassidy looked over her shoulder. She heard a boat roar from somewhere, but didn't see any near her. "Could you do it? If I escorted you there, could you do it?"

"I... yes."

"Where are you?"

"The Black Dolphin. I'll be in the lobby waiting for you."

"That's pretty far from where I am."

"Sorry, you're going to have to run. Miles will be watching you via the satellites."

"Okay," Cassidy said, looking down at her gun, realizing she only had so many rounds. "See you soon."

Cassidy tapped 'end' and ran across the bridge, then the next. She turned and after the fourth bridge, a boat careened past her, stopping just before it crashed into a lowered bridge. Two men with assault rifles lined up Cassidy in their sights. She shot to her left, blasting the windows of the nearest building. She jumped inside just as a spray of bullets pelted the ground she had been standing on. Cassidy heard gunfire, then an explosion. She peeked out around the windows. A second boat had a flaming hole in it and was sinking quickly, forcing its crew to jump off. Cassidy leapt out of the building and ran forward. As she neared the corner, she yelled, "Police!"

"Us too!"

Cassidy stepped outside. "Ajay?"

Ajay waved her over to cover. "How'd you get on?"

"Snuck on, I was just trying to get a ride out of New York."

Ajay looked over to where two cops were cuffing and beating down the criminals as they stepped onto even ground.

"Bet you didn't expect this! Anyway, since you're here, we're trying to pick them off as they tear through. You can help us out."

"No." Cassidy shook her head. "They are all headed to the major buildings looking for the central control. I've been informed it's on top of the Empire State Building. If they can take that over, they can stop the city dead in the water. I'm going to find Lei Xu, the one who made the motors. She said she can rotate the skyscrapers in a way that would make navigation impossible. Get all your men around the Empire State Building and keep them from boarding, otherwise the whole city could collapse into the ocean."

Ajay turned to the rest of his men. "Everyone move out, we're heading to the Empire State Building." He looked at Cassidy. "Good luck."

"You too."

Cassidy ran across the next bridge. A boat whizzed by, spraying bullets. She fell to the ground and felt glass shards fall onto her back. She looked down the long line of skyscrapers, knowing she had eight more blocks to go. *I'll never make it.*

"Cassidy!" a voice called.

Cassidy looked up. Alex stood in front of her on the side of a police patrol boat. "Get in!" he called, reaching a hand out to her. Cassidy ran to him and jumped into the boat.

She turned to the pilot and yelled, "We have to get to the Black Dolphin, we need to pick someone up."

"Cassidy," Alex began.

"I know what I'm doing, just trust me."

Alex bit his lip. He turned to the captain and called, "You heard her, get us moving!"

The cruiser tore through the canals. Cassidy heard gunfire and saw ships in the distance, but they managed to reach the Black Dolphin. Cassidy was about to call Miles when he and Lei stepped out of the lobby and ran up to the ship.

"About time." Miles held a gun at his side.

"Nice piece, do you know how to use it?" Cassidy called.

"No, I was just hoping to make loud noises and hope they ran away."

Cassidy turned to Lei. "Miss Xu? Ready?"

"Yes." Lei tried to sound brave as Alex and Cassidy helped her into the boat.

"Miles?"

"Good luck."

Cassidy gave him an evil glare. "I need as much help as I can get. In lieu of that, you'll do fine."

Miles looked at Lei, then back at Cassidy. "We're avoiding danger, right?"

"Yes, you coward. The gunmen should be focused on getting to the Empire State Building, so bypassing them should be easy enough. But once we actually arrive, that's going to be the hard part. Just follow my lead and try not to get shot, Lei."

Miles looked back at the lobby. He cursed himself and climbed up into the boat.

"To the Empire State Building," Alex passed on the order.

Alex, Cassidy, Lei, Miles and the three other officers kept their eyes peeled at the one building that towered over all the others as they tore south. The sounds of gunfire and explosions grew louder as they neared. They were one block away when a boat stalled in front of them with crewmen inside clamoring toward the front of the boat, firing madly forward. Cassidy noticed that the police had lowered the bridge in front of them, but that didn't stop the men from laying heavy fire down the blocks.

"Wait here," Cassidy ordered without looking back.

Alex put a hand on her shoulder. She met his eyes with dark

intensity.

"We do this together."

Cassidy nodded. They jumped out of the police cruiser and snuck up on the marauders' boat. They jumped in, guns raised. Cassidy ran up to the first man and put a gun to his head. Alex aimed his gun between the other two, who had just realized they had been boarded.

"Drop your weapons," Alex ordered. The three did. Cassidy picked up two assault rifles and slung them over her shoulder. She patted down the men, taking out two pistols and dumping them into the water. Cassidy and Alex holstered their pistols and hefted the assault rifles.

"Let's move," she ordered them off the boat and into the police cruiser behind them. Lei watched nervously as the men were cuffed and forced to lay on the deck.

The captain looked at Alex. "We can help you storm the building."

"The biggest threat shouldn't be inside," Lei's voice croaked. "The fact that the city hasn't fallen apart yet means they haven't taken over."

Alex breathed deep, trying not to show how much pain he was in. "Lei's right," he forced out. "Cassidy, we have to escort Lei up there. The rest of you, hold the oncoming hordes off as long as you can."

Cassidy, Alex and Lei stepped off the cruiser. Miles jumped out after them. Cassidy shot him a glance.

"You thought I'd stay behind and fight off the entire lower class of New York from a dinghy filled with gasoline and gunpowder?"

The four raced across the bridge to the Empire State Building and ran up the steps to the doors. Alex's head was spinning and he felt an immense pain shoot through him. He looked over his shoulder and watched the world split into three dizzying images. Boats were headed his way and the gunfire grew louder with every passing moment.

Lei was tapping her right hand outside the doors to the building. "Give me a second, I can get these open."

Cassidy lowered her rifle and fired through the glass. Lei and Miles walked through. Cassidy turned and saw Alex on his knees with a hand on the steps. "Alex?" She ran up to him. "Hey, buddy, now's really not the time."

A cruiser tore out of a side canal. Armed men raised their weapons at them.

"Come on!" Cassidy grabbed him under the arm and lifted. She struggled forward and the two hobbled into the building as a wild spray of bullets blasted through the entrance. The men leapt onto the block and ran after them.

"Miles, help him! Lei, get the elevators working quickly!" Cassidy yelled as she turned and fired upon the first man who entered. Cassidy fired left, right, center and left as the bandits began to stream in. Miles helped Alex take cover behind the marble reception desk beside Lei.

"Give it here," Miles grunted as he pulled off Alex's assault rifle. He stood up and fired blindly at the men entering. Alex grimaced painfully as he tried to focus. He saw Lei trying to hack into the elevators, but she was shaking violently and ducking with every sound of gunfire. Alex grabbed her right wrist and held it steady. Lei jumped and stared at him with eyes like a cornered animal's.

"You can do this," Alex breathed. "Just concentrate on what you're doing." Lei looked back to her hand. She tapped wildly.

Through the gunfire, there was a barely audible ring. Cassidy turned to see the golden elevator doors open to her right. "Go," she motioned.

Miles helped Alex to his feet and they ran to the elevator. Cassidy walked backwards, firing as she did. She jumped to the side as bullets hit into the marble counter, kicking up a cloud of dust. She retreated into the elevator, firing a few last shots as the doors closed, praying that the doors could withstand bullets. Then they were heading upward, to the top. The doors opened to a long hallway with a red carpet contrasting against the gilded walls and antique vases on either side.

"Go, Lei. I'm going to stay here and keep them from getting to the top."

Lei nodded and took off for the end of the hallway. Miles eyed Cassidy as she called the elevators and clicked the emergency stop button on each.

"You can go, too." Alex looked up at Miles.

Miles looked down at him and Alex could tell he really wanted to. "Sorry, mate, but I don't really trust you to hold them off yourself." Miles pulled out his handgun. "Can you still aim straight?"

"Mostly." Alex put a hand on his stomach, not caring to hide the pain anymore. Cassidy looked down at his hand and back up to his face. Alex was covered in sweat and his eyes were unfocusing.

"How are we going to do this?" Miles turned to Cassidy.

She looked around the room. "There are two stairwells. They should be up here in about ten minutes or so, once they realize that they can't use the elevators. I will take one and shoot at them as they march upward. You two take the other." Miles and Alex started to walk away when she added, "We should prop the doors open with the pedestals, that way we can hear each other better and call out the retreat if they get too close."

Cassidy turned to the nearest pedestal. She lifted the heavy vase and put it on the ground, then pulled the pedestal back until it fell backward and slowly tugged it towards the stairwell. Miles was holding the vase when it slipped in his hands and cracked, sending wet soil everywhere. He looked up at Cassidy.

"Those damn gangsters."

Under the strain of the pedestal, Cassidy nodded at the far upper corner of the hall and panted, "You're on camera, and the entire city government probably watched you break that priceless Chinese vase."

Miles looked up, his grin fading. He returned to his pillar and dragged it to his door, propping it open.

"Use your vantage point. If they do run up a hundred floors, they will be exhausted, their aim will be shit. If they overwhelm you, run, don't be a hero. I don't care if they make it up, just don't get shot; I don't want anyone coming up behind me without warning."

Miles nodded and helped Alex toward their stairwell. Cassidy went down a few steps in hers and looked down at the cavernous depths of the old building. After a few minutes, there was a faraway echo of footsteps and shouts. She sat down and mentally prepared. As she did, the building lurched forward, then turned and Cassidy grabbed onto the railing. She heard shouts of astonishment from far below her as she did. She looked up. *Come on, Lei.*

Lei ran out onto the open roof. She stopped and gazed out, marveling at the unsettling change in the horizon now that the Boroughs were behind them and Manhattan was still careening south. She walked towards the edge of the building and looked down. She saw miniature blasts of light, barely visible from so high up. The sound of gunfire echoed up to meet her, but was faint and distant-sounding. She clapped a hand to her mouth as she watched tiny figures fight in a constantly moving battlefield.

"You there, identify yourself!"

Lei jumped at the sound. She turned and saw a heavily-armed man on the ground, holding an assault rifle towards her. "My name is Lei Xu, I was the designer of the Poseidon motors. I am here to help."

Atop the observation deck in the center of the roof, a familiar face peeked out. "Lei?" the mayor yelled from an open window. The edgy man put down his gun. Lei ran up to the observation deck.

"Lei, what are you doing here? How did you get up here?"

"Running," she panted. "I got some help from a cop and Miles Buhari."

"What?" The mayor looked as if she had been slapped.

"Listen, I'm here to direct the skyscrapers."

Sophia shook her head. "We have that under control."

"No, you don't. There are a hundred ships coming straight for us. The news reported that all the ships in the Boroughs were burned to the ground, so no help is coming from there, either. We are on our own for at least another hour before the Navy arrives and we can't hope to hold on much longer with just this small police contingent, which is why we need to use the skyscrapers as a weapon. Close them in on each other so tight that it crushes the boats and turn the skyscrapers so that the canals are unmanageable to them."

The mayor looked at the captain, then back to Lei. "Can you do that?" *Without killing us all.*

"It's a better plan than inching our way south and hoping that the Navy double-times it."

The mayor couldn't argue with that. "Take over."

Without another word, Lei ran up to the observation deck and strode to the console. She immediately halted the movement of every skyscraper. After a minute, as the skyscrapers settled, she clicked on the Empire State Building and spun it. In a few seconds, the building began to turn. She turned her attention to boats scattered throughout the city and began closing in buildings and lowering bridges. She looked to her right and saw the security camera footage at the base of the Empire State Building. Two boats had been smashed by the building's base as the concrete block tore it into the next building. To her dismay, armed men jumped off and ran into the building.

Cassidy stumbled and grabbed desperately onto the railing. She looked down, all the way down. She heard shouts below her as a few armed men must have also been reeling from the suddenly spinning building. Cassidy tried to sway with the motion as best she could and dropped to the stairs, making herself as small a target as possible.

Footsteps echoed up from the base of the stairwell. Heavy panting soon followed. Cassidy smiled as she thought of how long they had to trek upward. *Good, they won't have the energy to dodge.* But as they slowly approached, she realized that the constant sound of footfalls wasn't an echo; there were dozens of them. She saw them approach and kept low. She wanted to fire desperately and she felt a sense of nervous dread as they approached. Alex's chest exploded in her mind.

That was a scared kid. These are killers who have handled guns before. She clutched her assault rifle until her hands went white. *I only have one mag left.* She cursed herself for emptying the assault rifle. *I need to make it count.*

Cassidy was lying on the ground as they neared. Their footsteps pounded in her ears.

"Thank... God... we're almost at the top," a voice called breathlessly.

Cassidy sprang from her position and fired, spraying a line of death down the stairs. She ran forward, firing all the way down. Her gun ran out of bullets and she dropped to the ground as a heavy stream of fire, blinding and deafening, echoed across the stairwell from below. She crawled to the nearest corpse and picked up another assault rifle. She turned over the body, hoping to find another magazine. Instead, she found a belt full of grenades. She pulled the first one out, removed the pin and threw. It bounced off one of the concrete beams, falling down the infinite stairwell, exploding uselessly below.

Fuck.

There were shouts below her. The footsteps were getting faster. Cassidy grabbed the next grenade, pulled the pin and threw. This one hit its mark and there were screams. More bullets flew and she was pressed against the ground as they ricocheted on the wall behind her. She grabbed the third grenade and threw. More screams, more death. This time, they weren't going to wait for her to attack again and she heard them bolt up the steps. They were so close she could feel the heavy footsteps race up the stairs. She pulled the last pin and held the grenade in her hand as the footsteps grew closer. Cassidy's heart skipped a beat. She glanced up at the death in her shaking hand. When she looked back across the stairwell, two armed men stopped, guns raised at her.

"Catch!" She threw the grenade, put her hands over her ears, closed her eyes and hugged the far stairs. A deafening explosion enveloped the world. She couldn't tell the ground from the sky as the rotating of the building and the earth-pounding explosion had removed all sense of space. When the world finally righted itself, Cassidy ventured a peek over the side. She rolled over just as the wall above her was peppered by bullets.

Cassidy lowered herself to the ground as much as she could and ran up the stairs, knowing they couldn't be held anymore. She threw open the hallway door and pulled out her pistol and held it forward. Miles looked back at her, rifle leveled.

"Oh, thank God it's you."

She looked behind him. The door had been closed, locked and Alex was placing the pedestal against it.

"Did you kill any of them?"

"A few. It's the first time I ever did." He saw the look in her eyes and realized there were more important things than his own existential crisis. "But there are more coming and I'm out of bullets."

"Okay, let's go." Cassidy ran down the hall.

"Shouldn't we brace your door?"

"No time, they're already here."

Miles turned and made to help Alex. He waved him aside and the three ran down the hall. Up on the roof, two men with assault rifles leveled their guns at them.

"I'm a cop," Cassidy shouted, holding her pistol out. "Cassidy Kikia." She looked up at the observation deck. "Didn't Lei tell you to expect me?"

One of the guards looked at the other. "No, she didn't."

"Show us your badge."

Cassidy heard a banging behind her and guessed that Miles' door was being forced open. She pulled out her badge. "They are coming, right now."

"Okay, okay." The guard waved them forward and closed the door.

"Miles, go up to the observation deck," she ordered. "You're done here."

Miles looked at her, wanting to help, but he realized he was useless without bullets.

She caught his glance. "Help him get up there." She motioned towards the observation deck. Miles nodded and put his hand around Alex's shoulders.

"How many can we expect?"

"Closest guess? A lot."

"What's the plan?" the guard on Cassidy's right asked.

"They are common criminals with big guns. Stay away from the doors. They are going to try to muscle their way through. Conserve ammo."

Heavy footsteps shook the ground. Bullets burst through the door.

"Get out of view," Cassidy whispered. A second later, machine guns were held out the door and fired wildly. She ran around to the other side and got to see the surprised looks on the men in the stairwell before she fired. A second charge came and she ran back to join her new companions. A stream of blood flew past her vision and she was left with one man shooting beside her. She fired towards the doors and looked down at her fallen companion. He was jerking, eyes wild, neck streaming blood. She grabbed his weapon and kept firing.

"Back up," Cassidy yelled. "Back to the observation deck."

They fired wildly at the door and then bolted back. The observation deck's massive windows were gone, the glass carpeting the roof in front of them. Cassidy ran underneath the deck, sprinting furiously as the sound of bullets followed her. She ran up the stairs underneath the deck. When she was in, her eyes ran across the terrified faces inside as they cowered behind tables and consoles, except Lei, who still piloted the ship with shaking hands. Cassidy looked past Lei to the floating image of Manhattan in front of her.

"It's over," a voice boomed from outside. Cassidy dared to look out. Five men with machine guns waited on top of the building. In the middle, Ezreal Redding stood looking up at them. He looked as if he were about to fall over, his old frame buckling under the journey. But his eyes lit up with triumph. "Come out. You cannot hide; the reckoning has finally come."

Cassidy ducked back down. "Are there any guns in here? Anything we can use as a weapon?" She called out to no one and no one responded. "You know what will happen to all of you if they get us? Do we have anything we can use as a weapon?"

Grim faces were her only response. Cassidy looked back out, seeing their defeat.

"There is something we can do," Lei piped up, her voice quivering. "I-I think I have an idea. But I need a distraction."

"For how long?"

"Maybe two minutes, I can't be sure."

Cassidy looked down. The assault rifle had run out of ammo and she didn't have much left in her pistol either. She couldn't buy two minutes with gunfire. "Okay," Cassidy breathed. "I'll hold their attention."

Cassidy walked down the steps, shaking even as she told herself to be brave. She held her assault rifle forward. That just might be able to deter them for at least a second as they shot her down.

"You put on quite a show, Mr. Ezreal Redding. Or is it Matthew Hammond?" Cassidy called as she stepped forward from under the deck, glass cracking underneath her shoes. She stared down the barrels of five machine guns.

Ezreal cracked a smile as he stared her down. "It seems like your side doesn't have much fight left if you're the only one standing between us and control of Manhattan," Ezreal's booming voice echoed past her, his eyes drifting towards the deck. "I assume you are their last bodyguard. You are a subject fighting for the very people who oppress you."

"I'm a cop."

Ezreal grinned disdainfully and Cassidy could see the troops around him tense with anger. "All the more reason for you to join us."

"And what are you going to do once you have control of the city?"

"We will give it back to the people of New York City."

"Until the army comes."

"Since when has an army ever been able to crush the will of the people? Afghanistan, Venezuela, Iran, Afghanistan again. No army can suppress the oppressed. We will fight, turn the canals red with blood and we will win. In time, New York will belong to the people, and not to a government that can't even keep its cities above water. Now step aside."

"You failed last time. Remember?"

His smile faded.

"Is that it, then? Some mad quest to restart the revolution that made you spend fifty years underground so your failure and everything you've done can be justified? God, you are pathetic."

"Step out of the way, girl."

"So pathetic that one person nearly brought you down all by himself. My partner, Alex Waverly, unraveled your whole plot with diving equipment and a harpoon gun. I am just finishing what he started."

"Is he up there?" Ezreal looked up to the observation deck. "Or did he not make it? Either way, I have plenty of bullets saved for him with more than enough for the rest of you."

Ezreal turned to the man on his right and began to raise his hand. Then the world trembled, ever so slightly but just enough to bring a look of panic to his face. His eyes glanced around, searching for whatever was causing the disturbance.. He looked over the building's side and downward and his eyebrows furrowed. Then a look of horror came upon his face. Cassidy looked over and saw the neighboring skyscraper heading right towards them. Foam kicked up from the Empire State Building's base as Lei readied it for the incoming colossal blow. The rest of Ezreal's squad had a second to look before the impact. There was a terrifying howl of steel on steel. The people on top of the building were tossed around like rag dolls and the building began to tilt to the east. Cassidy's assault rifle fell from her hands and off a thousand feet. Her body tumbled toward the edge. Wildly, she grabbed the edge of the building and held on for her life as it began to tilt even more. One of the criminals fell screaming over the side. The rest of the gang lay flat, holding themselves to the ground.

Cassidy heard a loud noise behind her and looked over her shoulder at a second skyscraper racing toward the building. She clung to the edge as tightly as she could. She had just enough time to think *Lei seemed so sane* when the second skyscraper hit. There were screams all around her, but she could only hear her own. Then the building held. Cassidy looked down and realized that the two buildings were stabilizing each other, even as the Empire State Building had tilted. Cassidy could guess what was going to happen next: Lei would try to push the Empire State Building backward, meaning that the building on the other side would ease back, as the skyscraper just below her would push it back upright.

Cassidy summoned all her strength and pulled herself up. She ran, keeping herself low. One of the men looked at her and aimed. She dove, grabbed him by the jacket, pulled him upright and kicked him square in the stomach. He stumbled and rolled off the building, spraying gunfire everywhere. The skyscraper in front of her backed off slowly, while the one behind her pushed forward. Steel screamed and massive shockwaves rolled through the building. The other armed men began to rise to their feet. Cassidy ran past them straight towards Ezreal. She tried to punch him, but she could hardly control her movements, so it turned into a wild tackle. They rolled together as the Empire State Building began to tilt the other way. Ezreal tried to break away, but Cassidy kept pushing them towards the edge. She looked over the side, ready to plunge, ready to kill them both.

Ezreal pushed her back and stumbled on the edge, his leg slipped and he fell to the ground, his lower half swinging over the edge. He reached inside his coat and pulled out a shiny silver pistol. Cassidy reached for her own gun, leveled it and shot him in the chest. His body went rigid, and with the next shaking of the building, he fell off the side. The building had nearly righted itself and the shaking had begun to stop. Cassidy looked over wildly and saw guns raised against her. She aimed at the nearest gangster and fired.

There was a metallic click that carried in the wind, but no explosion.

Cassidy shook as she stared into death.

Bang!

The first of the men dropped.

"Put your guns down!" Ajay shouted behind the remaining gangsters. They turned and saw five cops with guns drawn. They dropped their weapons.

"On the ground! On the ground!"

They did as they were told and Ajay slapped handcuffs on the pair. "Larry, hold them here. I think we'll get the elevators running before we take 'em down." Ajay looked at Cassidy. "What the hell was all that shaking about?"

Cassidy could barely stand. She smiled, insanely. "They had us outnumbered, outgunned. Lei thought maybe we could get them thrown off the building by knocking them together."

"Great goddamn plan," Ajay grumbled, just as amazed as her that they were alive. "I nearly took a dive down the stairwell."

"We got the guy in charge of it all. Well..." She looked over the side of the building. She turned back to him and smiled.

Ajay laughed. "You are one hell of an officer. I can't believe you snuck on board this skyscraper, ran all the way across town to get Lei, then ran up the entire Empire State Building. Are you a superhero or something?"

"I didn't run up; we took the elevator and then broke it."

Ajay gave her the most disgusted look she had ever seen. "Fuck you! We had to run up the entire goddamn building to get here!"

Cassidy clutched her side, laughing. She was the only one.

Manhattan continued its southward trek in peace as the city council and national government decided that the safest decision was to keep sailing as far away from New York as possible before taking a brief stop to let medical personnel from the Navy arrive. Just an hour later, they were preparing a ceremony to honor the brave police officers who had protected the city inside the Empire State Building. On the second floor in the gilded reception hall, all the officers left in Manhattan were congregating around Cassidy. She kept trying to move away from them and had even backed up towards the window, but the crowds had circled around her. She felt sorely underdressed in a muddied jacket and jeans, though she had managed to wipe some of the blood stains off in the bathroom. From the corner of her eye, she saw Alex step out of the room. She put a hand on Miles' left shoulder as Lei was leaning against his right and beaming up at him.

"Tell them how much of a hero you were, I have to use the little girls' room." Cassidy took off toward the exit.

"Alex!" she called just as the door to the stairwell shut. She raced to it, threw it open and jumped down the stairs two at a time, a difficult task since the entrance was a debris-filled wreck. She found Alex standing on the sidewalk as the same police cruiser they arrived in bobbed in the water.

"Alex!" she yelled as she ran out to him. He turned as she rushed to his side. "You weren't going to just leave me, were you? Not without saying goodbye?"

Alex turned and smiled. He opened his mouth, but stopped.

"Well? You don't have anything to say?" She noticed he was clutching his stomach and softened. "Are you going to be all right?"

Alex snickered. "I came here to ask you the same thing. But then realized maybe it was never my place to ask."

Cassidy met her partner's eyes. Her hair gently tousled in the seafoam breeze as the towering steel monoliths cut through the water. "And?" she asked, hoping he had something to say.

"I was worried that you were sneaking into Manhattan because you were desperate and lost. But now that I think about it, maybe even if you came here for bad reasons, it'll all work out. Or... maybe that's just what I'm hoping for myself."

Cassidy gave him a questioning look.

"I'm leaving with Haley. Packing up and heading to the mainland. I was supposed to be there already, but I needed to make sure you were okay."

"Do you think we can just leave New York behind? The Boroughs, I mean."

"Before Ezreal and his men left, they burnt down nearly all the boats in New York. And the Navy has opted to guard Manhattan, which means that there are about twenty thousand National Guard who are trapped back at home indefinitely with no organized crime left to fight. I think the Boroughs just became the safest place on Earth."

Cassidy shook her head. "Damn, we should have left years ago."

Alex smiled. He looked over at the police cruiser. As he turned back, Cassidy had her arms around him. She let go and looked up at him and for the first time, her eyes softened. Her lips formed a sad half-smile and behind the pain in her look, there was hope.

Alex shook his head, smiling. "We don't have to miss each other; I'm just going to look forward to when we meet again."

Cassidy began to laugh and choked it back.

Goodbye to you too, Cassidy. He turned his back on her and stepped onto the police cruiser and took off back for the Boroughs.

It was a short run from the piers to Haley's house, one that Alex made despite the burn in his stomach. Each step made him feel lighter as he knew he was finally leaving. He was near-delirious with pain when he reached the house. With the last of his strength, he knocked on the door. It opened and an angry-looking man with fading gray hair looked down on the panting Alex with his arms crossed.

"Haley…"

"She's gone," he replied. "She spent hours waiting for you, crying, saying you were leaving her again."

"I told her to wait for me."

"She must have stopped waiting."

Alex shook his head. "Where'd she go?" The reality was sinking in and a worse, hollow pain was replacing the sharp stinging.

"The ferry, she left about half an hour ago. Packed her bags and everything."

"She didn't call me…" Alex muttered more to himself than anything. He looked back up at Haley's father. Alex didn't have anything else to say to him, and he didn't seem in the talking mood. Alex walked away and heard the door slam shut. *No, how could she? I was coming back, I came back…*

He brought up the neural interface and called her phone. It went directly to voicemail. *No… no… Haley…* He felt the world grow heavier and he collapsed to his knees. Then a thought came to him. He brought up the ferry schedule. The new 'Boroughs to Shore' ferries left on an hourly basis. *She only boarded five minutes ago.* He went back into his phone app and called up the police cruiser. With newfound strength, he sprinted back towards the pier.

"Men, the job isn't over yet," he called.

"What is it?"

"I have reason to believe there is a bomb on the ferry going to the mainland. We have to chase it down."

Alex watched the police cruiser swing into the docks and leapt in. It tore off in the water until in the far distance, Alex saw the slow-moving ferry, which had stopped a few hundred meters from the shore, so close the passengers could have jumped out and swum to the coast. The police lights flashed on. A hundred people looked out curiously at the small ship. Alex and two other officers boarded the ship and his eyes raced madly around the deck.

"Remain calm!" Alex called as loudly as he could. "We're in a heightened state of emergency since the attack on Manhattan, we need to inspect the ship before letting you go, remain calm."

His eyes finally found her. Haley looked at him with a shocked expression, a stuffed suitcase near her feet. Alex looked to his left and right and watched the other two cops disappear below deck in search of the non-existent bomb. He gave up all pretenses and walked up to her, smiling.

"I can't believe you," she whispered. "You called in a fake bomb threat?" She looked out to shore. "We were almost there!"

"I wanted to step onto shore with you."

Haley looked back up into his eyes and he saw the hurt in hers. "I thought you said you weren't stupid enough to leave me again."

"I'm still stupid, but I'm not so much that I have to get shot three times to know you're better than whatever I'm holding onto back there."

There was a sound of heavy footsteps from behind and the two cops walked up to Alex. "There's no package here," one of them said. "Must have been false information."

"Well, better safe than sorry," Alex replied cheerily. "I think I'll take the ferry out, watch over things, just to be safe. "

The officer nodded and the two hopped over the other side. The cruiser roared away and the ferry started moving closer to land.

"I'm done stalling. I'm stepping onto dry land. If you want to go your own way once we get there, that's fine, but you've been the only important thing in my life. There is literally nothing else."

"Nothing?" Haley replied. "No work left? You don't still have to save the Boroughs?"

"It doesn't need saving. The conspiracy is gone, the army has turned the Boroughs into a thousand floating fortresses..." He stopped mid-sentence. "I don't know when it started, but at some point, I knew there was nothing there for me. Even the important things I did all felt like stalling. When I first met you, I thought about leaving. But then I went back to work and I must have figured you were too good to be real." He smiled coyly at her. "I understand if you don't want to go out with me, but if you're wondering if there's anything standing between us again, the answer is nothing at all."

The ferry slowed with a small lurch. The doors at the end of the boat opened. Haley leaned over and kissed him. She pulled back and grabbed his hand. The two walked out together onto dry land.

Epilogue

Manhattan split up the longer it traveled down the coast. By the time it passed the Carolinas, the once mighty fleet had turned into a few dozen titanic monoliths edging slowly down the coast until there were only four. Samantha and Rodney finally had an unobstructed view of the coast as their building slowly drifted down the Eastern Seaboard.

Then the day finally came.

Rodney couldn't wait any longer and stepped into the bathroom. "Cassidy's already down there waiting for us. You look fine, Sam."

"I want to look better than fine," she remarked as she added another layer of lipstick.

Rodney walked over to her and put his arms on her waist while kissing her neck. "You're going to miss it."

"All right, all right."

Rodney led her outside the apartment, down the stairs and into the lobby. The whole room was crowded with people who stared out at the shore. The entire horizon turned a blood red that dimmed the distant Appalachians purple. At the foot of the mountains were dark green forests.

"You look beautiful!" Cassidy exclaimed as she stepped up next to Sam. "I wish I had brought a dress with me."

"Thank you! If you want to borrow one of mine, we could run up really quick. It might not be a perfect fit, but—"

"No, it's fine, I wouldn't want to impose. Are you two ready?"

"Definitely," Rodney interjected. "I've had enough of the sea."

"Poor baby." Cassidy smirked. "Some hearty southern food should settle your stomach."

Rodney felt a wave of queasiness come over him. It must have been visible because Sam cooed, "You'll be fine! More than fine, the food down here should finally put some meat on your bones."

"I hope so. In between the frozen dinners we've had for the last couple of weeks and the bobbing of the sea, I'm about done with food."

"Look, Mommy!" a small girl's voice called out. Lights appeared on the horizon, first a few, then a million as they approached Savannah. The skyscraper slowly wheeled in and headed straight for the city's heart. Sam and Rodney edged closer, squeezing next to the window. There was a loud boom and there were gasps in the room.

"Fireworks!"

A hundred more exploded into the night sky. As they neared, Rodney could see individual people in apartments leaning over their Parisian-style balconies. He waved and watched a few wave back. Near the port were thousands of people. Even from afar, Rodney could hear music and see steam rising from barbecues large enough to feed thousands. The skyscraper stopped its motion. A loudspeaker from behind them announced, "It is now safe to disembark."

Sam beamed at Rodney, eyes filled with wonder. The three rushed out alongside a hundred others as they clamored toward the festival. They met the crowd awaiting them in the square and soon they were eating and drinking, dancing and attempting to remember a hundred names as people tried to introduce themselves through the sounds of music, fireworks and exuberant hysteria. Rodney looked around and realized they had lost Cassidy. He grabbed onto Sam's hand and followed her as she weaved through the crowds until the sun rose again and he knew he had spent his first night on dry land.

About the Author

Gary Girod has published short stories of all genres for the past decade. He also founded the French History Podcast, which covers the history of France from three million years ago to present. He is currently finishing his doctoral dissertation at the University of Houston and divides his time between writing fiction, world-traveling and wearing a suit while monologuing about the deeds of dead people.

CPSIA information can be obtained
at www.ICGtesting.com
Printed in the USA
LVHW111004140520
655602LV00001B/95